Strange Police

REG GADNEY

Strange Police

When eras die their legacies
Are left to strange police
Professors in New England guard
The glory that was Greece
CLARENCE DAY

faber and faber

First published in Great Britain in 2000
by Faber and Faber Limited
3 Queen Square WC1N 3AU

Photoset by Parker Typesetting Service, Leicester
Printed in England by Clays Ltd, St Ives plc

A CIP record for this book
is available from the British Library

ISBN 0–571–20292–6

2 4 6 8 10 9 7 5 3 1

Στὴ Φαίη μὲ ἀγάπη

By collecting these remains of antiquity for the benefit of my country, and by saving them from future destruction, which threatened them inexorably if they had remained for many years the prey of malevolent Turks, who mutilated them for a senseless pleasure or with the aim of selling them off piece by piece to passing travellers, I was not impelled by the search for personal gain.

LORD ELGIN

In her sooty vitals, London stores these marble monuments of the gods, just as some unsmiling Puritan might store in the depths of his memory some past erotic moment, blissful and ecstatic sin.

NIKOS KAZANTZAKIS

Cooled in summer by the breeze from the gulf, the great screen of the Taygetos shuts out intruding winds from the north and east; no tramontana can reach it. It is like those Elysian confines of the world where Homer says that life is easiest for men; where no snow falls, no strong winds blow nor rain comes down, but the melodious west wind blows for ever from the sea to bring coolness to those who live there.

PATRICK LEIGH FERMOR

Author's Note

The distinguished Greek novelist Apostolos Doxiadis has given me most generous help in the correction of this manuscript. Apostolos has my thanks.

No character in this book is based upon the living or the dead. The conjugation of Greek names has been simplified for English readers. If there are errors in the text, then they are my responsibility and I apologise for them, especially to Greeks whose country I love.

R. G.

LONDON AND TSERIA, 2000

Strange Police

i

Alan Rosslyn sat at the edge of the deserted Kardamyli quayside and watched the splendour of the sunrise across the Messinian Gulf. The line of the horizon was violet and indigo, the ocean's shifting surface turquoise. The morning swim would be his last before taking the flight from Kalamata to London.

Bronzed and fit after three weeks in the Mani, Rosslyn reckoned he deserved to feel at ease. Yet indecision was disturbing him. Instinct was telling him to stay here in Greece; to continue his love affair with Cleo Ipsilanti, a Greek divorcee in her early forties and an experienced former agent of the British Secret Intelligence Service.

Either common sense or conscience warned him to take the plane home later in the day and escape the heat of summer in the Peloponnese. To take a break from the affair and the possible risks of revelation and embarrassment. Others could well construe their passion as unwise and unprofessional; better, perhaps, had it never ignited. How much easier had he simply stuck to his primary purpose here in Greece: to advise upon the protection and security of Cleo's private estate above Kardamyli on behalf of the London firm of private commercial investigators, Tunim Associates.

Now it was too late for any self-recriminations and his professional, more matter-of-fact commitment to the brothers Tunim had to be completed.

ii

Campbell and Menzies Tunim were an ambitious pair. They treated Rosslyn with a wary respect and, as their subordinate, with some condescension. Rosslyn had experience of the public sector: Customs and Excise; the Security Services, MI5, MI6; and the Metropolitan Police. And the brothers Tunim did not.

Campbell Tunim was hefty, paunchy, with a cherubic face and curly hair. In his forties, he was some ten years Rosslyn's senior. The accent was a cultivated drawl, but after a few drinks Campbell would loosen his floral bow tie and the vowels soon betrayed the south London family origins. There was also something of the unhealthy couch-potato bully about him. It showed in the narrow, porcine eyes, which seemed to glint when he jabbed you in the ribs with his fist, a little too sharply for comfort, in his favoured gesture of greeting. Like his brother Menzies, Campbell had a previous career as a City banker. Also like his brother, he served part-time in the Territorial Army.

As for Menzies Tunim, plausibility was perhaps his most distinctive asset. The grin was wide and boyish, which made his occasional fits of anger somewhat the more surprising. Menzies, who insisted his name be pronounced Ming, was a Freemason, so-called judo aficionado and a non-playing member of Surrey County Cricket Club, which allowed him to claim spurious friendship with former prime minister John Major.

It was hard to say quite how much of his background Menzies had embroidered. There were the exaggerated examination successes, the self-proclaimed sporting achievements of his minor public schooldays, and the Duke of Edinburgh Award for Leadership and Outward Bound Adventure. No one, as if it mattered anyway, seemed to have scrutinized the written record. Up at Cambridge he claimed to have been spotted as likely material by an SIS recruiter, his Senior Tutor and Director of Studies at Churchill.

Rosslyn had no idea quite why the Secret Intelligence Service finally rejected Menzies. Perhaps it had to do with a fellow student of his, Marion Shaw, who had entered the secret world with ease. They were said to have been lovers in their days at Cambridge, and Menzies would talk about her with almost pathetic admiration, as if she were some sort of celebrity.

The woman Menzies Tunim eventually married was a decade

4

older than himself, a Polish woman from Wimbledon who had four teenage sons by her previous marriage. The father and former husband had a prison record, mostly convictions for minor fraud. When Menzies came into her life she had at once changed her name from Sharon to Charlotte-Anne and had resigned her job as a cosmetics salesperson and beauty products demonstrator in Self-ridges. He blamed Charlotte-Anne for his expanded waistline. Judging from the pasty complexion, the sloping shoulders and the paunch almost as large as his older brother's, it was hardly surprising that he was a man who always sat when he might have stood, drove his car when he could have walked, and spent his weekends in his dressing gown seated in front of cable TV with sweet white wine and pizza. Though he was inclined to boast of such domestic contentment, Menzies was afflicted with a nervous condition he was at some pains to hide. The condition showed itself in the roughness of the flaking skin on his forehead, wrists and hands. Invariably he wore white silk gloves to hide the blemishes. The gloves were pearl-buttoned at the wrists and he would shoot his cuffs like a sleight-of-hand *artiste* and say, 'The pearls. Charlotte-Anne's idea. Brilliant.'

The Tunims could have opted to recruit one of the many former MI6 officers new in the City of London marketplace. But the redundant spies (mostly from the MI6 counter-terrorist and Middle East departments) had formed their own rival consultancies, offering advice to oil companies, defence contractors and banks on their dealings with Third World markets. 'Strategic advice and intelligence that cannot be obtained from the usual government and commercial sources . . .' was what they provided to their clients. Disingenuously, they claimed 'never to employ current MI6 contacts'. The Tunims maintained that this effectively tied the hands of their rivals behind their backs. Anyway, what else was left for the irredeemably institutionalized former spooks to employ? Hardly brain power.

Rosslyn, however, was a very different animal, even more useful to the Tunims than a former officer from the secret world.

Private-sector creatures, the brothers Tunim pursued profit and, indeed, they had achieved it with some success. During the twenty-two months Rosslyn had worked for them, they had delegated some difficult cases to him; mostly these had involved fraud. There had been the nasty case of blackmail involving a junior cabinet minister's wife, and two or three jobs for a firm of Anglo-Saudi accountants. So far, Rosslyn's previous experience had not been tapped and, in recent weeks, with rumours of recession in the air, he had wondered if his two-year contract with them might not be renewed. Whatever the case, Tunim Associates continued to be one of the more effective commercial intelligence-gathering consultancies in the UK. Europe too.

The culmination of their success had been a trade-off, the result of secret and prolonged discussion with SIS, a trade-off of considerable financial advantage to the Tunims, arranged by SIS Deputy Assistant Director Marion Shaw. The deal, one of several arranged between the public and private sectors of the intelligence-gathering industry, was that they would furnish SIS with intelligence if and when they gained it. At arm's length and in return, Marion Shaw furnished Tunim Associates with lucrative commissions and, from time to time, informally left selected files open on the desk for the benefit of the Tunims' eyes alone.

Rosslyn reckoned that the Tunim Associates' juniors would know nothing of these trade-offs with Shaw and her friends at Vauxhall Cross. Perhaps the Tunims' accountant knew something of them; or the freelance technician the brothers employed to hack into any computer system in the universe so long as it was connected to a telephone. But the accountant's loyalty to the Tunim brothers was unimpeachable and the morose and silent computer man buried himself in the investigation of City frauds for the benefit of companies who had no wish to expose their troubles to the Fraud Squad.

As far as MI6 or SIS was concerned, Campbell and Menzies Tunim dealt directly with Marion Shaw. Rosslyn, of course, knew of her: an angular and conviction-driven career intelligence officer. With secrecy in the blood, she was tipped as the possible occupant of the big office at Vauxhall Cross, a future Director of the Secret Intelligence Service. 'A Cambridge contemporary of mine,' Menzies would brag.

'One of the inner circle. One of the Oxbridge movers and shakers. Thanks be, dark and light blue still count for something in this old world of ours.' Rosslyn doubted it.

On Shaw's recommendation, SIS paid fees into the offshore holding company, Schneider-Portland Investments. The arrangement provided the cover for SIS's white-laundered payments to Tunim Associates. Financially, at any rate, the arrangement was good news for the Tunims. It was Marion Shaw who had approved Rosslyn's commission to survey the security of Cleo's estate and recommend the means for her protection.

iii

Cleo Ipsilanti had been one of MI6's most valuable agents in Greece, Albania and the Balkan states.

MI6 had told the Tunims that her presence in Greece seemed to be regarded by some unfriendly parties as more than a little case-sensitive. Campbell Tunim told Rosslyn that he 'had the feeling our friends at Vauxhall Cross value her more than they let on. Leaving aside Kosovo, it seems there's the continuing problem with the P17N.'

P17N was the provisional wing or splinter group of the Greek 17 November terrorist group. 'As if to underline the sensitivity of Ms Ipsilanti's position,' Campbell Tunim had said, 'there have been threats to kidnap one or other of her two teenage daughters. Cleo has passed the anonymous letters to her former paymasters in MI6.' According to Tunim, SIS had their reasons 'for keeping a wary distance'. Reasons, apparently, not unconnected with P17N. So SIS called on Tunim Associates to advise on precautionary security measures for Cleo Ipsilanti's estate without attracting the curiosity of any Greek government intelligence agency or police, or their counterparts in Albania or in any of the Balkan states. SIS and their American friends wanted to keep everyone as sweet as possible.

Rosslyn left London for Greece and took a room with a sea view at Lela's Hotel and Taverna in Kardamyli.

During his first days in Greece, Rosslyn found the Peloponnese to be the undiscovered treasure of Greece. It was astonishingly beautiful. So was Cleo Ipsilanti. He had not imagined that she'd be dark and slim, with gypsy good looks and such a warm, wide smile.

One of her two daughters, Olympia, was staying with her. The other, Demetra, was apparently in Athens with her father, Cleo's ex-husband Ioannis. He headed a long-established and successful Athens law practice, founded by his father, the Greek patriot and big shot Stamatis Kostas Ioannis Ipsilanti.

Cleo's estate, above Kardamyli, was a forty-minute drive through the mountains from the largest city in the Peloponnese, Kalamata. The approach to the estate was along narrow roads above the small village of Tseria. The wild isolation of the land immediately beneath the Taygetos mountains afforded natural and spectacular protection. In the surrounding villages, several of the Maniot stone houses were owned by retired and amiable British and German expatriates. A few of them lived here all year round.

Cleo's land included several thousand acres of olive groves overlooking the Vyros gorge to Exohori on the golden mountainside to the south.

The neighbouring estate was one of several owned in Greece by the aristocrat and good friend of ex-King Constantine, George Vayakakos. Cleo's closest friend, Vayakakos was presently undergoing treatment in a private London clinic.

The climate, as befits an area prone to earthquakes, was severe. In summer, the temperatures regularly climbed to 100 degrees. Sometimes even more. The mountains and the Vyros gorge seemed to be permanently in the grip of the daytime iron heat. Cleo had told Rosslyn that in winter the cloud was very low, the rain heavy and the rivers in the gorges swollen. If it were not for the stoves she'd installed and the wood that burned day and night, the stone walls of the houses would be damp for months on end.

At the heart of her estate, set in the olive groves, were the three family residences. They were converted stone houses and overlooked the gorge. Precipitous paths and goat tracks twisted down through rocks and thorn bushes, past hidden springs, to Kardamyli and the coast of the Messinian Gulf.

Rosslyn gathered that Cleo shared her apparently idyllic existence with her lover, Nicos Nezeritis. There were several photographs of him around the house. The striking Greek was some years younger than his mistress. Like Demetra, he was an accomplished mountaineer. The photographs showed him standing on summits in the Himalayas, the Alps and the Andes. One showed him in the Taygetos with Demetra. Cleo employed Nezeritis apparently as her personal assistant. She told Rosslyn that Nezeritis had been away for the past weeks on unspecified business in Paris. Olympia had something of the intensity of her mother's eyes and shared her wide mouth, flared nostrils and dark skin. The aura of the gypsy somehow belied Cleo's age. It struck Rosslyn that she had successfully deceived the years.

As to the installation of the discreet system of security, she told him 'she would welcome the construction of the new electronically controlled entrance gates and other protective devices'. She drew the line at boundary fences of steel mesh topped with razor wire or anything else that might attract the hostility of the locals. She was Greek. She loved Greece. She trusted her own and was anxious not to cause offence. She hinted, without naming names, that several of the nation's senior ministers, foreign servants, industrialists and shipping magnates were secretly in her debt. She wanted, for whatever reason, to preserve the low profile of her estate.

V

The experienced agent keeps deception simple. And, with two exceptions, everything Cleo told him during their encounters beneath the Taygetos mountains was true. The first lie she told him concerned the present whereabouts of Nezeritis, her erstwhile lover, assistant and mountaineer; and Demetra, her daughter. To be fair to her, Cleo had no idea about their precise and day-to-day whereabouts at the time.

The second lie was not so much a falsehood as an understandable omission, caused by her refusal to confront the reality that Nezeritis had turned his attentions away from her to Demetra. It seemed to Rosslyn to be a measure of her self-control that she never once gave him a clue to this betrayal. Conspiracy, he observed correctly, was in her blood.

But it was perhaps to her self-control, coupled with her consummate ability to control others, that she owed her survival as an agent in the chaos and bloody turmoil of Balkan conspiracy. Rosslyn could only guess at it. As for her, perhaps somewhere in her mind she entertained the hope that this love affair between Nicos and Demetra, the result of the other intrigue in which they were engaged, would soon enough flicker out.

vi

Every three or four days Menzies Tunim telephoned Rosslyn from London. He took the calls in the privacy of his hotel room and gave a brief report on the progress of his work. He told Menzies that Cleo's estate would be easy enough to protect. He had found nothing especially untoward. True, he had noticed one or two strangers in the vicinity. But he had seen no reason to be particularly concerned about the figures carrying cameras and field glasses. They had seemed to be foreign tourists, bird or butterfly watchers, botanists, or just passing ramblers in the mountains. A couple of them had photographed Cleo's houses, the panoramic view of the gorge and distant coastline. Menzies had advised him to photograph the innocent strangers if he got the chance. To use discretion: 'You can't be too cautions.'

With a light laugh, Rosslyn said he had already done so. 'One or two of them have photographed me as well. Some women. Possibly Germans.'

'What about the Ipsilanti woman?' asked Menzies. 'Has she been cooperative?'

'Very,' said Rosslyn.

'What's she like?'

'Warm, outgoing, friendly.'

'Alan, what else has been going on?' said Tunim. 'You're not personally involved?'

Rosslyn felt Menzies Tunim had probably guessed something of what had been happening.

vii

Cleo and her daughter had proved generous hosts. Olympia readily accepted that, whenever possible, she should remain on the estate during Rosslyn's stay, and afterwards until the security systems were installed. Given the threats of kidnap, it wasn't an unreasonable rule to impose and easy enough for her to follow. When she wanted to make an excursion to the local pebble beaches or to spend a day walking in the Taygetos, and there had been several all-day treks up the goat paths of burning stone to the cool of the mountain ridges, Cleo and Rosslyn had accompanied her.

viii

From high up among the rocks, the views of the coastline ribbon and shimmering lavender-blue sea were breathtaking.

On these excursions, they took packed lunches of tomatoes, bread, cheese and carafes of the local wine. Rosslyn noticed that Cleo always kept a loaded double-barrelled shotgun within reach. There was something slightly erotic about the way she kept the gun with her.

He found Cleo more irresistible than ever. They travelled the precipitous roads that looped and spiralled through the mountain wilderness, affording sanctuary and calm. There was the celebrated clarity of light. The fierce blue sky and relentless heat of day, followed by the cool nights when he had never before seen the stars so clearly.

She had shown him many of the coastal and isolated mountain villages set in the arid Maniot landscape. She said that the imagination could easily transport you back to the Middle Ages, and Rosslyn reckoned she had it right. Glancing into the eyes of the old people in the villages, he began to understand the intensity of passion that inflamed the Byzantine family feuds.

The backdrop to this civilization, Cleo said, was totally appropriate. Volcanic rock is all too prone to violent earth tremors. She showed him ruined villages not far to the south, tiny churches and the chill caves at Cape Matapan, the mythical gateway to hell itself.

It was on the small pebble beach beside a deserted cove after a lunch of bread and wine that they had first made love beneath the windless sky.

ix

By night, accompanied by the din of the cicadas, there had been the dinners with Cleo and her daughter on the terrace beneath the clouds of moths dancing around the lights and the enormity of the night sky pricked with stars.

Afterwards, they sat at the table beneath the vines and talked far into the night.

x

On his last night in Greece Cleo prepared dinner. The priest called in to say his farewells. He said he owed his good English to practice with Cleo. Rosslyn warmed to him.

Once the priest had left, the women performed party pieces.

Olympia, wearing a sweatshirt emblazoned with a portrait of Elvis, sang 'Always On My Mind'. Cleo danced barefoot, a long gold Victorian watch-chain swirling from her long neck. Dressed in white silk, she looked ravishing in the candlelight. Rosslyn never took his eyes off her.

Then, together, Cleo and Olympia sang the lament by Papadia-
mandis:

'This was little Akrivoula,
Granddaughter of Mother Loukaina.
Seaweed is her marriage-crown,
Shells are her dowry.
The old woman still laments
Her ancient child-bearing
As if the world's pain and sorrow
Could ever end, ever end.'

xi

The voices seemed to echo across the empty gorges to the summits
of the mountains in the darkness. By candlelight, they each dropped
a pebble into the deep well on the lower terrace and made a secret
wish, vowing never to tell each other what they'd wished. Cleo was
the last to drop a pebble in the well. 'I want this to go on for ever,'
she said.

Rosslyn helped her replace the wooden cover. He caught the scent
of her perfume and felt the white silk of her dress brush his knees,
and then, as if she were making a secret sign, felt her hand squeezing
his. With that, the fun beneath the stars was over. And barking dogs
fell silent.

Accompanying Rosslyn to his hire car, Cleo said, 'Come back to
the Mani, Alan. Treat it as home from home.' Then she added, 'I've
never really asked you quite how much you know about my
previous existence. My secret career.'

'Only what little you've told me about it. You asked me not to ask
questions of a professional nature. Wasn't that what you said? You
said it's not something you're allowed to talk about.'

'Perhaps you've guessed about it already,' Cleo said. 'But I doubt
you've guessed the disappointment. Too much lost. Too many of my
friends. Too many lives.' She looked back at the night-lights of the

estate's houses sparkling through the olive trees. 'I was advised to give all this up, Alan. Perhaps I should have done so for safety's sake. Sold up. But I love it. Nicos doesn't want to settle with me in England and I can't say I blame him for that. Perhaps I will have to disappear. With or without Nicos. What's confusing me . . . well, let's say the person who has confused me is you, Alan.'

If the mention of Nicos Nezeritis pained him, Rosslyn did not let on. 'I can understand,' he said. 'But I don't want to be the source of your confusion.'

'Be careful how you drive back down to Kardamyli,' she told him. 'You've had a fair amount to drink.'

'Thanks to you,' he said. 'Too much. You've been very kind to me. In every way.'

'My pleasure,' she said, her face in the dark shadows. 'You've made me very happy, Alan. Promise me that you'll come back here.'

'One day,' he said. 'Yes.'

'Good,' she said. 'Then take this.' She handed him a sealed package. 'Open it when you get safely back to your room. Before you go to sleep. And don't ask me.'

'Don't ask what?'

'If you can stay here tonight.'

'You read my mind.'

'I know mind-reading. It's a gift I have. One day I'll let you in on the secret of my confusion.'

xii

He drove fast along the spiralling roads bordering the mountain gorge down to Kardamyli. The music on the cassette full blast.

With Cleo on his mind, London seemed to be a thousand miles away.

xiii

Alone in his hotel room Rosslyn opened the package Cleo had given him. Inside it, a letter:

Alan,

Tonight you'll be back in London and the real world. But whenever you wish to come here to me and next time to my bed instead of the wet softness of the grasses in the Vyros gorge, you only have to say. I enclose 3,000 dollars to cover your expenses. Treat them as an emergency fund to be used when you can come back to me. I cannot tell you how much it has meant to me to be your lover. Forget everything you know about my past. As you know, I have spent too long in the dirtiness of the ordinary world. I am so inordinately in need of you that I will not tell you. Now burn this. Keep the gold chain for ever. Wear it when you return to show me nothing's changed. I am in love with you and I don't want you to break my heart.

  Cleo

PS: I enclose a photograph. Please keep it with you.

xiv

In the photograph Cleo stared into the camera's lens. She was standing in a stone doorway. Brushed slightly to the right, her hair was shining. The skin of the forehead was unlined. The eyebrows, though thick, were long and even. The eyes seemed to be very slightly unaligned. It was as if she wasn't just staring into the camera lens but penetrating it. The nose was perhaps a little too long. The nostrils were flared and perhaps it was they that suggested the gypsy origins. The shoulders were a little too wide. Around her neck she wore a gold chain and the sunlight sparkled on several of the links. Her breasts were firm and full. Her stomach was not quite firm: a small roll of flesh was visible beneath the navel. She was wearing worn and dusty leather sandals. Otherwise, she was naked.

XV

He opened the parcel she had given him and inside it found the antique gold chain wrapped in several layers of tissue. And there was the bulky envelope containing the high-denomination US dollar bills.

The gold chain touched him. But the dollars he had no need of made him feel uncomfortable. It was the first time a lover had given him money like this. Something about it made him feel compromised. He had said his goodbyes to her in his way. He had promised to return. He had told her that he loved her. But there was no reason for him to visit the estate tomorrow to find the convenient moment alone with Cleo to return the money to her. Anyway, because of visitors she was expecting later in the day, she had asked him not to go there.

He heeded the warning voice telling him to return to London.

Part One

On 2 March 1998, exactly on schedule, building contractors moved into the heart of the British Museum. This marked the first stage in the construction of Lord Foster's Great Court. When it is completed in autumn 2000, it will instantly become one of the sights of London.

Our great poet Yannis Ritsos expressed the feeling of our entire people when he wrote:
Αὐτὲς οἱ πέτρες δὲ βολεύονται μὲ λιγότερο οὐρφνό
[These stones cannot make do with less sky.]
I believe that the time has come for these marbles to return to the blue sky of Attica, to their natural place, to the place where they form a structural and functional part of a unique ensemble.

TOP SECRET
The Trustees of the British Museum have no entitlement to give away the Elgin Marbles.

1

On the third Saturday in May, many of the demonstrators who had arrived in Bloomsbury seemed reluctant to accede to the instructions of the police and leave their makeshift banners outside Conway Hall. Dense with traffic fumes and pollen, the atmosphere seemed to increase the edginess of the police officers standing by the entrance. They were eyeing the arrival of the several hundred demonstrators who had come to hear an address by the Cambridge Professor of Classical Archaeology in support of the restitution of the Elgin Marbles to Greece.

The meeting began shortly after three o'clock. The professor's tone was more like that of a speaker at a memorial service than a public agitator's. What he had to say seemed to pain him. Certainly, there was not the slightest hint in his address of the violence that followed later that afternoon.

'The lamentable history of the Elgin Marbles,' he said, 'is generally well known to all of us here. For those of you, ladies and gentlemen of the media, who seek the facts on which our case is based, a press release will be handed to you as you leave and before we march from here to the British Museum and then on to Downing Street to hand in the petition signed by many thousands.'

Speaking without notes, he issued a grave but not entirely necessary reminder to the audience: 'We are here to remember that Lord Elgin, the British Ambassador to the Ottoman sultan, arranged for whole sections of the marble sculptures, indivisible elements of the Parthenon, to be wrenched off with great and almost casual violence. He then had them summarily shipped to Britain, where they arrived in 1802. Financially embarrassed, Lord Elgin sold them to the government in 1816. And the Marbles have remained in London for almost 200 years.' Stabbing the air with an accusatory finger, he said, 'Looted by Elgin, the Marbles represent the highest point in the cultural history of Greece. Some say the world. They are arguably the highest artistic achievement of mankind. A world treasure beyond price. And the demands for their return have been persistent, and the arguments for and against as passionate as our own. It is such demands, the demands for restitution to Greece, that, in the name of all right-thinking people throughout the world, we support.'

This was greeted with a round of vigorous applause.

'Let no one be in two minds,' he added, 'that the monument to which they belong is in Athens.'

Cheers interrupted him.

Once they had subsided, the professor went on, 'The world can be sure that the government of Greece will ensure that the Marbles are properly housed near the Parthenon. This will enable the many millions of people who visit the Acropolis each year to see the temple almost in its entirety. The Marbles will be in safe hands. That is guaranteed. The British have an obligation, not just to Greece, but to the cultural heritage of the world, to return them to the Parthenon, which also happens to be the emblem of UNESCO. There can be no sensible disagreement whatsoever with the argument for restitution on aesthetic grounds: namely, that as many of the sculptures that remain outside Greece as possible be brought together with those still in Athens, thus putting an end to the disfigurement that Elgin started.'

There were cries of 'Hear, hear.'

'Neither need there be any suggestion whatsoever that to hand the Marbles back will begin a flood of requests, or other such demands, for the holdings of the world's museums and galleries to be similarly restored. Restitution of the Elgin Marbles will not begin some form of cultural musical chairs. On the contrary, we are talking of unique works of art. A unique situation. The unique remedy.'

Sustained applause followed.

'The Greek government maintains that the new Acropolis Museum will receive the sculptures. The Greek government will cover the costs of transportation from London to Athens, as well as those incurred by making a complete set of copies for the British Museum.' He paused, before raising his voice again: 'My friends, we ask that a wrong be set right.'

The applause was warm and prolonged.

The chairman of the meeting then thanked the professor and said that the Minister for Culture, Media and Sport had been invited to attend the afternoon's proceedings but had declined. This announcement was received with jeers.

'Similarly, the Trustees of the British Museum said they were unable to send a representative.'

More jeers.

Once they had subsided, the chairman announced that both he and the Cambridge professor would be happy to take questions from the audience.

The first questioner identified himself as a journalist from *The Times*.

'Isn't it true,' he asked, 'as Greek ministers themselves recognize, that many more people see the Marbles in London than ever would in Athens?'

'With very great respect,' said the professor, 'that's a hypothetical question. Even the British Museum's attendance figures are, to put it politely, vague.'

'What about conservation?' asked the journalist.

'What about it?' said a heckler.

'Greece has much to learn about it,' said the journalist.

'Is that a statement or a question?' the chairman asked.

'Sit down,' the heckler yelled.

'A question and a statement,' said the journalist.

This prompted a woman to rise quickly to her feet. She introduced herself as being from the Greek embassy in London. 'It is a proven fact,' she said, 'that for several decades the British Museum has undertaken restoration work that was misguided. The Marbles were cleaned to the point at which the original paint was stripped away. And many features of the original carved surfaces that might have allowed scholars to ascertain the work of individual sculptors have been removed.'

'Let me suggest,' the professor intervened, 'that the only lesson Greece needs about restoration from the British is not to follow our own example.'

Then a woman, an American 'from the *New York Times*', said, 'The aesthetic case for restitution made by Mr Louis de Bernières looks pretty thin, doesn't it? I mean, on view in Athens, the Marbles will be invisible from the Parthenon, won't they?'

'Balls,' a heckler shouted.

The professor took up her point carefully. 'There is, of course, the argument that the Marbles are central to the rebirth of classical Greece as seen through foreign eyes. I have already, I hope, made it clear that they are indeed unique – uniquely the common property of Western civilization. It is not, however, it seems to us, the British Museum that made them so. And it is not within its halls that they should remain.'

While the chairman waited for anyone else to put a question, the tall woman who had been standing to the rear of the hall left unobtrusively.

Outside the hall, the police officer who had been ordered to make random checks on those attending the meeting asked her to identify herself. The woman showed him a printed ID card. It read:

Marion T. S. Shaw

Foreign and Commonwealth Office

Downing Street

London SW1A 2AL

Inside the hall there were no more questions and the chairman said it was now time for the march to the British Museum to begin. After that, he said, they would proceed to Downing Street to deliver the petition. (As it turned out, the petition never was delivered, and it is not known what eventually happened to it.)

Under the eyes of the police, the march to the British Museum began as a relaxed and orderly affair.

In their hearts perhaps, the distinguished Cambridge Professor of Classical Archaeology and the demonstrators, however voluble, however passionate, all silently recognized that the combination of long-standing political inertia and the old quasi-legal maxim that possession is nine points of the law would always apply. There was something of the lost cause about the case presented by the professor. No matter that Byron and Shelley, and even Thomas Hardy, had inspired people with the idea of restitution; or that the voices of distinguished academics, journalists and major international figures in the arts and sciences have, for many years, been continuously raised in favour of restitution.

The police had agreed in advance that the marchers could assemble at the back of the British Museum in Montague Place. To the surprise of the organizers, several hundred other protesters, youths with less peaceful intentions, had already gathered there.

It seemed that the youths were expecting trouble. And among them were at least two dozen ugly figures resembling football supporters with Union Jacks painted on their shaven foreheads. Police, who had already erected crowd-control barriers, surrounded the youths and the painted shaven heads in turn. More than a hundred tourists from half a dozen buses and other curious bystanders had gathered to see what was happening. To one side of what was already in effect a police cordon were two police officers mounted on horses.

With some awkwardness, the professor used a portable amplification system to address the faithful and began a shortened, and somewhat more rhetorical, version of the address he had already made in Conway Hall. It was when he reached the passage about the British having an obligation to the idea of justice and so forth that the can of beer was thrown hard into the professor's face. Stunned, he staggered, and a woman standing directly to the professor's right, wearing an Indian shawl and linen hat, succeeded with difficulty in taking over the microphone.

'It's that sort of British vandalism and irresponsibility which we deplore,' she cried out. '*Please*. This is a peaceful demonstration.

'Cow,' one of the phalanx of shaven heads shouted at her in chorus.

The woman cried, 'We are here to persuade the British government to restore to Greece what belongs to Greece. *Please*.'

The police did not at once make a move. They allowed the shaven heads to continue the catcalling and bawling. Some of the thugs had now worked their way among the banner-carriers and when, without great difficulty, they snatched them, they began to smash the banners and force a line of several dozen demonstrators against a van that was selling hamburgers and cold drinks.

Heavy boots went in at once as if on cue. Several demonstrators collapsed against the wheels of the van and its owner started yelling out in panic. Soon the van was entirely surrounded by shaven heads and other youths who joined in an attempt to overturn the vehicle. The violence seemed oddly orchestrated.

'There are people trapped beneath it,' someone shouted, only to be met with a wave of catcalls and raucous laughter.

A woman's voice screamed: '*Help!*'

Moments too late, uniformed police tried to separate the youths and shaven heads from the demonstrators, who were anyhow retreating in shock and disbelief. Two, perhaps three, bloodied demonstrators, badly hurt by flaying boots, had managed to crawl beneath the van. To safety, so they believed.

The mounted police officers brought their horses closer to the van, which now seemed to be the centre of the violence. Voices were raised asking for calm and were suddenly distorted. Heads butted heads. There was the sound of breaking glass. Ugly shards were jabbed against bare arms and against hands raised to protect faces spilling blood. And still another voice was yelling at the owner of the van to get clear. Many of the demonstrators backed away in shock, falling over banners and their colleagues in retreat. There were more cries of anger.

Then smoke was gushing from the open windows of the van and, as if people sensed the imminent disaster, panic spread. Screaming children were lifted into adult arms as the police sirens began to wail.

The explosion that engulfed the van must have been powered by the ignition of the petrol tank. It was a single and deafening thud, followed by a gigantic spit of flame that seared eyes and faces.

Within seconds many suffered appalling burns and two people lay dead.

At this point, the woman who had identified herself to the diligent police officer at Conway Hall as Ms Shaw was watching the conflagration from a safe distance in Malet Street. Well out of earshot, Marion Shaw was on her mobile phone, talking to the Director General of MI6. Her tone conveyed not a trace of regret for what had happened. When she said she would be speaking to the police contact about the investigation that would inevitably ensue, the DG asked her to give him time. He would speak to the 'relevant police officer personally' and 'get back' to her. Shaw told him she was heading home to rejoin a woman friend, her weekend guest.

Pigeons rising in front of her, she hurried to her car, which was parked near Russell Square. With leather shoulder bag in one hand and mobile phone in the other, her knuckles were white, her jaw set.

2

Just over half an hour later, Marion Shaw arrived back at Frognal. Hers was the top floor in the early-twentieth-century annexe of the Old Mansion, the nine-bay brick house of two storeys set back from the steep road.

She made her way up the stairs and let herself into the darkened hallway. 'Christiane?' she called out. But there was no reply from Christiane Prevezer, the Second Secretary and resident SIS officer in Greece, on a few days' leave from the British Embassy in Athens.

She found her asleep beneath a duvet and quilt on the living-room sofa. There was a bottle of whisky and a glass on the floor and next to them an open bottle of sleeping pills. Only when Shaw opened the shutters did the other woman stir and begin to cough.

'God, look at the time,' Prevezer said. 'Why didn't you wake me when you left?'

'I tried to,' Shaw said. 'I'll make some coffee.'

Wrapping the quilt around her shoulders, Prevezer followed Shaw into the kitchen. 'What happened?' she asked.

A thin figure, Prevezer had narrow, sloping shoulders. Her dry skin was pale, the backs of her hands freckled and the fingernails bitten to the quick.

Shaw told her. 'It got totally out of hand. The meeting became a demonstration. And the demonstration became a riot. At the last count there are certainly two dead, maybe more, and God knows how many people suffered serious burns. They set fire to some van selling junk food.' She shook her head.

Dark and slim, Shaw was an attractive if rather severe-looking woman in her thirties. She would not have been out of place as the matron of a private clinic. The husky voice with the affected drawl of some older generation did not entirely succeed in disguising the West Yorkshire flat 'a's.

There was a look of desperation in her eyes now as she said, 'It was complete chaos.'

'I'm sorry,' said Prevezer. She lit a cigarette. 'It's not your fault though, is it, Marion?'

'No one's fault,' Shaw said bitterly. 'Not mine. No one's fault. Not the DG's.'

'He already knows what's happened?'

'I told him,' said Shaw. 'There'll be the inevitable police investigation. And that may be too close for comfort for all of us. For the DG. Downing Street even. And perhaps, let's face it, Christiane, for you and me.'

'What, you think the DG may be having second thoughts?' Prevezer said. 'Surely not?'

'No. At any rate, not yet.'

'Who were the people who died?' Prevezer asked.

'Two elderly women,' said Shaw. 'I don't know who they were.' She filled a glass with mineral water.

'Do you have any painkillers?' Prevezer asked.

Handing the glass to Prevezer, Shaw said, 'In the cupboard. Help yourself.' She began to pace around the kitchen.

Prevezer swallowed two tablets. 'Are you quite sure the DG isn't having second thoughts? If so, you must tell me, Marion.'

'He only knows what you and I know. It's my love-child. When the operation begins we'll pin the blame on bloody Greece. They will be the criminals.'

Prevezer considered Shaw's remarks in silence for a while, then said, 'You don't think the DG could conceivably know that you have a personal agenda in all of this?'

'What do you mean?' Shaw asked quietly.

'Or that someone at the office has been dragging up our past?'

'I'd know about it if they were,' said Shaw. 'There's no possible way they can find out.'

'And my past too?' Prevezer asked.

Shaw shook her head. 'No.'

'I hope you're right,' Prevezer said. 'If you don't mind me saying so, it'll be dangerous if you allow this blood thing to show.'

'What are you getting at, Christiane?'

'How deeply you want revenge on the Greeks. Don't let anyone see it's a blood thing.'

'Who do you mean by *anyone*?'

'The DG. Don't let the DG see the poison. It's OK for you to show your deepest feelings to me. But, Marion, don't let anyone else see them.'

Shaw smiled. 'You think it shows?'

'Well, I see it, yes. But others . . . who can tell whether anyone suspects that you're facilitating this robbery in order to obliterate the horror of your past?'

'I can sense suspicion when it's around,' Shaw said. She raised an eyebrow. 'And you, Christiane, isn't that what you're doing too?'

'I don't have to tell you about me.'

With that, Shaw began to laugh. 'You don't have to tell me,' she said, 'about the bloody awful mess you're in.'

'That's my point,' said Prevezer. 'As I said last night, I do wonder how wise it was to have engineered the man Rosslyn's visit to Cleo Ipsilanti.'

'Last night you drank too much, Christiane,' Shaw said. 'Far too much. In fact, I'm surprised you can remember anything at all, let alone what you said about Rosslyn. You leave him to me. He's the puppet and I'm the one who pulls the strings. I control the Tunims. I control Rosslyn.'

'And the DG?'

'I know him better than he knows himself.'

'But you didn't succeed in controlling the demonstration.'

'I didn't intend to, did I?' said Shaw. 'It's served its purpose. You'll see.'

'I hope so. Let's face it, we need each other, don't we, Marion?' Prevezer said. And as though doubting it, she added, 'We still need each other very badly.'

'I know,' Shaw said sharply. 'And that's why I want you back in Athens. Rosslyn isn't going to cause me any difficulty. Neither is

Cleo Ipsilanti going to be a problem. She's a woman with a secret past and present, and there are parts of them she doesn't want exposed. Chapters in her past and present that neither she nor the DG want bringing into the open. And they are very personal. There you have it. No one will be a problem, Christiane. No one. Enough said.'

Prevezer found something troubling about Shaw's conviction. Sometimes there was something cruel in those dark eyes. Her driven and ambitious friend and colleague in the secret world was beginning to show signs of the fanaticism of the solitary, and it frightened her to be quite so deeply in Shaw's thrall. True, Shaw was brilliant. You had to admire her mind and the passion for extraordinary Byzantine conspiracy that matched the obsession with Greeks and Greek politics and history. But even for a senior SIS officer, and Prevezer was familiar with most of them, Shaw's impenetrable coldness and ruthlessness were virtually unmatched. It was as well, Prevezer had good reason to know, to have Marion Shaw as your ally and not your enemy. And she knew that in both her professional secret life and her secret personal life, Marion Shaw exploited people's weaknesses incessantly; Christiane Prevezer was no exception.

She was about to ask Shaw about those chapters in Cleo Ipsilanti's past and present which 'neither she nor the DG want bringing into the open'. The chapters that she said were 'very personal'. But she could tell that the moment had passed, and anyway, had Shaw wished, she would have elaborated on them. Christiane Prevezer sensed that whatever the problems were, Shaw was keeping them up her sleeve for a rainy day.

3

The emergency services took several hours to clear the scene in Bloomsbury. Forensic experts performed their duties. Statements were taken from witnesses. Six shaven heads and three demonstrators were held at Holborn police station, where they were questioned. The police proffered no charges and later released all nine.

By midnight, salvage teams had removed the burnt van and, under the eyes of police officers, council cleaners cleared all traces of the violence. The story made the front pages of the early editions of the Sunday papers. The Elgin Marbles had once more become an issue and the editorials about the violence in Bloomsbury succeeded in having something of the propaganda effect that Marion Shaw wanted. A tabloid headline yelled: YOU'VE LOST YER BLOODY MARBLES, GREECE.

The police established the identities of the two people who had died in the violence. It seemed an especially poignant twist of fate that they were Greek tourists, two elderly sisters who had unwittingly paid their last respects to the Elgin Marbles. To some degree, the poignancy was exploited in the secret exchange of letters between the British Prime Minister and the Director General of the Secret Intelligence Service in London and the Prime Minister of Greece in Athens.

Prime Minister, Greece, to Prime Minister, United Kingdom

Dear Prime Minister

It is with profound regret that the government of Greece has been informed by the United Kingdom Secretary of State for Foreign and Commonwealth Affairs of the death of the two Greek nationals that occurred outside the British Museum on Saturday afternoon.

We trust that your government, its authorities and the British police will take the fullest possible measures against those agitators and bring to justice the murderers of the innocent Greek nationals who died.

The tragic and disgraceful events that took place in London do nothing to advance the case of the British government and people, who have for many years understood full well the case for the restitution of the Parthenon Marbles to Greece. We have drawn your attention on numerous occasions to the suitability of returning the Parthenon Marbles in the year 2004, the date of the Athens Olympiad. The Parthenon Marbles remain the symbol of national deprivation. They must be returned in the name of ancient title and aesthetic sense, and such claim has its basis rooted in law, justice and likelihood. Scholars acknowledge them the world over to be a milestone in European and world culture.

You may be sure, Prime Minister, that the two tragic deaths that have occurred in London will not have been in vain or be seen to have been in vain come the day the Parthenon Marbles are rightfully returned to Greece.

The President of the Hellenic Republic and the government of Greece feel sure that, under your leadership, justice will prevail.

Moreover, the people of the world await the gesture of selfless courage, the gesture you can make, to restore confidence in the stated wish of the British government to demonstrate its belief in a united Europe and reaffirm its commitment to set right the wrongs of history.

TOP SECRET
Prime Minister to Director General, MI6

The draft of my reply to the letter from the Prime Minister of Greece is enclosed. If you require alterations or emendations to be made you should communicate these by return. You will recall our brief and unminuted discussion with the Secretary of State for Foreign and Commonwealth Affairs concerning Greece. Our firm position is that the status quo concerning the Elgin Marbles must be preserved.

TOP SECRET
<u>Draft</u>
Prime Minister, United Kingdom, to Prime Minister, Greece

Dear Prime Minister

Thank you for your letter. Her Majesty's Government deeply regrets the tragic accident that occurred outside the British Museum last Saturday. We deplore the violence that resulted in the death of two innocent bystanders and serious injury to many others.

You may be sure that the Secretary of State for the Home Department is personally monitoring such investigations as are necessary. Equally, you may be sure that the police are taking whatever action is necessary to apprehend those who are responsible for this outrage.

It remains impossible for the government of the United Kingdom to accede to your request for the restitution of the Elgin Marbles or any further discussion of the issue in either the short- or the long-term future. Further, it is clear that such restitution has no basis either in law, in justice or in likelihood. Your remarks do little to advance your case for restitution.

The Trustees of the British Museum have no entitlement to give away the Elgin Marbles.

While former colleagues may, in the past, have suggested some measure of willingness to support your case, please rest assured that no such willingness now exists and that no policy alteration will be entertained by Her Majesty's Government either now or in the foreseeable future.

TOP SECRET
Director General, MI6, to Prime Minister

New Century House
Vauxhall Cross
PO Box 1300
London SE1 1BD

Dear Prime Minister

Thank you for your letter and enclosure. There is nothing, from my point of view, which needs alteration in your letter to PM Greece.

The officer with overall responsibility for this matter in so far as it relates to Greece and the Balkan area is Ms Marion Shaw, who is in close contact with her subordinate at the Athens embassy, Ms Christiane Prevezer. Ms Shaw continues to keep Chairman Joint Intelligence Organization informed on a regular basis.

Ms Shaw remains directly and exclusively answerable to me alone for whatever operational action requires to be taken.

You may be sure that Ms Shaw is an officer of great ability in the Service. She is held in high regard by staff at all levels and has much experience of Greece and the Balkan states. Likewise, I have complete confidence in Ms Prevezer.

I recall our discussion with the Secretary of State for Foreign and Commonwealth Affairs and our agreement that such future discussion remains unminuted.

Widely reported in the world press, the deaths of the two elderly Greek women excited still further calls for the restitution of the Elgin Marbles. For some days, the British media continued to maintain that the United Kingdom had the right to keep them in the British Museum and that there was no possibility of restitution. Letters presenting both sides of the argument appeared in *The Times*, whose editorials supported the British Museum's case to keep the Marbles. Various compromise plans were mooted. The Department of Culture, Media and Sport was said to be considering the proposal that the British Museum open a branch in Athens and that the Marbles be housed within it, but they wouldn't be given to the Greeks outright. Thereafter, that summer at any rate, the public debate about restitution seemed to have reached stalemate. What might or might not happen to the Marbles was a matter for speculation and the future.

4

Beneath the leaden London sky the British Museum looked more like some impregnable and majestic furniture repository undergoing repair than one of the world's greatest treasure houses. Majestic treasure house, maybe. But not impregnable.

Originating in 1823, the building is itself a symbol of the ideal of a museum and arguably one of the finest examples of nineteenth-century Greek Revival architecture in the world.

Throughout 1998, the massive task of restoring and transforming the museum continued and, unlike the situation with the Millennium Dome at Greenwich, the progress of construction had so far attracted no controversy and went largely unreported. It had, however, been scrutinized, in conditions of the greatest secrecy, by the criminal Athens syndicate that had commissioned the clandestine entrance of two intruders.

At much the same time as the criminal syndicate formulated its aims, the removal of the British Library to its new site at King's Cross took place. This gave the Trustees of the British Museum the opportunity they had long hoped for: the transformation of the central space of the courtyard into what would be the core of the new museum's extensive buildings.

Work to enhance the vision of the original architect, Robert Smirke, a massive undertaking of restoration and improvement, was on schedule and the display on the hoardings informed the public what in general was taking place:

- Removal of the late-nineteenth-century Front Hall extension.
- Building of a new portico of neo-classical design on the south side of the courtyard.

- Creation of new public spaces.
- Restoration of the Forecourt, Front Hall, Great Court, former North Library, the Montague Place entrance.

In addition there was the installation of new lifts and a monumental staircase to lead the millions of visitors to a walkway linking the Great Court with the main museum's upper galleries.

This space – and some said that it was destined to be the greatest exhibition space in the world – would soon enough be enjoyed by visitors to new display areas, lecture halls, restaurants and special events. The court scheme alone, costing almost £100 million, the work of architect Lord Foster, was as gigantic in ambition as it was magnificent in concept. The painstaking restoration by a workforce of many hundreds continued apace. Some 16,000 tonnes of cement were brought on site; 2,000 tonnes of Portland stone, the single largest piece weighing eight tonnes, were quarried and finished to cover the 6,000 square metres of courtyard façades. The construction of the roof of the inner courtyard, as large as a football pitch, required the manufacture of 3,500 individual pieces of triangular glass, no two of the same measurements. These were some of the statistics of construction taking place behind the massive hoardings, mostly out of public view.

The most visible tools of construction were the two gigantic tower cranes. Manufactured by Wolff in Heilbronn, they were painted bright red and had extraordinarily long reaches – no less than seventy-five metres. They were forty-six metres tall, a metre more than Nelson's Column, and were capable of lifting enormous weights. These tower cranes seemed to dominate the whole area, immobile and inactive, in the dark dawn of the last Sunday in May.

5

The streets surrounding the British Museum were damp and silent. And because it was early on Sunday, none of the construction force was on site. Not far distant, the clock of St Pancras Parish Church was chiming the morning hour of six when the two masked intruders set about the start of their clandestine business. The climb over the outer wall.

The lead climber, Nicos Nezeritis, wore similar clothing to his companion, Demetra Ipsilanti. Black nylon mask with slits for the eyes and mouth. Drab, close-fitting top. Wild Country harness dyed black and, dangling from the climbing harness, a chalk bag filled with dark grey powder to increase friction on hand-holds. Each wore black stretch tights and high-friction Asdo butyl rubber-soled rock boots. Each carried grey nylon climbing rope coiled around their chests. Their heavy backpacks each contained micro-weight Natsume combination stone cutters and vacuum units. Cement guns. Eye shields. Lightweight hammers. Additionally, they were both carrying well-hidden, loaded .45–calibre handguns.

The two intruders had precisely sixty minutes to break into the British Museum, to complete their work inside and to get out again unobserved. They felt secure in the confidence of their climbing skills; the walls of the British Museum, even though wet and slippery, amounted to a grade E3 climb, nearing the limits of free climbing.

Using the protruding edges of bricks and flutings as holds, they climbed to the top of the first wall. Then, looping the rope round a protruding pipe, they abseiled the ten metres to the ground inside the museum's service area. Landing between a pile of tarpaulins and tall steel garbage drums, they then left the rope fixed to the wall. The rope would allow them to make quick their departure within sixty minutes once their morning's business inside the museum was finished.

Their business was by way of preparation and was crucial to the final stage of the robbery. Timing was of the essence. Nezeritis defined the crucial sixty minutes as the *zone*, consisting of a maximum of five minutes for their entry into the Duveen Gallery, then fifty minutes for work inside: loosening the Elgin Marbles' wall attachments and the undetected insertion of easily removable adhesive cement.

Their work inside the Duveen Gallery was intended to enable the final assault team to complete the task with care and absolute efficiency. Scheduled for a date and time as closely guarded a secret as the militaristic methods of final removal and transportation of the Marbles from the British Museum.

There were additional fail-safes in place, precautionary measures that had been arranged to afford the intruders protection against being caught. For example, the circuitry of the museum's alarm and surveillance system, linked to the security room and the Metropolitan Police, had been disabled – the result of inside information. Likewise, the locking system of the high glass interior public access doors to the Duveen Gallery had been disconnected. If any of the duty night guards, on patrol throughout the interior of the museum, were alerted to something untoward, then these heavy glass doors would stay locked and prevent the guards from taking emergency action against the intruders. The intruders would be able to complete this preparatory mission in safety, secure, unseen and uninterrupted.

In the silence of Sunday morning, the pair were climbing well within the limits of their technical expertise. One part of their mind concentrating on technique. A second on the result of a fall. And a third on the procedures to be followed in the event of either of them being injured, apprehended, or both. Although we may be forgiven for thinking differently, in their own minds no mystique attached itself to the undertaking. While not quite like any other job, to them it was still a job.

Few climbers prepare themselves mentally in the same way, and the two Greeks were no exception. Perhaps they visualized the crucial moves, thinking of them as far more difficult than they were, so that the reality of what confronted them would turn out to be less intimidating. The most frequent cause of failure is loss of confidence: say, the reluctance to climb for short periods without protection, or without complete concentration. They were well aware of the need to avoid such shortcomings.

During the past few months in Greece their preparations had been exacting. They had undertaken intensive and solitary night climbs of buildings with sheer stone walls. Bridge embankments. Telecommunications masts outside Athens. They had completed the necessary weapons training on a former Greek Army firing range in Sparta. They had also developed endurance and a mental state cool enough to suppress the debilitating fear of unforeseen accidents or pursuit by the British authorities. If they were seen or caught, they would have only their skill, their considerable physical strength, their handguns and their wits to assist in the getaway.

As it happened, they had suggested to their paymaster that the task of preparation for the eventual robbery might best be carried out by a single individual. But the paymaster had insisted that they must work as a pair. To carry in two sets of equipment in case of technical failure. To complete the work within the *zone*. It went without saying that they could not risk capture. If the notion of failure or disaster ever entered their minds, then it would only be failure of a technical kind. The stark fact was that if one of them were incapacitated and thus unable to leave, the other would need to see to the casualty's dispatch. If this dreadful possibility crossed their minds, it was understandably left unspoken.

They moved together quickly across the service area of the British Museum.

At the western side of the museum complex they reached the nearest section of the exterior wall of the Duveen Gallery. The well-practised diagonal approach at ground level was executed in silence, out of line of the security CCTV cameras fixed to the wall above.

Next to an electricity conduit, Nezeritis fastened the rope to the fine black cord hidden behind a downpipe. The cord was the undetected and solitary remnant of two previous and successful Sunday morning clandestine entries.

Some twenty metres above them, at the roof's edge, the cord passed through the eye of a single small piton driven hard into a crack in the exterior of Portland stone. Nezeritis hauled the cord to pull the rope through the eye of the piton above, and kept on hauling until he retrieved the other end of what was now a loop. Checking it was secure, he leaned backwards, with his feet against the stone wall, and allowed the rope to take his weight to test its anchor. Then he began the Jumar ascent of the sheer wall up to the edge of the roof above him, sliding the ascendeurs progressively in the doubled rope. Here, he secured his footing and paused a moment. He beckoned Demetra to follow.

Moments later both were standing on the northern edge of the glass roof of the Duveen Gallery. They left the rope in place and began to crawl along the surface of the parapet.

When they neared the far edge and northernmost corner of the roof they found the glass panel that had been loosened previously to allow them access. Nezeritis carefully raised it and gently set it to one side. From this position, the pair had a good view of the roof space beneath the exterior roof of the Duveen Gallery.

Completed like a marble mausoleum in 1962, the Duveen Gallery houses the frieze sculptures Lord Elgin had removed from the Parthenon. The rectangular panels, the metopes, and the pedimental figures are displayed in two transepts, one at each end. Of glass, the shape of a tent, the roof looks like an inverted V, and it covers the length of the large central gallery; its base consists of more glass panels. These form the translucent glass ceiling of the interior that houses the chill mausoleum dedicated to the preservation of the world's greatest works of art. It was here, to one side of the pinnacle of the inverted V, that Nezeritis fastened his rope to a steel support, making sure that the anchor was secure.

He lowered himself about four metres to a girder providing a secure foothold. Next, he set aside a second glass panel above the bank of display spotlights. Once this was lifted aside, the space allowed him access by rope straight down, at an angle of ninety degrees, to the marble floor of the gallery some twenty metres below.

Now the morning's work, this third stage of the loosening of the wall fixtures of the Elgin Marbles, was about to begin.

With his feet over the parapet, one hand on the climbing rope, Nezeritis clipped his ascendeur into it, checked it and nodded to Demetra. The nod indicating that he was now ready. Then he abseiled silently to the marble floor. Seconds later, Demetra followed Nicos down in silence.

For fifty minutes, wearing eye shields, they used the micro-weight Natsume combination stone cutters to cut away the fixtures of the Marbles on the south wall. They employed cement guns to insert the adhesive cement that would hold the Marbles in place, allowing them to be the more easily detached during the final raid. They then used the portable vacuum units to clean up the tell-tale signs of stone dust. That done, without hurrying, they concentrated on the execution of the return route.

They climbed the walls again using Jumars. To the top. Then down. And out to Montague Place.

Phase Three complete, they called the Athens number they had memorized. The number belonged to one of the world's wealthiest tycoons, in whose mind the plan for Strange Police was coming to fruition: Constantine Dragos.

6

In Athens that Sunday morning, Constantine Dragos calculated that Phase Three, the preliminaries inside the British Museum, should by now have been successfully completed. He was waiting for confirmation that the plan for Strange Police could be moved forward: for the call from Nicos Nezeritis in London to say Green. Or Yellow, if it had been completed with a minor setback. Or Red, if they had hit trouble and the mission had been aborted. He waited with a greater sense of unease than usual. The demonstration in London must surely, he believed, have persuaded the authorities to intensify security at the museum. If the protection of the Elgin Marbles had been his business, he certainly would have insisted on still greater security measures.

He sat on the wrought-iron balcony of his neo-classical Athens home, chain-smoking together with his boyish partner, Miltiades Zei. The sun caught the edges of the tiled roofs, the *akrokerdmata* or terracotta Medusa heads and goddesses, turning them the colours of a ripe apricot. Yellow, gold and slightly pink. There were distant sounds of stallholders in the flea market around Monastiraki.

The glass doors to the rooms of the upper level were open. Inside, on the floor of the spacious front room, lay body-building and weight-training equipment. Beyond an arch was a room with desks laden with state-of-the-art communications technology. Above the desks electronic maps and charts showing the Dragos Messinian Air international routes lined the walls. Small red lights pinpointed the present position of the airline's Boeing 737s and opposite the electronic charts were floor-to-ceiling photographs and interior plans of the latest aircraft purchased by Constantine from Boeing in Seattle.

The view from the top storey of the house in the Plaka across to the Acropolis in the south was magnificent. Dressed in white cotton robes, the two men gazed at the mass of limestone rising in all its glory from the plain of Attica and at the Parthenon: Chamber of the Virgins. Softened by the haze, its magnificence fuelled their mood of anticipation.

Zei followed Dragos's gaze to the open skies and saw, painted with the distinctive bright blue of Messinian Air, the Boeing 737 climbing high above Elikinon Airport, bound for Amsterdam. 'I know what you're thinking,' said Miltiades Zei. 'Don't worry, Constantine.'

'You're right,' said Constantine.

He was thinking of Nezeritis and Demetra somewhere in London and the companion Boeing on stand-by in the United Kingdom to bring them home again to Greece. Once Nezeritis came on the line with the codeword Green, Constantine as paymaster would be able to wake his father, Alexios, aboard *Hellenic*, the forty-six-metre family yacht built in the shipyard at Pisa by Andreatta-Rizzo. The luxury motor yacht, with its steel hull and aluminium super-structure, was moored in Piraeus at the Zea Marina between *White Knight of Araby*, from Road Harbour in the British Virgin Isles, and *Marala*, from Panama.

Green, and Constantine would report success. The son would have once again earned his spurs and the father could not fail to be pleased with his sole heir. This, as his grandfather, erstwhile friend of a frail Sir Winston Churchill in the years of senility, might have said, marked the beginning of the end of the beginning.

Forty-two years old, Constantine Dragos was managing director of the Messinian Shipping Corporation (MSC), the worldwide ship-ping line and air transport conglomerate, of which his father, Alexios Dragos, was chairman and life president.

Educated privately in Switzerland, at Balliol, Oxford, and at the Harvard Business School, Constantine could effortlessly have pursued a career as an academic of some distinction. Indeed, possibly believing that with him on the faculty they would benefit from the Dragos millions, Harvard had offered him a research post. But, like his father, Constantine considered the academic life to be ultimately escapist. The real world called. And the reality of increasing the family's wealth. Courteously, he declined Harvard's offer.

The origins of the enormous Dragos fortune could be dated to just after the Second World War, when Constantine Dragos's grandfather Stelio owned the Dragos Line. The most spectacular increase in the family's wealth came in 1979, coinciding with the jump in oil prices which followed the Iranian Revolution.

Then, in the early 1980s, MSC diversified. Constantine supervised the expansion of the fleet of ships, Japanese-built bulk carriers and oil tankers. The MSC ships were Liberian-listed to minimize tax payment, because Liberia, unlike Panama, keeps no register of companies. To ameliorate the possibly enormous cost of insurance liability and disaster claims, each ship was owned by a separate company, established by the Trust Company of Liberia in New York. Simply out of courtesy, when in Piraeus the ships of MSC flew the flag of Greece.

With the 1990s, Constantine turned his energies to the streamlining of Messinian Air, the airline of some thirty-five Boeing 737s, offering highly competitive tourist, corporate and business flights from the United Kingdom's Luton and Stansted Airports.

The financial management of Messinian Air, Constantine's baby, was, as with its parent MSC, to say the least, secretive. Monies were funnelled into the Dragos-owned Zemitz-Schmidt Bank in Vaduz, Liechtenstein, which owned substantial London freeholds in Mayfair and Knightsbridge, others in Manhattan, and still more in Sydney. The Zemitz-Schmidt bank also controlled the finances for funding the plan for the restitution of the Elgin Marbles.

There had been no doubt in the mind of either father or son that Constantine Dragos would succeed his father, just as Alexios had succeeded Stelio. When Constantine returned to Athens from Harvard, to his house with the view of the Acropolis and his office in Piraeus, he applied himself with monastic zeal to the stewardship of the Dragos fortune. He also determined, even more actively than his driven father did, to pursue their shared obsession: the restitution of the Elgin Marbles referred to in the secret codicil of Stelio Dragos's Last Will and Testament. Where successive Greek governments, the generals and the newer politicians had so conspicuously failed, the Dragos family would succeed. By whatever means necessary, they would make the gesture that would write the name of Dragos into Greek history for all time.

The Elgin Marbles would become the Dragos Marbles. The Dragos gift to the new museum of the Acropolis. To civilization and the world. Retribution for two hundred long years of arrogant British vandalism and philistinism would be achieved with the success of the robbery: Strange Police. And Constantine would share the triumph with his young lover, Miltiades Zei.

Together, after many months of research in London, Constantine Dragos and Miltiades Zei conceived a plan of great brilliance and daring. Central was an element of good fortune. The British played, as it were, into the hands of Dragos *père et fils* – Alexios and Constantine.

Constantine Dragos was his obsessive father's son. Unusually tall for a Greek, he had lost his right hand dynamiting fish with friends off Crete. Attached to his right elbow, a metallic and sharpened claw served as an effective replacement. A practitioner of martial arts, he had on several occasions, it was rumoured in Athens, allowed his anger to get the better of him in island bars and he had employed the claw to blind two armed Albanian illegal immigrants before they had a chance to draw their guns. The Albanians' companion, a hapless Turkish merchant sailor, had been taken to hospital minus the ears Constantine had severed, with his lower intestines so severely punctured that the wonder was the man survived five days in intensive care before he died. Charges against Constantine for triple murder had never been brought. Substantial payments to local police secured their silence and the media reported that Constantine, far from having committed murder, had selflessly intervened in the violent brawl. Others, who kept silent, knew better. Unwritten wisdom said that it was best to keep in the good books of the family Dragos or, if possible, keep out of their books altogether.

Alexios Dragos was nowadays only infrequently seen in public. He wore heavy dark glasses and shared his life with the diminutive Mitsuko, the Japanese companion who rarely left his side.

Father and son kept in constant communication by mobile phone, or by means of satellite telecommunications wherever in the world they might be. Like his father, Constantine was, in spite of his inheritance, a driven man, and the aura of urgency and violence about him was sometimes almost frightening in its intensity. Both men shared a passionate dislike of Great Britain and the British. Bordering on hatred, it found expression in their determination that the Elgin Marbles be returned to Greece. Many other Greeks thought and felt similarly, yet they seemed powerless to act. Time and again, promises to achieve restitution had been broken by Greek ministers, just as they had been by their British and European counterparts.

There were, of course, those British philhellenes, worthy liberal academics like the Cambridge Professor of Classical Archaeology, and a clutch of serious journalists and romantics who still argued unsuccessfully for the Marbles' return. With these people Dragos father and son had no contact. The time for talking was over. Direct action was needed.

Something else significant fuelled the Dragos family's obsessive dislike of the British. Alexios felt he had been personally humiliated by them, and by Constantine's mother no less. The British woman had cuckolded him in favour of Austrian financier Wolfgang Bruch, of Bruch AG. She had successfully sued Alexios for sixty million dollars after a legal wrangle and prolonged divorce case, the outcome of which he referred to as The Drop in the Ocean. A bitter reference, given that shortly after the divorce settlement had been made she had fallen from Bruch's motor yacht off the Azores and drowned in what many felt to have been doubtful circumstances.

With another woman, there was even said to have been a love-child: the daughter whose paternity Alexios Dragos vehemently denied. Whereas, of course, Constantine's paternity was sure and open, it was said that only Naumann Bartenstein, the premier firm of Viennese lawyers, were privy to the girl child's identity. There were those elderly women retainers of the Dragos household who maintained that the girl was the living reflection of the mother and that was why Dragos wanted nothing to do with his offspring. Others maintained that all of this explained why, whereas the Alexios Dragos Public Cultural and Educational Foundation awarded substantial scholarships to academics in Hellenic Studies in the United States, France, Italy and Russia, none would ever be given to a Briton. The British were the enemy. To be reviled. Scorned. Fought.

Since the departure of The Unmentionable, a veil of secrecy hid Alexios Dragos's personal relationships. The word, in those Athenian circles where such things were mulled over, was that he had fathered the children of several high-class Greek women already married. There were the rumours that he had struck deals with the compliant husbands, whose wives enjoyed Alexios Dragos's sexual athleticism. Now and then some Greek journalist or other would prepare a colourful story about these Dragos conquests, only to discover soon enough that the Dragos lawyer, Ioannis Ipsilanti, had obtained a writ against the proprietor of the hapless newsman's paper. The articles were spiked. Inevitably, at best, the newsman was sidelined; at worst, he was sacked without explanation or notice. Though the rumours would hang in the air as seven-day wonders for the diversion of Athenian socialites, none seemed to have a clue about the exact focus of Alexios Dragos's campaigns of seduction. There were also the jokes, none entirely wholesome, about those men who had fallen under the spell of the metallic claw of Constantine and the devotion of his lover, Miltiades Zei.

In the manner of his father, while waiting for the London call Constantine Dragos brooded on the secret meetings scheduled to take place one week from now in the Piraeus offices, on the fifth floor of Messinian Shipping Corporation of Liberia in Platonos Street. The clandestine unit of Greeks would assemble in the offices behind closed doors. He would give them the final briefing and this would be followed by the inspirational address, the call to action, given by Alexios Dragos.

Neither father nor son were under the illusion that the restitution would be easy or come cheap. On the contrary, the operation had been planned with military precision and vast sums of money had been earmarked for its completion. Loyalties had been bought on pain of death with the resources of the Dragos family in the Thrace Bank.

The clandestine unit comprising former Greek commandos, a military engineer and a Greek Air Force pilot was ready to go in response to the call of Constantine Dragos at a moment's notice.

For over eighteen months, again assisted by Miltiades Zei, Constantine Dragos had been secretly making painstaking inquiries throughout Greece about possible recruits from among experts who possessed the necessary skills. They had perused the authoritative trade journals, *Covert Action*, published in Washington DC, and *For Your Eyes Only*, the regular and up-to-date summary of intelligence on current military matters, published in Amarillo, Texas. He found that most of those he short-listed showed a preference for steering clear of direct involvement in combat operations. Rather, they sought the safer option: the offer of military training and strategic advice.

In strict secrecy, they had drawn up a list of private military companies in the United States, United Kingdom, South Africa, Israel and France. Including Sandline International, there had been at least ten firms in London to consider, with 8,000 former British soldiers on their books and combined overseas contracts worth more than £100 million. European Security Operations, based in Westgate, Kent, told Dragos that they could provide him with a protection team within forty-eight hours. But protection was not what Dragos and Zei had in mind.

Finally, there was the choice of personnel. A patriotic matter. One of important principle. 'We are Greeks. It is a blood issue.' Common sense finally prevailed. The personnel for Strange Police would be exclusively Greek, and Nicos Nezeritis with Demetra Ipsilanti, who undertook the preparatory missions, completed the necessary training with flying colours.

Now, as he waited for the call from London, Constantine had

good reason to be pleased with the men whose services he had bought with the greatest care. The efficiency of the hired guns, their skill, sheer professionalism and even brutality had to be admired. Constantine believed he had chosen well. But one crucial problem still remained: how best to penetrate the security and protection of the British Museum. As he waited for the call from Nezeritis, it was the security that caused Constantine unease.

The initial resolution of the security problem he reached had been as simple as it would be difficult to effect. Somehow, one or other of the British Security Services had to be penetrated. The question was: how could this be achieved in a short period of time? The answer had been found closer to hand than expected.

7

The Dragos arm, at first charming and then with a firmer grip –
symbolized, as it were, by Constantine's sharpened metal claw
– was discreetly applied to Ioannis Ipsilanti, the family lawyer. And
it never let go until the lawyer came up with the name.

Through the good offices of Ioannis Ipsilanti they found their
woman at the British Embassy in Athens. Second Secretary
Christiane Prevezer, colleague and friend of Marion Shaw. Ms
Prevezer, with her love of Greece. They offered the Second Secretary
and MI6 officer financial recompense. Feigning offence, she at first
refused to accept it. *What do you take me for? A traitor? Typical. If I
were a man you wouldn't be treating me with such contempt. This is a kind
of cheap abuse.* But once her tirade had finished, Ioannis Ipsilanti
mentioned the divorce files, the transcripts.

The transcripts were of the lawyer's interviews with the bisexual
and promiscuous Christiane, who had consistently betrayed her
wealthy husband, the senior security adviser to the British Cabinet
no less, in the bed of two Corsican separatists: one male, one female.
Prevezer's admissions had been full and frank. Greek rhetoric
slammed into the weakened target. He kept on repeating her name.
*Christiane, you're bent. Christiane, you're in every kind of serious trouble.
Christiane the Secret Servant, the British diplomat and pervert, exposed to
ridicule. Christiane, Christiane, wise up to reality.* By the end of it he
had reduced her to tears.

Alone, working nights in her second-floor office at the back of the
British Embassy, it took her four long days to access the information
from Vauxhall Cross.

Second Secretary Prevezer had been thorough. She downloaded

the results of her handiwork on to a disk for Ipsilanti. The disk contained detailed plans of the British Museum. Details of the electronic security systems. The technical drawings of the alarm circuits. Names of the chief security personnel, two of them from the firm in the private sector who had been under surveillance on the sex tour they had joined in Frankfurt for Manila the year before. The monthly 'Top Secret Sit-Reps of MI6/MI5/Met/Home Office'. Briefings as they applied to 'Level 3 Red Targets: UK, London District and Home Counties'. She made the single copy and took it home to her Piraeus flat above the Mikrolimano on Vasileos Pavlou Street. There she added her appraisals of the security and surveillance systems, the routines of the guards, the hierarchy of responsibility for protection and copied the lot on to a second disk.

Over breakfast on the roof terrace of the Hotel Castella above the Mikrolimano, a short walk from her flat, she handed the latest airmail *Guardian Weekly* to Ioannis Ipsilanti. Wrapped inside the newspaper was the second disk.

Ioannis Ipsilanti gave the Prevezer disk to Constantine Dragos the same morning in the Piraeus offices of MSC.

'Gold' was how Constantine Dragos had described the quality of the secret intelligence that the compromised Prevezer had given him.

Finally, the call from London came through and Constantine heard Nicos Nezeritis say the word: 'Green.'

Dragos and Zei relaxed together in the shower.

This Sunday was also the day that Christiane Prevezer would be joining them for lunch at one-thirty. Constantine Dragos was looking forward to seeing her. They would celebrate the success of Phase Three.

Early in the afternoon, Prevezer was seated opposite Constantine Dragos and Miltiades Zei on the veranda of the flat with the view of the Parthenon. She wore a crumpled linen suit, a cheap man's watch and canvas shoes. The blue and white striped silk shirt was open at the neck. Her eyes were still puffy from sleep. Broken veins in the pale cheeks revealed something of whisky drinking to excess. Her straw hat was on the table. An air of the sour and the smug hung about her.

'There's something,' she announced, 'that I think perhaps you should know. To do with Ioannis Ipsilanti's former wife. Cleo. I assume you realize she worked for the Embassy?'

'Yes. On the cultural side.'

'The truth is slightly different. She may be retired now. But before that she was an officer in MI6. One's colleague. And she's still of considerable interest to the Service.'

'Why are you telling me this?' Constantine asked.

'You already know,' Prevezer said, 'about Cleo's former role?'

'Yes,' said Dragos. But that was a lie. He did not know about this role of his lawyer's former wife. If the information unnerved him, he was careful to show no signs of it. 'What is the problem?'

Prevezer said, 'The Service has a man out here in Greece advising her on personal protection.'

'Who is he?' Dragos said.

'A London security consultant,' said Prevezer. 'Alan Rosslyn.'

Dragos looked at her with a frown. 'Who exactly is he?'

'Rosslyn? Oh, just what you'd expect. Professional. Experienced. A hard man. I'm simply telling you that if he's got the slightest wind of Strange Police then he'll pass the intelligence straight to London.'

Dragos stared at the Englishwoman. She was, unfortunately he felt, a necessary evil. It was hard to see quite what those Corsicans found physically attractive in her and her breath reeked of stale alcohol. She gave him a wry smile. 'Have I disturbed you?'

'You don't disturb me,' said Dragos. But, of course, she did. He added, 'Call me when you have any news from London.'

Prevezer left and Constantine Dragos stared towards the Acropolis and the Parthenon. He felt the unwelcome sense of growing fear.

Miltiades Zei could see it in his lover's eyes.

'This man Rosslyn,' Dragos wondered aloud, 'this business of the protection of Cleo Ipsilanti. What the hell can it be about?'

'Ask Ioannis,' Zei advised. 'Why not?'

Dragos called Ioannis Ipsilanti on his mobile phone. Watching the

51

sunbeams on the Acropolis, he told the lawyer quietly that he was not a happy man. He needed to know exactly what the Englishman had been doing in Greece. How far could Cleo Ipsilanti be trusted? Ioannis Ipsilanti was silent.

'You should know, Ioannis,' Constantine Dragos told the lawyer. 'You were married to her. What is the Englishman doing?'

'I don't know anything about him.'

'I do, Ioannis. He's working for the British Secret Intelligence Service. Find out what he's been doing here.'

Ipsilanti was evasive. 'Find out what, Constantine?'

'I've told you,' said Dragos. 'You're still fond of her, aren't you?'

'You know that, Constantine.'

'She was the one who left you for Nezeritis, wasn't she?'

'You know she was.'

'And you hate Nezeritis. Why?'

'You know why, Constantine.'

Dragos twisted the knife. 'So, say this man Rosslyn's been screwing the mother of your children.'

'What do you want me to do?' said Ipsilanti, his voice shaking.

'I've already told you, Ioannis. I want you find out everything about the reason for the Englishman Rosslyn being in Greece. In Kardamyli. And, Ioannis, I mean it. *Everything.*'

8

On this final morning then, on the jetty at Kardamyli, overlooking the magnificence of the Messinian Gulf: the short swallow dive Rosslyn executed was graceful. The splash sent out ripples edged with white and silver. He swam away from the shore with a slow and relaxed crawl. At first the sea felt warm. Then, because fresh water spouted far below from fissures in the volcanic seabed, it turned freezing cold. A surprising and heady mixture of water temperatures, both comforting and bracing. After a few minutes he trod water, breathed deeply and squinted at the rising sun.

Later, beneath the shade of the vines on the veranda of Lela's Hotel and Taverna, he breakfasted alone on thick yoghurt, fresh eggs, honey and bread. The light breeze stirred the bougainvillaea and giant geraniums. Wasps, attracted by the rich waxy honey, soon cut breakfast short. He was halfway across the hotel veranda when the sound of the approaching Toyota jeep broke the silence.

When the vehicle came into view Rosslyn recognized the driver as the priest from Tseria. He watched the priest's approach with a slight sense of apprehension.

Without so much as a good-morning, the priest asked anxiously, 'Have you seen Olympia?' He was tapping his foot on the dusty gravel.

'She'll be up at the house,' Rosslyn said.

'No one's answering the phone and the place is locked.'

'Maybe no one's awake yet.'

'Then why has the phone been dead all night?' said the priest. 'Other people's phones are working. My wife says the lights were on in Cleo's houses all through the night. If it's all right with you, I think we should go there together. I don't wish to enter the house without you. I think there's a problem. Something's wrong.'

'Let's go and check it out then,' said Rosslyn. 'Wait here for me while I put some stronger shoes on.'

He returned to his room. Changing into different clothes, he remembered the package containing the US dollars. He would return them to Cleo. It seemed only fair. Taking the package with him, he returned to the priest, who was waiting for him at the wheel of the Toyota with the engine already running.

The tyres hummed on the sun-baked new tarmac road out of Kardamyli. The priest turned on to the empty, twisting mountain road for Prosilio fast and the Toyota raised dry dust against the walls covered in the painted blue graffiti proclaiming the favoured political colour of Maniot Royalists. He swerved to avoid a woman dressed head to toe in black. She was shouting something at the goats in the scrub beside the road.

'Take it easy, Father,' Rosslyn shouted above the din of the engine. He could see the apprehension in the priest's dark face.

9

Beneath the mulberry trees, Rosslyn and the priest opened the iron gates to the estate. Rosslyn had with him the package containing the US dollars.

Each of the four stone houses had its own separate stone terrace linked by a series of wide smooth rock steps. He saw that all of the night-lights on the stone walls were still on. The lights the priest's wife had presumably seen burning through the night.

Heat enveloped him. So did the heavy fragrance of the jasmine surrounding the trickling fountain in the main courtyard. The scent was so heavy, Rosslyn thought, its sweetness was almost sickly. Droning insects hovered above the surface of the oval pond. Some flicked against his sweating forehead. The silence, broken only by cockerels crowing in the distance, seemed to be a warning sign. There were no dogs barking in the yards above where they were supposed to stay at night until either Cleo or Olympia called each by name and took them out for exercise in the olive groves. No dogs. And there was no sign either of the usual tribe of playful cats. Even the lizards seemed to be hiding.

'Bruno?' the priest called out. The dog made no reply. *'Bruno?'*

'Take it easy,' Rosslyn told him. 'Let me go first. Just in case there's someone unwelcome here. We'll look at Cleo's rooms first. Stay close to me.'

He approached the first house and the narrow door of solid wood, pushed it open slowly and stood still, waiting for his eyes to adjust to the gloom. Listening. He called out, 'Hello? Cleo? Anyone at home? Hello?'

There was no answer.

He knew the layout of the house. Cleo's bedroom was at the back.

The cool room had once been a stable and two of its walls were of solid rock. Opening the door, he caught the familiar fragrance of her scent. Instinct: some sense of premonition seemed to warn him against what his eyes were seeing. He heard the buzzing of insects in the fetid air. Outside, from somewhere in the distance, he heard the sound of a chainsaw's motor and the voice of a melon seller distorted by amplification. As his eyes grew more accustomed to the gloom, he saw the porcelain bowl containing peaches and next to it the glass vase of dry wild flowers. Flowers they had picked together at Cape Tenaro. And then, in the dark shadow, the contours of the animal. Breathing evenly, he fought for self-control.

Feet and paws. He was staring at the twisted body of the dog. The dead animal lay sprawled diagonally across the wide bed. The white linen sheets were drenched in blood. It had been shot at close range. Half of its left shoulder had been blasted clean away. Oddly, or so it seemed at first to Rosslyn, the animal's eyes were closed.

He stooped down to where the telephone lay on the marble floor and lifted the receiver. The line was dead.

To his immediate left was the door to the shower room. He had to look in there too. Nauseated, he stumbled over a dish of dog food on the floor, and found the door difficult to open. Something was blocking it on the inside. Opening the door against the pressure, feeling something move away, he felt a wave of coldness numb his spine. Perhaps it was Cleo's body that he half expected to find lying on the floor. The saliva had dried up in his mouth. His throat and lips were parched. He tried and failed to swallow. He switched on the shower-room light and, instead of Cleo, he saw it was another of the dogs that had obstructed the door. Shot dead, the smashed and bloody body lay in a twisted heap across the white floor tiles. Covered in shattered glass. It seemed as though the gunman had blasted open the vanity cabinet containing Cleo's cosmetics, make-up and containers of painkillers and vitamin pills. The glass had showered the dog. Had he been looking for drugs or something else? Money? What? But why kill the dogs? Where was Cleo?

He backed out of the shower room. Fear was generating a fierce throbbing in his temples. He recognized the corrosive weakness spreading downwards from his thighs to his feet. Through the doorway, he caught sight of himself in the cracked mirror. His face stared back at him open-mouthed. Instinct told him to throw open the shutters of the windows in the bedroom. To let in the air. But before he did so, struggling against the sickness rising from his stomach, he stood in the middle of the bedroom, looked about and then took another long look at the dog on the bed. Who had done this?

He saw an open box of paper tissues on the floor next to a striped towel and a pile of underwear. And Cleo's briefcase, lying on the floor near to the legs of the bedside table. It was half-open and he noticed the slim leather wallet. He quickly looked inside it. Flicking through the thick wads of drachmas, dollar bills and fifty-pound notes and fingering the half-dozen or so credit cards, he concluded that this was no kind of hit-and-run robbery gone very wrong. Even Cleo's open leather jewellery box containing diamond rings stood invitingly and apparently untouched on the bedside table's lower shelf. And there was her laptop on the writing desk, untouched. His eyes pricked with what felt like anger. He heard himself repeating, 'O God, O God,' as if it were a mantra.

He set the package containing the US dollars on the table by the bed and, holding his breath, gently covered the dog with a corner of the linen sheet. How could he leave it here, alone, in this dreadful silence? He crossed the room to the windows and threw open the shutters. The glass doors clattered against the stonework. Outside all was quiet again. Even the insects seemed to have fallen silent. So too the chainsaw and the melon seller had moved on, his amplified and distorted voice now out of earshot. Silence. Until he heard the priest yelling, 'Alan, come here.'

Sensing what the other man must have found, he ran out of the house. He ducked his head to avoid the branches of the fig trees. Took the stone steps two by two. Passed the ornamental pond, to the open door of the nearest house.

Open-mouthed, hands covered in blood, the priest was trying to speak, but words escaped him. Motionless, standing just inside the doorway, he stared into Rosslyn's eyes. Like a broken gargoyle, his head seemed to nod towards what was inside. Trying to bar Rosslyn's entry, he croaked, 'Don't look, don't look.'

Rosslyn, his face set, touched the priest's arm. Fear seemed to drain his heart of blood. 'Steady,' he said softly, his dry lips quivering. 'Let me see.' He did not want to look, to see, but he pushed gently past him and went into the room. Bracing himself, he waited for his eyes to adjust to the gloom. Then, still squinting, he looked about him.

The marble floor was a sea of blood, and his shoes seemed to drag on the stickiness. He needed to touch something and reached for the metal of an ironwork chair to steady him. The sour-sweet smell of blood filled his nostrils and he heard his own breath wheezing and rattling in his throat. He stepped across to open the shutters of the nearest window.

Carefully, he moved the bed away from the wall. Some training text he vaguely remembered from his previous life as a Customs and Excise investigations officer: *Murder is 99 per cent domestic in origin. Almost invariably it follows some prolonged and violent struggle and the victims, almost always female, have sustained injuries to the face or arms or hands as they struggled desperately to protect themselves. The attacker most often knows the victim.*

But there was no body. Only Olympia's discarded sweatshirt and the bloodied image of Elvis Presley.

Outside, he sank his hands and forearms into the water of the ornamental pond, splashed it into his face and breathed heavily.

'Where are they?' the priest pleaded.

'I don't know,' said Rosslyn. 'All we can do now is find a phone and call the police.'

'The blood . . . is it Olympia's?'

'I don't know, Father,' said Rosslyn. 'I just don't know.'

'But we have to find them.'

'We can take a look around,' said Rosslyn. 'But it really will be best if we let the police do the search.'

'I have this feeling that they're dead, Alan,' said the priest.

'There's no sign of them in the other houses. I think they've been kidnapped, Alan. You know about the threats?'

'Yes, I know. Perhaps someone saw whoever spilled the blood. The police'll find out who. Let's look around. Then we'll get the police up here fast.'

Leaning against the stone wall of the veranda, he looked down to the terrace and across the olive groves, shimmering in the heat.

'Do you realize the Mercedes has gone?' said the priest. 'Someone must have taken them away in it, Alan.'

Which was what Rosslyn was thinking until something caught his eye: sun glinting on varnished wood. Black metal. The buckle of the dull canvas strap of the shotgun. The weapon lay on the flagstones beside the well on the lower terrace. Then he saw that the wooden lid of the well was askew.

The priest followed his gaze. His eyes caught Rosslyn's and they must have had the same thought simultaneously.

They walked down the steps to the lower terrace and looked at the shotgun. 'Don't touch it,' Rosslyn told the priest. 'It'll have fingerprints on it. Leave it where it is.'

He lifted aside the cover to the well and peered down into the darkness. Lichen covered the sides and some fifteen metres below was the patch of still, dark water reflecting the light of the sky and the blur of his own head and shoulders. He froze. He was staring at a white silk dress.

'The dress,' said Rosslyn. 'It's Cleo's.

The priest looked down into the well. 'Why? Why?' he said.

Rosslyn looked again. Far below, to the dark pool and the floating white silk. Short of breath, he felt his legs weakening, his body shuddering. He tried and failed in his imagination to piece together what must have happened. The blood. The dogs. And Cleo's body dumped in the fetid water of the well. He squinted into the darkness. There was the dress all right. He looked harder. He could see no head. No limbs.

Perhaps it was shock that prompted him to take the gold chain from his pocket and drop it into the well. He heard the tiny splash and heard himself saying, 'We must call the police.'

After he had made the call from the priest's house to the police in Kardamyli, Rosslyn telephoned Menzies Tunim in London. He told him what he had seen. The blood. The dead dogs. Cleo's dress at the bottom of the well.

'No,' he said in reply to Menzies Tunim's question, 'I didn't see her body. Look, the well's too deep for me to start climbing down to look. For Christ's sake, Menzies.'

He could hear the sound of the priest's wife wailing in the next room.

'Stay by the phone,' Tunim was saying. 'I'll call you back. Give me fifteen minutes.'

The strong light of the afternoon sun hurt his eyes and even in the iron heat he felt cold, almost feverish, grief rising in his chest in spasms.

The priest was standing in the doorway. 'What can we do?' he asked.

'Wait for the police.'

'Nothing like this has happened in living memory,' the priest said. 'I think we must go to the house and stay with the dead.'

'Yes, we should,' said Rosslyn. 'I'll come with you once I've taken the call from London.'

The priest looked baffled. 'London?'

'Yes. It's important I speak to my office again. They're calling me back. I'll wait.'

The priest seemed unable to fathom out what London and Rosslyn's office might have to do with the calamity.

'Would you fetch me a glass of water, please?' Rosslyn asked him.

The priest sighed and left the room. He returned a moment later with the glass of water and a small dish of figs. But the offering did nothing to assuage Rosslyn's grief. The cold water tasted metallic and the warm figs bitter. He felt a confused sense of shame and desperation.

Some ten minutes later, not fifteen, it was Campbell Tunim who called back from London. 'How are you feeling, Alan?'

'Terrible.'

'Are you alone?'

60

The priest was still standing in the doorway, hands folded across his chest.

'No,' said Rosslyn.

'Can they hear any of this?'

'Only what I say.'

'Then be careful what you reply to me, Alan. Just yes or no. What with the shock and everything, are you OK to drive?'

'Yes. Why?'

'Because you have to get out of there at once, Alan.'

Rosslyn thought of Cleo. Of Olympia. Of what he had said to the priest, that he would accompany him to the house. The priest was right. To leave Cleo's body up there alone would be an insult, a betrayal. 'I can't leave.'

'Alan, you must.'

'The police will want to talk to me.'

'Exactly. That's why Shaw wants you out of there. And now.'

'It's nothing to do with her,' said Rosslyn sharply.

'It most definitely is. Listen to me. You must get the hell out of there now.'

'I can't.'

'You can. You will. And don't take the flight you booked out of Kalamata.'

'What is it Shaw wants me to do?'

'To drive straight to Kalamata. Do not go back to your hotel. Drive straight to the railway station. It's near the avenue Leoforos Aristomenous. Between the esplanade and the bus terminal. You'll be met outside the entrance to the station. Our friend will be waiting for you in exactly one hour's time. And she'll stay there till you arrive.'

'Who is she?' said Rosslyn.

'Prevezer.'

'Sorry, who?'

'Some woman colleague of Shaw's from the Athens embassy. Christiane Prevezer.'

'She can't get to Kalamata from Athens that fast.'

'She's already there. You'll recognize her. One of the women you saw taking photographs. Your fail-safe watcher. She'll see you safely on a private flight out of Kalamata. Don't speak to the daughter any more or to anyone else. Just get the hell out of there. And fast. Find Shaw's friend, Prevezer. I'll meet you off your flight tonight. You'll be landing at RAF Northolt. Special delivery.'

This is something. They must be rolling out the red carpet if it's to be Northolt.

'We'll go up to the house now,' Rosslyn told the priest. 'Let's wait for the police there.'

They left the cool of the house for the heavy heat outside and walked up the steep and narrow road in stony silence. The sun was very high above the mountains. The heat colossal.

Broad and powerful, the priest walked with the agility of the mountain man. Stumbling, unused to the rough surface, Rosslyn led the way, forcing the pace, knowing that the police would arrive shortly. It would be touch and go whether or not they arrived before he left and he prayed that the priest had, in his confusion, left the keys in the Toyota.

Another uncertainty began to nag him: *Suppose I pass the police en route to the Kalamata road? They will surely recognize the Toyota being driven by a stranger, stop me and ask why I'm leaving the crime scene . . .* A voice in his head told him it hadn't happened. And he felt an overwhelming urge to take one final look at Cleo. To be there when the police raised her body from the well. Lizards darted for cover beneath a white limestone rock. *No, he told himself, no. Get out of here.*

Overhead, very high above the mountain ridges, two buzzards floated, carried by the currents of the air, hovering.

The Toyota was parked where the priest had left it. He saw the keys in the ignition. 'If you don't mind, Father,' he said, 'I don't think I can face looking at the scene a second time.'

'I understand,' the priest said gently. 'Why don't you wait at my house?'

Rosslyn muttered his thanks. He watched until the strong, black-robed figure had climbed the stone steps and was out of sight, then opened the gates and, quickening his step, returned to the Toyota. He slipped into the driving seat, started the engine and did not once look back.

Turning off the road hard right, he drove the Toyota up a narrow track and killed the engine. Listening to the silence, broken only by the bell clanging from the neck of some distant goat, he stared at the heated rocks and crags. Some, like broken jagged bones, protruding from the green scrub.

Far below, beyond the cypresses and shimmering rocks, lay the sea: blue turning silver at the sweep of the horizon. Then the sound of the approaching vehicle on the road below concentrated his mind. As he had expected, he saw the white police jeep leaving Prosilio fast on the twisting road below and the cloud of yellowish dust behind it.

It passed by suddenly and he waited a moment before restarting the Toyota, reversing, turning and then heading away down the track, in the direction of Kalamata. The wind and dust in his raw and stinging eyes only added to the pain.

Kalamata, largest city in the southern Peloponnese. Scarred and sterile way-station recovering from the earthquake that laid waste to it a decade ago. The air was thick with dust from building works and petrol fumes. The sounds of the traders at the market stalls. Dour men with wrinkled skin. Gold teeth glinting in the sun. Endlessly flicking worry beads, clack-clack, around their hairy hands. Girls in tight shorts riding pillion on the motorbikes. A smiling priest holding hands with two laughing small girls. Beyond the happy trio he saw the thin woman with the straw hat who was standing beside the black BMW.

She shook Rosslyn's hand limply and introduced herself as 'Christiane Prevezer, British Embassy, Athens' . . . while at the same time holding open the passenger door of the BMW. Shifty and prissy at the same time, she managed to convey the message that she was going to be very pleased to be shot of him.

She drove to the airport at high speed. The interior of the car was filthy. It reeked of cat and stale cigarettes. An empty Coke can rattled around his feet and there were stains where its contents had dribbled across the floor.

'London's rather upset, to put it mildly,' she said.

He cleared his throat.

'Do you know who could've done it?' she asked briskly.

'No idea,' said Rosslyn. 'Did you know the Ipsilantis well?'

'Only Cleo. By reputation. It's terribly sad. You must be feeling awful.' This was the practised show of sympathy from the woman who's seen it all before.

'You could say so. Who wouldn't be? I still am.'

'Did you get to know Cleo well?' asked Prevezer.

'Yes, I did,' said Rosslyn. 'And, by the way, there's some fairly sensitive material in my hotel room. Along with my passport and personal belongings.'

'They're the least of your worries,' said Prevezer.

'You'd better collect them,' Rosslyn told her.

'I already have,' said Prevezer wearily. 'Swept up. That's my job. The eternal sweeper-upper. That's the easy bit. Housework. A woman's work is never done.'

'Where are they now then?'

'Quite safe,' she said abruptly, adding, 'Your canvas bag is in the boot untouched.'

'And there's the little matter of the Toyota I took and the hire car I left in Kardamyli.'

'I know,' said Prevezer. 'My problem. All taken care of. No need to fret.' She parked away from the terminal at Kalamata Airport, near the military and Greek Air Force buildings. 'If you'd come with me, Mr Rosslyn.'

He followed her to the buildings in the heat. 'The plane isn't due for a few hours,' she said. 'I've arranged a room for you where you can pass the time. By the way, if you're worried, you won't need a passport or a ticket.' Then, as she showed the uniformed sentry her ID, almost as an afterthought, she asked, 'Are you hungry?'

'No.'

She led the way along a corridor. A door opened into a vacant office with a small TV on a desk. She opened a small fridge beside the washbasin. 'Pity you're not hungry,' she said. 'There's a packed meal for you in here. You can pass the time with TV. Oh, and there are some cold drinks. I have some calls to make.'

The wait seemed interminable. When Prevezer eventually returned she handed him some of yesterday's London newspapers. 'I'm afraid the plane's been delayed,' she announced. 'It'll be here in the early hours.' She looked at her watch. 'You should be arriving at Northolt in time for breakfast.'

11

Greece seemed to sink away from him beneath the clouds. He stared down at the blotches of olive groves in the parched and moonlit landscape. The harsh contours of the mountains were softened by the perspective from above.

The Royal Air Force steward brought him coffee in a plastic cup and, grinning stupidly, muttered something about there being no Duty Free on board. Rosslyn said nothing to him and was left alone with his thoughts and the moonlit view of the coastline of Albania. Later the mountainscape of the Alps. Lake Geneva.

There would, of course, be questions asked by the Secret Service people in London. Perhaps he would be asked to return to Greece to assist the police with their investigations. *What the hell use would that be?* In his mind he could see Cleo. And, noticing that the steward was lolling off to sleep on a forward seat, he looked again at the picture of her naked that she had given him. The eyes penetrated his brain as the pilot announced cheerily that they were making 'good progress over the south coast of Blighty . . .'

The steward had returned to his senses and came forward to make sure that Rosslyn's seat belt was fastened. 'Everything been all right, sir?' he asked.

'Thanks,' said Rosslyn.

The sight of the British summer rain at dawn was joyless.

As the RAF 125 CC3 began its descent over London to the main runway at Northolt, the empty London dawn also saw the beginning of Phase Four of Strange Police.

12

That Sunday morning in June, as the RAF plane brought Rosslyn to Northolt, the arrival of Nicos Nezeritis and Demetra Ipsilanti at the British Museum was witnessed by a Bloomsbury vagrant, as innocent as he was unreliable.

The squat Irishman in his fifties was tucked up beneath a pile of sodden blankets. He had sheltered through the night next to the railings beside the Malet Street entrance gates to the London University Senate House and Library.

A heavy sleeper, ignored by sewer rats, the police on night patrol and student revellers from the party at the School of Oriental and African Studies, he had spent a quiet night. Even the burglar alarm that had been ringing continuously through the night in nearby Gower Street had failed to wake him. He finally stirred, as was his habit in the summer months, some time before six that rainy morning. Peering with bloodshot eyes from between the sodden layers of stinking blankets, he saw the two masked figures standing on the wet pavement across the street.

This first view of them caused the vagrant a moment of concern. Obviously, they were up to no good, and he saw that they seemed to be staring across the street to where he lay. Worse, with the agile stride of the trained athlete, the taller of the masked figures had begun to cross the street towards him. Nerves on edge, the vagrant pulled the blankets over his matted hair. The swollen eyes in his bruiser's face shut and he lay still. He was unable to hear the tread of the man's approaching footsteps on the wet tarmac. It was a disturbing moment. With legs crossed at the ankles, arthritic filthy fingers intertwined and resting on his chest, he remained rigid in the position of some marble effigy of a medieval knight upon a tomb.

When he reckoned the coast was clear, he coughed into his hand. Then, his eyes just above the edges of the blankets, he peered out once more. Across the street, next to the red telephone kiosk, at 1 Montague Place, where the sign on the entrance door said British Museum Photographic Service, he saw the two masked figures had begun to scale the black iron railings.

They wore the same clothing and carried the same equipment as before. Otherwise, the one major difference this Sunday morning was the heavy rain.

Once more they abseiled the ten metres to the ground inside the museum's service area. Landing between a pile of tarpaulins and tall steel garbage drums, they left the rope fixed to the wall.

In the pouring rain, they moved together quickly across the service area to the exterior wall of the Duveen Gallery. That well-practised diagonal approach. Executed in silence, out of vision of the CCTV cameras.

Once on the northern edge of the glass roof of the Duveen Gallery, they began to crawl along the now very slippery surface of the parapet. The summer wind had risen. Even after the heavy rain, there were dust flurries which reduced their vision and made the crawl along the edge more dangerous than on their previous entries.

Until now the early morning rain seemed to be an ally, offering camouflage. But as they neared the far edge and northernmost corner of the roof of the Duveen Gallery, their vision became blurred. The wind too seemed to have become an enemy.

They found the glass panel that had been loosened previously to allow them access. Nezeritis carefully raised it, gently set it to one side and looked down again briefly into the Duveen Gallery. Lowering himself some four metres to the girder providing a secure foothold, he set aside a second glass panel above the bank of display spotlights.

It is hard to say whether it was over-confidence, so certain were they of success that Sunday morning, that led Nezeritis to fail to check his figure-of-eight descendeur. The screw-gate karabiner was half-open, allowing it to pop out from his harness as it took his full weight. Coolly, Nezeritis anchored the abseil rope to the girder. His feet over the parapet, hands on the climbing rope, he nodded to Demetra, the nod indicating that he was now ready to abseil to the marble floor.

At the same time, dust gusted sharply into Demetra's eyes. It caused her to flinch and she stepped back. The rope took the strain of Nezeritis's weight. Suddenly it went slack and the dust blinded Demetra. She grabbed at the rope and to begin with it seemed to hold his weight. But then with a jerk, as if cut by a jagged edge, it loosened. Still blinded, eyes stinging, she was instantly alerted to the danger of the tell-tale movement. But there was nothing she could do to prevent what followed.

No longer sure-footed, she crouched awkwardly and succeeded in gripping the wayward rope. But the impetus of Nezeritis's sudden fall increased. Hopelessly, she peered down, tottering on the slippery surface; she too was off-balance. As she regained her footing, with the rope tangled around her legs, Nezeritis was toppling down head-first. The rope in her hands was limp.

Within seconds she heard the dreadful impact against the marble floor below.

When she looked down she refused to believe what she was seeing. Nezeritis had been quite unable to prevent his collision with the marble floor. He lay spread-eagled, his legs twisted in apparently impossible angles beneath him. He was very slowly raising his head. Demetra could hear him moaning quietly and saw him try, and fail, to raise his arms in a desperate plea for help.

She checked the abseil rope, clipped on and dropped swiftly to the marble floor below, where Nezeritis lay moaning. It was all too clear that both his legs were smashed. Bloodied bone splinters protruded from his climbing tights.

He whispered, 'I can manage. Let's get out of here. You take my backpack.'

Demetra looked around hopelessly, as if the eerie silence was a warning.

'Let's go,' Nezeritis said, his voice echoing in the empty gallery.

'Just take the backpack.' The eyes in the slits of his mask seemed twisted in pain. 'Give me a lift.'

Even though she was a strong woman, it was plain to Demetra that there was nothing she could do to save him.

'For Christ's sake,' Nezeritis pleaded. 'You can get me up and out of here.'

Demetra realized that there was no point arguing with him. She had to leave him. But leave him alive? It would be the fatal risk. Her companion's identity would soon enough be discovered under interrogation. 'I should take your gun,' she said.

'No,' said Nezeritis. *'Get me out of here.'*

Demetra hesitated for a final moment. Then, trying to cause the minimum of pain, she began to remove his backpack.

Nezeritis whispered, 'Let's just get back up and out of here. You have to try . . .' With a great effort, he managed to grab Demetra's sleeve. 'Come on. We have to go.'

But she freed herself from his clutch and touched him gently on the forehead. 'I'm sorry.'

Crouching down beside him, her hands sticky with blood, trying to avoid the look of panic in his eyes, she searched his clothing for tell-tale signs of identity. In an inner pocket she found his false passport. She removed his handgun and holster and strapped his backpack to her own.

His face contorted, Nezeritis was rolling over into the foetal position. The elbows were strangely hunched around the head and the neck was raised backwards and upwards. Choking, he was making a last and desperate attempt to stand. It was hopeless. The pain was far too great and he fell backward and sideways against the marble floor, losing consciousness.

As he collapsed, Demetra drew on a pair of black leather gloves. She took her handgun and forced it into Nezeritis's weakened grip. Opening his mouth, she drove the nozzle of the gun between the teeth and squeezed the trigger.

The echo of the single gunshot was muffled. Its impact blasted a stream of flesh and blood and shattered bone from the head and skull across the marble floor.

Demetra got to her feet. Shaking and breathing heavily, she waited. Hating what she had done, she told herself to think of the task she had performed simply as a mercy killing. Something to be done in the line of duty to ensure that the captor learned nothing and the wounded would be relieved of further suffering. She took little consolation from the certain knowledge that Nezeritis would have done the same to her. Then she turned away and began the climb back up the wall to the gallery's first edge.

Realizing that the British police would launch an immediate investigation, there were certain measures to be taken. Primarily, the vital task of covering tracks had to be completed. No traces left of the preparations they had made previously. As far as possible, the hunter's trail needed to be confused. If the British police and Security Services ever discovered that the intruder had been Greek, then at least the evidence that he had shot himself suggested the involvement of P17N. The Greek syndicate had contrived the story to cover the sort of emergency that had just occurred. However thin it seemed, it was the one they had agreed upon. Likewise, the next precautionary measures Demetra Ipsilanti took.

Gripping the finger-hold in the brickwork firmly, she kicked in several of the glass panes. The glass easily shattered and shards fell to the floor and fragmented. That made it seem that Nezeritis had fallen, fatally injured himself and, in his agony, put a bullet through his brain.

Looking down at the sight of the stream of blood slowly spreading from the corpse, Demetra paused for a moment. Surely the final assault would, at the very least, have to be postponed until the task of loosening the remaining marbles had been finished, to facilitate their ultimate removal. Or, at the worst, the whole attempt would have to be aborted.

They had never considered the possibility of failure. They had discussed technique. Each move. The meaning of the hand signs. The rule of silence. Even that, this morning, had been broken. Now failure had been cemented with the single fatal gunshot. This was not how it should have ended. There were supposed to have been no surprises.

71

Without hurrying, Demetra concentrated on the execution of the return route. Strapping the handgun to her harness in readiness for anything else untoward, she made her way back along the route of entry. Up the rope. Over the walls. To the top. Then down. She felt, as she climbed, a sense of desolation and anger as she yanked out the pitons that would inevitably reveal their means of access. Her eyes narrowed against the London wind and rain.

The death of Nicos Nezeritis would surely serve to increase the determination of the Athens syndicate that the robbery must end in triumph. Nezeritis, the first fatality, had lost his life to the great cause. Only ultimate success would avenge his death and carve his name in history.

13

Constantine Dragos listened to what she had to tell him from London. They were careful not to call each by their names.

'Red. I'm leaving.'

'Do you need assistance?'

'I may do.'

'Are you being followed?'

'I don't think so.

'Then all of you return. Now. Separately.'

Demetra cleared her throat. 'I have to tell you there's been an accident.'

'Accident?'

'Yes.'

'What accident?'

'Our friend is dead.'

Dragos's breath caught his throat. 'Dead. Where did it happen?'

'Inside the target area. He fell. There was no alternative to what I had to do.'

'Very well. I understand what you're saying,' said Dragos quietly. 'Talk to no one. Only get out of there.'

'I will,' said Demetra. 'There's the problem of the equipment's disposal.'

'Leave no trace. Dump it.'

14

In London at seven-forty a.m. Demetra bought two large black plastic garbage bags at the Open 24 Hours shop in Grafton Way. At the rear of the shop, to the left of the refrigerated unit packed with milk, pies and sandwiches, making sure she was out of sight of the assistant at the counter, she crammed the backpacks into separate bags and tied both securely. Her knuckles white, she twisted the necks of the bags with the gesture of a strangler. Minutes later she tossed them into a builder's skip. Then she made her way on foot to King's Cross and caught the train to Luton Airport.

15

Constantine Dragos lit a cigarette. Logical he might be and calm. But the extreme seriousness of the setback in London was undeniable. Now he needed the Englishwoman's advice on damage limitation. Restraining the bitterness and anger he was feeling, he put through a call to Christiane Prevezer's flat in the Athens outskirts.

16

In her down-at-heel Piraeus flat on Vasileos Pavlou Street above the Mikrolimano, Christiane Prevezer was woken abruptly from her sleep by the ringing telephone. The ginger cats scampered from her bed. Constantine Dragos was telling her they had to meet immediately. 'Find a cab,' he said. 'Leave it some distance from my house. Walk the rest of the way. Make doubly sure you're not being followed.'

'Is there trouble?' asked Christiane Prevezer. Her mouth was parched.

Dragos told her the news was bad. Beyond that he did not elaborate.

Her head ached. The result of last night's ferocious drinking binge.

17

Fifty minutes later, on the veranda of the flat with the view of the Parthenon, Prevezer's straw hat was on the table between them.

'The sun,' she said, 'is my enemy. I prefer the moon.'

Constantine Dragos thought she was talking gibberish.

'I can understand your disappointment,' she drawled with studied calmness, eyeing Dragos through her cigarette smoke. 'Are you going to postpone the operation?'

'Not if it can be avoided,' said Constantine. 'What do you suggest we do?'

'One,' said Prevezer, counting on her fingers, 'postpone the Piraeus meeting. Two, give me enough time to make some soundings in London. Indirectly, you understand. See what they know. Whether, obviously, they have any idea the Marbles have been tampered with.' She hesitated. The weary smile showed malformed teeth and reddish gums. 'You look doubtful.'

'This is going to use up valuable time. I can't keep the team waiting indefinitely.'

'You won't have to. I can see what London has to tell us today. Would you be prepared to tell me the identities of the casualties?'

Dragos was unsure of her and muttered something about Prevezer not needing to know the name.

'Or the person they were working with?' she asked.

'We have a rule of anonymity,' said Dragos.

'I understand,' Prevezer said. There was no sign of sympathy in the blue eyes. 'Have you had Cleo Ipsilanti dealt with?'

'She won't say anything.'

'And the daughter?' Prevezer asked.

'Nor the daughter.'

Prevezer continued, 'If she or any of her friends is involved, then the timing of what's happened in London could prove a little awkward for you.' She paused. 'You ought to be concerned about Rosslyn.'

'I know. That's why we pay you.'

'I appreciate that,' she said. Getting up to go, she added, 'You can rely on me.'

Dragos stared at the departing Englishwoman in silence. The eyes seemed to say: *I hope you're right, Prevezer. If not, you're dead meat.* 'Here,' he said. 'You forgot this.' With his metal claw he handed Prevezer her straw hat, and the gesture seemed to cause him a stab of pain.

'Thanks. But if I'm to be of help,' Prevezer said, 'it really is important that you be as absolutely frank with me as possible.' She gave him that wry smile.

'The man Rosslyn,' Dragos said slowly, 'needs to be neutralized. See to it, my friend.'

18

Menzies Tunim collected Rosslyn at the RAF Northolt administration block and drove towards central London through steady rain. The roadside trees glistened and the greenness seemed strange. The hedgerows in the front gardens were full. The sky lowering. Thunder was none too distant.

'I'm sorry, Alan,' said Tunim. 'I'm afraid you're going to have to face some nasty questions.'

'I am?' said Rosslyn. 'What about the bastards who killed Cleo?'

'Shaw tells me that the investigation into the Ipsilanti woman's death is already in the hands of the Athens police.'

'They must get whoever did it,' Rosslyn said.

'Yes,' said Tunim. He hesitated before adding, 'I'm sure they will.' Something about the hesitation in his voice suggested to Rosslyn that they were both facing serious trouble. 'The police in Athens have already held an informal press conference with selected Athens journalists.'

Rosslyn looked at Tunim incredulously. 'Why so soon?'

'Because they're steamed up about inflaming further Greek hostility towards illegal Albanian immigrants. Something about making the Balkan mess even worse than it is already. Worrying that the Greeks will put two and two together and unravel the link between us, SIS and you.'

'The Greeks couldn't do that.'

'That's as maybe. MI6 is pretty angry. Presumably about the mess your friend Cleo had got herself into. They're treating it terribly seriously.'

'So they should.'

'I think we can trust them to bat on our side,' said Tunim. 'Don't you?'

'I've never trusted them,' said Rosslyn. 'They don't take prisoners.'

'That's your opinion,' said Tunim. 'I must say that I'd rather have them on our side than not. We need them, Alan, and you know it as well as I do.'

'And their funds too,' said Rosslyn. Perhaps it was the turmoil of his emotions that generated the comment.

'They want to talk to you first. By way of debriefing. Right away.'

'Can't it wait?'

'I'm afraid it can't, Alan.'

Rosslyn could tell that Tunim was holding something back.

'They're waiting for us with friends at a service flat in Marylebone,' Tunim said. *Friends*, Rosslyn assumed, meant intelligence officers. 'The usual kind of place,' Tunim continued. 'The halfway house. Off-limits. Marion Shaw wants to talk to us both at some length.'

'About having pulled me out of Greece as if I were a wanted man or what?' Rosslyn said.

'I dare say that, and other things besides. Other things. That's what Shaw's saying. She has one of her people on the case in Athens. Day and night. A woman called Prevezer.'

'I met her.' Rosslyn looked sideways at Tunim. 'She's minor. Who are the others . . . Shaw's friends, the visitors?'

'The American, Riley, is CIA. Riley I know. The other man, Georgiadis, is from the Greek Embassy. They're needing help.'

Rosslyn was familiar with the coded rating of urgency. When Tunim spoke of 'needing' rather than, say, 'wanting' help, it meant serious shit had hit the fan and someone was required to clean up. He flipped through the wavebands on the radio for the news. Perhaps Tunim was under instruction from Marion Shaw not to pass on her view of events in Greece before the debriefing. He was driving carelessly.

'By the way,' Tumin said, once they reached the Westway, 'she'll tell you about the incident at the British Museum. Some poor sod blew his brains out. Shaw seems to think you'll be able to identify him. She seems to believe there's a connection with what's happened in Greece. We'll see what she has to say.'

'Before then,' said Rosslyn, 'would you mind slowing down a bit?'

They drove the rest of the way in silence.

Parking the car in Great Portland Street, Tunim said, 'All we have to do is listen. We needn't commit ourselves to anything if we don't want to.'

The brass plates beside the entrance of the building at the junction of Great Portland Street and Weymouth Street bore the names of consultant surgeons. The only one without the name of an individual said 'Advisory Services'. Tunim pushed the button and gave his name. A voice told him to take the lift to the top floor.

19

Marion Shaw opened the door to the flat. The handshake was powerful. 'Alan, how very good to see you.'

Rosslyn set his locked canvas bag down beneath the coat-stand by
the inner door.

Walking straight-backed, like a trained dancer, Shaw led Rosslyn
and Tunim to the service flat at the far end. There were CCTV
cameras in the corridor. Rosslyn noticed that she slipped a plastic
card into the locking mechanism of the outer door, then a different
card into the second door.

Perhaps some consultant surgeon really used the flat during the
day. It smelled faintly of disinfectant and fresh paint. Yet there was
no couch. No weighing scales. No screen or washbasin. There were,
oddly, several telephones and two fax machines beside a bunch of
paper roses in an oriental vase. A mahogany sideboard took up one
wall. Opposite, next to a wall-clock, was a reproduction eighteenth-
century mirror. There were framed prints of watercolours on the
walls. Landscapes of Windsor Castle and Balmoral by the Prince of
Wales.

Campbell Tunim was there with two other men. Shaw introduced
them. First, the darker man, Theo Georgiadis, the Greek with the
smoker's cough, the intelligence officer from the Greek Embassy.
Then Jon Riley, the American, with an open boyish smile. US
Embassy. CIA.

'It must have been appalling for you, Alan,' said Shaw. 'I'm so
very sorry.' She turned to Tunim. 'I wonder if you'd mind finding
some coffee in the kitchen, Menzies? Or perhaps something stronger
for Alan here. A brandy perhaps. Privilege of the expert witness?'

'Nothing for me,' said Rosslyn.

'I think I'll give in to temptation,' said Shaw. 'If that's in order. A small glass of brandy.' She turned to the American and the Greek. Georgiadis said he'd like a glass of brandy too. Riley said he'd like coffee. 'Regular, no milk, no sugar.'

'Campbell, before we start,' said Shaw, 'I wonder if you'd be good enough to look after our friends here in another room for a while. I'd like to talk to Alan on his own, if that's in order.'

'Fine,' said Tunim.

'Let's sit at the table, shall we, Alan? ' Shaw said as the others left the room.

Rosslyn sat at the head of the table facing the heavily curtained windows.

'I'm so sorry about Cleo,' said Shaw. 'Hard to believe it, isn't it?'

'Yes,' said Rosslyn. 'It is hard. Very hard.'

Menzies Tunim returned almost at once with the bottle of brandy and the glass for Shaw.

'This may take some time,' said Shaw for Menzies Tunim's benefit, adding with the hospital matron's tone of warning, 'Keep our friends entertained, if you wouldn't mind.'

20

Shaw asked, 'Get on well with Christiane Prevezer, did you?'

Rosslyn was well aware that officers in the Secret Intelligence Service, like lawyers, rarely ask questions to which they do not already know the answers. 'She was friendly enough.'

'A fine officer,' said Shaw. 'We agreed it's for the best that we got you out fast. I'm sure, in the circumstances, you understand the general reason.'

'What I want to understand is what *happened*,' said Rosslyn.

'We don't know,' said Shaw. She was looking at the carpet by the wall like someone alerted to vermin in the skirting. 'Ioannis Ipsilanti, Cleo's ex-husband in Athens, is handling the family angle. There we are, Alan. Dreadful.'

'And what about your woman, Prevezer?' he asked. 'What's she doing?'

'She's keeping in the background. She has very good connections within the Greek police. We can regard the police as allies. Up to a point.'

'Have they got any leads yet?'

'None worth mentioning,' said Shaw.

'What are they doing?'

'The best they can,' she said. 'The best they can.'

'And what does that mean?'

'They've organized extensive house-to-house interviews in the area. There's a forensic team in place. There'll be the usual collection of fingerprints, hair and blood and DNA samples. They've started checking car-hire bookings and airline reservations and the railways. A description's been circulated of the missing Mercedes. There are roadblocks set up on all the major roads. They're checking hotels and campsites. The military and air-sea search people are involved. At the moment that's about the sum total of it.'

'Doesn't anyone have any idea who could've done it?' asked Rosslyn.

'It's anyone's guess,' said Shaw. 'The killer or killers in the plural had the means. And the opportunity.'

'But what could've been the motive?' said Rosslyn. 'Even the dogs.'

'Tell me, Alan,' said Shaw. 'What's your view?'

'I haven't got a view . . . yet.'

'I mean,' said Shaw, 'it's not as though there was any history of instability in Cleo's make-up, was there?'

'On the contrary,' said Rosslyn.

'How well did you get to know her?'

'Well,' said Rosslyn. 'It's terrible, what's happened. She was so full of life.'

Shaw narrowed her eyes. A wry smile across the face. 'You grew fond of her?'

'Yes. She was very likeable.'

'She was always the consummate professional,' said Shaw. 'But personally, Alan, what did you make of her *personally*?'

'I've told you. She was very likeable.'

'What about her weaknesses?'

'Weaknesses?' Rosslyn hesitated, as if refreshing his memory and finding it empty. 'Such as what?'

'Well, for example, would you say she drank?'

'Yes,' said Rosslyn. 'But not to excess, if that's what you're asking me. She didn't have a problem in that department.'

Shaw pushed her chair away from the table. She crossed her knees. Rosslyn noticed the sheer silk black stockings. The short ankle boots of soft black leather. 'There's a history of men friends, isn't there?'

Rosslyn breathed deeply. 'There's a partner called Nicos Nezeritis.'

'Yes, we know.'

'By the way, someone ought to tell him what's happened.'

'Yes,' said Shaw, with studied nonchalance. 'But let's think about Cleo. She was a highly attractive woman. Did you find her so?'

'Yes, I did.'

'And the relationship with her ex-husband?'

'I don't know anything about it.'

'Didn't you meet Ioannis?'

'No. There was no reason why I should have done.'

'And Cleo's man, Nezeritis.'

'Nicos Nezeritis.'

'Did you come across him?'

'No. I believe he's in Paris.'

'And Demetra?'

'I guess she'll be in Athens with her father.'

'How do you know that?'

'How do you think?'

She lowered her voice almost to a whisper. 'You tell me, Alan.'

'Because Cleo told me.'

'Things all right between them, were they?'

'I didn't pry.'

'And you really knew nothing about the relationship between Cleo and her husband?'

'No,' said Rosslyn. 'You tell me about it, if you want to.'

'We gather it was always perfectly amicable,' said Shaw. 'He made substantial financial provision for both Cleo and her daughters. We can discount the ex-husband, don't you feel?'

'You mean as a suspect?'

'Well, yes, Alan. What else?'

'I didn't know him.'

'Do you suppose that Cleo could have lost her head, done something silly in the heat of the moment?'

'What are you saying?' said Rosslyn

'That she might conceivably have done the thing herself and committed suicide.'

'No, I can't believe that. No.' What little goodwill he had so far shown her was fast evaporating.

'So you'd say one can eliminate the murder-suicide scenario?'

86

'I'm not a police officer or a shrink.'

'Of course not,' said Shaw, 'but you knew her intimately. You were the last person to see her alive.' She got up from the table and walked to the door. 'If you don't mind,' she said. 'I need to have a word.' She didn't say with whom and left the room.

Leave it out, black eyes. Spare me this. You have a dirty mind. You're not pointing your painted little fingernail at me, are you?

When Shaw returned she offered no explanation for her absence.

'I don't know who the last person was to have seen them alive,' Rosslyn said.

Shaw inclined her head. The nod of approval. Knowing. Manipulative. Detached. Patronizing. The bedroom-eyes wide open. 'You don't?' The sarcasm was heavy.

'The killer saw them last, didn't he? The person who did it.'

'Ah, yes,' said Shaw. 'Yes. Unfortunately '

'We don't know who it was,' Rosslyn interrupted, 'do we?'

Shaw rubbed her eyes slowly. 'On the other hand, if we trawl back through her dealings with sundry Greeks and Albanians, then we could very well be looking for the proverbial needle in the haystack.' She was trying to alarm him into an admission.

'She never discussed her previous career with me.'

'Never?' Shaw asked with a look of wounded disbelief.

'You said it – she was a professional, wasn't she?'

'But, Alan, you said you got to know her well, didn't you?' she asked, lowering her voice again in accusation.

'That,' he said very slowly, 'is what I said.'

'You see, that's why I've asked for a private word with you.' She leaned across the table and reached out. For a moment Rosslyn thought she was about to take his hand. 'What you say to me,' said Shaw piously, 'will go no further.'

I wonder. Are you looking for some sort of confession?

'Alan. She was a highly attractive woman, wasn't she?'

'She was. Common knowledge.'

Shaw leaned even further across the table. Rosslyn could see the cleft of her small, pale breasts. The white skin. Pretty moles. 'And you had an affair with her, didn't you, Alan?'

What is this? Cleo's not even in her grave. Her daughter's missing. And you, pretty face, sit here asking me if I had an affair with her?

'Greece,' said Shaw. 'Sun. Sand. And a bit of the how's-your-father. It would be very natural, Alan. You're an attractive man and unattached.'

'I don't need a lecture on what's natural from SIS or anyone else. You're totally out of order.'

Once again Shaw smiled. The lips were very dry. 'Did you just once make love to her?'

'Oh, please.'

'Forgive me.'

'For what?' snapped Rosslyn.

'If I've made you lose your temper.'

'I haven't lost my temper. You're just being impertinent.'

The studied look of hurt crossed Shaw's face. 'But you seem so terribly uneasy,' she said. 'Like a grieving lover. Uneasy. Tense. Oh, I do understand, Alan. You have my sympathy. I'm on your side, believe me. I'm a friend.'

'So what's this interrogation for then?'

The question seemed to sadden her. 'An attempt to gain some understanding,' she said. 'Experience tells me you show the sadness and anger of the lover. You look exhausted.'

'So would you if you'd seen what I saw,' Rosslyn said slowly. 'Now leave it out. Get to the point. Tell me what you people are doing. That creep of yours in the straw hat. Prevezer. A third-rate spook poncing around in Greece like some kind of cheap tour guide. What are you people doing? Cleo was one of yours. One of her daughters has disappeared. Why?'

Shaw remained silent.

'It was unspeakable,' Rosslyn continued. 'I saw it. You didn't. And there's the other daughter. Worried stiff, I dare say. So now, you tell me. What the hell are you doing about it, apart from putting me on the block?

All sweetness, Shaw asked with exaggerated patience in her voice, 'What do *you* suggest we do, Alan?'

'For starters, have you checked her previous main contacts?'

'Any that could be relevant,' said Shaw. 'Yes. And we're double-checking again and all the rest. No one person presents himself or herself as an obvious suspect. If there were one we most probably wouldn't be here now. And if they were suspect Greeks or Albanian associates of hers from the old days, then you can be sure it's not something we'd like to publicize. We wouldn't want to give them advance warning. And the Greek Intelligence Service wouldn't want us to either.'

'Is that the sum total?' asked Rosslyn.

'About the sum total of the present situation,' said Shaw with condescension. 'Look, I know Cleo's a dreadful loss.' She looked into the distance. 'There really isn't anyone else like her we can use to help. Fluent in Russian, Albanian and Serbo-Croat. Did you know that?'

'No, I didn't,' he answered dully.

'Believe me. She knew her way around the shifting alliances of terrorism in Greece and the Balkans like the back of her hand. She was the one who knew the webs of organized crime throughout the region. It's a very distinguished record. She was a courageous woman.' She cleared her throat. 'Still, all of that'll have to go unremarked upon. If there are the inevitable awkward questions from the press, then the Athens ambassador will say whatever he's told to say.' Again her mind seemed to wander. Back to the secret past. 'No one's going to say,' she continued eventually, 'that over the years Ipsilanti's not been responsible for the disposal of some pretty nasty individuals. Such truths are best left unsaid, Alan. But the truth is this. There's quite a bloody trail across Albania, Bulgaria and Turkey. If you could follow the footprints you'd sooner or later find those of Cleo Ipsilanti's friends. You could say that she's left her shadow across Greece unremarked upon. But we can't speak the truth, can we?'

'If you say so,' said Rosslyn with a weary smile.

'And, as you'll perfectly well grasp, we prefer that her relationship with us remains that way. The hidden shadow. Her death and the manner of it are more besides. We can't even say it's the work of some known psychopath or some terrible family matter.'

There was an awkward silence. Shaw's dark eyes darted. Like a predatory animal circling its prey. Too long in the night. Watching. Waiting for the crippled victim to make a move. Waiting for exhaustion to take its toll.

'There has to have been a witness,' she said at last. 'You'd think so, wouldn't you? But without being glib, you could say the only living witnesses were the infernal cats. Unfortunately, they don't talk. And the dogs are dead.' She was biting on the nail of her little finger. 'Then there's you, Alan, isn't there?' The slow smile spread across her wide mouth. 'You, Alan.'

'I've very little useful to tell you,' Rosslyn said. 'Do you have a suggestion how I could help?'

'You'd like to help, Alan?'

He smiled, vaguely enough, he hoped, so that she might not gather the extent of his resentment. 'If you say so.'

'I need to ask you one or two more routine questions. It'd be helpful if you'd tell me if there's any written record of contact concerning professional matters.'

'Such as?'

'Such as your commission in Greece?' she said.

'There's nothing written down.'

'And about Cleo. Forgive me for returning to my original tack, but I must know. Was she under any sort of stress? That sort of thing. Whatever stress and strain a man as perceptive and intelligent as you might notice in a client?'

'No, she wasn't under any stress.'

'And Cleo's partner, Nicos Nezeritis. What did you make of him?'

'I've told you already,' he said fiercely. 'I never met him.'

'I do have to ask again, Alan. It's very important to us to know whether or not Cleo may have discussed her past with you. Any aspect of her work for us, or anything that may have related to it. However small.'

'All I know about her is what very little I've told you already. What exactly has this got to do with what's happened?'

'As it turns out,' said Shaw, 'quite a lot.' She folded her hands together. 'I know it must be painful for you, but think back to

Greece. Two of our people, the Danish couple, tried to see you at your hotel. That was after the discovery of the killings. Luckily for us, our Danish friends got to your hotel before the Greek police. When you didn't show up, they went up to your room unannounced. They found your possessions. You'd already packed.'

'I know all this,' said Rosslyn. 'Prevezer told me. Did they find the report?'

'Yes. Fortunately they did. If I may say so, it wasn't terribly wise of you to leave it lying around, was it? They recovered the draft of it. Let's say we'll overlook that little slip. That's the good news.'

'And what's the bad news?'

'We've discovered something else,' said Shaw. 'About you and Cleo.'

Rosslyn narrowed his eyes. 'Tell me then,' he said. 'About this discovery.'

'The bad news,' Shaw continued for the prosecution, 'is that our friends found a plain white envelope addressed to you in Cleo Ipsilanti's hand. Inside was a personal letter addressed to you.'

Rosslyn flinched. *You can't have seen it. I have it here in my pocket.*

'Nothing else,' Shaw continued quietly, 'except there is the missing sum of dollars that she refers to in the letter. Dollars apparently intended for you. Some 3,000 dollars. Quite a sum. Is this correct?'

'Yes.'

'And where are they, Alan?'

'I think I left them at the estate.'

'You *think* you left them there?'

'That's what I've just said.'

Shaw shook her head in disbelief. 'You see, our friends went back to the estate. They made a copy of the hard disk from Ipsilanti's computer. We've been able to paint a picture of her last hours. They made a print-out of her files and the last one, the one she saved some time before she died, we have a copy of it here.' She produced a folded A4 sheet of paper from her pocket. 'This is addressed to "AR". That's presumably "Alan Rosslyn", isn't it? And it refers, among other things, to the gift of a gold chain. And when our people took a look at the scene of the killings, they found the package containing exactly 3,000 dollars had been left near the bodies of the dead dogs. So you must have returned the money to her. My question is, did you return it to her before or after she died?'

'After.'

'So one's naturally tempted to ask oneself what Cleo was doing, paying you 3,000 dollars, and why did you seek to hide the fact of the gift by returning it?'

'I have nothing whatsoever to hide,' said Rosslyn. 'You say you've read the letter. It's all down there. Read it yourself.'

'I have read it, Alan. Believe me, I have.'

'What's your problem then?'

'I don't have a problem. Rather, *you* have a problem. That's why you've been lying to me.'

'In what respects?'

'Let's get to the nitty-gritty. You two were lovers, weren't you?'

There was a long silence.

'Lovers, Alan,' she said, adding with great emphasis. 'You and Cleo.'

Rosslyn shrugged. It was a gesture of admission. 'If you don't know that, then your people poking around weren't doing much of a job.'

'Let's say events overtook them,' said Shaw. 'Let's go back to the scene of the crime. The Greek police eventually showed up. As you'd expect, fortunately our people left nothing disturbed. No trace that they'd been there. What I'm keen to know is the subtext of the payment to you. What was it for exactly? What are we to suppose she was paying you for? Not your silence, surely?'

'The money was a personal matter,' said Rosslyn. 'Something of her own devising. A gift.'

'Your idea?'

'Her idea,' said Rosslyn. 'It's in the letter.'

'I see,' said Shaw. She let the silence hang a moment. Finally, she said, 'It would be helpful to us if you'd give us the broader picture. What sort of wider game were you two playing? The murders are one thing. But your involvement, whatever it may be, isn't something that we terribly want to get involved in.'

You wouldn't think so, thought Rosslyn. *Not from this line of questioning.*

'You could say it's a question of resources,' said Shaw, 'and our not wanting to get tied up too intimately with the Greek government. Their Intelligence Service. Police. And their on-the-ground investigations. If you had some private agenda, then I have to say it's gone spectacularly wrong. There is one woman dead out there. One of ours. And her daughter's missing. It's very bad, Alan.'

'You don't have to tell me,' said Rosslyn.

Shaw was not letting go. 'The murder victim's lying in some stinking Greek morgue in Kalamata. Your lover. The daughter's vanished off the face of the earth, trailing blood behind her. You can't honestly expect anyone not to wonder what in God's name you'd got yourself tied up in.'

Rosslyn said nothing.

'Alan, you of all people should appreciate that it's a simple matter of keeping the hands clean. Let's face it, the basic spadework commissions we give Tunim Associates must represent a healthy slice of the Tunims' revenue.'

'That's down to them.'

'And in no small measure down to you too.'

'What are you driving at?'

'This needn't get in the way of our cooperation, if you follow me.'

'I don't *follow* you,' said Rosslyn.

'You've taken Cleo's pay-out or pay-off, whatever you want to call it.'

'What do you want me to do?' asked Rosslyn. 'Prevent the SIS history of playing stupid buggers in Greece and the Balkans from leaking out.'

'That's my problem,' said Shaw bluntly. 'I'll put it another way, if I have to,' she added with apparent reluctance. 'There's us. There's you. And to date the arrangement with Tunim has worked well.' Once more she seemed lost in the dark shadows of her private thoughts. 'But we can always pull out of it at a moment's notice. Best to get out while we're on top, in the clear, with no blood on our hands. Don't you feel I'm right?'

'Pull out, is that what you want?'

'That might be an option. But it would terminally damage the Tunims professionally, wouldn't it?'

'You'll have to ask them about that.'

'I will. Our little holding company has the controlling interest in Tunim Associates. We can wind up Schneider-Portland at a moment's notice. It's not the Tunims' company. It's ours. The bottom line is that we own you. That's why you get juicy fat commissions from us.' She tapped her chest. 'Through me personally. Look at it how you will, you're in our silk-lined pocket. And you? Tunim Associates is still in debt to Coutts. And who holds the purse strings? We do. We call the shots.' She closed her eyes.

'What is it you want me to do?' Rosslyn asked. 'Say sorry to the Tunims. Tell them their business is washed up. Is that what you want?'

Before Shaw could reply, the telephone ringing on the mahogany sideboard interrupted her. 'That'll be for me,' she said. 'Athens. The embassy.'

He watched Shaw take the call. Her dark eyes unblinking. Then she turned away to gaze from the window and continued listening motionless. Finally, rather curtly, she said to the caller, 'Thanks. I'm sorry.' She returned to her table and stared hard at Rosslyn. Yet, Rosslyn noticed, when she said she was sorry, there was a flicker of a smile on the very dry lips. 'The Athens police have put out a warrant for your arrest.'

'For what?' said Rosslyn.

'Murder,' she said quietly. 'Tell me, Alan. Tell the truth. We can help you. We're both on the same side, aren't we?'

He held her stare and said nothing. Somewhere in the room there was the noise of ticking. A clock, the hidden turning tape? Unsure which, Rosslyn felt the anger rising in his chest.

At last Shaw said, 'The embassy hasn't been able to find out the precise wording of the charge. The informed guesswork seems to suggest that it's probably murder or conspiracy to murder.' Shaw raised her hand to the silver chain around her neck. 'You're up to here in it, Alan. They've got some pretty hard forensic evidence

94

against you. Fingerprints on the shotgun. The gold chain recovered from the well. A white silk dress sent away for DNA tests. Suppose it was to show traces of your semen on it?'

'Leave it out,' said Rosslyn, his anger rising.

'It's all in the hands of the Greek police, Alan. And there's also the unfortunate fact that you fled the scene of the crime.'

'On your instructions. You can't call that fleeing the crime scene.'

Shaw shrugged. 'The Greeks don't know that, do they?'

'Why don't you tell them then?' Rosslyn's voice had a sharp and accusatory note.

'I rather think it would be a touch unwise,' Shaw observed. 'Not our style, Alan. Tourist murders. No. No. Who do they think we are? Police informers? No. It's facts we deal in. Facts and hard evidence. And you know as well as anyone, that's one thing at least we have in common with the police.'

'Also, I assume, to at least try and find the truth.'

'That goes without saying,' Shaw countered harshly.

'What about the embassy coming out with it?' said Rosslyn.

'The embassy? Ah, well, as far as the practicalities are concerned, there won't be too much the embassy can do. There we are.' Again, the patronizing strain in her husky voice. 'Meanwhile, and do correct me if you feel I'm wrong, there can't be a single major client who will like the idea of having the Tunims' firm on board if one of the leading freelance investigators is up on a murder charge. I'd have total sympathy with that view. The same goes for us, doesn't it?'

Lawyer-speak. It was infuriating.

'Let's not go round in circles any longer, Alan. If the charges are dropped then everything's fine and dandy. If not . . . There's the chance of an extradition order being applied for for your summary return to Greece. What will you be looking at? Say, twenty-five years in a Greek jail?' Shaw shook her head. 'I think it's time to call the others in, don't you?'

'Wait a second,' Rosslyn said. 'You don't think I did it?'

'No, my first impression is that you didn't do it. I can't imagine why on earth you would have. So there you have it. I don't think you did it.'

'And why the hell did you go through the personal aspects when you've got a copy of her letter?'

A look of triumph on her face, Shaw was already heading for the door. 'Because I wanted to discover just how good a liar you are. And I'd say you're good. Bloody good. I couldn't care less what you and Cleo did together in private. You'll find I'm broad-minded when it comes to what issues from beneath the navel. I just needed to be sure of you. Now I am. As well as being a top-flight investigator, you're a bloody good liar. But one thing, Alan. Never lie to me again. Do you follow? Don't lie to me about anything. If you value your freedom and your future, remember what I've said. Never lie to me again.' With one hand on the door, she stared back at Rosslyn. 'I want you to listen to what the others have to say.'

Rosslyn was about to say something. But Shaw brought a finger to her tight, dry lips. *Hush-hush. Whisper who dares.* Rosslyn watched her with a look of disgust. Then she called down the corridor to the others to join her. It seemed to be an order, not a request, as if she had asked the jury to return to announce the result of their deliberations. A verdict which she already knew.

21

Shaw set the photographs face up on the narrow conference table: glossy colour photographs, close-up shots of the head and shoulders of the man who had shot himself in the British Museum. The disfigured face seemed familiar.

'The problem of formal confirmation of the man's identity is finally one for the coroner,' said Shaw. 'Until we've established his identity, the hearing will be delayed. But we already have a strong suspicion we're looking at Nicos Nezeritis. Cleo Ipsilanti's erstwhile partner. Lover. Call him what you will.' Shaw stared at Rosslyn hard. 'Do you think this is Nezeritis?' she asked him.

'As far as I can tell,' said Rosslyn. 'These look something like the photos I saw of him in Greece.'

'Cleo must have known what he was doing,' said Shaw.

'Maybe.' said Rosslyn. 'But I don't, do I?'

Shaw shook her head. 'One would have thought you might,' she said. 'If that's true, Alan, we're not going to find out now, are we?'

There was a silence.

'Alan,' said Shaw, 'you have to know why this is important to us.' She turned to the Greek, Georgiadis. 'Why don't you explain, Theo? Tell us about 17 November. The .45–calibre handgun. And P17N.'

Georgiadis was toying with a packet of cigarettes. 'Let's assume the dead man is Nezeritis. He killed himself with the .45–calibre handgun that was found next to him. That's for sure.' He lit the cigarette carefully. 'The .45–calibre handgun is the trademark of the 17 November terrorist group.'

'The calibre could be coincidental,' said Rosslyn. 'Nezeritis could have been acting alone. If he was acting with others, then what?'

'It suggests that 17 November or one of its splinter groups has established an operational unit in the UK.'

'Why?' said Rosslyn. 'To attack the British Museum?'

'It isn't necessarily the obvious choice of target,' Shaw interjected. 'More likely they'd be aiming at a bank. Some commercial interest. One that the general public would be, shall we say, less likely to hold in any great affection.'

'How do you know they were intent on sabotage?' Rosslyn asked.

'We don't,' said Shaw. 'Nothing was found on or near the body to suggest that he was planting, for example, an explosive device. In fact, discounting his hard-weather clothing, the only incriminating evidence was the handgun he killed himself with. So logic suggests that he was engaged in some form of preliminary reconnaissance. The broken panes of glass in the roof suggest that he slipped and fell. Then hit the floor. Fractured his legs. And, realizing he'd never get out, he shot himself.'

'The British Museum could just be one of the first bomb targets,' the American, Riley, interjected. 'Which is why our embassy and various other high-risk US interest targets, commercial interests and banks, are also on Red Alert.'

'You know about these 17 November people?' asked Georgiadis, his voice thickening.

'A certain amount,' said Rosslyn. 'We did a security job for a shipping company in Piraeus. After the murder of Constantine Peratikos.'

'Show him the short history lesson, Theo,' Shaw said, smiling thinly.

Georgiadis passed Rosslyn a small folder headed TOP SECRET.

Embassy of Greece
1a Holland Park
London W11 3TP
Tel: 0171 229 3850

Counsellor: Theodoros Georgiadis

P17N
Named after the November '73 student uprising against the military. Splinter group or breakaway cell of the 17 November terrorist organization. The main 17 November organization is essentially anti-USA, Turkey, NATO, Germany, Britain.

AIMS
The removal of all US and UK military and commercial interests in Greece.

PREVIOUS ATROCITIES
Murder of CIA Athens station head Richard Welch, US Navy Captain George Tsante, US Defense Attaché William Nordeen.

MAJOR TERRORIST ATTACKS
Thirty-five recorded terrorist attacks, including coalition targets in Greece during Gulf War. Three-man hit squad assassinated Turkish Press Counsellor Omer Sipahioglu. Shooting of Constantine Peratikos in Piraeus (Peratikos family own the Piraeus-based Aran Shipping and Trading Company and London-based Pegasus Ocean Services). Anti-tank rocket assault on Greek television network building.

MAIN AREA OF OPERATIONS
Athens: variously launched missile attacks on the US Embassy, army depots, tax offices, multi-national corporations, General Motors dealerships, McDonald's fast-food outlets.

DISTINGUISHING FEATURES
After all attacks police found .45-calibre shells at
sites. Expertise suggests military training in the
Middle East. One thing distinguishes them from other
terrorist groups operating in Europe and America: in
over twenty years not a single 17 November member has
been arrested. Their identities remain unknown.
Papandreou had suspicions about those involved, but if
he knew who they were, he took the names with him to his
grave.

ORGANIZATION
Highly secretive, tight-knit, unseen.

COUNTER-STRIKES
None to date. International security services are
waiting for them to make a mistake before further full-
scale launches of terrorist attacks against UK, Greek,
Turkish, German and US personnel, not only in London
and Athens, but elsewhere.

Shaw lobbed the ball into Rosslyn's court. 'You've had experience of these sort of people,' she said. 'The IRA, for example. What do you make of the evidence?'

Rosslyn once more examined the photographs. 'There isn't very much,' he said. 'The dead man. Suicide. The weapon. Beyond that, who knows? There's nothing else I can tell you.'

'Are you protecting her?'

'Protecting who?'

'Cleo. I repeat, are you protecting her? If so, we have a problem.'

'You certainly do,' said Rosslyn.

'Exactly,' said Shaw. 'And your refusing to tell us what you know about Nezeritis doesn't make it any easier.'

'I've already told you what I know. And that's next to nothing.'

'Not next to nothing. Nothing,' she said, with the smile of the interrogator who is wholly convinced the subject is lying. 'You have told us nothing about Nezeritis.'

'What is it you want me to tell you?' Rosslyn said, exasperated.

The American, Riley, was staring hard at Rosslyn. Perhaps he felt he should take the more amiable and positive line. 'We have formed the search and investigation team,' he said. 'Marion here. Theo and myself. We must find out just who Nezeritis was and who he was answering to, without the Greek intelligence hierarchy knowing that any of us are involved.'

Georgiadis tapped the table with his knuckles. 'My seniors must have no idea of this. If, for one moment, they think that we've got near them, then we risk reprisals. Sudden and full-scale terrorist attacks. I too, Mr Rosslyn, am taking a risk.'

Rosslyn looked at the Tunims. Then at the others. 'If you have no objection, I'd like to have a word with Campbell and Menzies in private.'

'By all means,' said Shaw. 'Go ahead.'

22

In the narrow corridor Rosslyn said quietly, 'What the hell are they getting at?'

'They want you to tell them what you know,' said Menzies.

Rosslyn leaned against the wall. 'I've nothing else to say,' he said. He shook his head. 'That's the truth.'

'It's your decision, Alan,' said Menzies. 'You can always go back in there right now and say *adios*, I won't cooperate, piss off and good night.'

'And if I do?'

Campbell Tunim shrugged. 'We'll survive.' He hesitated a moment. 'Alan, if you don't mind me asking, you were Cleo's lover, weren't you? I'd say that you owe it to her memory and the daughters. I think you should do the business, Alan. Tell them what you know.' He put his hand on Rosslyn's shoulder. 'Shall we get back in there and you tell them the rest of it?'

'Listen,' said Rosslyn, 'I had nothing whatsoever to do with Cleo's death. I know nothing about Nezeritis. Nothing. That's the truth.'

'We believe you, Alan,' Menzies said sourly. He was rubbing his white-gloved hands together. 'Oh, we do believe you.'

'I don't give a monkey's toss whether or not you believe me. I went out there to do a job. I did it. I formed a relationship with the client. That happens. I know nothing.'

'In this case,' said Campbell, 'it's, shall we say, a shame. The people we deal with are special. Our enemies are special. Their operations are special and we can smell them on the breeze. This one smells powerfully of betrayal. You took a sweetener from her, didn't you?'

'Are you suggesting Cleo's betrayed MI6?'

'No one's exactly suggesting anything,' said Campbell Tunim. After a pause, he added, 'Not yet.'

'Shall we rejoin the others?' said Menzies Tunim. 'Shaw has a constructive suggestion to make.'

'Does she now?' said Rosslyn. 'Tell me, you two, whose side are you on?'

'Yours, Alan.' The flatness in Campbell Tunim's voice seemed calculated. 'Yours, Alan.'

For the first time in their relationship, Rosslyn sensed that they were being neither open with him nor, worse, quite honest; and they had become his enemies.

23

Rosslyn and the Tunims once more took their seats at the table.

Shaw began. 'We understand, naturally, the difficulty you're facing.' Now she seemed to be more consultant surgeon than prosecuting counsel. The tone infuriated Rosslyn.

'You *understand*?' he said. 'Before you tell me any more about it, I have to say, in the name of God, I had nothing – I repeat, nothing – to do with Cleo's death. On the contrary, I'd have done anything in my power to prevent it. I know nothing about Nezeritis.' The outburst stunned the others into silence. 'Look,' he continued, 'there are plenty of people you could get to find the truth about her murder. And whether there is or isn't any link between the two deaths. Or any P17N terrorist operation. Undercover investigation officers at Customs and Excise might help you for a start. They have some top-class men and women. And there's MI5. That's their job. And your own people, Shaw. What about your people? Cleo was one of yours.'

'It's no use being wise after the event,' said Shaw. It was almost a murmur.

'What the hell do you mean by that?' said Rosslyn loudly.

'I mean that had one known that you would, as it were, have gained the ear of Cleo we might have asked you to question her discreetly. But we've lost the chance now.'

'Then was Nezeritis known to you?' asked Rosslyn. 'Was he on your books? Was he some kind of lunatic?'

'Not as far as we know,' said Shaw.

'Then how did you identify him?' asked Rosslyn. 'You knew who he was even before you had me confirm his identity.'

'Because that's our business,' said Shaw, 'to keep an eye on Cleo. For her sake as well as ours.' She smiled knowingly. 'In just the same way, Alan, as we came up with your name in the first place. I don't have to tell you yet again about the anonymous threats to Cleo and innumerable others among our agents in Greece and in the Balkan region as a whole. Alas, too late, the killing of Cleo was carried out.'

Riley interjected, 'I've already said that Washington's profoundly uneasy about the probability of still more attacks on our embassies and consulates. Worldwide. On diplomats and families. Businessmen too. We've lost eight women and children in the last three months alone.'

'I know all that,' said Rosslyn. 'Let me ask you again, who are you all looking at?'

The silence was very awkward.

'We don't know who to look at,' said Riley. 'Who knows what contacts the terrorists have established? With Muslims. Algerians. God knows.'

Seeking some sort of confirmation, he looked to Georgiadis.

'Who knows?' said Georgiadis with a shrug.

'They could have established some sort of cooperation,' said Shaw, 'with any kind of fundamentalist terrorist organization. One with substantial cash applying the pressure. Remember the press photos of the outrages. We have a responsibility to bring the murderers to justice. We've thought about everything very carefully, Alan. We agree that I should put a proposal to you.' The intonation had shifted once more. Back to that of the judge about to pass sentence. 'We agree that it will be for the best if you remain within a thirty-kilometre radius of London for the immediate future. Let me be completely straight with you, Alan. Firstly, the Greeks may well apply for an extradition order against you. If your connection with us were to be made public, then we face an embarrassing situation. Secondly, none of us here tonight feels that you have been as completely straight with us as we have been with you.'

'Everything I have told you is the truth,' said Rosslyn.

'That's something for us to decide upon,' said Shaw. 'We need some more time to make our own additional investigations in Greece. Into Cleo. Into Nezeritis. We want to put you on ice. Keep you out of sight, protected.' She turned to Riley. 'Perhaps you'd answer the second part, Jon.'

The American stretched his neck. 'One of our agents in Algiers has traced a key connection. Let's say a fuse has blown. We've followed the wires and they lead to Athens. One or other of the NATO embassies has someone, we don't know whether man or woman, who's under pressure. Most likely it's blackmail. Intimidation. We don't know whether we're looking at a grudge scenario. Or even whether the target is within our embassy or yours.'

'That's your business.'

'It's the truth,' said Riley.

'What has all of this to do with me?' asked Rosslyn. 'Faked murder charges. And now you sit here saying I have to be kept under some kind of house arrest.'

'It's a matter of your protection,' said Shaw.

'Thanks all the same,' said Rosslyn. 'You happen to be looking at one man who can protect himself.'

'Alan,' Shaw said softly, 'you've been specifically mentioned as a target to be eliminated. And that's why it's so important that you tell us everything. I mean everything. All that took place during your three weeks in Greece. Names. Conversations. Dates. Times. Everything.'

'I've told you,' said Rosslyn, enraged. 'I've told you everything I know.'

'Take it easy,' said Riley. 'OK. Supposing that's true.'

'It is true.'

'Or supposing it's not,' said Riley, 'you have to realize there are others who want the information. What was Nezeritis doing? Why P17N?. What in hell was Cleo doing with Nezeritis? What did she know? Either we get to it first or they will kill to get it. And they may even kill you if you don't give it them. Right, Theo?' Riley looked at Georgiadis, who nodded in confirmation. 'So, listen to me, why not give it to us?'

Rosslyn's eyes were burning. 'You listen to me. I can get myself a lawyer. Go back to Greece. Stand up and be counted. You think I want, even for one moment, Cleo's daughters or anyone else to believe I had anything whatsoever to do with her murder? It's bullshit. I know it. You know it. What conceivable motive would I have for even thinking of doing her harm? Jesus Christ, I am, I was, in love with her. OK, if those people want to question me, let them. The police. P17N. Why would they want to kill me?'

'Why would they want to kill you?' Riley echoed with greater urgency. 'Because, see, they think you will give it to us. So you need to be kept in the icebox. Safe. That's what Marion here is saying. We've treated you as a friend. One of us. But we can only be your friends if you agree to be ours. It takes two, right?'

'Why don't we take a short break?' Shaw suggested. She gave Rosslyn the matronly smile. 'Leave you to collect your thoughts. Would you like a drink or anything?'

'No, thanks,' said Rosslyn. 'Let's get this thing straightened out.'

Without replying, they left him on his own.

24

He tried to remember what Cleo had said to him that final night in Kardamyli. *I've never really asked you quite how much you know about my previous existence. My secret career. I doubt you've guessed the disappointment. Too much lost. Too many of my friends. Too many lives. I was advised to give all this up, Alan. Perhaps I should have done so for safety's sake. Sold up. But I love it. Nicos doesn't want to settle with me in England and I can't say I blame him for that. Perhaps I will have to disappear. With or without Nicos. What's confusing me, well, let's say the person who has confused me is you, Alan.*

Perhaps I will have to disappear was echoing in his mind. It had seemed a throwaway comment. Now he wished he had asked her exactly what it was she had meant.

He felt like saying to Shaw that he'd be happy to cooperate with her. But what was the point? He'd already cooperated. He had nothing to hide from these people. It was they who were hiding something from him. And the Tunims? True, they were in thrall. To SIS. To Shaw. Maybe that was why they had stayed quite so silent.

Someone, of course, was desperately protecting someone. But who? Perhaps most extraordinary of all was that Shaw, Riley and Georgiadis were being so tight-lipped, so evasive. Or was he quite simply expendable? Were they baiting some kind of trap?

Underneath it all, did they want him to go back to Athens and face the charges? Maybe they really didn't know what Nezeritis had been doing in the British Museum. Maybe nothing at all had happened and this was a game. Part of some preliminary move in a strategy of their own sick invention.

But the voice for the prosecution in his head insisted: *There's no evidence of any credible sort that establishes the defendant's innocence. On* the contrary, ladies and gentlemen of the jury, look at it carefully. Take your time. Make up your own mind. The fingerprints. The dress. The jealous lover, Rosslyn, who, unable to face the idea that Nicos Nezeritis would soon return, decided, in a moment of utter savagery, to end the life of the one he claims to love. The scenario is, alas, all too common. Nezeritis, in an act of tragic despair, took his own life. Let's leave him aside. We cannot, alas, allow ourselves to think of what may have been going through his sadly troubled mind. No. Simply, ladies and gentlemen, consider the evidence, if you will, objectively. Without passion. There is no room for doubt, is there? None. He had motive. Means. Opportunity. We have established all three and the forensic evidence is incontrovertible.

Then the voice for the defence. It was vaguer. Kinder. *It hasn't happened. It didn't happen. There are indeed photographs of Nezeritis, but who knows what he was doing in the British Museum? Oh, yes, of course the story would seem to be absurd. Yet there are no photographs of Cleo. It hasn't happened. She may not even be dead. The Greeks say they have her body. But I need to see it to be sure. Sure, they might need, as custom has it, to bury her as soon as possible. But we're talking murder. So burial will have to wait. And has Olympia seen it? Where's Demetra? I need to know, beyond all doubt, that Cleo is dead. And if she is, then I want her killer brought to justice. If she isn't, I would like my life to continue as before, however hard and painful the hideous events have been. Therefore, ladies and gentlemen of the jury, I need to find Olympia, see Demetra. On their own ground. And there are others too, are there not? Her former husband. Her friend and neighbour, Vayakakos. No stone can be left unturned. If that means going back to Greece, so be it.*

Trial adjourned. *Sine die.*

He told himself to follow for the moment whatever orders Shaw might give. As for the Tunims, they owed him. The least they could do was offer an explanation for why they wouldn't deny he was a murderer. What was making them stay so silent? As for Cleo, if only he could speak to her. Ask her what, in the name of all that's holy, she was really involved in. Was what they had just a summer fling? What was it she wrote? *I cannot tell you how much it has meant to me to be your lover. Forget everything you know about my past. As you know, I have spent too long in the dirtiness of the ordinary world. I am so*

inordinately in need of you that I will not tell you. Now burn this. Keep the gold chain for ever. Wear it when you return to show me nothing's changed. I am in love with you and I don't want you to break my heart . . .
It seemed a long time ago.

And now there was the sound from the corridor of the others returning. To his surprise, Rosslyn saw Campbell and Menzies Tunim standing in the doorway. They were alone.

25

'They've left,' said Campbell Tunim. 'They've asked us to explain the situation.' He pulled up a chair. 'Shaw's gone so far as to make arrangements for you to be protected by SO10. You know the sort of thing she's talking about?'

Rosslyn knew. SO10, the Metropolitan Police's Crime Operations Group. The provision of protection for witnesses whose evidence places their lives at risk. The protection involves the witness being relocated. Given a new identity. He or she quite simply disappears.

He nodded. 'You don't say?' The look he gave Campbell Tunim was one of professional appreciation rather than respect. It reflected little of the trouble in Tunim's eyes. It was as though he were reasoning: *Well maybe, Alan, maybe you are telling the truth. And I don't know what to do.* It was not in the natures of the Tunim brothers to admit failure or that they might be in the dark. They both looked very angry indeed.

'The alternative, Alan,' Menzies said, 'is that you leave here and the devil takes the hindmost. You may think you can handle that. But the plainer, if not more brutal, fact is that neither Shaw nor I can afford to lose you.'

'She needs your help,' said Campbell. 'Her people need you to ask one or two people some awkward questions.'

'Such as who?'

'Some of Cleo's close associates,' said Menzies, 'and a few of her former colleagues.'

Rosslyn thought: *George Vayakakos.* 'You have a name?' he asked.

'No names,' said Campbell.

'Once you're established in your relocation,' said Menzies, 'they want you to undertake some interviews.'

Rosslyn shrugged. Neither in agreement nor in disagreement.

Menzies Tunim got to his feet and walked to the window. He drew aside the heavy curtains. 'There's a black Audi parked down there across the street,' he said. 'There's a protection officer waiting for you in the car. Her name is Winter. An armed plain-clothes woman police officer. You'll leave this building alone. From now on, to the rest of the world, she'll act as your companion. To all intents and purposes, you're under house arrest. Believe me, it's not how we wanted things to end.'

'You have to understand,' said Campbell, 'that Shaw's made it very plain to me that you can no longer remain with us.'

Rosslyn's eyes narrowed. 'I'm fired then?'

'She's asked us to forward you a sum in lieu of three months' salary,' said Campbell. 'That's so long as you cooperate with her people. I doubt it will be terribly onerous. The usual stuff. Question and Answer. Q and A. A and Q.'

Controlling his anger, Rosslyn got to his feet. 'You two. You've gone along with this?'

'No alternative,' said Campbell. 'Believe me, Alan, it's very painful. As painful for us as it is for you. But we have to say you dug a hole that even we can't get you out of.'

Rosslyn crossed the room to the window and drew aside the curtain. There was the black Audi in the rain and the woman driver, who was little more than a blur. There had to be a way out of the building the police officer would not see. He let go of the curtain and let it fall back into place. His right fist was clenched. The anger boiling. Behind him, Campbell Tunim sighed. Menzies had his back to him.

Rosslyn began to turn sideways slowly. Then stepped back a pace. There was the look of the bully on Campbell's face. The slight smile. The cheap regret.

The sideways turn Rosslyn had begun became a spin. The clenched right fist hammered into Campbell's stomach just below the ribcage, causing the bigger man to buckle. As Campbell's face fell, Rosslyn's clenched left fist struck home to the side of the jaw.

Staggering backwards, Campbell's head crashed against the table and he slid, his legs buckling, to the floor, unconscious.

'What the –' said Menzies Tunim. But before he could finish the question, Rosslyn swung his fist at him. The first blow missed. Menzies Tunim flayed out wildly with his white-gloved hands. 'You stupid fu –' he began. This time first Rosslyn's left fist, then his right struck the other man in the mouth. He fell back, unable to steady himself, eyes closed.

Grabbing his canvas bag, Rosslyn found the emergency exit stairwell beyond the lift. He took the stairs fast, two by two.

The front entrance doors were in full view of the policewoman in the Audi across the street. Even in the rain she would almost certainly see him leave. He made his way to the end of the corridor on the ground floor. Pushing through the swing doors, he found himself in a passage. At the end of it were the fire-exit doors. He pushed the bars downward and the doors opened. As they did so the alarm went off. It was still blaring out as he turned left into an alleyway and, at the end of that, left again, running at full speed through the rain.

26

The alarm was still ringing when Winter, the plain-clothes police officer, found Menzies Tunim yelling at her from the entrance. When the pair of them reached the top-floor apartment Campbell Tunim was semi-conscious. Her efforts to get Menzies to explain exactly what had happened proved useless. He was beside himself with fury. Finding no sign of the man she was under orders to protect, Winter first called up SO10 on her mobile phone to report him missing. Then she called Shaw, who had just reached home in Frognal.

Shaw told her to call an ambulance for the injured Tunim, then to remain where she was until she got there. Menzies Tunim likewise.

Winter advised Shaw to give her permission to alert the Metropolitan Police Air Support Unit, TO26. There would be a duty helicopter patrol airborne and she could make immediate contact with Scotland Yard's Central Communications Complex.

'You have my authority to do whatever's necessary,' Shaw told her. 'Find him.'

Then she called Deputy Assistant Commissioner Special Branch (SO12) Liaison MI5: 'He will be trying to leave the country,' she told him. 'Have P Squad alerted at Heathrow, London City Airport, Gatwick, Stansted, Luton and Waterloo International Terminal. I want him found.'

27

Constantine Dragos concluded that Phase Four of Strange Police, the necessary work of loosening the remaining Elgin Marbles, would have to be completed on the day of the robbery itself. With the undertaking now on schedule, it fell to Miltiades Zei to renew old acquaintances, to make substantial purchases and call in favours. The size of the Dragos budget would ease his progress across Europe. None the less, he needed to be careful to spread expenditure, so the passage of money would be well nigh impossible to follow. His closed world resembled that of the super-mercenary purchasing ordnance such as new and second-hand armaments. When one or other interest group starts spending money it attracts attention. To avoid this, using assumed names, he utilized a web of different banks and currencies. He took the utmost care to avoid attracting the attention of international intelligence agencies as he kept secret appointments.

28

Miltiades Zei, dapper in a lightweight Gucci suit, met the agent for Hanakawa Transport, Nobuyoshi Matsumoto, in the bar of Gdansk's Marina Hotel on Ulica Jelitkowksa. He struck the deal for the purchase and immediate delivery to Messinian Air of the Hanakawa MCFTU: the sophisticated mobile combined forklift and transportation unit. The Japanese took the substantial personal sweetener in US dollars. No record of the transaction would be kept.

In Moscow, Zei was the guest of Lev Rybakov and Anatoli Chernov of Belorusskaya Armaments at the Alexander Blok Casino. The deal involved the purchase of American MI6 Armalite rifles and white phosphorous grenades. Rybakov would personally transport the arms to Athens. Payment to the Russians would be made to an offshore company in Jersey in a selection of European currencies.

In Switzerland, Zei met up with Dr Lutz Farenkamp of Austrian Engineering and Construction International at the Hotel Schweizerhof on Bahnhofplatz in Zurich. Farenkamp chauffeured Zei in his Mercedes due west from Zurich to Thalwil, the railway junction for the Chur and Luzern-Gotthard lines. It was there, for Zei's benefit, that he demonstrated the workings of two Wolff tower cranes, twins of the cranes in use in London in the British Museum construction area. The gigantic WK 8036, as its trade designation suggests, had a jib span of eighty metres and a lifting capability of 3.6 tonnes. The other crane's jib was seventy metres, with a lifting capability of 3.1 tonnes. Both were powered electrically from the cockpit, in which the operator sits alone some thirty metres from the ground, controlling the crane's manoeuvres with the joystick. Communication with the ground construction supervisors and his partner in the cockpit of the second crane was by short-wave radio.

Zei familiarized himself with the control and operation of the world's most powerful tower crane and the movements of the horizontal trolley and counter-jib. Dr Farenkamp's silence came dear. He paid in Swiss francs.

In the United Kingdom, outside Maidenhead, he placed an order for the Mercedes-Benz Actros, the multi-wheeler truck. Weighing some forty-four tonnes, the state-of-the-art wagon had electronically controlled brakes on all its wheels and a flame-retardant Megaspace cab. The one important extra that Zei ordered was the detachable roof to the rear section. He arranged for delivery of the truck to the administration block at Altenhall. Perhaps, he suggested, Mercedes would be good enough to provide a tarpaulin in addition. The dealer was happy to oblige. So Zei bought the vehicle there and then, using an electronic bank transfer to the account of Messinian Air in Luton.

At the Southampton offices of the Falklands Campaign veteran Air Commodore Bill Knott, Distinguished Flying Cross and Bar, RAF (Retd), Chairman of ATWS Ltd, Air Technology World Services, Zei finalized the purchase of the Boeing Vertol MH-47E Chinook on behalf of Messinian Air.

The payment was made up of US dollars and MSC shares in the ZBC Angola diamond mine that Cape Consolidated had sold to Dragos. The paperwork would to completed on Air Commodore Knott's behalf by his family stockbroker in Leadenhall Street.

The summer weather was postcard perfect when Zei surveyed the helicopter landing ground east of Colchester and then the Altenhall airfield in Norfolk.

The airfield originally opened in 1940 for Second World War fighter operations. Having served as a base for Lightning F-1s during the 1960s, it was then bought by a private consortium. In the late 1980s Messinian Air purchased the controlling interest in the airfield and leased aircraft, freight storage and maintenance facilities to major European importers and their agents. Most of the varieties of aircraft that used the airfield were on ramps outside the hangars. Lined with hedgerows, a network of quiet country roads surrounded the airfield, which was situated in flat agricultural land. The B1150 road formed the eastern boundary and other minor roads allowed easy access.

Zei selected the two hangars to house the Chinook and the other purchases. He checked that they could be satisfactorily secured under the armed protection of Strange Police personnel. Satisfied that he was intimate enough with the disposition of the Altenhall runway, flight control procedures, runway and local geography, he committed the details to memory. Come the night of the execution of the robbery, only in an emergency would he have need of maps and charts.

After a substantial English breakfast at the Norwich Forte Posthouse hotel, he left East Anglia and took the train from Norwich to London's Liverpool Street station. From there he took a black cab direct to Heathrow.

The scheduled afternoon Olympic Airways Athens flight was boarding when he reached the Terminal Three departure lounge. Next time he left the United Kingdom it would be in altogether different circumstances. Meanwhile, there was the ultimate briefing to attend at noon the following day.

29

Soon after Zei left Heathrow for Athens, Constantine Dragos telephoned Nicos Nezeritis's mother in Corinth. 'Nicos gave his life for Greece,' he told her. 'When each day the sun rises over the Acropolis in its magnificence and when it sets, Nicos will be remembered by all future generations born of Mother Greece.'

Mrs Nezeritis insisted that she wanted her son's body brought home for burial.

'It will be done,' said Dragos.

But it would be several months before the body arrived unceremoniously back in Greece in a pauper's coffin.

30

The following day, along with Demetra Ipsilanti, the four other key members of the final assault group came to the Dragos family yacht, *Hellenic*, moored at the Zea Marina, Piraeus. At the last minute, as a precautionary measure, the location of the briefing had been switched from the Platonos Street offices. The first to board the yacht, Grigoris Stratis and Yannis Tselios, came to Piraeus from Chios in the Aegean; Adonis Abatzi arrived from Crete and Stefanos Kalaris from Hydra in the Dodecanese.

Before the light lunch served on the shaded sun deck by Alexios Dragos's Japanese companion, Mitsuko, Constantine Dragos and Miltiades Zei introduced the new arrivals to each other for the first time and then to his father. Altogether, including Constantine Dragos, Miltiades Zei and Demetra Ipsilanti, the assault group now consisted of seven Greeks.

After lunch Constantine chaired the meeting, behind the closed doors of the *Hellenic*'s main saloon.

Panelled in bird's-eye maple stained salmon pink, the vast saloon was furnished with sofas and easy chairs upholstered in pale gold and crimson. They were arranged in a square on a thick white carpet. In the centre of the square was an ottoman standing on an Indian rug. On the walls were replicas of the Elgin Marbles and on the marble plinth at the far end of the saloon, reproduced in Pentelic marble, was the 'River God, Illissus or Eridanos' from the Parthenon's west pediment.

With his one good hand Constantine turned his worry beads over and over again. 'First,' he said, 'there's the loss of Nicos. The setback none of us could have foreseen. We've lost one of our personnel who would have been a key member of the final task force. Not only that, but the loosening of the Marbles is incomplete and will have to be undertaken during the mission. Moreover, there's the additional problem that certain of the British now realize who Nicos was. We are reliably informed that the British Secret Service in liaison with CIA and the Greek Intelligence Service is considerably exercised by perceived threats from P17N, the provisional arm of 17 November, the group that had issued threats to Cleo Ipsilanti. We also know that British SIS commissioned a firm of London security consultants to survey her estate with a view to recommending the installation of security systems. Hence the arrival in Greece of their man, Rosslyn, who formed an attachment with her. We cannot be sure whether or not she gave Rosslyn any indication of Nezeritis's involvement. In the meantime, we are able to conclude that the intelligence services believe Nezeritis was in no small measure connected with P17N. Not with us. That's the line they are pursuing and why SIS got Rosslyn out of Greece immediately. We have to face the fact that the man Rosslyn remains a wild card. But we believe he'll be kept on ice.' He looked around the table. 'Any questions?' There were none. 'Meanwhile, to the plan in detail –'

He took over an hour to talk the plans for the operation through in detail. There was military brevity about the presentation. His explanations were succinct. Referring to large-scale ground plans, he described the surrounding area and layout of the British Museum. Descriptions of the interior of the museum and Duveen Gallery were based upon the up-to-date plans that Prevezer had obtained for him; details of the electronic security he described originated from the same source, as well as the layouts of the alarm circuits. Beside the names of the chief security personnel detailed biographical information had been added.

Turning to the building work taking place at the museum, he said that everything was on schedule. He and Zei had hacked into the computers of JCLC, the engineering contractors based in South-ampton. Thus they were in possession of daily progress reports covering all aspects of the building and engineering work, and these included the various security arrangements jointly supervised by the museum and JCLC. He added that he had 'received confirmation that none of the security officers was armed. Moreover, as perhaps everyone present is aware, in so far as construction and engineering works are suspended from twelve noon on Saturdays until seven a.m. on Mondays, only a skeleton security unit mans the site. The preliminary security preparations for neutralization are covered on the pages headed Operational Security.'

Here he asked again if anyone had any questions. Again, there were none. He then opened the dossier in front of him and passed copies of two photographs around the table. 'One: the sky view of the target. The glass roofs of the Duveen Gallery are to the left. Two: the interior of the gallery itself.'

There was a general discussion about the work achieved to date by Demetra Ipsilanti and Nezeritis. Demetra elaborated and gave a full account of the fatal accident.

'Now I turn,' Dragos continued, 'to the basic premise of the operation as it relates to timings.' He took the meeting stage by stage through the timings. From the moment they left Greece to landing at Altenhall. The onwards lift by Chinook to the airfield in the Colchester area. The journey in the container wagon to the museum itself. The work to be achieved inside the museum and the transportation of the Marbles by container wagon to Colchester and then to Altenhall. The loading of the Marbles into the waiting Boeing. The return flight to Sparta.

Here he backtracked to discuss the use of the two cranes. 'You will see the section plan of the Wolff WK 8036 tower crane.' He distributed copies of the drawing of the crane's design supplied by Dr Farenkamp. 'Lifting massive loads on to the construction site, the crane has been operating for several months. But, looking at the JCLC plans and time schedules, you'll see that it is operational within the south and south-eastern areas of the complex. Not the north. The second crane, in the northern area, has a span that will encompass the Duveen Gallery. This is the crane that we will employ.' He set his claw hand on the dossier in front of him and continued, 'The UK assault group including container wagon drivers will consist of seven personnel. Call signs: Alpha, Beta, Gamma, Delta, Epsilon, Zeta, Omega.' He outlined the chain of command. 'I will be overall CO.

Arrival at the target area is scheduled for a Sunday at three a.m. From now on we should regard the operation as being on alert status Green. To recap here, the first phase is entry through the glass roof from Montague Place. The first group of Demetra, with you, Grigoris, and you, Yannis, will scale the walls, break and remove the glass panels and metal roof supports. Then the remaining fixed Marbles will be attended to. Gaining control of the crane is the second phase. A two-man team will achieve this. Miltiades and myself. The crane will be employed to lift in the Hanakawa mobile combined forklift and transportation unit, the HMCFTU. This will be manned by you, Adonis. You will enter with the HMCFTU. Then follows the lifting of the HMCFTU into the Duveen Gallery. This will move the Marbles to the position enabling the crane's lifting platform to be lowered. Following that the Marbles will be raised by the crane and installed in the container wagon on stand-by with you, Stefanos, in Montague Place. We then regroup. From here the Marbles will be transported by freight wagon to the RV collection point north of Colchester in Essex. This is a highly dangerous procedure.' They perused the road maps. 'Roads from Colchester to Altenhall are regularly patrolled by the Essex, Suffolk and Norfolk police authorities and wagons stopped and searched at random. Therefore, I've put in place a staged transportation procedure. We fly the cargo out of the Colchester area by a Boeing Vertol MH-47E Chinook to the disused airfield in Norfolk at Altenhall, some twenty-four kilometres north of Norwich, off the B1150 between the city and the north Norfolk coastline. You should appreciate the three types of flight clearance available to get around UK-controlled airspace. IFR or Instrument Flight Rules, VFR or Visual Flight Rules and Special VFR. Our flight routine will employ VFR clearance, providing our own separation from other aircraft between 0.300 and 0.400 hours. The advantage is that if we accept our own responsibility by asking for VFR clearance, we will prevent delays. VFR clearance in class D airspace is five kilometres. Given the time of year of the operation, we foresee no serious meteorological obstacles. And given we have control of the Altenhall airfield, there will be no conflict over landing orders. There is more than adequate taxi and runway capacity for take-off for Greece. The Marbles will be loaded on to the Messinian Air Boeing, which will then airlift the cargo to the final RV in Athens. Obviously we have to consider the variable meteorological conditions in the UK. The likelihood of prolonged high winds is remote. Piloted by me, the Boeing will fly at a ceiling of 35,000 feet.'

There was a long silence. With a silk handkerchief Constantine wiped the moisture from his sharpened hand claw.

Grigoris Stratis eventually spoke up. 'And once the Marbles are back in Athens, what then?'

'They will be taken immediately to our secure warehouse here in Piraeus.'

There were nods of silent approval around the table. The only sound was the clack-clack of Alexios Dragos's worry beads.

Constantine continued, 'I have to remind you that there will be a window of only some twenty minutes in which to complete the lifting in the target zone. If we were to need several attempts then the elements of surprise and swiftness would be lost. So it will be one lift. Not two. Ideally we would have recommended that the Chinook lift the Marbles out, but flying restrictions and the strong likelihood of unwanted identification over London make that of course impossible. That is why we will utilize the on-site crane. The wagons. The Chinook north of Colchester and then onwards to Altenhall for the final stage of transportation out of the United Kingdom.' He took a sip from the glass of mineral water in front of him. 'I have two teams of general and supplementary personnel in waiting. Each consists of six people. In the interests of security we do not intend to brief substitutes or personnel at Altenhall until twelve hours before commencement. Even then they will be known only by their call signs.'

Adonis Abatzi asked about arms and protection.

Constantine explained, 'Personnel will carry 203s and American MI6 Armalite rifles, and those at the vehicle checkpoints, RVs and final RV will be equipped with 5.56 light-support machine-guns, Minimis with 500 rounds each, and white phosphorous grenades for smoke-screen purposes.'

Abatzi looked impressed.

124

'The covert transportation of the MH-47E Chinook to the United Kingdom,' added Dragos, 'and its assembly for operational duty . . . Miltiades will oversee all of it.'

Here Alexios Dragos spoke for the first time. 'I suggest,' he said, 'we take a break. Perhaps you'd care to adjourn to the deck bar for refreshment.'

31

Immediately the saloon doors were closed, Alexios Dragos said to his son, 'I know those British Secret Service bastards. Is there any chance Prevezer could be stringing us along?'

'No,' said Constantine. 'We have enough personal dirt on her to wreck her life. She's up to her neck in it. She isn't going to talk to anyone else, believe me.'

'You'd better be right,' Alexios muttered.

Constantine fingered his worry beads. 'She's mostly served her purpose.'

'I remain concerned,' said Alexios, 'about what the British Secret Intelligence Service may learn from the man Rosslyn.'

'That's a risk we have to take,' said Constantine.

'How can you be so sure of it?' Alexios said with persistence. 'We have to know what this Rosslyn's told the British. We have to find out.' The eyes were red-rimmed. He sat back in his chair, his legs apart. 'Rosslyn,' he said, 'is the sole issue that remains an obstacle.'

There was a prolonged silence.

Alexios shook his head. There was the glint of gold in the lower teeth. 'London is three hours away,' he said. 'This Rosslyn, Constantine. There is no alternative. We have to kill him.'

Constantine breathed deeply. Looking at his watch, he said, 'Let's talk later.'

'You agree?'

'I hear what you're saying.'

'Good,' said Alexios. 'Good. I have to say I'm proud of you.'

Constantine smiled silently. His adrenalin raced. He was exalted. It was all Green.

'And one other important matter,' said his father quietly. 'One that

I have to explain to you now. A matter you will have to agree with. It concerns precautions, Constantine, both in London and here in Athens . . .'

Constantine listened to his father with a look of increasing fear and disbelief.

32

It was in the early hours of the following morning that Yannis Simopoulos, the Athens police chief, drove Alexios Dragos and Demetra Ipsilanti in an unmarked police car to the darkened house in the Kypseli district.

Without consulting either the Foreign or Public Order Ministry, Simopoulos had placed the Kypseli house under heavily-armed guard under the provisions of the Greek Police Witness Protection Scheme. Simopoulos's purpose was to remain one of the most closely guarded secrets of Strange Police.

33

In London, alert to the air and ground police search he believed would already be under way, Rosslyn had stayed out of the way in the twenty-four-hour Gerrard Street Chinese private bar and eatery. Stacked crates of pak choi, lotus roots, red chillies and Australian lychees advertised as fresh obscured the entrance to the basement club, near the Shanghai Great Hairdressers Salon. Smells of barbecued pork and duck with hoisin sauce were heavy in the air. Strictly 'Members Only', the neon-lit establishment had 'Notices of Warning' pinned to the walls: 'We have an alarm connected to the police station', 'For your own protection and ours, you are being videotaped', 'Banknotes tendered here will be tested with the Counterfeit Money Detector Pen.'

Without asking questions, Michael Lo took Rosslyn's canvas bag and showed him through the kitchens. He led the way to an alcove in the comfortable back room and bar, where, away from the prying lenses of the CCTV, the gambling was in full swing.

Lo could see at once from Rosslyn's face that he was in some sort of serious danger. They had shared trouble before, but he had never seen such intensity in Rosslyn's eyes.

Once secure inside the club premises, Lo said he was available to do any other favours needed. He offered Rosslyn a bed and use of the bathroom upstairs, and declined his offer of payment.

This was the same Michael Lo who, in danger of his life, had helped Rosslyn, the former undercover Customs and Excise agent, nail the Black Shell drugs cartel operating out of Macao to Portugal and all the way to Felixstowe in the late 1980s. In return, Rosslyn had brought charges against the half a dozen Chinese hit men who had torched Lo's Sueng's Club One. Along with their families, the six Chinese hit men had been summarily deported and Lo was eternally in Rosslyn's debt. The Anglo-Chinese knew Rosslyn to be a fine investigator: wry, methodical, hard, possessed of the keen intuition that raised him far above the natural abilities of your average detective. The professional investigator who was no time-server and no friend of bureaucrats. Nothing seemed to intimidate him. Perhaps what most of all drew Lo to Rosslyn was his sense of honour. He was the investigator who was as good as his word. And he was a good listener, warm and painstaking no matter what calls were made upon his energies, day or night. Rosslyn never seemed to sleep. He could stay awake three nights and three days and still his mind showed ferocious concentration.

Now Lo detected edginess in Rosslyn and he supposed it had something to do with the swollen knuckles of his right hand. It was plain to see he had recently hit someone or something very hard indeed. The investigator's mood was blacker than he ever remembered seeing it.

Over beers at the alcove table in the back room, Rosslyn said he wanted one or two urgent favours, 'maybe more'.

'Whatever you want of me, Alan,' said Lo, 'you only have to ask.'

'I have five and a half thousand dollars in a deposit box,' Rosslyn told Lo. 'I'd like you to get the cash for me first thing in the morning. I don't want them to see me take it out. There's a coded number that allows anyone who gives it to the supervisor to get the cash.'

Lo removed his glasses, wiped them with a white silk handkerchief and said, 'I can give you that much now. Then I can collect it later. That's if you're in some kind of shit.'

'You could say so,' said Rosslyn.

'I can tell,' said Lo. 'Listen. Which deposit service are we talking about?'

'Occidental.'

'Shaftesbury Avenue,' said Lo. 'I know them. You realize they take the numbers of currency they hold?'

'You're kidding?'

'No,' said Lo.

'I never knew.'

'Now you do. I can have the dollars collected. We can change them into another currency without the deal being traced.'

'I'd like you to do it for me.'

'Then what currency do you want it in?'

'A thousand in francs and lire, say, and the rest in drachmas.' Rosslyn gave Lo the coded number of the deposit box.

'That's no problem,' said Lo. 'I have francs and lira in the safe and there are some Greek investigators my brother knows in Bayswater who can supply us drachmas.'

'How reliable are they?'

'They're OK. No problem. One of them, Kostas Lambrakis, is married to a cousin. They're unlicensed, but OK. Good.'

'How good?'

'I've used Lambrakis once or twice. He's efficient and careful.'

'Could he find someone in London for me? A man I need to talk to?'

'Sure. I can ask him for you. Who is he?'

'Write this down. A Greek called George Vayakakos. He's an aristocrat and friend of ex-King Constantine.'

Lo wrote the name down on the back of his business card.

'It shouldn't be too difficult to find him,' said Rosslyn. 'He's a patient in some private clinic or hospital in London. Most likely Harley Street. It'll be one of the major ones. Try the Harley Street Clinic. King Edward VII Hospital for Officers. The Princess Grace. The Wellington Hospital in St John's Wood. I need to see him as soon as possible. And if this Lambrakis can tell me anything about him, I'd be pleased to hear it.'

Lo pocketed the business card. 'What else do you need from me?'

'If you want to know, I need a passport. New identity. A car with non-British plates and papers. To be collected in Calais or Boulogne.'

'And you're going to say –' Lo pointed his fingers at Rosslyn, the fingers held to form the shape of a handgun.

'No,' said Rosslyn. 'Not that.'

'Then how long have I got to deliver?' asked Lo.

'Thirty-six hours,' said Rosslyn. 'Maybe forty-eight at the most.'

'That doesn't give us long,' said Lo.

'Do your best,' said Rosslyn. 'And I need to stay off the streets.'

'Remain here. Upstairs. It's secure.'

'How secure?' said Rosslyn. 'I mean, do you have an arrangement with the Met at all?'

'Like?'

'Any off-limits deal? The no-go area?'

'No, we don't,' said Lo. 'Things have changed since your day at Custom House. But as far as the police go we're whiter than white. They don't come here.'

'And your staff,' said Rosslyn, 'are they discreet?'

Lo smiled. 'Family. You have no worries on that score.' He thought for a few moments. 'The car in France I have no problem with. But this new identity you need . . .'

'Do you have a problem with it?'

'Only if you've used one in the past.'

'None that need concern us. Not in the long term.'

'In the short term?'

'Once I used a Canadian passport.'

'I'd keep it simple,' said Lo. 'Stay British.' He paused before saying, 'You look exhausted, Alan. If I were you, I'd get some sleep. You want me to show you the upstairs room?'

'If you wouldn't mind,' said Rosslyn. 'One more thing. I'd like you to take a look for me at my flat in Claverton Street. See who's there. Then let me know. I'll stay up.'

Lo handed Rosslyn a mobile phone. 'I'll call you.'

34

After he had shown Rosslyn to the upstairs room, Lo went to the kitchens of Sueng's Club Two and packed a Special Meal for One into silver-foil containers. Carrying the containers in a white plastic bag, he left the club by the back entrance and headed off on his motorbike in a south-westerly direction.

In Pimlico, a short distance from the address in Claverton Street, he parked his motorbike and went the rest of the way on foot. Among the cars parked opposite the entrance to Rosslyn's basement flat he saw the black cab. The driver at the wheel caught his eye and at once continued reading his newspaper. Lo noticed that the driver was managing to read the newspaper and make a call on his mobile phone at the same time.

As if not quite sure of the address he was seeking, Lo hesitated at the gate in the railings that opened on to the stone steps leading to the basement. He looked up and down the street. Sure enough he saw, some twenty or thirty metres away, a black car parked. A Ford. The driver was a woman and she had one passenger in the front seat and another in the back. Lo noticed all three faces turn in his direction. Without further hesitation, he opened the gate, went down the narrow steps and rang the bell. He saw the curtains in the windows were drawn across.

The door was opened with a suddenness that suggested the black man in the doorway had been tipped off about his arrival. Lo went into Chinese humble mode and thickened up the accent. He held out the white plastic bag. 'Your take-away, sir. OK?'

The black man in track suit and trainers turned his back and called, 'Anyone order a Chinese take-away?'

Lo noticed the black man's police-issue mobile phone. He edged inside the entrance to get a better view. He saw a second and then a third man appear in the corridor. The third man was pulling on his jacket. Lo just had time to make out the holster and the handgun.

A voice said, 'We haven't ordered anything.'

Lo said, 'My mistake.'

Alone again in the street, he glanced at the cab, then at the laughing faces in the black Ford.

He rode his motorbike to Victoria, came to a stop outside the station and then, making sure he was unobserved, he called Rosslyn. 'Your place is alive with Special Branch,' he said. 'Stay put.'

'Did they photograph you?'

'Not as far as I could see.'

'Any CCTV?'

'If there was, it was well hidden. But I don't think so.'

'No helicopter?'

'No.'

'You did well,' said Rosslyn. 'Thanks.'

'Get some sleep now,' Lo said. 'You're going to need it.'

35

Rosslyn lost track of time, and memories haunted his dreams. Cleo and Greece. Greece and Cleo. Likewise, the voice of his old chief at Customs and Excise, the Sea Captain, Gaynor, who would say, 'Never get caught in the yellow box without an exit without a gun.'

The idea that he was unarmed troubled him. Yet the risk of carrying a weapon to the Continent was not worth taking. It was bad enough that the police would soon have a photograph of him to hand. And if he were found to be carrying a weapon in Greece it would look even worse when they read the murder charges out to him in some stinking Athens police station.

There were the equally persistent questions: Why would anyone have wanted to kill her? What was the motive?

The means seemed obvious. She had been shoved into the well and presumably drowned. And yet . . . He had not seen her body. Just the white silk dress floating on the murky surface in the semi-darkness. The white silk against Cleo's flesh that had so aroused him.

She had that shotgun to hand. Why? Why had it been left there by the well's stone wall? He tried to remember whether it had been fired and found he was undecided about that. Then there was the opportunity. She had said she was expecting visitors up at the estate. But who? Were they the same people who had sought to frame him? But why? And what threat had his presence there represented?

The wanted man, he was caught in the yellow box without an exit. The way ahead seemed booby-trapped. The Greeks had a warrant out for his arrest. He could not afford to remain in London for very long. Shaw and her kind would have alerted the police to the search for him. And there was no chance of moving sideways, turning to

Campbell and Menzies Tunim with a plea for help. It seemed he had made enemies of everyone. He had walked into the net of iron and had no idea how wide it might be.

The exhausted voices in his mind told him to stick to facts. The one thing he knew was that he had no part in Cleo's fate. Half asleep, he began to wonder what sort of deal the Tunims must have done with Shaw and about the extent of the damage he had inflicted on the brothers who had betrayed him.

He fell asleep feeling white silk enfurling him; Cleo's mouth against his; her breath filling his lungs.

36

Campbell Tunim had been admitted to the London Clinic and it was there, shortly after noon, that he woke to find Menzies with Marion Shaw in the private room. She had brought him a bunch of flowers.

'What happened?' she asked.

'I couldn't have been more reasonable with him.'

'You told him what we want of him?'

'Yes.'

'Did you give him any names?'

'No, I didn't,' said Campbell.

'We got the impression he realized he was being marginalized,' said Menzies.

'He already has been,' Shaw said.

'I told him he couldn't stay with us,' said Campbell. 'I made him the offer of three months' money. He seemed so, well, reluctant to cooperate. I told him, frankly, that he'd dug himself into a hole he couldn't get out of.'

'And then?'

'The bastard went berserk. He hit me. It was totally unexpected. The next thing I knew was that Menzies and the protection officer were standing over me.' He fingered the bruises to his jaw. 'I hope you've got him.'

'Not yet,' said Shaw.

'He can't have gone far,' said Menzies. 'Surely you could arrest him at his flat. It's in Pimlico.'

'He hasn't returned there yet.'

'Have you got people watching it?' asked Menzies.

'Yes, we have,' said Shaw. 'But I rather doubt he'll return there in the immediate future.' She went to the door and asked the nurse in the corridor to bring coffee for two. She returned and sat on the end of the bed. 'I don't suppose you'll be surprised to hear that my people are none too pleased about what's happened.'

'Neither are we,' said Menzies.

'I can imagine,' said Shaw. 'It's unfortunate to say the least. I've been told to bring our arrangements to an end.'

'If that's really the case,' said Menzies, 'you realize that we'll be out of business.'

Shaw got up and walked to the window. 'I can't allow that to worry me, I'm afraid.' She fingered the hem of the curtain. 'Tell me, did either of you ever really get on with him?'

'Not personally, no,' said Campbell.

'But we didn't exactly think it would end like this,' said Menzies.

'Or that he'd be the one to drive you out of business?' said Shaw.

'Certainly not,' said Campbell. 'On the contrary.'

'We always thought you approved of him,' said Menzies.

'True.'

'Look,' said Menzies, 'I do realize that none of us is indispensable. We'd very much appreciate it if you'd reconsider what you've just said. I mean, about terminating our business arrangements with your people.'

'Oh, it's not up to me, you understand,' said Shaw. 'No. Somehow I have to make very sure that Rosslyn keeps his mouth shut and keeps his fingers out of what's happening.'

'I'm sorry, what exactly are you talking about?' said Menzies.

'You remember that I spoke to him alone in the Marylebone flat last night?'

'Yes,' said Menzies.

'What would you say if I told you Rosslyn maintains you've been double-dealing?'

'I'm sorry?' said Menzies.

'That you've been playing both sides. Selling our intelligence to some of our wayward children in Bonn and Frankfurt and Berlin.'

'That's a complete fabrication,' said Campbell.

'Look,' said Shaw, 'let's not pretend that our games are played by the Queensberry Rules. I don't expect you to tell me that you've been acting dishonourably. Obviously, there'll be an investigation into his allegations.'

The nurse brought in the coffee on a tray. Menzies Tunim waited for her to leave and close the door. 'Rosslyn's lying.'

'I wonder,' said Shaw. 'You seemed quite content to get rid of him, didn't you? And he obviously entertains a considerable dislike for you.'

'Is that what he told you?' said Campbell.

'It's what I inferred from what he had to tell me.'

'What precisely did he tell you?' said Menzies.

'I'm afraid that's strictly a matter for the board of investigation to consider. Obviously it will be painstaking and fair. Rosslyn will be called as the key witness.'

Campbell Tunim raised his hand like a police officer halting traffic. 'In no sense whatsoever are we guilty of malpractice. Believe me. You asked us to sideline Rosslyn.'

'We followed every one of your instructions to the letter,' said Menzies. 'And, I have to say, without being told by you anything of the background to what may or may not have transpired in Greece. Now you tell us he's accused us of some malpractice of which we know nothing whatsoever. I repeat, nothing.'

Shaw shrugged. 'Suppose,' she continued, 'I were to take your line? Say, act in your defence. Or even persuade my chief that you were deserving of immunity.'

'Immunity from what?' said Menzies.

'Why, prosecution.'

'For God's sake,' said Campbell.

'No, let me finish. The slate is effectively clean. Suppose we consider the avoidance of the long-drawn out investigation and immunity from prosecution?'

'What's the alternative?' said Menzies.

'Make me an offer,' Shaw said.

'Square things with Rosslyn?' said Campbell.

'What do you mean?' asked Shaw.

'Get him to tell the truth,' said Campbell. 'Get him to admit he's lied and lied again.'

'Only we don't know where he is, do we?' said Shaw.

'No,' said Menzies. 'But you people have the resources to find him, don't you?'

'I wonder,' said Shaw. 'It's not strictly a job for us. Rather, it's one for the police. And I can tell you that the involvement of the police is something we wish to avoid. We do not want the Greek police involved either.'

'What makes you so sure they will be?' said Campbell.

'You know why. Because there's the warrant out for his arrest.'

'You really believe Rosslyn murdered the Ipsilanti woman?' said Menzies. 'You see, we don't.'

'No, neither do we,' said Shaw. 'And we're not even completely sure she's dead. Our officer in Athens, Prevezer, has been forbidden access to the mortuary. But who can tell? If and when he tries to prove his case, Rosslyn may not be given access either. But given his involvement with her, you can be sure that he'll do his level best to establish what happened and get the charges dropped.'

'What happened to her?' said Menzies.

'I can't tell you.'

'You think Rosslyn knows?' asked Campbell.

'We think he'll sure as hell try to find out,' said Shaw. 'That will involve his going back to Greece. And I have to tell you that we don't want him to return there and get in the way of our operations on the ground. We want him found and silenced. Our first attempt resulted in the failure of last night. And, believe you me, it will not happen again. And that's where you come in. You have the chance to defend yourself against him. And the best method is attack, or, in this case, complete silence.'

'Tell me then,' said Menzies Tunim, 'what is it you have in mind?'

'To remove the threat of investigation,' said Shaw.

'And then?' said Campbell.

'There'll be some formalities to be completed, governed by the Official Secrets Act. Paperwork and so forth. Then some briefings.'

'After that?' asked Menzies.

'I think we should get you discharged from here. Meanwhile, it will be best if you talk to no one about our discussion or our meetings. By no one, I mean no one, Menzies. Not even Mrs Tunim, Charlotte-Anne. Then I can progress the immunity authorization and you'll be in the clear.'

Menzies Tunim removed his white gloves to scratch at the flaking skin of his raw fingers.

37

Outside the London Clinic, Menzies Tunim accompanied Shaw to her car. Holding the door open, he said, 'Marion, I've known you as well as anyone in this trade. Tell me, there's something very wrong, isn't there?'

'I can't deny it.'

'I mean, it's personal. I've never seen you like this. Something's on the line.' He put a restraining hand on her elbow. 'What is it? Are they about to fire you? Are you going to do a Shayler or a Tomlinson?'

'C'mon, Menzies. Grow up.'

'I'm serious,' he said.

'Then what do you think?' she asked.

'I think that P17N shit is a cover. You're playing some quite different game.'

'What makes you think so?'

'Because of what you once told me,' he said. 'Way back in history.'

'When was that?'

'At Cambridge.'

'What did I tell you, Menzies?'

'About Greece, Marion.'

'Greece?' she said.

'That you had Greek blood in your veins. You never knew who your father was. You told me he was Greek. Now there's all this. Greece. Rosslyn. The Ipsilanti women. You're looking anorexic. What the hell is going on, Marion?'

'Cambridge was a long time ago,' she said. 'Would you mind letting go of my arm? Please. And your remark about me . . . that's bloody rude, even by your standards.'

'Whatever it is that's happening, don't let them get to you. Don't go putting your head in the oven or doing something stupid.'

'I don't have a gas oven at home,' she said. 'And you once said I had the opposite of a stupid mind. You said you loved me for my mind.'

'Always was my line with tight-skirt totty.'

'I think I realized that,' she said.

'Then don't do anything stupid, OK?'

'Like what?'

'Like carrying out that threat to kill the bloody Greeks.'

Pigeons were diving at scraps of bread thrown from an upstairs balcony. 'Did I say that?' she asked.

'Yes, Marion, that's what you said. One summer evening along the backs. You were pissed out of your brains.'

'I don't remember,' she said.

'You don't? I'm reminding you, Marion. You know what else you said to me?'

'What did I say?' she asked.

'That I had an incredible memory for people's asides, the casual remark. That it could be useful in the Foreign Service.'

'Well, it hasn't turned out like that. And now I'd say to you that, if you're not very careful, that gift of memory of yours could get you into very deep shit indeed.'

'Really? With whom?'

'With me,' she snapped.

'Then I'm right. This isn't only operational, is it? It's a bloody personal war you're fighting, isn't it? And I think you're losing it. You are in every kind of personal trouble.'

She stared at him in silent fury.

'Perhaps I'm right,' he said. 'I owe you a favour. I can help you.'

'Say again.'

'I can help you,' he repeated.

'No thanks, Menzies,' she said. 'Tell me, what was it I told you at Cambridge?'

'You said you intended to find your mother and your father. That those people who fostered you were in, where was it, Huddersfield?'

143

She was on the edge of tears. 'Harrogate.'

'Right, Harrogate. That some friend of theirs had confirmed the story about your mother and Greek blood.'

'This has nothing to do with anything, Menzies. *Nothing*.'

He positioned himself between her and the car door. 'I wonder. You know what the word is in the trade, Marion? Oh, not at your exalted level. Not in the Bishop's Babylon Palace. No, among the choirboys. You know what's being said?'

'Is this personal?'

'No. Operational. You should know it, if you don't already.'

'What should I know, Menzies?'

'Some Greek with more money than you or I can dream of has taken soundings in the States, here in the UK, in South Africa, Israel and France. He looked over Executive Outcomes and Strategic Resources in Pretoria. Gurkha Security Guards in St Helier, Jersey. Military Professional Resources Inc. in Virginia. Sandline International here and ten other UK firms in London. European Security Operations in Westgate, Kent, told him that they could provide him with a protection team within forty-eight hours. And this guy was on the verge of accepting them when he went totally quiet.'

'Don't waste my time, Menzies.'

'Take it or leave it, sweetheart. I'm telling you that a Greek syndicate has been spending like it's going out of fashion. Gdansk. Moscow. Zurich and here in the UK.'

'Oh yes. Who are they?'

'I've told you, Greeks.'

'I mean, how do you know they've been in those places?'

'Because we were commissioned to find out.'

'Who by?'

'By the stockbroker of a man called Knott. Bill Knott, ex-RAF. Chairman of Air Technology World Services. He asked us for a rundown on these people and where their funds were coming from. He's been offered some dodgy shares in Greek stocks.'

'And where's the money coming from?'

'Thrace Bank, Vaduz, Liechtenstein. The bank, Marion, the Thrace Bank. Don't you see it? Two Greeks own it. Alexios and Constantine

Dragos. Father and son. Owners of the Messinian Shipping Corporation and Messinian Air. And you want to know who their lawyer is? It's a man called Ioannis Ipsilanti. Former husband of Cleo. You want me to tell you who she is too, or have you forgotten already?'

'I haven't forgotten, Menzies,' she said, struggling to collect herself. 'Tell me one more thing, though. Have you by chance ever heard of a firm in Vienna, lawyers called Naumann Bartenstein?'

'No. Why?

'Forget it. Meanwhile, if you value our relationship, I suggest you take no more interest in this. If not, let me tell you, you will be in trouble that will break your neck.'

'And Rosslyn?'

'Screw him,' Shaw said.

'And the Greeks?'

'Not my problem,' she said with venom.

With so much venom that Menzies Tunim realized, without knowing the nature of the target, he had scored a bull's-eye. Indeed, from the cauldron of emotions he saw in Shaw's face, he might as well have destroyed the target altogether.

38

When Rosslyn woke, Lo was offering him a mug of sweet tea, some sliced French bread stuffed with an omelette and the early edition of the *Evening Standard*. The newspaper was open and Rosslyn saw his own face staring up at him from the page. An old photograph above a short article saying that Alan Rosslyn, a private investigator, was being sought by the Metropolitan Police in connection with an assault in Marylebone.

Lo looked at him uneasily. 'Alan, do you feel like telling me what this is all about?'

So, over the food Lo had brought, Rosslyn explained. When he had finished, Lo reiterated his offer of assistance and stuck to practicalities. He said the dollars had been changed into the currencies Rosslyn wanted. He had made provisional arrangements for Rosslyn to be provided with a Volkswagen in Calais. 'Everything will be ready in just over forty-eight hours,' he said and then added, 'Two other things. You should travel with a shadow. I have someone in mind.'

'I prefer to work alone.'

'Given the extreme seriousness of the position you're in with the Greek police?'

Rosslyn thought about the proposal, then asked, 'Who are you suggesting shadows me?'

'A former officer in the Hong Kong Police. My sister-in-law, Ethel Chang. She'll need paying. But we can settle that on your return.'

'I'll think about it,' said Rosslyn doubtfully. 'And the other matter?'

'Vayakakos. Lambrakis found him. He's a private patient in the Wellington Hospital in St John's Wood. He is awaiting heart surgery.' Lo unfolded some A4 sheets of paper. 'This is Lambrakis's initial report.'

Rosslyn read:

GEORGE THEODOROU VAYAKAKOS.

Born 20 October 1927, Kalamata, Greece.

Entered Military Academy in Greece in 1946. Graduated in 1948. Commissioned into infantry. Took part in operations against Communist forces during Communist Wars. Wounded and decorated.

Volunteered in 1951 for Greek Regiment in United Nations Korean expeditionary force. Three times awarded American Bronze Star and twice the Silver Star. Highly decorated by Greek government.

Trained subsequently in United States at Fort Benning, Georgia. Later served as senior instructor at Military Academy of Greece and instructed the then Crown Prince, Constantine.

In 1958 appointed ADC to Crown Prince Constantine.

Appointed Chief of Military Household of the Crown Prince in 1960. Held position until accession of Crown Prince to throne as King Constantine. Served as Private Secretary to King Constantine until military coup in 1967.

In 1967 arrested and held by the Colonels at military headquarters until his release was negotiated by King Constantine.

He served as Military Attaché to King Constantine until the failed counter-coup in December and then escaped to London.

The Greek military government sought Vayakakos's return but he declined to return to Greece. Subsequently, he was court-martialled in his absence and threatened with immediate arrest should he return to Greece.

King Constantine remained in Rome until he was deposed finally in 1973. He maintained regular contact with Vayakakos and when the king came to London in 1974, the same year the Greek monarchy was abolished by referendum, Vayakakos assumed the role of Private Secretary and Deputy Director of the King's Private Office.

In the meantime, Vayakakos had taken a postgraduate degree at London University in Greek Art and Archaeology and submitted a thesis entitled 'The Iconography of the Parthenon Sculptures'.

He has been active on several international committees seeking the restitution of the Parthenon sculptures, the Elgin Marbles, presently housed in London in the Duveen Gallery of the British Museum.

The late Melina Mercouri, who persuaded the Greek government to allow him to return with his wife during the 1980s to the small Vayakakos family estate in Kardamyli, Messinia, Greece, applauded his work for this cause.

His wife, Maria Arianna Vayakakos, died in 1978 in Kardamyli. There were no children of the marriage. His closest relatives are his cousins by marriage, Alexios and Constantine Dragos, owners of the Messinian Shipping Corporation, Piraeus, Greece.

Rosslyn's immediate reaction to the background on Vayakakos was, no matter what the risk, he had to see him. 'Does Lambrakis have any idea how serious the man's condition is?'

'Not really,' said Lo. 'Lambrakis did say that, according to the ward sister he saw, Vayakakos has received visitors on a daily basis. Friends who are looking after his affairs while he's hospitalized. Lambrakis doesn't know who they are.'

'Do you mind getting Lambrakis to call him? Have him say he has some confidential business that needs attention. Keep it simple. Something about papers needing a signature. Perhaps one of the friends could see to it. I want to know who they are.'

Lo said he understood what was needed. Lambrakis could be relied upon to make the approach with the necessary discretion.

'Meanwhile,' Rosslyn said. 'I'm going to risk the streets. I'd like you to shadow me as my rear-view eyes. In case anyone is following me. We're paying a visit to the British Museum.'

39

Summertime in Bloomsbury. The light breeze. Clear air. A perfect day. With Lo keeping him in sight, Rosslyn joined the first lecture group of the afternoon in Gallery 8 of the British Museum. The Duveen Gallery.

'The Parthenon sculptures,' said the woman lecturer, 'are dedicated to the patron goddess of Athens, Athena.' She must have given this talk a thousand times. She had a practised drawl, with a tendency to drop her final g's. 'The Parthenon itself, a temple, was built in the fifth century BC. The carvin' of these marble sculptures, the most beautiful in the world, was the work of many hands, supervised by Phidias.'

Rosslyn positioned himself at the back of the group. He was looking up at the glass panels through which Nezeritis was said to have fallen and at the floor where he had died.

'Today,' the lecturer was saying, 'we know them as the Elgin Marbles, because it was Lord Elgin who brought them to London in the nineteenth century.'

Moving to the eastern wall, he peered behind the panel labelled 'Heifer led for sacrifice at the Great Panathenaic festival' to examine the wall fixings.

Suppose he had been trying to steal one of the marble panels? The one he was looking at was securely fixed to the wall by what seemed to be heavy-duty white plastic cement. No ordinary thief could remove it. Let alone transport it out of here unseen. You'd be looking at a full-scale operation. No one could get away with that. Nezeritis had to have been thinking of something else. But what?

'Many of the sculptures you see here,' the woman lecturer continued, 'are really panels which originally belonged to the frieze on the temple's exterior. You will also see fragments of sculptures which were situated on the pediments. And also the metopes, the space between triglyphs – incised stone blocks in a Doric frieze occurrin' at intervals. These are from the south wall of the Parthenon.'

Rosslyn wanted to ask her how much the whole lot weighed, but he doubted that she would know.

She was warming to her subject. 'There are many intriguin' interpretations of the frieze. Clearly, we can see the procession of horsemen and votaries. Some scholars argue that what we see is a representation of the Panathenaic festival. This was held to mark the birthday of the goddess every four years. Some say there may have been two processions depicted. Others that, like the Theban Sphinx, the frieze embodies some great secret. We hope that one day some papyrus or stone inscription will be found to explain things.' She turned her attention to a small gang of spotty teenage boys wearing the colours of AC Milan. 'There you are, young men. And who knows? You may be the very ones to solve the great mystery.' The Italians youths blushed. 'Now, if you'd like to follow me, we can look at some of the sculptures in detail. This is, of course, the unique opportunity the British Museum affords us. The supreme close-up view that would have been quite impossible in fifth-century Athens. Let us consider the mysteries.'

Rosslyn hung back and decided to inspect the Marbles for reasons that had nothing to do with the mysteries of art history. Staying with the flow of the crowd in the Duveen Gallery to hinder possible recognition, he put his silent questions to the ghost of Nicos Nezeritis with the intensity of the spiritualist conjuring up the voices of the dead. *So, then, Nicos, how did you kill yourself? You must have been lying, or maybe squatting, or even sitting on the floor when you stuck the gun inside your mouth. Come on, Nicos. Speak to me.*

Wedged between two gawking Australians, Rosslyn looked up to the glass panels in the roof. *And that's where you fell from. You must have slipped sideways. Fallen hard on a section of the panels, which then gave way. And then you fell landing on the legs, which crumpled underneath you. Is that it? And then? How long afterwards was it that you shot yourself? Is that what you really did, Nicos? In the circumstances, it was a pretty weird thing to do, wasn't it? I mean, you must have been in terrible pain. You'd have to be very unstable or very sick to end it like that, Nicos. Or brave to the point of lunacy. And who found you, dead man?*

He made a mental note: it must have been the duty security guard who found him. It wouldn't be too hard to find out which one. And what did a duty guard do when faced with the horror of a blood-soaked, twisted corpse lying on his patch? He would have done what we all do when we stumble upon the dead. Seek the company of the living and those who can help. His voice echoing in the empty halls of the museum, he would have called out for his colleagues. And then, collecting himself together, he would have called the police. What did they then make of this awful scene?

He stayed close to another group of visitors, two German families. And he looked around the gallery, his eyes taking in the infrared lights of the security system and the most probable line of Nezeritis's fall.

He reminded himself to check the security system. To check why an alarm didn't go off. What about the fire exit? That wooden door. How secure was it? Locked from the inside in spite of Fire and Emergency Regulations. Had it been locked that Sunday morning? Couldn't Nezeritis have obtained a key somehow and saved himself that crazy climb? And he saw the CCTV camera above the door. Why was there no record of Nezeritis on the video? Or was there a record that someone was keeping quiet about?

He called to mind the forensic photographs Shaw had produced for him to make the identification of Nezeritis: photographs that showed Nezeritis's bloodied body covered in shards and splinters of glass. Perhaps he had hit the floor and some of the bits had fallen a few seconds later.

Wrong. Because how come his face, even after he had shot himself, was covered in a thousand glass splinters? The photographs showed that the glass had broken after and not before Nezeritis crashed down to the floor. Why did the glass fall afterwards? And what about the closed-circuit TV? Was there really no record of his entry, his fall, his death? And if not, why not?

He stared at the CCTV cameras. Each was on a revolving base. He made a mental calculation of the angles of vision. There was no reason why those cameras couldn't have picked him up. Somewhere there must be a video recording of what happened. Unless there had been something seriously wrong with the CCTV system that morning. Or did Nezeritis know in advance that the bloody things would be out of action?

Once more, he looked up to the glass roof. Nezeritis fell in here from the sky, that was known. As for the facts of his entry . . . Fact one: he didn't walk through the glass doors. Fact two: he didn't bust in through the fire exit. Could someone else have been here waiting for him? A bent guard, say. Who was it waiting for Nezeritis? Was it one of the museum's executives or officers or security people? Had Nezeritis been acting quite alone?

Rosslyn could not imagine that Nezeritis climbed up there alone. Even though he was an experienced Alpinist, a veteran of the Himalayas and familiar with the rocks of the Taygetos. He wouldn't be making the climb alone.

He considered how the evidence might show Nezeritis had entered with a companion. After the twisted body was stretchered out to the mortuary or police corpse-storage refrigerators off Pratt Walk, what happened then? Was his clothing DNA-tested? Of course it was.

He tilted his head to stare at the glass panels of the roof. There were no broken panels now. But there were signs that some of them had been replaced. Fair enough. They would replace them. Safety reasons. Conservation reasons. Did the police examine the smashed glass panels before the repairs were made?

He followed the tide of foreign visitors to the sexy statue of Iris in Pentelic marble at the far end of the gallery. What about the art then? Iris here, for example? Had Nezeritis been intending to vandalize her and then commit suicide? But the suicide doesn't usually do the business with someone else around. Suicide's a solitary act.

Was he being stupid or had he just been bloody unlucky, and then perhaps realized he'd get caught? With two busted legs, he wasn't going to get out of here in a month of Sundays. But what if he had a companion with him up there when he fell? What was he going to do? Try and hoist Nezeritis up and out? Let's go one step further. Nezeritis must have had a back-up man covering his moves.

Tell me, Nicos. You weren't alone in here, were you? Come on. Your soul will never rest in peace until you tell me.

40

He left the British Museum and headed for the gates to Courtyard B, in front of the museum director's offices, where there was a security man on duty. He looked up at the massive Wolff tower cranes. They were very impressive feats of engineering. Then he glanced at the faces of the passers-by. Africans. Japanese. Across the street he saw a couple of Arab women, their faces masked. And behind the Arab women, hands in his pockets, there was the distinctive figure of a tall and angular man. Belted Burberry raincoat. Probably an East European. The weightlifter's neck and sloping shoulders. With his back to Rosslyn, the man was apparently staring into the shop window of the Oriental and African bookseller, Arthur Probsthain, at 41 Great Russell Street. There was something strange about the way he stood slightly back from the window; the stance of a man whose eyes are focused not on what he sees in the display window but on what is reflected in the glass. The Welsh voice behind him said sharply, 'Can I help you, sir?'

Rosslyn turned and smiled at the guard, who was standing like a sentry in the doorway to his hut. Wearing a blue anorak over his uniform, with silver hair and in his late fifties, he looked at Rosslyn with a certain caution.

'I'm a journalist,' said Rosslyn.

'How can I help you then?'

'I'm covering the story of the man who died in the museum.'

'The suicide in the Duveen Gallery?'

'That's the one.'

'Sunday morning, yes,' the Welshman said. 'What do you want to know then?'

Rosslyn produced his wallet. 'I'd like to talk to the person who found him.' He held out his hand. In the palm there was a twenty-pound note.

The guard shook Rosslyn's hand and the note was transferred. 'Man called Eddie. That's who found him. My younger brother, Eddie.'

'Could you fix it?'

'Sure. He's in the canteen. Do you want me to call him now?'

'I'd really appreciate it if you would.'

Rosslyn waited while the guard made the call. Turning slowly, he looked back again across Great Russell Street. He was staring straight into the face of the angular man who was pushing dark glasses up to the bridge of his nose with one hand. His other hand was tucked awkwardly in his coat pocket. And once Rosslyn engaged his stare, the man walked slowly away with an air of affected boredom.

Within five minutes the other guard, Eddie, approached the hut. The brothers talked quietly and Rosslyn produced a second crumpled twenty-pound note.

'What is it you want to know exactly?' said Eddie.

'I'd like to take a look at the exterior of the building,' said Rosslyn. 'The general vicinity of the exterior of the Duveen Gallery and the roof above it. Where it happened. The death. Sunday morning. Where the man fell in.'

'Follow me.' Eddie showed him through the barrier. 'Best go this way,' he was saying. 'Mr –'

'McLaren,' said Rosslyn. 'Chris McLaren.'

He followed Eddie along the western side of the museum, past a loading bay, until they reached an iron fire escape.

'Up here,' said Eddie, 'and you'll have a fairly good view.'

'You found the body?'

'Yes. Bloody awful.'

Together they climbed the iron steps. At the top, next to the fire-exit door, Rosslyn said, 'When you found the man, what did you make of the layer of busted glass that covered him?'

'The broken glass?' said Eddie. 'There was a lot of it. Smashed to bits. Splinters of it. You should have seen the blood. The gun he did it with. Terrible. He was covered in it. And there was those broken panels above.'

'What about them?' said Rosslyn. 'What did you make of them?'

'They looked, like, odd . . . You know, they looked to me like they'd been kicked in somehow. That's what I thought. I mean, if he'd fallen through them they wouldn't have been smashed so badly. And I thought later on, well, suppose he'd just stumbled and slipped. Well, that glass is tough. I don't think his fall would've smashed the glass, like, of its own accord.'

'Let's talk about him in a minute,' said Rosslyn. 'What time was it when you found him?'

'Sunday morning. Shortly before eight o'clock or thereabouts. The fall didn't trigger the alarms.'

'You mean you think he kicked in the glass and then he fell and *still* the alarms didn't go off?'

'That's what happened. I'd say so. Mind, it didn't strike me that he'd fallen, did it?'

'You tell me.'

Eddie shook his head.

'Which is what he had done, isn't it?' asked Rosslyn.

'You can say that again. Yes. Then he shot himself. The wonder was that he had the strength left in him to fire the gun at all. You'd think he'd have knocked himself unconscious, wouldn't you?' The Welshman paused. 'Finding him there and that. Makes me sick to think about it. You understand? Not something I want to see again, Mr –'

'McLaren,' said Rosslyn. 'I can imagine it must have been a shock.'

'You're telling me. Bloody hell.'

'So where do you reckon he got in then? Before he got up on the roof? How did he, well, get there?'

'Take a look,' said Eddie. 'That's something of a climb at the best of times. And that morning it was pissing down. I wouldn't fancy my chances at that game. No way.'

'You really think he was mad, some sort of sicko person?'

156

'No. I think he knew what he was about all right. Oh, yes. But *what* was he doing?'

'You tell me then.'

'I don't know,' said Eddie. 'I just don't know. I heard say he was Greek. But that was another rumour. Then they said he was an Arab. Who knows?'

'You think he was Greek?'

'Greeks. Arabs. You see them all in here. They all look the same to me. I wouldn't know.'

'What do you reckon his exact point of entry was, then?' asked Rosslyn.

'Search me. This place is a fortress. Anyway, the TV cameras would've picked him up. You know, recorded him on the video. As I told you, they didn't. Eddie's Law. They weren't working. Or, if they were, then no one's saying what the video showed. The police can't work it out and neither can our people.'

'They did question you, though, didn't they?'

'Yes. The coppers. Special Branch. Security Service people.'

'Do you remember any of the names of the officers who question-ed you?'

Eddie shook his head again. 'No.'

'How do you know the Security Services were interested?'

'Because that's what they said they were. Officers of the Security Service.'

'What about the fire exit in the Duveen Gallery, that wooden door? How secure is the fire exit?

'As a matter of fact,' said the Welshman, 'I asked myself about it. It shouldn't be locked from the inside. But it was. Still is.'

'Was it definitely locked that Sunday morning?'

'Yes, it was. As far as I know, yes. Definitely.'

'Could the man have obtained a key?'

'No.' He paused. 'Well, I suppose we don't know if he did, do we? In any case, there's a CCTV camera outside above the door. Like above the glass box where there's the key for emergencies and suchlike. There's no record of him there on the video. That was working. Well, I think it was. I couldn't be totally sure. But then, you know, what with the shock and all. You get confused in that kind of situation. Someone dead. The blood.'

'And what about the closed-circuit TV?'

Eddie's face twisted in confusion. 'As I say. Believe me, there's no record of his entry, his fall, nothing. No.'

'Why not?'

'Because the cameras don't cover the interior of the roof or the floor.'

'That's a shame.'

'You're telling me. And still they've done bloody nothing about it.'

Rosslyn remembered the CCTV cameras. The revolving bases. He recalled the mental calculation of the angles of vision he had made. There was no reason those cameras couldn't have picked up what was happening. There must be a video recording of what happened.

'There was absolutely nothing wrong with the CCTV system that morning?'

'Nothing. That's what I'm saying.'

'You're quite sure?'

'They were tested and retested. Special Branch told us there was nothing wrong with them. Made a point of that, they did. But that was later.'

The key seemed to lie somewhere in the confusion. Some said they were working. Then along came others who said they weren't.

'That's what the museum's internal security people and the police tell me,' Rosslyn lied. 'It's a state-of-the-art system. They're rather proud of it, aren't they?'

'Bleeding pride before the fall, I'd say. Wouldn't you?'

'Yes. I can agree with that.'

Rosslyn paused. So Nezeritis fell from the sky. Again. Fact one: he didn't walk through the glass doors. Fact two: he didn't bust in through the fire exit. Could someone else have been here waiting? A bent guard, say?

Eddie was saying, 'I can tell what's on your mind.'

'What's on my mind then?'

'Us. The guards. Let me tell you. We're whiter than white. No one's covering anything up. We weren't responsible. You think we want to lose our pensions? Oh no.'

'What about the curators or museum officers or whatever, are they responsible then?'

'No. No. The same. Pure as driven snow.'

'Tell me then,' said Rosslyn, 'given your experience, are you certain, quite certain, the intruder was acting alone?'

'There's no evidence to say he wasn't, is there? The Special Branch went over all of that. They even, what's it . . . DNA-tested the clothing. Man told us. That's what they did, see. To see if there was a sign anyone else had touched him. And the buggers DNA-tested my gear too. Yes. That's what they did. Negative, they said. No traces of anyone else, I heard. Nothing.'

'Who did you hear that from?'

'I don't know. It was another one of those rumours that get put about.'

'And the broken panels?'

'The panels, they've all been replaced. Safety reasons.'

'And do you remember if the police looked at them before the repairs?'

'Yes, they did. They took away samples in plastic bags.'

'They didn't find anything, I suppose, anything that you heard about?'

'Nothing that I know of. No. The whole thing's as good as closed. Though I imagine there'll be the inquest and all of that.'

'Yes. And you'll probably have to give evidence, won't you?'

'I've done that before.'

'Have they given you the date and time so you can attend?' Rosslyn asked.

'No, they haven't. Not yet. Dare say they've postponed it or something. Still, it's not that long ago since he died.'

'Tell me,' said Rosslyn, 'do you reckon the intruder had been intending to vandalize the Marbles or something?'

'Search me,' said the Welshman. 'There are some odd buggers about. The ones who want them sent back to Greece. There was that demo. A few of us looked on. It wasn't nice. The police were watching. They even had some armed officers up on the roofs. They must have been expecting trouble.'

Rosslyn surveyed the buildings, the roofs, the waste-disposal area and the perimeter walls. 'Perhaps. The walls to the rear face down on Montague Place, don't they? It's one hell of a climb. There's no way an ordinary person is going to get into this place. Can we look at the roof itself?' he asked.

'Sure. There's another fire escape over there.'

From the top of the fire escape, Rosslyn could see enough of the roof of the Duveen Gallery. As a climber Nezeritis had to have known precisely what he was doing to get up there.

'Can you find me a ladder?' Rosslyn asked.

'Maintenance is closed. They've gone off home.'

'OK then. Let's take a look at the exterior walls.'

'From the outside, you mean in Montague Place?'

'No. Show me them from the inside. Down there.'

They stood among the pile of tarpaulins and dented garbage drums of rusted steel. Rosslyn calculated that the wall between him and Montague Place was about ten, maybe twelve metres high. Eddie, who was looking inside the nearest of the garbage drums, had been exaggerating the height. None the less, in the rain it must have presented a formidable obstacle even to an experienced climber. There must have been a rope. If Nezeritis had been there alone it would still be there. Rosslyn looked up to where the nearest building's exterior wall towered above him. There was, of course, the clear blue sky, with wisps of cloud, and, just visible in the distance, the summit of the red Wolff tower cranes.

Then he saw the rope. Part hidden by a drain pipe and electricity conduit, it dangled from the parapet of the building almost to the ground. He decided not to draw the Welshman's attention to it. Like trying to fathom out the meaning of the Marbles inside, as the scholar says, it's a matter of looking, looking and looking again. Given the presence of the rope, he was persuaded, temporarily at least, that Nezeritis had been acting on his own.

Yet, surely if he had climbed in alone, the pitons, like the rope,

160

would also have been left behind? But there was no sign of pitons. Someone had removed them from the brickwork.

He decided he would take one more look later on. At about the same time Nezeritis entered the museum. Some time between six and seven in the morning. In the removal of the pitons lay the proof that Nezeritis had been there with someone else.

He thanked the Welshman for his help and gave him another twenty pounds for his trouble.

Outside the museum, in Great Russell Street, Eddie was closing the gates when Rosslyn saw Michael Lo waiting discreetly to one side of an ice-cream van.

41

He sauntered towards Tottenham Court Road, pausing ostensibly to stare at shop displays, using the reflections in the windows to see who else could be lingering with peripheral vision focused on him.

Lo left the side of the ice-cream van and kept his distance.

The crowds on the pavement became Rosslyn's allies. Few of the pedestrians were standing still, unless you counted the Japanese couple anxious to find a cab. There were two women peering into a computer store. And there was the elderly man with an eyepatch flogging the *Big Issue* at the entrance to the subway at St Giles's Circus. And now there was the curly-headed man behind him. What was he, twenty metres or so away, across the street? Wearing an expensive black leather jacket, white silk scarf, designer jeans and dark blue trainers. He was carrying a small metallic camera. Possibly he's Italian, thought Rosslyn. Even maybe Greek.

At the entrance to the subway Rosslyn bought the *Evening Standard* and then walked down about five steps and suddenly dropped his newspaper. Gathering the pages together, he turned briefly and looked up. Curly stood there at the top of the steps. Behind him, silhouetted against the dull evening light, he glimpsed the disappearing figure of the belted Burberry heavyweight he had seen in Great Russell Street. Curly beat a quick retreat and the big man did likewise.

From St Giles's Circus Rosslyn took a black cab to the corner of Gerrard Street. From there he walked the rest of the way to Sueng's Club Two. He was as sure as he could be that his followers had suspended observation of him. At any rate, for the time being. It would be characteristic of Shaw, as the professional, to have put tails on him and yet, if these were two of her lackeys, why hadn't they gone the whole way and snatched him from the streets?

It turned out that Michael Lo had the answer.

42

In the upstairs room above Sueng's Club Two, Michael Lo said in triumph, 'I photographed the pair of them. We'll have the pictures within the hour. I called Ethel and she picked up on the surveillance in Mayfair. She's got her pincers into them. The Scorpion, it's in her blood. She won't let them out of her sight.' His ringing mobile phone cut him short. 'Friends of Vayakakos.' Lo wrote them down and handed the note to Rosslyn.

Rosslyn flinched: Shaw/Riley/Georgiadis.

'Are you going to tell me who they are?' asked Lo.

'Secret Intelligence Service,' said Rosslyn. 'CIA and the Greek Embassy. Probably their secret intelligence, KYP, station head in London.'

'Maybe that explains why Vayakakos has been given protection.'

'Is Lambrakis sure of that?' said Rosslyn.

'So he says. There's a police officer stationed outside Vayakakos's room.'

'All the time?'

'Twenty-four hours,' said Lo.

'No exceptions?' asked Rosslyn.

'Lambrakis's man says the only time Vayakakos is alone is when he uses the bathroom or when he leaves the hospital each day at six in the evening.'

'What happens then?'

'It seems he's driven to Moscow Road and the Greek Orthodox Cathedral of St Sophia.'

'And the protection officer drives him there, so he's not alone then?'

'Yes and no. Vayakakos stays there about an hour with the priest.

Then he's driven back. The protection officer stays outside in the car. Vayakakos won't let him inside the cathedral. They talk and pray together or whatever behind locked doors.'

'You say your man's sure he's alone with the priest, and the cathedral is locked?'

'That's what he told me.'

'Somehow I've got to see him alone. And see him fast.'

'Seems like you're going to have a problem with that.'

'Tough,' Rosslyn was saying. He was unfastening the canvas bag. He took out his journal with the photograph of Cleo and handed the picture of her to Lo. 'When you collect the pictures of those two who were on my tail, have a copy of this made. Just the face. And while you're at it buy me a really decent bunch of flowers. Bring the photographs and flowers back here. I need to be at that Greek Orthodox Cathedral by five-thirty and I'd like you to shadow me. In case the protection officer gives me any grief.'

Michael Lo looked admiringly at the photograph of Cleo. 'Is she the trouble?'

'You could say so.'

'Lucky you,' said Lo carelessly.

'She's dead,' said Rosslyn sharply. 'And Vayakakos may be able to tell me who killed her.'

'If he doesn't?'

'I think there are too many people out there who'll have a go at me. Or, looking at the brighter side, there'll be every kind of copper searching for me desperate to slam a murder charge on me.'

'For what?' said Lo.

'For the murder of the woman in that photograph. Oh, and charges of conspiracy, avoiding arrest, assault. You name it.'

'Is it really that bad?'

'Yes. That bad and worse.'

For the first time the look of unease in Michael Lo's eyes was undisguised.

Part Two

I dared to suggest that these Marbles should return to Greece. Since then, a small tempest has raged.

MELINA MERCOURI

Come to the grave, brothers; let us see the ashes and dust from which we are formed. Where now do we go? What have we become? Who is poor, who rich? Or who in power, who free? And are we not all dust? The face's beauty has rotted, and death has withered every flower of youth.

THE ORTHODOX SERVICE FOR THE
BURIAL OF THE DEAD

43

At five-thirty p.m., in the Byzantium, the Moscow Road café frequented by Greek exiles in London, Rosslyn settled the bill. Carrying the photographs in separate brown envelopes and the flowers, he crossed the road, careful to avert his eyes from Lo, who was ostensibly making repairs to his motorbike.

To the east side of the presbytery, he found the back entrance to the Greek Orthodox Cathedral of St Sophia. The exterior of the imposing domed building is of striped red and yellow brick. Since 1932 it has been the Greek Orthodox Cathedral of Western Europe. The doors were locked. Looking round, he saw a curtain lifted aside in the nearest of the presbytery's ground-floor windows. Before he could catch the man's attention the door opened.

'Yes?' a voice inquired.

'I wonder if I could see the Papas?'

'He has an appointment,' the man in the doorway said in a thick Greek accent.

Wearing a grey suit, white shirt and slim black tie, he was stockily built. Rosslyn assumed he was the caretaker.

'He is expecting a visitor,' the man said, the dark eyes squinting beneath heavy eyebrows.

'Yes, I know he is,' said Rosslyn. 'An acquaintance of mine, George Vayakakos.'

A look of recognition flashed across the man's dark face.

Rosslyn held out the flowers and the brown envelope containing the photograph of Cleo. 'I'd like the Papas to give him these personally. I've just returned from Greece. I have to leave again tomorrow for Athens. It's a rather urgent family matter . . . private, you understand.'

'Why don't you come inside then?' the man said. 'I'll talk to the Papas. What name shall I say?'

'McLaren. Chris McLaren. From Kardamyli.'

'Ah,' the man smiled. 'The Peloponnese.'

'Yes. It's a lovely part of the world. Are you from there?'

'No. Thessaloniki.'

'A beautiful part too,' said Rosslyn. 'You know the Taygetos?'

'Yes,' the man said, smiling even more. 'Mr Vayakakos will be here soon.'

Rosslyn handed over the flowers and the photograph of Cleo. 'Perhaps you'd tell him I'd value the chance to give him a personal message?'

'Very well. I will ask the Papas. I will have to lock the door if you don't mind. The insurance. And please, if you don't mind, don't light a candle. The insurance.'

'Thanks, I won't,' said Rosslyn.

'You shouldn't have to wait more than ten minutes. Mr Vayakakos is always punctual.'

'I don't mind waiting,' said Rosslyn.

'Very well,' said the man, and he locked the door as he left Rosslyn alone to wait and pray that Vayakakos would see him.

Rosslyn walked slowly into the silent and dim interior of St Sophia's. The scent of lilies and incense hung heavily in the air. He peered closely at the mosaics and icons. Wall-paintings by Greek, German and British hands. The thin beam of sunlight caught the edges of the red glass candleholders in the three-dimensional metallic cross, an imitation of the cross in St Sophia, Istanbul. He would have liked to light a candle for Cleo, as they had lit candles in the small and deserted churches of the Mani. The caretaker's prohibition caused him a stab of grief. Absent-mindedly, he turned over the small, four-page folded pamphlet issued by the Archdiocese of Thyateira and Great Britain in Greek and English. It contained the record of last Sunday's sermon by Father Elias and the text from St Luke.

Rosslyn sat in a high wooden seat and read: *While he was still speaking, a man from the ruler's house came and said, 'Your daughter is dead; do not trouble the Teacher any more.' But Jesus on hearing this answered him, 'Do not fear; only believe, and she shall be well.'*

The creak of the church door interrupted his reading and Rosslyn saw the stooped figure walking slowly towards him. He was alone. The effort of walking obviously pained him and it seemed he was using his rubber-tipped walking stick to feel his way as if he were a blind man. Or perhaps the frail figure was fearful he might slip on the floor of polished marble. The man said quietly, 'George Vayakakos.' You would not at once have taken him for a Greek. The thin frame supported the expensive tailored suit: Savile Row cut in grey Huddersfield worsted with slanting jacket pockets, the trousers narrow. The brushed white hair seemed to have been oiled sideways in a single streak across the skull.

Rosslyn got his feet. 'My name's –'

Before Rosslyn could get his name out, Vayakakos said, 'I've been expecting you.' The voice had the note of uncertainty of a man unsure of what degree of formality was appropriate. 'Though, I confess, I did not think that we would meet in circumstances such as these.' Choosing his words with great care, he spoke slowly, as if between clenched teeth, without the slightest trace of a Greek accent.

Rosslyn stood back a little, his hand outstretched in an offer of assistance suggesting the older man might care to take a seat in the nearest pew.

Vayakakos turned and said, 'I think we should talk in the robing room, where women are strictly forbidden entry. Perhaps you understand that I have, as usual, been accompanied here by an armed woman police officer in plain clothes. She sometimes enters the cathedral with the caretaker during my private prayers with the Papas. The caretaker will prevent her from entering the robing room. It will be for the best that we talk there. As a precautionary measure.' He led the way into the semi-darkness of the robing room and, once the door was closed, said, 'We can talk for no more than thirty minutes.'

Rosslyn held back a chair from the table for him.

'Thank you,' said Vayakakos. Sitting down heavily, he folded his thin hands on the crook of the walking stick. 'I'm afraid I am no longer the man I was. As you can see perhaps, the doctors have told me there is nothing they can do to help me.'

'I'm very sorry.'

'No, don't be sorry. My misfortune is your good fortune. Otherwise, if time were not running out for me, I would not have been willing to talk to you. Now, I'm bound to say, there is nothing left for me to lose. And quite why your security services seek to waste their time and money on a dying man escapes me.' He glanced at the clock ticking audibly on the wall. 'Thank you so much for the flowers and particularly the beautiful photograph of Cleo.' The voice caught in his dry throat and Rosslyn filled a glass from the washbasin for him. Swallowing pained him. 'Tell me briefly, Mr Rosslyn,' Vayakakos said, 'what it is you want of me?'

He listened to Rosslyn's summary of events. Cleo's fate. The interview in Marylebone. The circumstances of Nezeritis's death and the conclusions he had reached after his reconnaissance at the British Museum. The expression of concentration remained the same throughout and was impossible to interpret. It occurred to Rosslyn that the frail Greek had already heard the news about Cleo.

Vayakakos cleared his throat and said, 'None the less, the evidence you can give the police in Greece might settle the matter once and for all.'

'What evidence, other than what I found when I reached the house with the priest? The police will have questioned him in depth and will have seen everything I saw and maybe more. What conceivable motive could I have for wanting Cleo dead?'

'Who can tell what will be in their little minds?' Vayakakos said. He was breathing with difficulty. 'More importantly, perhaps, you have been wondering why I said I was expecting a visit from you?'

'Yes, I have. Who told you?'

'Olympia. She telephoned me and told me the police want to interview you about what happened to her mother. She told me that she had spoken by telephone to her mother at some length.'

'Where is Olympia?'

'She didn't say. She was being uncharacteristically cautious. She didn't enter into much detail. It seemed to me that someone might have been listening to her call with me.' He shifted slowly on the chair. 'But I have no doubt,' he continued, 'from something of what Olympia said, that her mother is definitely still alive. That Cleo did not in fact die in that well at the estate. You could understand the situation. She knows too much. But to kill her before she revealed what she knows would have been a strategic error not even a Greek would make.'

Rosslyn shook his head in disbelief.

'Indeed, while I believe your account in its entirety,' Vayakakos continued, 'you never once told me that you actually saw Cleo's body. You say you saw the dress. You say you saw blood. But no body. So whose blood? The dogs?'

'Yes.'

'You and the local priest, the two of you saw the dress. Neither of you saw Cleo lying in the water dead. Only the dress. Isn't that the truth of it?'

'Yes. That's correct. But –'

'There is no but, Mr Rosslyn. Without conclusive evidence of death, it is unwise – let us say too early – to jump to serious conclusions.'

'With respect, Mr Vayakakos, there's a corpse in the Kalamata morgue and the police have said it's Cleo's.'

The tired eyes looked at Rosslyn kindly. They seemed to be taking stock of him. 'I accept your respect, Mr Rosslyn. In return, let me give you mine. Tell me, just how long exactly were you in Greece?'

'Three weeks.'

'Not quite enough time, was it, to have familiarized yourself with the workings of the Greek police? The spider's web of the Ministry of the Interior – or whatever unpleasant organization may now have replaced it – and the senior ranks of the Greek Intelligence Service into the bargain. Understand that little really changes in Greece when it comes to enforcement of the law. And if some false identification needs making and some lie told, silence bought, believe me, my friend, the power of the drachma makes all things possible.'

'Our people at the Athens embassy have been in close contact with them.'

'I don't doubt that the embassy has acted honourably. But as I

173

know to my own personal cost, some of their people act out of, shall we say, British interest, as is their duty. Others may act out of self-interest. And with your experience of the SIS, which is more up to date than mine, I imagine that you don't need me to sit here telling you about that.'

'Then what happened to Cleo?'

'I don't know.'

'And how do you explain what happened to Nezeritis?'

From outside in the street there was the sound of a police siren. For a minute or so they remained silent, until the sound faded.

'Nezeritis?' asked Rosslyn.

'Nezeritis, yes,' said Vayakakos. 'The British Museum. Consider perhaps the hypothesis that some other person accompanied him. I knew Nezeritis only too well and you, I think, did not. He was not a man made to blow his own brains out. And as a former soldier who only too often has been trapped in life-endangering situations of many differing kinds, I can tell you that, with two fractured legs and the agony such injury causes, I doubt he had it in him to kill himself so soon. So I am bound to agree with you in general. He must have been there with someone else. Except, as far as you know, there was no witness to the break-in.'

'As far as we know,' said Rosslyn. 'And why were they there, what were they doing?'

'Your version of what happened subsequently, the interviews, well, I think you should examine motive more closely.'

'That's why I have to return to Greece.'

'I understand that,' said Vayakakos. 'But you do realize it will be very dangerous?'

'Yes. But what's the alternative? No one else will clear my name. Do I remain here as some sort of exile in my own country waiting for the next blow to fall? And what of Cleo?'

'I sympathize with your predicament. Some might even say it is not dissimilar to my own. In your case you should look again with care at the motive for what's happened.'

'And all roads lead back to Cleo,' said Rosslyn. 'First, the written threats from P17N passed on to SIS.'

'Yes, I know about those threats,' said Vayakakos. 'Cleo told me about them.'

'What about her murder?' said Rosslyn, the bitterness rising in his throat.

'Assuming that she has been murdered.'

'You don't believe it?'

'I only believe what I know,' said Vayakakos. 'Take Olympia first. She's disappeared. At any rate, we are led to believe she has. Bearing in mind the doubt I've raised, I think you should be more optimistic on both scores. And still, you must consider Cleo. Her past. Her friends. Her intimates.'

'In all three of which you played a part.'

'Yes, indeed I did, as it seems to me you did too.'

'Yet you doubt she was murdered?' said Rosslyn.

Vayakakos shrugged.

'Look, Mr Vayakakos,' Rosslyn said gently. 'All I know about you is this.' He handed over the report prepared by Kostas Lambrakis.

It seemed to take an eternity for the older man to adjust his half-moon glasses and even longer for him to study it. 'That's the bare bones of my misspent life,' he said finally. 'There are, I am afraid, some matters which I cannot discuss even, my friend, with you.'

'I only want to know, to know very badly, which matters have a bearing on what's happened to Cleo.'

Vayakakos was looking closely at the photograph of Cleo. 'Up until the day of what we can call the incident, she telephoned me here in London regularly. She naturally mentioned you. How very much her daughter liked you. And I have to say I gained the impression that after the difficulties she'd experienced with Nicos, you seemed to be something of a breath of fresh air. It struck me that she was more than just a little fond of you.'

'And vice versa.'

'I don't doubt that. Many people have fallen in love with her. The ex-husband, Ioannis Ipsilanti, is a weak man. A creature of compromise. Quite different in that respect from his father, Stamatis.' He looked again at the Lambrakis report. 'Then there is the matter of our friend, Alexios Dragos, and his son, Constantine. How much do you know about them?'

'Nothing,' said Rosslyn. 'What was Cleo to those people?'

'Simply put,' said Vayakakos, 'it was the affair between Alexios Dragos and Cleo that put paid to her marriage to Ioannis Ipsilanti. The result of that, apart from the vastly expensive divorce from the British woman who was his wife and whom Dragos still, I believe, calls The Unmentionable, was that Constantine developed an abiding hatred of Cleo.'

The noise of children's voices from outside caused him to turn his head. His mouth bore the traces of the beginnings of a smile.

'And I see no reason why,' he continued, 'you shouldn't know it, but it is Alexios Dragos, not Ioannis, who is the father of Demetra. To the considerable chagrin of Constantine, it is to Demetra that Alexios has left the major and substantial part of his shipping empire, along with freehold properties here in London, in Manhattan and, I dare say, elsewhere too. It is a profoundly unhappy family . . . not so much at war, but let's say on the verge of war with itself and others too.' He coughed and the effort contorted his features. He struggled to prevent the whistling in his throat. 'More water, if you please.'

The water Rosslyn gave him seemed to provide relief. Choosing his words still with great care, he continued, 'About a year ago, before I left the Mani and was forced to seek the advice of doctors here in London, a man called Theodoros Georgiadis paid me a visit in Kardamyli. Subsequently, as you seem to be aware, he was posted to the Greek Embassy here in London. Georgiadis was, of course, privy to the history of Cleo's career with SIS. He was also deeply involved with the fruitless investigations into P17N that had led nowhere. He questioned me at length about threats to Cleo and her daughters. Under the definite impression that these originated with P17N, he asked me if I would be good enough to report back to him anything untoward, such as –' He managed to restrain his cough. 'Such as people in the area, aside from the inevitable tourists, who might be showing undue interest in Cleo. Though I agreed to be of help, my efforts, for what they were worth, yielded nothing. Frankly,

I didn't believe the threats originated with any terrorist group.' He paused. 'After all, the threat of kidnap is pointless unless it is connected to some specific issue. Rather, the threats, so it seemed to me, constituted a kind of harassment and no more, and I was somewhat disinclined to take them too seriously.'

'Did Cleo take them seriously?'

'Yes, of course she did.'

'And Demetra?'

'I don't know,' said Vayakakos. 'She is a creature of obsession. With her father. With the nobility of Greece. Its past, its present and its future.' He paused. 'You must forgive me, but we are running short of time.'

'Would you prefer to continue some other time?'

'No.'

'I can arrange it.'

'Perhaps you can, Mr Rosslyn. But no. Let me finish. It's you who is running out of time. You see, the death of Nezeritis points up whatever dreadful fate Cleo is facing. Like you, I cannot tell what may, or may not, have happened at the British Museum last Sunday morning. I would say, though, that the British authorities seem to have acted with admirable and unusual speed. That in itself is highly suggestive of the extreme importance they attach to what is happening.' He paused again. 'To be as concise as possible, I do not for one second believe, as you or others like Georgiadis and his American associate may, that the matter is to do with P17N. No. On the contrary, I am perfectly certain that it is all to do with both Alexios and Constantine Dragos. No matter whether the killing of Nezeritis was deliberate or some sort of tragic accident.' He took another sip of water. 'What you seem to be entirely unaware of is the answer to a question you haven't put to me.'

'What is it?' said Rosslyn.

'Think. Why do you imagine I am being protected around the clock by armed police officers?'

'Tell me.'

'Because someone is afraid I will talk of Dragos. Of what I will say in public. And you may wonder why I seek to visit the Papas here.

Oh yes, we say prayers together. We read from the Divine Liturgy. He is preparing the way ahead for me. To relieve the sting of death. More than that. I am dictating to him my version of the events that have also led to your being here with me alone this evening. And what I am dictating to the Papas is by way of being not so much a Last Will as a Testament.' He broke off to cough again. 'The essence, the very heart of it, concerns the obsession, you might even say the mania, of the Dragos family, by foul means or fair, to see the Elgin Marbles once and for all returned to Greece. It is a cause with which I too have been associated in an academic and, shall we say, gentler way. Excuse me, a moment –' He was struggling for breath. 'May we sit in silence for a while?'

Once he had strength enough to continue, Vayakakos said, 'Demetra shares the obsession, like Nezeritis. It is a mission fuelled by a sort of fanaticism that is almost religious in its intensity. And, believe me, Alexios Dragos, perhaps more than any Greek in modern times, has the gigantic and necessary resources to achieve its end. Indeed, his father, Stelio, Constantine's grandfather, made provision for the establishment of the secret organization that pursues the aim.'

'How do you know this?'

'Because my father, Alexander Elias Vayakakos, was a signatory as witness to the Will of Stelio Dragos. He was one of the executors. You ask who told me. He did. My father did.'

'And Cleo, what part has she in any of this?'

'She has no part in it.'

'But surely she knows about it?'

'Of course she does. Remember, as if I need to tell you, Mr Rosslyn, that Nezeritis was her lover.'

'Of course. I realize that.'

'It was not terribly difficult for her to find out about those so-called trips to Paris of his. He very rarely went there, if at all. He was engaged on quite other business. Business undertaken on behalf of the Dragos interests. Dragos has him in his grip. Just where he wants him. I leave it to you to imagine the extent of the perversity. And yet, I suppose, like many men of tremendous wealth, there is something magnificent, however dark it may seem to you and me, about the sheer intensity and energy of his driving passion to see the Elgin Marbles returned to Greece. You can be sure that Cleo felt it too. But there is no sense, none at all, in which she can be held responsible for the actions of either Dragos or Nezeritis or for the latter's death. None at all. But you do not, I think, know why the relationship ended?'

'No, I don't.'

'You should. Nezeritis. Fortune hunter. Lothario. Call him what you will. Nezeritis seduced Demetra. It broke Cleo's heart. It inflamed both Alexios and Constantine Dragos.'

'Then why the association of Nezeritis with them in this mission of theirs?'

'Put it down to the Greek way of learning from the enemy. Better to stay close to him. The ruthlessness and brutality, the cruelty and genius for self-protection, of Constantine and Alexios Dragos, you need to understand, were honed in the years of the Colonels.'

'Why haven't you informed the British authorities of this?' said Rosslyn. 'Or perhaps you have.'

'No. You can be sure I have thought about that with the very greatest care. And, perhaps because I feared for Cleo's future, I decided that discretion was the wisest course to take.'

Rosslyn saw that tears had formed in the exhausted eyes.

'I love Cleo as a father.'

'I can understand.'

'Can you?'

'Yes. I too feel deeply about her.'

'So she told me,' said Vayakakos. 'You see, whatever crisis Alexios and Constantine Dragos may be initiating, she has finally fallen foul of them. Constantine Dragos's hatred for her I have explained to you. Had it not been for the last few weeks, I'd have been somewhat baffled by Alexios's attitude. But then, remember, though Cleo opened very little of her, shall we say, professional mind to me, she spoke to me from the heart. And I could tell, easily and with clarity, that she loves you with a considerable and genuine passion.'

Rosslyn looked at him in silence, feeling, after what seemed to have been for too long an eternal chill, warmth and something approaching ease.

179

'I have to say, Mr Rosslyn,' said Vayakakos, staring at him intensely, 'that it will be her passion for you that has incited the fury of Alexios Dragos against you and all you represent. Oh, I suppose he could tolerate Nezeritis, perhaps because he was Greek. But you are something altogether different. He will, as it were, want you neutralized. And so far, as you must admit, he has achieved that with considerable skill. But you must believe me, I know the workings of his mind. This minute he will no doubt be sitting aboard that yacht of his somewhere in the Mediterranean arranging for some other hand to kill you. And he will be worrying in his nasty mind just how much Cleo has told you of his mission to steal back the Elgin Marbles for beloved Greece.'

'She told me nothing,' Rosslyn said, as if he were paying Cleo a compliment.

'So the more she protests that, the harsher will be his efforts to force an admission from you.' There was a dull disquiet in what he was saying. 'Look, he is a man of passion. Love and hate. And the borders between them are very narrow . . .'

The ticking of the wall clock seemed ever more insistent.

Rosslyn said, 'What is to prevent you and I calling the Security Services right now and passing on all you've told me?'

'Nothing at all,' said Vayakakos with a sudden tone of warning. 'Nothing, other than that we need hard proof, objective proof, evidence and witnesses to whatever expression Dragos may have made of his thoughts. And we have none, do we? And you can be very sure that Dragos has seen to it that he will have left no trace. And anyone who is party to his thoughts will be all too well aware that if they show one blink of disloyalty, give even the smallest hint of a preparedness to betray, why, Dragos will kill them. And that, I am afraid, goes for Cleo. And say the British already know of Dragos's determination, why, they might play the waiting game and catch the robbers in the act. What clearer argument could be given to the international community that the United Kingdom and not Greece is the proper steward of the greatest works of art on earth?'

Rosslyn watched Vayakakos raise himself. He was leaning on his stick.

'There you are. I think I can read your mind. I wish you good fortune in Greece. Above all, I trust you are able to give Cleo the freedom and peace of mind she so richly deserves. If I were a much younger man, I'd volunteer my companionship to you. But that time, alas, has long since past.'

'I'm very grateful to you for all you've told me.'

'Not at all. If I were a wiser man I should have persuaded you to abandon your plan to go to Greece and find her. But then I can tell your mind's made up.' Vayakakos walked carefully to the door of the robing room and unlocked it. 'Oh, one more thing. This –' he was clutching the photograph of Cleo – 'may I keep it? Without, you understand, explaining how it came into my possession.'

'Of course,' said Rosslyn. 'I'm sure Cleo would wish you to have it.'

'I would like to think so,' said Vayakakos. 'Thank you.' He clutched the photograph of Cleo as if it were a cherished talisman. 'I suggest you wait here for ten minutes. The caretaker will show you out once I have left. In spite of everything, I have enjoyed our meeting. Good luck to you.'

'You too,' said Rosslyn. 'And don't believe all the doctors tell you. Fight it.'

Vayakakos smiled wanly. 'I am afraid that I do believe them. But you can be sure that it won't prevent me fighting. Goodbye, Mr Rosslyn.' He hesitated. 'One last thing. You may hear about me from a Marion Shaw.'

'I may?'

'You know her?'

'Yes, I do.'

'She entertains a lasting hatred for Alexios Dragos. Mark my word, she has good reason. Oh yes. I would be wary of her. There are many stories of her relationship to Dragos.'

'What relationship?'

'She has a personal agenda. Be wary, you understand. Be wary of Marion Shaw. There's a streak of the thwarted fanatic in her. The streak of cruelty. Her passion for conspiracy is somehow admirable in its intensity. Her knowledge of Greece and Greek politics and history is remarkable. But there is a coldness, a ruthlessness, about her. Better to have Marion Shaw as your ally and not your enemy. She exploits people's weaknesses without cease. Now time's run out.' He looked exhausted. 'Remember my advice, my friend. Goodbye.'

Rosslyn waited until Vayakakos had left the cathedral before walking to the small anteroom beyond the hanging metallic crucifix. He wondered what the relationship between Shaw and Alexios Dragos might conceivably be. Personal? Business? Operational? He could have been the causal agent. How was it linked to Cleo? The endless web of loyalties and betrayals seemed Byzantine in complexity. The web that had now trapped him too.

Standing to one side of the narrow windows, he looked across the street to where Michael Lo was on look-out duty. The Chinese was sipping from a plastic cup. There was no sign of the woman police officer and it was the sound of voices being raised elsewhere outside the cathedral that explained why. A female voice was demanding to be allowed admission. And the caretaker was firmly denying what the woman was calling her legal right.

Rosslyn walked quietly across the marble floor the better to listen. He heard the caretaker declare, 'This is the house of God,'

'And I am a police officer.'

'You will have to make an appointment like anyone else.'

'I believe there may be another person in there.'

'There is not.'

'If I am right, you understand you will be in serious trouble?'

'You are wrong. This is the house of God and I am right. This is God's house.'

'I don't care whose house it is. We have our rules.'

'So do I. God's rules.'

There was a long silence. Perhaps the police officer had decided the best course of action was to assume proper responsibility for her charge. To take him back to hospital, where he belonged. Perhaps she would return and, who knows, maybe even test the record of last Sunday's sermon for fingerprints. *By which time I will be out of the country. Out of sight. Bound for Greece.* Rosslyn retreated to the shadows behind the pulpit to wait for the coast to clear outside the cathedral.

Splinters of red light in the glass of the polished metal crucifix hung above his head like warnings. *Find Dragos and his cronies.* The investigator's mind unpicked the fabric of Vayakakos's story and it stirred a sense of optimism. *Prove the charge of murder empty. No matter that the Greek police will fight to save dignity and face. With the passion of the convict protesting bogus innocence, they'll press even harder to make the charge stick.* The fear the thought inspired in him seemed to reinforce the sense that, like Vayakakos, there was a death sentence hanging above his head. George Vayakakos's words echoed in his mind: 'The essence, the very heart of it, concerns the obsession, you might even say the mania, of the Dragos family, by foul means or fair, to see the Elgin Marbles once and for all returned to Greece.'

44

During the same afternoon, the United States Department of State in Washington issued the following statement for immediate circulation to all its embassies. It was the first indication that the US government was on renewed alert for terrorist attacks being launched against its worldwide interests.

The text of the statement read:

GREECE COUNTER-TERRORISM REWARDS PROGRAM:
OFFERS RENEWED *Office of the Spokesman, US Department of State*

The Government of the United States of America, as part of its efforts to work in close cooperation with the Government of Greece, is renewing its appeals to the Greek people for information regarding terrorists acts against American persons or property under the Counter-Terrorism Rewards Program. The program offers up to five million dollars for information leading to the arrest and conviction of persons or groups who have committed terrorist acts against American individuals or property.

The Embassy and the Government of the United States asks any person who may have knowledge of past or planned terrorist activities to contact the Embassy.

Persons with information about terrorist activities can contact the Embassy directly:

Telephone 720–2490 or 729–4301

<u>Or write to:</u>

The Embassy of the United States
Attention: HEROES
91 Vas. Sofias Avenue
10160 Athens, Greece

In the United States, people may write to our post office box
address:
HEROES
PO Box 96781
Washington DC 20090–6781 USA

<u>Or call:</u>
1.800–HEROES-1 (1–88–437–6371)

<u>E-mail:</u> *heroes@heroes.net*

45

At the same time in London, at the Foreign and Commonwealth Office, the Minister of State listened carefully to what the visitors from the SIS, the Greek Intelligence Service and the CIA had come to tell him about P17N.

Prompted jointly by Marion Shaw and Jon Riley, ·the CIA's London head of station, the Director General of SIS had sought the urgent meeting with the Foreign Secretary and requested that he receive them alone. Making no bones about the inconvenience, the Minister had agreed. The meeting soon turned sour. Within minutes the Minister's mood of irritation turned to anger and, to the embarrassment of the Director General of SIS, the hostility was directed towards him.

'I cannot for the life of me understand,' said the Foreign Secretary, 'why you haven't produced a report on this before for me. Surely by now you know the lines of ministerial responsibility as well as I do, don't you?'

'Yes, I do, Minister,' said the Director General of SIS.

'Then you could have spoken to the Secretary of the Cabinet, Secretary of State or Home Secretary or Intelligence Coordinator, couldn't you?' Anyone, he seemed to be saying, except himself.

'Well –'

'There's no *well* about it.'

'But –'

'No *but*. The Intelligence and Security Committee isn't going to receive this kindly, is it? You're bringing far too little far too late, aren't you?'

'With respect, Minister,' said the Director General of SIS, 'I don't think that's strictly fair.'

'I'm afraid your respect is of no great interest to me.'

'I'm trying.'

The Minister examined his fingernails. 'Trying what?'

'Trying to explain that up till now our American and Greek friends here considered that we should heed the signs of the activation of a Greek terrorist cell in the UK.'

Before the Minister could reply, Riley weighed in with support for his British colleague. 'State, sir, has renewed the offer of a reward to anyone providing information about the terrorists. We have reason to believe –'

The Minister interrupted him sharply, repeating, 'Thank you. Thank you. Thank you. That's a matter for Washington, my friend. I fail to see why a suicide here in London should lead us to perceive some threat to UK interests.'

'The evidence –'

'There simply isn't enough of it on the table, is there? This isn't, it seems to me, an issue that needs to be raised with the Prime Minister. Or one demanding any action by me.'

'The Prime Minister,' said the Director General of SIS, 'if I may –'

'No. No,' said the Minister. 'First, you listen to *me*. My advice to you people is this. If there's any genuine evidence pointing to the possibility of some serious action that I should know about, well, then I've no doubt, between the three of you, you'll find it. And you will place it first on my desk. Do you understand?'

The Director General of SIS nodded.

'Does that mean you agree?' said the Minister.

'Yes,' said the Director General of SIS.

'Then we have nothing more to discuss at this point in time,' he said with a thin smile. 'If you will excuse me I am already late for a meeting with the Chancellor.'

From the Foreign and Commonwealth Office building, the three intelligence officers went their separate, silent ways into the London dust and heat. Variously to the US Embassy in Grosvenor Square, the Greek Embassy in Holland Park and SIS headquarters at Vauxhall Cross.

Shaw took a call on her mobile phone. The head of SO – Crime Operations Group – wanted to see her urgently. Jaw set, clutching her shoulder bag, her knuckles white, she made off in the direction of New Scotland Yard.

46

The Chief Superintendent was waiting for Shaw in his office with the woman police officer, the protection officer who would normally have been on duty at the Wellington Hospital in St John's Wood. On the orders of the Chief Superintendent, she had been temporarily relieved by another officer and had spent the last few hours trying to establish the identity of the Chinese she had seen waiting outside St Sophia's in Moscow Road.

Had it not been for the caretaker's insistence that she stay out of the cathedral she might never have been the slightest bit suspicious of the Chinese. But the man's presence there and the caretaker's attitude had troubled her.

She had reported her unease to the Chief Superintendent. And, as he put it to her, it was better to be safe than sorry. He had told her to check with SO4, the National Identification Bureau. The NIB, funded by the Home Office, contains the records of some five and a half million people in the United Kingdom, one adult for every ten Britons convicted of imprisonable offences. The records office has a 700–strong staff, fifty of them police officers, the rest civilians. The Method Index contains computerized files on 50,000 offenders guilty or suspected of serious crime or connected with it.

Disclosure of their contents can be made only on grounds of national security, or what the police consider to be in the public interest; what they call probity – to do with the administration of justice – and with a view to protecting members of the public considered to be vulnerable.

The entry on Lo – or, to give him his full name and occupation, Michael Nelson Lo, Club Proprietor of Gerrard Street, London w1 – straddled the two categories: suspected of serious crime and protection and vulnerability. The NIB 1988–9 records revealed briefly and somewhat vaguely that Lo had been of invaluable assistance to HM Customs and Excise Investigation Division. The outcome had been the successful prosecution of the Black Shell drugs cartel that had operated out of Macao and Portugal. The place of arrest was given as Felixstowe. The NIB file contained the photograph of Lo, and the woman police officer identified him as the Chinese she had seen in Moscow Road.

There was always the possibility that his presence there was no more than coincidence. But the request for information about Lo's connection with Customs seemed to rule it out. The officer responsible for handling Lo had been Alan Rosslyn.

The woman police officer had reported the connection to the Chief Superintendent and he, in turn, called in the protection officer who had been assigned to Rosslyn at the personal request of Marion Shaw. 'Lo has to be shielding Rosslyn,' the Chief Superintendent conjectured.

'Unless he's left the country already,' said the woman police officer.

The Chief Superintendent looked doubtful. 'What makes you think so?'

'That's what I'd do if I were he. He's gamekeeper turned poacher.'

The Chief Superintendent muttered something about hunches and women's intuition and his not fancying their chances of finding him.

'But we can bust Lo,' said the woman police officer.

'What was he doing in Moscow Road?' said the Chief Superintendent.

'Waiting. He wasn't doing anything specific.'

'Yes. But waiting for what?'

'More to the point,' said the woman police officer, 'waiting for whom? There has to have been someone inside the cathedral with Vayakakos.'

'You think Vayakakos will tell you?'

'Vayakakos? No. He doesn't talk to me. And I don't think Shaw got very far with him either.'

'OK. Let's put it to Shaw,' said the Chief Superintendent. 'Though don't rely on her telling us much that's helpful. I know her kind.'

Five minutes later, Shaw arrived at New Scotland Yard.

47

With dreadful slowness, the Chief Superintendent reviewed the theories. He said that Rosslyn would most probably have quit the country already. So there now seemed little chance the police would succeed in finding him. 'Your people might though,' he said, as if he were betting on Shaw winning this week's National Lottery rollover.

Shaw surprised the woman police officer. Not, however, the Chief Superintendent. She had little to say and seemed friendlier than usual. 'We already have a contingency plan in place,' she said without further elaboration or making any mention of the Tunim brothers.

'Where do you reckon he'll go?' asked the Chief Superintendent.

'It would most likely be Greece,' said Shaw, with a mean smile. 'If it weren't for the fact the Greek police want him on a murder charge.'

'Who was it?' said the Chief Superintendent. 'The victim?'

'His lover,' said Shaw. 'One of our former officers. The rest of it involves the Service. It needn't bother you.'

The look on the Chief Superintendent's face seemed to suggest he'd heard that one before. If Shaw noticed it, she showed no sign.

'I advise you to let us bring in Lo for questioning,' the Chief Superintendent said. 'And to allow my colleague here to speak to the caretaker of the cathedral in Moscow Road.'

To the Chief Superintendent's demonstrable irritation, Shaw said she would prefer to wait.

'We may lose Lo,' the Chief Superintendent said. 'And then it'll be too late. I know the Chinese.'

'I think he'll just carry on with life as usual,' said Shaw. 'Let's wait and see.'

This was too passive an approach for the Chief Superintendent. He wondered what games Shaw's people were playing. Here was a man wanted by his police colleagues in Greece, where his wife liked to holiday in summer. The man was wanted for murder. In addition, he had assaulted two people, his own employers. Shaw had said she wanted him effectively placed under house arrest. Now here she was, for God's sake, having been given a major lead, saying, 'Let's wait.' He reckoned she had got things very wrong. 'Thank you, Ms Shaw,' he said with bland sweetness.

The dark eyes stared at him and she left without another word.

48

With Rosslyn still at large, Marion Shaw prepared herself for a sleepless night. She put through two calls. The first was to Christiane Prevezer's apartment in Piraeus. But Prevezer was either not answering or she was out. So Shaw left the message telling Prevezer, no matter what time of day or night, to call back as a matter of great urgency.

The second call was to the Director General, SIS. Shaw confirmed that all of those who had been party to Rosslyn's cross-examination were aware that what had happened at the British Museum was connected with P17N.

'They inferred nothing else?' said the Director General.

'Nothing,' said Shaw. 'Though Rosslyn may be the one who makes connections.'

'You have to find him. And Prevezer, is her cover secure?'

'Yes, it is.'

'What has she told you?'

'I can't get hold of her at the moment. We have the routine arrangement that she's to call me.'

'Let me know what she says. The PM has asked me some awkward questions. The matter of the demonstration. The casualties. The rather abrupt termination of the police inquiries. It isn't going away, Marion, is it?

'You can put his mind at ease,' said Shaw. 'The only threat is Rosslyn.'

'Then, for God's sake, find him. He's your baby. And so is the goddamn rest of it.' There was a bitter silence. 'You must get the full picture from Vayakakos. If you don't, who knows what will be leaked? If that happens, if the press get hold of it, the whole thing will explode in our faces.'

'I'm seeing him in the morning,' said Shaw.

'Just as well,' said the Director General. 'It isn't looking good, Marion, is it? Not for you at any rate.'

'You did give the plan your approval,' said Shaw.

With that the Director General cut the call off. He then turned to another telephone to get on the direct line to the Prime Minister in Downing Street.

49

Marion Shaw sat in her study staring at the flickering screen of her PC. Finally, after several neat whiskies, she lowered her head to the surface of the desk, forehead on folded arms, listening to the wind rattling the windows, haunted by her secrets. *Have I overstepped the mark?* She longed for some reassurance in her loneliness. Solitude she regarded as her friend. But the loneliness was another thing. It seemed to taunt her. It felt as if the secret life she loved was unravelling in front of her aching eyes. The secret life she loved fuelled as it was by other secrets, deeper obsessions. The container of her weakness, as she thought of it, lay in the tomb that was housed within the mausoleum of her past. How grateful she was to the Service that kept her sane, the community of secrecy that kept her mind from wandering back to the family she had never had. The nightmare. The fear of drowning. The dreadful spectre of Death in Unknown Circumstances. DIUC. Even the acronym, this Achilles' heel, sounded Greek, and there was no one on God's earth she could turn to for the help she needed so desperately to assuage the inner pain and sense of loss. Devoid of compassion, the friendless secret world makes no humane allowance for confession. She said aloud. 'It was my fault.'

It was perhaps the combination of the pain and alcohol that led her involuntarily, somewhat automatically, in her loneliness to search for comfort among the secret and hidden letters.

The photographs lay in Lilley and Skinner shoe boxes beneath the floorboards. The dry cardboard boxes wrapped in green felt that held the contents of the tomb. *My fault.*

She drew back the grey worn carpet and raised the oak floorboard.

Then she reached among the electric cables in the dust until her hand gripped the felt.

Here they were. The photographs of her mother, whose likeness she had inherited. The resemblance was uncanny. The similar dark hair. Eyes. Lips. Teeth. Here she was on Paros. Hydra. On Santorini. In Crete. The guitar-playing flower child of the 1960s. Dippy-hippie. Beads and bangles. Beautiful and serene. *I am doing this for you*, she said with prayerful fervour.

Here were the photographs of her mother swimming naked in the Aegean. Her mother's hair was long and wet. She rummaged among the brownish tissue paper for the bracelet from Cartier. *He gave it to you.* It was fashioned in heavy gold, like one part of a handcuff. *He tried to trap you, didn't he? He found out the names you'd used and he'd had some Bond Street jeweller engrave them in this gold.* The names were Somersley, Seddon, Salisbury, Setty. She stared at the silver napkin ring with the date of her mother's christening. St Edmund's Church, Southwold. And your real name: Susan Mona Maureen Shaw. *Born on the cusp of Capricorn and Aquarius. And here's me. My birth certificate:* Marion Tamsin Somersley Shaw. *I am born on the cusp of Capricorn and Aquarius. Neither one thing nor the other. Shoved out to the foster parents, Bertram and Rita, in Harrogate. Here's me at Harrogate Ladies' College. 'Do say the haitch, Marion, dear. Remember. Now after me: Hertford, Hereford and Harrogate.' I have your eyes, don't I, mother? But nothing of your freedom.*

She unfolded the letter of final proof. She read:

Naumann Bartenstein   Attorneys at Law
Jaurèsgasse #386, Vienna, Austria

My darling child,

In the event of my death I want you to have possession of these boxes. I have decided, in the interests of complete confidentiality, to deposit private papers with my solicitors here in Vienna,

Naumann Bartenstein, on the helpful advice
of Wolfgang Bruch. They go some way to
explain who you are and who I am and who your
father is. It is for the best that you have no
contact with him.

I write this at a time of my life when I am
hated by your father, Alexios Dragos, even
to the extent that he denies your
existence.

I understand something of your present
professional status in the British Foreign
Service. It will not be difficult for you to
ascertain that Alexios Dragos is a proven
criminal who has been responsible for much
suffering. And I feel sure you will not want
the contents of this letter made known.

I am sorry that this letter will cause you
pain and sadness. But I think it best you
know the truth. You are a child of secrecy.
But that in no measure clouds my loving
thoughts of you.
In Peace and Love,

Susan Shaw

Back at her desk, she unlocked the slim top drawer and drew out the
box containing the Sig Sauer P226 handgun she kept hidden for
emergencies. She unwrapped the chamois-leather cloth and the one-
piece stainless-steel slide glinted. Slowly she fitted the double-
column magazine loaded with twelve rounds and then sat staring at
it. *If thine eye offend thee, pluck it out.* The only wild card, the rogue
virus, that might now prevent the realization of her greatest need
was Rosslyn. *Pluck it out. Get a grip, woman,* she told herself. *Sit it out
till morning.*

There was the night to be faced and she shivered, finding nothing
that would comfort her or relieve the gnawing of her obsession.
Prevezer has to be got out and home to safety.

Finally, leaving it loaded, she folded the weapon into the chamois-
leather cloth and set it carefully in its box, before replacing the box in

the drawer and locking it. Kicking off her shoes, she padded through the flat, swaying slightly, to her bedroom.

At five-thirty next morning she was woken by the telephone at her bedside. The ward sister from the Wellington Hospital in St John's Wood was on the line. 'I'm very sorry to have to tell you that George Vayakakos died an hour ago.'

The rising sun brought with it the dawn chorus across north London. Marion Shaw, still fully dressed, eyes swollen from weeping, felt that her world had begun to fall apart.

50

Rosslyn woke after a sleepless night.

Lo had attached a Post-It note to a mobile phone with two numbers for Rosslyn to ring in case of emergency. One was his; the other was Ethel Chang's. He had added a postscript: *Best stay out on the streets until tonight. I'll be here from six.*

He was at the British Museum entrance in Montague Place when the St Pancras Parish Church clock chimed seven. The streets and pavements were deserted. By the entrance gates to the London University Senate House and Library in Malet Street, the Irish vagrant peered out from beneath his blankets.

Just beyond the red telephone kiosk, next to 1 Montague Place where the sign on the entrance door said British Museum Photographic Service, he saw the man heaving himself on to the top of the iron railings. The vagrant cursed. For the second time within the week here was someone up to no good. Once again, he saw that the intruder seemed to be staring, like the others had, across the street towards him.

Leaning over the iron railings, the intruder peered for a long time at whatever lay beyond. Then he turned and began hurriedly making his descent to the pavement. With a firm stride, the man crossed the street and approached.

The vagrant pulled the blankets over his head. Once he reckoned the coast was clear, he peeped out, his eyes just above the edges of the blankets. This time he was looking into weary battered eyes. The man was saying, 'Mind me asking if you doss down here regularly?'

'You could say so. What's it to you then?'

'Were you here last Sunday?'

'I wasn't anywhere else,' the vagrant said, the suspicion rising in his voice. 'Who are you?'

Rosslyn produced his wallet. 'I have nothing to do with the police, the council or any political or religious organization. There's a greasy spoon round the corner. Do you fancy eggs, sausages, bacon and sweet tea? The works?'

'What do you want then?'

'To give you breakfast and have a chat.'

Gulping tea and smoking a cigarette, the Irishman fell on the heap of breakfast food with the appetite of a wild animal. 'You're a gent,' he said, chewing with his mouth open.

'Others might not think so,' said Rosslyn.

Unable to endure the vagrant's stench, two shift workers at the next table took their trays of breakfast to a table by the front window.

'Let's talk about you,' Rosslyn said. 'Last Sunday morning some people climbed into the British Museum. They most probably climbed in not far from where you were sleeping.'

'That's what they did,' the vagrant said.

'Do you remember what they looked like?'

'I didn't see their faces. They were wearing masks. Stockings or balaclavas or some such.'

'What else?'

'I don't know. Looked to me like, maybe, army or mountain climbing clothes. Carrying backpacks. I'd say they knew what they was doing.'

'What else do you remember about them?'

'One was this thick-set bloke. Heavy. Big. Big shoulders. Hard. The other looked smaller. Slim. I'd say a young woman.'

'There were two of them?'

'Right. Two.'

'Did you see them again?'

'Yes. But there was only the woman that came out. The other one wasn't with her. She left in a hurry. Carrying an extra pack at the time she left. They was to have nicked something and the other fella must've left another way. See, I've done that too in the good old days. Mind, not that I broke into a place like that museum. Never my league, was it? I worked the suburbs till the arthritis here got hold. See, that's the problem.'

'Do you remember anything else about them?'

'No.'

'Did they speak to you?'

'No.'

'You to them?'

'No. I didn't like the look of them, did I?'

'Has anyone, apart from me, asked you about them?'

'No.'

'Have you told anyone else about them?'

'No.'

'You're sure about that – you're sure the police haven't spoken to you?'

'You're joking. They don't speak to me. Buggered if I'll speak to them. Good luck to the bastards. I hope they lifted something. What's the point of all that stuff in there? They should share it out for the rest of us, shouldn't they?'

'Maybe,' said Rosslyn. 'OK, thanks for your help.' He handed the vagrant a ten-pound note.

'Could you run to another of the same?'

Rosslyn handed over another ten pounds and left him to the rest of his breakfast.

That makes two. Nezeritis and Demetra.

At nine a.m. he joined the rush-hour crowds at Euston station. There was no sign of the pursuers he had last seen at St Giles's Circus the previous day.

He'd decided to kill time: take a train to the Midlands and return to London during the evening rush hour. Tomorrow, once Lo had the arrangements in place, he would leave for Greece.

He boarded the train for Birmingham. Settling with the newspapers, he searched for any continuation of the story. To his relief he found none.

He caught the announcement just after nine-thirty. The woman's voice on the tannoy apologized for the delay to the nine-forty-five train to Birmingham New Street; it was now expected to leave in one hour's time.

At five past ten the entryphone bell to the office at Sueng's Club Two sounded. Michael Lo expected it to be either Ethel Chang, who had been due to arrive at ten, or Kostas Lambrakis and his assistant, Lina Avolites. Not the man who introduced himself: 'I'm a friend of Alan Rosslyn,' he said. The accent was foreign. Lo could not place it. It was unlike Alan not to have mentioned there would be a caller.

The foreign voice said, 'Alan's asked me to deliver a package to you in person.' Had the delivery been for Lo, part of the normal run of business, he would have told the man to meet him downstairs, where there was a CCTV camera. As this had to do with Alan, it was better that no record of the visit should exist. He told the man to come to the office on the first floor.

Crouching, Lo had just secured the office safe when the office door behind him opened. He was getting to his feet when the metal claw struck his ear. He fell sideways, curling himself up, arms shielding his head, when the claw came down against his head a second time.

Unfortunately for Lo, Ethel Chang had been delayed in the solid traffic around Marylebone. There would, however, have been little she or anyone else could have done to prevent the brutal force or curtail the speed of the assault.

51

At ten-thirty a.m. Rosslyn was alerted by the mobile phone Lo had provided. It was Ethel Chang. 'The police and ambulance service are at the club,' she said. 'There's been an accident. I can't speak long.'

He could tell she was very frightened. 'What's happened?' he asked.

'I've spoken to Lambrakis. He's told me to find the new arrival –'

'Who?'

'That's you.'

'He knows about me?'

'Not your name. Just that Michael has been doing favours for an important friend. And Lambrakis for him. Listen to me. For God's sake, don't go back there.'

'I have to somehow.'

'If it's the things Michael had for you in the safe, I've got them with me. We have to talk. Where are you?'

'Euston. You?'

'Middlesex Hospital. I've just seen Lambrakis.' She paused. 'I'm very sorry . . . I have to tell you that Michael's dead.'

He closed his eyes.

Michael Lo. Dead.

'I have to see you.'

He felt the anger and the guilt mixing in his chest. Once more the pain for which he felt himself responsible.

'Meet me in Regent's Park,' he told her. 'By the bandstand. I'll be waiting for you. Watch your back.'

52

Ethel Chang stood next to him on the new-mown grass in Regent's Park. Wearing sunglasses, a lightweight black suit and white shirt, the jacket slung over her right shoulder, she cut a diminutive and frail figure. She was breathless and had been weeping. They stood close together near the bandstand, a short distance from the elderly audience listening to a detachment of the Regimental Band of the Coldstream Guards playing Eric Coates's 'Knightsbridge March'. The scent of the grass was in the air and there were cumulus clouds developing to great heights in the sky.

Chang said, 'The animal bastard must have used a hammer of some kind on his face and neck.'

'Who found him?' Rosslyn asked.

'Lambrakis. The man was still there when he arrived with Lina Avolites. He pushed past them and got out.'

'Did he say anything?'

'Not much. Only that they should piss off out or something. Lina Avolites thought the accent was definitely Greek.'

'Who's Lina Avolites?'

'Lambrakis's assistant,' Chang said. 'Lambrakis told her to tail him.'

'Does she know where the man went then?'

'He's on his way to Luton Airport. She followed him to King's Cross and found out from the ticket desk what sort of ticket he'd bought.'

'Didn't the police follow him?' said Rosslyn.

'No,' said Chang. 'They didn't. They only got there once he'd left.'

'And Lambrakis,' said Rosslyn, 'did Lambrakis tell the police that Lina Avolites was on to him?'

'No.'

'Why not?'

'Because he has his reasons for not wanting to get involved with the police.'

'Have you heard from Lambrakis since?'

'No,' said Chang. 'But he's told Lina Avolites to call me.' She showed Rosslyn her mobile phone. 'If and when she can get a name.'

'What did he look like, Michael's attacker?'

'Lambrakis told me he was around six feet tall. Slim. One hand in his pocket. Presumably to disguise the weapon, the hammer or whatever. Lambrakis isn't much more than my height and size. He wasn't going to fight. Meanwhile, here's what Michael wanted you to have. Michael told Lambrakis and he got it from Michael's safe and passed it to me to hand to you.' It was an envelope containing the 5000 dollars in mixed currencies. 'I've made arrangements for the VW to be available for you at Calais,' said Chang. 'And Lambrakis thinks it'll be safer for you to leave the country by plane. Not by ferry. And Michael reckoned it'd be sensible for you to travel with a companion. That's me. He was very serious about it. So's Lambrakis. But both of them told me you prefer to work alone.'

'Quite right, I do.'

'But if the police at the airport are looking for you, they'll be expecting you to be alone. I think Michael had it right. I should travel with you, Mr Rosslyn. Will you need a gun?'

'Once I get to Greece maybe.'

'Do you have a dealer there?'

Rosslyn shook his head. 'No, I don't.'

'We do,' said Chang. 'Lambrakis does. Outside of Athens. But he won't sell a gun to you direct.'

The audience was applauding the Coldstream Guards' band.

'He'll sell to you?' asked Rosslyn. 'Is that what you're telling me?'

'Yes. He'll sell to me.'

'How much?' asked Rosslyn.

'To me on behalf of Lambrakis,' said Chang. 'We're looking at 500 dollars.'

'Including rounds?'

'Including rounds, yes.'

'To you, even though Lambrakis won't be around?'

'Yes. To me. No problem. Two handguns and the rounds will be 750 dollars.' She lifted the dark glasses from her eyes. 'What's it to be then?'

'You handle the cancellation of the car in Calais. Michael was right. I don't believe I have the time to drive to Greece. I have to bank on the Greeks thinking that's the last place I'll go back to right now.'

'Do you need me to go with you?' Ethel asked.

'Yes,' said Rosslyn. 'And no.'

The Coldstream bandmaster announced Coates's 'Elizabeth of Glamis' from *The Three Elizabeths Suite*.

Rosslyn continued, 'I don't want to involve you in unnecessary difficulties with the Greek police. You have to know that there's some bloody warrant out for my arrest in Greece. For murder. I need the gun. Maybe you should do that for me in Athens. It looks like the risk I have to take. After that, you can get out of Greece and leave the rest of what I have to do to me.'

'Whatever you want,' said Chang. 'That was what Michael said.'

'It's not that I don't appreciate your help,' said Rosslyn.

'You're welcome,' Chang said. 'Then you'll go by air?'

'Yes. I suggest you get two tickets to Milan Linate. Then two more. Milan Linate to Athens. Just as soon as you can –'

Chang's mobile telephone interrupted him. He watched her take the call. It was Lambrakis's assistant, Avolites, calling from Luton Airport. Chang repeated what Avolites was saying for Rosslyn's benefit: 'Constantine Dragos. Greek. Flying Athens direct. Messinian Air Flight MA 466. Departure delayed. Rescheduled departure tomorrow at 10.30. Dragos accompanied by Miltiades Zei. Greek. Employee of Messinian Shipping Corporation. They've taken a cab to the George Hotel, Luton . . . Hang on –'

'Have her check out the rooms,' said Rosslyn. 'Use her nous. Pay reception whatever's needed to get the adjoining room for her tonight. Plus one more for you and me near to it.'

Chang relayed the instruction to Avolites.

'You want surveillance on them?' she asked Rosslyn.

He nodded. 'Can Lambrakis supply the necessary?'

'Yes,' said Chang, and spoke again to Lina Avolites: 'Call Lambrakis. Have him courier you a B1 Zeitz amplifier, contact mikes and steths. Ask him to connect to the hotel-room telephone.' She paused. 'Hang on again . . .' She turned to Rosslyn. 'She has photographic ID of both men.'

'Good,' said Rosslyn. 'Tell her to listen in to everything she can get for us. We'll call her with the RV time in Luton. And thank her. She's done well.'

The Coldstream Guards band had finished the lunch-hour performance by the time they left Regent's Park.

'You've done this sort of work before?' Rosslyn asked.

'Sure. That's what Michael paid me for. I have to earn a living. Like you, I guess.'

'I can think of better ones.'

'Maybe,' said Chang. 'But, like me, it seems right now you don't have too many choices. That right?'

'I wouldn't argue with you.'

53

Ethel Chang checked in at the front desk of the George Hotel in Luton with Rosslyn as her companion. They were given Room 385 on the third floor.

'Ms Lina Avolites is in Room 387,' the receptionist said pleasantly.

Rosslyn prayed that Avolites had done the business, that Dragos and Zei were in Room 386.

They took the lift to the third floor. Rosslyn admired Chang. She was fighting hard to keep grief at bay.

They had spent a long afternoon behind drawn curtains at her small house in Edgware. After securing the passport photograph, they waited for Lambrakis to check the Dragos background. Finally, it was a tall order, but in the very short time available he was to look for any strand in the web that might connect Miltiades Zei to the Dragos family interests, Nicos Nezeritis and Cleo Ipsilanti. Perhaps Rosslyn had expected the result of Lambrakis's electronic trawl would be disappointing and in the event Lambrakis came up with nothing. Perhaps, he ventured to Rosslyn, Vayakakos knew more than he had revealed.

From Room 385, Chang called Lambrakis. Getting no answer from any of the several telephone numbers he used, she left a message for him to call her at the hotel. Then she called Avolites in the room along the corridor. She took some time to answer, but when eventually she did she said she was ready and waiting for them.

'I don't like it,' said Chang. 'Twice she asked me if she needs to dress for dinner.'

'She doesn't,' said Rosslyn. 'Not in this place.'

'She said she only had a *black* dress,' said Chang. '*Black* is the slip word that means I can't talk and there's serious trouble. We should wait a few minutes. See if she calls back. If she doesn't, then I really think we have to abort the surveillance.'

'Let's give her five minutes,' said Rosslyn.

They finally gave her ten minutes, but still she didn't call. They then tried Lambrakis again. No reply.

'I don't like it,' said Chang. 'Lina can look after herself all right. *Black* is *black*. I'm sorry, we have to leave.'

'I'll take a look,' said Rosslyn. 'You stay here.'

Chang sat on the edge of the bed and watched Rosslyn go to the door. He was opening it slowly, cautiously, when it was pushed with great force into his face.

The bright light dazzled him. Before he could slam the door shut, a voice yelled, 'Police. Don't move.'

Eyeball to eyeball with three armed police officers. No Contest. Raising his arms above his head, Rosslyn showed the police his empty hands. Two more police officers barged into Room 385 and arrested Ethel Chang.

Escorted by police cars, the two armoured police vans drew up in the delivery bay at the back of the George Hotel.

Standing by her car, Marion Shaw watched the arrival of the police vehicles with satisfaction. 'Give the drivers their orders,' she told the Chief Superintendent. 'Chang and Avolites to be taken to Holloway. Rosslyn and Lambrakis to Whitemoor Prison, Cambridgeshire. I want Rosslyn held indefinitely in the Special Security Unit and made available for interrogation by me at a later stage.'

She made a hurried departure. She wanted to prepare herself for what could be a decisive meeting with the Director General.

54

In Athens, the absence of Constantine Dragos and Ioannis Ipsilanti delayed the meeting in the Piraeus boardroom of Messinian Air and the Messinian Shipping Corporation. Once again the location of the meeting was withheld from the members of the assault group as a precaution. Twice, as they waited for Constantine and Ipsilanti, Miltiades Zei told those already seated around the table that Constantine would be joining them 'all in God's time'.

When it came to saying where the two men were or why they had been delayed, Zei skirted round the subject. His evasions exposed some of the first cracks in the mood of high expectancy, also the tension between himself and Alexios Dragos. The relationship had never been as easy as Zei would have liked. Something of the difficulty now began to show itself. Alexios said calmly that, as far as Ipsilanti was concerned, no one knew where he was, and this was indeed the truth of it. There was some further small talk among the group, some further discussion of specific operational duties, until, with uncharacteristic suddenness, Alexios threw the big card on the table. Saying that he would start the proceedings without his son, he announced, almost casually, 'We start the final phase on Sunday.'

'You mean this Sunday coming?' said Zei.

'Sunday, three a.m.' said Alexios. 'British Summer Time.'

'Too soon,' said Zei. 'Not without Constantine's approval. The final preparations cannot be hurried.'

'We've decided on the manifest of equipment,' Alexios said. 'We've chosen the transportation. Facilities here and in the UK. Armaments. Communications procedures. We will stick to the letter of the plan and timings with minor embellishments of our own choosing.

Nothing will be altered. You people must be on stand-by for Sunday.'

'Our agreement,' said Zei, 'is that the final choice of timings be approved tonight.'

The telephone rang. Zei took the call and passed the receiver to Alexios, who listened. The others waited for him to speak.

Alexios announced, 'That was Simopoulos.'

'Who?' asked Zei, in a tone that suggested he recognized the name anyway.

'Chief of Athens Police,' said Alexios for the benefit of anyone who did not know.

Zei took a deep breath. 'What does he want?'

Alexios got to his feet. 'Let's talk for a moment in my office.' He headed towards the door. 'If the rest of you will excuse the two of us a moment.'

Alone with Zei in his office, Alexios said, 'He wants me to give him the whereabouts of Cleo and Olympia.'

Only Zei's thin laugh broke the silence. Then, after a pause, he said, 'What the hell is this about?'

Alexios was silent.

'Well?' said Zei, his gaze fixed on the other man.

'I will be in a position to tell you later,' Alexios said.

'Come on, you're saying they're both alive?' said Zei.

'I'm saying nothing.'

'I don't believe it.'

'You can believe what you will.'

'If they are.'

'If they are, then what?' said Alexios with the flicker of a smile.

'They'll go straight to the British.'

'They can't,' said Alexios, studying his worry beads. 'You haven't listened to me.'

'Does Constantine know they're alive?'

'There are some things you were never meant to know. Some things you will never know. They will not go to the British. Why? Because I have ensured that they won't. They won't go anywhere until I say so. Until we have completed the mission in London. Cleo needn't give us grounds for concern.'

His lips wore the mocking smile that said, *I told you all along, didn't I?*

'Who else was it, do you suppose,' he said, 'but the British who contrived their disappearance? Let's talk practicalities, shall we? You have to look to Prevezer, don't you?' Suddenly the smile fell from his face and there was a brutality about the set of his jaw. 'I'm one move ahead of you. That's why Constantine isn't here. Prevezer's passed her sell-by date. And in the interests of security Constantine's setting that straight. See? Right now, I suggest we wait a little longer. We aren't taking any chances with *anyone* who may have talked. No chances. Period.' He tapped the surface of his desk with his fingertips. The slow drumbeat. 'Prevezer has to go. And by "go" I mean whatever it takes to get her silence. We need the human shield, right? And it sure as hell isn't going to be some loose-mouth British diplomat. Listen to me, she's screwed. Rosslyn's screwed. Even so, I'm telling you, we don't take one single unnecessary risk. I've been down this path in my life before.'

The anger was stirring, rising. He walked to a side table and fingered an ugly-looking, brand-new and high-powered fishing spear gun.

After a moment, he continued, 'Do you know why his firm's directors, two men called Tunim, have been on your butt? Do you?' Touching the tip of the lethal-looking spear gun's arrow, he let the question hang. Then he said, 'There are those in London who know of your itinerary in Europe and wherever else.' He returned to his seat at the table. He was gesticulating now. Jabbing the accusatory finger. 'Do you know?'

'No,' said Zei.

'Of course you don't know,' spat Alexios. 'You listen to me. It's my business to know. Fortunately for you, they found nothing, right? Nothing. But it's my money that's on the line. I don't get paid for losing. Only for seeing that other people lose.'

55

Constantine Dragos climbed the stone steps to the apartment block on Vasileos Pavlou Street. Dogs sniffed wheeled bins of sour garbage. He carried a short, hard length of black rubber in the pockets of his baggy canvas trousers, along with a roll of industrial adhesive tape, red enamel paint in a spray can and a pair of transparent plastic gloves. Beneath his lightweight black cotton jacket, taped to his left side just above the waist, he had the loaded .45–calibre handgun and a length of detonation cord.

He found the gateway entrance to the apartment block and crossed the small courtyard, his boots squelching red juice from fallen fruit on the paving stones. The entrance was open and there was the bell marked CP.

In the dim front parlour of the ground-floor apartment, an old woman turned away from the blaring TV.

He gave her an inquiring look.

'She has a visitor,' the old woman said.

'She does?' said Constantine. 'That's nice for her.' *Not too good for me though.*

The old woman shrugged and turned back again to the TV screen.

Then his mobile phone sounded. He glanced at the old woman. Reckoning that she would be unable to hear him above the din of the TV, he hunched his shoulders and took the call.

It was Alexios Dragos. 'Is she there?'

'Yes, and she has a visitor.'

'Take him out.'

'I will.'

'Tell Prevezer we've aborted. Make certain she tells London it's aborted.'

'I hear you.'

'Then kill her.'

The glass entrance door to the apartment block was open. He went inside, pulling on the transparent plastic gloves as he climbed the wooden stairs to the fourth and top floor. The windows in the short passage to Prevezer's flat were curtained. Drawing one of the curtains aside, he found it covered the door to the fire exit, which was unlocked. Outside, the rusted iron spiral steps led down to the back alleyway.

The Citroën saloon parked beneath a line of trees belonged to Ioannis Ipsilanti. That was good. He would not need to use Prevezer's car. He hoped the tank was full.

Outside the door to her flat he paused and listened. Inside he could hear the sound of voices, though not what was being said. Then he rapped on the door and waited.

The door opened. It was on a restraining chain and Prevezer was standing to one side.

'Christiane?' Constantine asked.

'You should have rung before coming here,' she said, her eyes wide with fear.

'It can't wait,' said Constantine.

He peered inside the flat. Three ginger cats stood in the hallway by the cat-litter tray and Ipsilanti's jacket was slung over the low sofa. The door to the bathroom was ajar and he saw it being closed from the inside. He jammed his heavy boot between the door and frame. 'Unfasten the chain,' he told her.

'You can't come in' said Prevezer.

He could smell the whisky on her breath. Then he heard the telephone ringing and he saw the door to the bathroom drawn shut. The telephone stopped ringing. Slipping his hand inside his jacket, he said, 'I have a card for you.' He palmed the card towards her and she reached out her hand for it. Instantly, his hand clamped over hers, wrenching back her fingers.

'Ioannis,' she yelled.

'Shut up,' he hissed. 'Now, open up or I will break your fingers.'

With her free hand, she slipped the door chain and let him in. 'Let go of me.'

He jerked the .45 from the holding tape, closed the door and locked it. From the bathroom he heard Ipsilanti speaking on the phone.

'Who's in the bathroom?' he said with a smile.

Her bloodshot eyes held his. 'No one.'

With his left wrist-bone squeezing against her throat, he frog-marched her, choking, towards the bathroom door.

Inside the bathroom Ipsilanti was speaking on the phone in desperation. Constantine could not afford to wait. The zone for interrogation was only fifteen minutes. For the execution of Prevezer, say, another three. Now Ipsilanti's presence meant the business would take longer.

Increasing the pressure on Prevezer's throat, balancing himself against the side wall, he turned in a slight crouch sideways and, with all his weight behind it, aimed the kick with his rubber boot just above the handle. The lock broke away and the door burst open, slamming against the ceramic shelf, throwing bottles of scent and medication to the floor, where they shattered and spilled their contents.

Ioannis Ipsilanti shouted, 'Don't move!' Legs wide apart, he was pointing a gun at Constantine, who smiled.

'You too, Ioannis?' he said quietly. He held Prevezer tight. 'You want me to kill her, Ioannis? What's it to be? Do you want to put one in her?'

'Get out,' yelled Ipsilanti, petrified.

'Sure,' said Constantine. 'What's in it for you to kill me?'

'Get out.'

'Ever killed a man, Ioannis? Like, face to face?'

'I have someone on the phone,' said Ipsilanti. 'Call the police,' he shouted.

'Ioannis,' said Constantine quietly, 'put the gun on the floor, OK?'

'Do what he says,' said Prevezer, retching.

'Slowly now, Ioannis,' ordered Constantine almost inaudibly. 'Then hand her the phone.'

Ipsilanti did as he was ordered. Taking the cordless phone, Constantine kicked the gun out of reach and then handed the phone to Prevezer.

'Talk,' whispered Constantine. 'Say it, say it.'

Prevezer cleared her throat. 'Hello? Marion. Oh yes. Yes, it's me.'

Constantine pressed the snout of the gun into the back of her neck. 'Stay calm.'

'No,' she said into the cordless phone. There was a dry clicking in her throat. 'Everything's fine now. There was a slight row. I have a friend here. That's all. Yes, really. Look, why don't I call you back? Fifteen minutes? Fine.'

'Good,' Constantine said, taking out the roll of industrial adhesive tape. 'You wind this round his eyes.'

He handed her the tape. She was trembling violently. Her eyes still wide with shock.

He stooped down and retrieved the gun that was lying on the floor among the shards of broken glass. 'Now, Christiane, move it. The sooner we get this over with, the sooner you two walk out of here alive. We have fifteen minutes, see, Christiane. Fifteen minutes.'

She began to wind the tape around Ipsilanti's head.

'Faster. Tighter. *Tighter*. Around his eyes. Nose. Leave the mouth. You'll be talking to me soon, Ipsilanti. Now the hands. Put your hands behind your back, shit-face. OK. Now the ankles, Christiane. Take off the shoes. Good. That'll do.'

Constantine shoved Prevezer to one side, her feet scrunching broken glass. Then he launched his boot into Ipsilanti's groin. 'You can feel, Ioannis. But you can't see. And you sure as hell can't run.' He aimed a kick at Ipsilanti a second time and the Greek turned over, his face pressed against the broken glass. 'You move and you cut your mouth to shreds. So don't you move, right.' He picked up the cordless phone. 'Don't move until I come back.'

Grabbing Prevezer by the hair, he closed the bathroom door. Taking the cordless phone, he led her by the hair into the dimness of the front room, where the curtains were drawn across. He turned his head. Squinting. Looking for any signs of a rape and attack alarm. Taking in the personal computer on the desk. The hi-fi on the wooden shelves. The open bottle of Glenfiddich whisky and tumblers on the low glass table. The piles of British newspapers and magazines scattered on the floor.

'Sit on the sofa,' he told her. 'Sit.' He could have been talking to a dog. 'Sit. Take off your clothes.'

'Take off what?'

'You understand English. Strip.'

'You're not –'

'No, I haven't the time or inclination.'

'You're an animal.'

He showed her the hand claw. 'Then don't encourage me.'

Naked, she curled up, crossed her legs, covering her breasts with her arms.

'Help me get this over with quickly,' he told her.

Drawing up a low chair, he sat facing her like a dentist in close. He showed her the hand claw. The broad thumb caressed the hooked point and he jabbed it suddenly towards her eyes and then pointed at the dark between her legs.

'Think, Christiane. Use your brain. Think names. Cleo Ipsilanti. The daughter, Olympia. Your friend, Rosslyn. The place up there in the mountains. Think Simopoulos. Think why, you stupid bitch, you did the deal with Simopoulos to let her out. Think.'

He took out the can of red spray paint and pointed it in her face.

'Think. You got Rosslyn out. We dealt with Cleo and her goddamn daughter, and you screwed up with only days to go. Tell me, now. Right?'

He squirted a small gush of red paint across her knees.

'It's cold.'

'What have you told your people? Shaw, right? The Marion on the phone. What have you told her?'

'The truth.'

'What's that supposed to mean? You tell *me* the truth.'

'The truth is that Cleo Ipsilanti knows your organization inside out. Demetra's her daughter, isn't she? Olympia's her daughter. I don't need to explain anything to you, do I? You're not stupid. It's staring you in the face.'

'I'm staring *you* in the face, Christiane. What the hell are you covering? Have you and Ioannis had second thoughts? Is that it?'

'No. Believe me, our government, we want to see the Marbles returned to Greece.'

'Bullshit.'

'And the way's been made easy for the operation to succeed. That's what Marion Shaw wants. What happens after that is none of my business.'

'And your people in London? Oh, *please*, Christiane, please don't make this so painful for yourself. You answer to us.'

'I answer to Shaw.'

'And us.'

'And Ipsilanti, who's he playing for now?'

'I don't know what you're talking about.'

'Come on, Christiane. What have you told them?'

'I answer only to Shaw.'

'You mean you've betrayed us?'

'I've told you. I answer only to Shaw.'

'Don't keep on saying that, Christiane.'

'It's the truth.'

'What game are you playing? You expect me to believe that somehow Shaw's in this thing with my father?'

'I didn't say that. Don't let your imagination run riot. It's not my job to ask her what her agenda might be.'

'And you expect me to call her back in fifteen minutes and ask her? Is that it?'

'If you wish. It's up to you. Do what you will.'

'Don't you tell me what to do. Like hell. It's up to you. You'll be the one to tell her the plan is aborted, right? You'll tell her while I listen and make sure of what you tell her, right?'

'It seems I have no choice.'

'That we can agree. Now why's the Ipsilanti woman, Cleo, been let out?'

'I don't know.'

'You knew this was going to happen, is that it?'

'No. You know about the fight she and her daughter put up. You know what happened there at her house. Come on, Constantine, we're in this together. We're partners.'

'That's good,' said Constantine. 'That's good. Here.' He handed her the cordless phone. 'Call Shaw. Tell her the operation's aborted. *Finito.*'

'She will need to know why.'

'Tell her that the technical resources are inadequate.'

He stood over her, the snout of the .45–calibre handgun at the base of her skull. 'Call her.'

56

Shaw took the call in her office at Vauxhall Cross.

'Marion?'

'Are you sure you're OK?'

'Fine. You have to know the operation's been aborted.'

'Totally?'

'I believe that to be the case. Totally.'

'Who told you?'

'Alexios Dragos.'

'Why?'

'The technical resources are inadequate.'

'Is that the reason?'

'I believe that to be the case.'

'When did you find out?'

'A few minutes ago. They were here with me. There was a row.'

'Is Constantine Dragos with you?'

'No.'

'Armed?'

'No.'

'What was the row about?'

'Something between themselves. I believe that to be the case.'

'Who was saying "call the police"?'

There was a silence.

'Are you in trouble?'

'No.'

'Is that the truth, Christiane?'

'Yes. Look, I'll call you back later.'

'Is Ioannis still there?'

'No.'

Prevezer carefully set the phone down on the floor. Then she turned. And she had just finished saying, 'There you are. Is that what you wanted?' when Constantine Dragos squeezed the trigger.

57

BRITISH DIPLOMAT KILLED IN ATHENS SHOOTING

Athens (Reuters) Suspected urban guerrilla shot dead British Embassy official, Christiane Prevezer, and her companion, Athens lawyer Ioannis Ipsilanti, 45, today in her private apartment.

Police said Prevezer, 38, had been taken hostage by the killer in her apartment in Piraeus, Greece's main port near Athens.

'We believe it is the work of the terrorist group P17N, but until we have ballistic test results we cannot confirm this,' Athens Police Chief Yannis Simopoulos told Reuters.

Both the 17 November and 1 May leftist groups have staged similar attacks in the past.

17 November has killed twenty-one Greeks and foreigners, including the US Central Intelligence Agency station chief and the US military attaché, and staged a rocket attack on the US embassy in January 1996.

Police found .45-calibre shells in Prevezer's apartment. P17N use trademark .45-calibre pistols to sign attacks and remote-controlled bombs and rockets.

'This was the first indication that this could be a terrorist attack,' police chief Simopoulos told reporters at the scene.

None of its members has ever been arrested.

'It is an extremely tragic event. I express my sorrow and am awaiting a detailed report from the Public Order Ministry,' the Prime Minister told reporters.

'I saw a man as he arrived at the British woman's apartment. He was a very large man with a German accent,' a close neighbour told Greek television.

Hospital officials said that Prevezer was shot at point-blank range and died before reaching Piraeus's Tzanio hospital. Ipsilanti was fatally shot while bound and gagged.

But the Director General had already received the news.

58

At Vauxhall Cross the Director General closed the unpleasant confrontation in his office with Riley and Georgiadis. Protesting that Shaw had been given far too few resources to penetrate and combat the P17N presence outside Greece, the American and the Greek seemed entirely to overlook the fact that it had been a British officer, Prevezer, who had been shot dead in Athens. Worse still, Georgiadis was claiming that, without any proper consultation with the Greek Foreign Ministry or Public Order Ministry, Prevezer had engineered some deal with Athens police chief Yannis Simopoulos concerning the investigation into the case of Cleo Ipsilanti.

Now, moreover, considerable doubts had been raised about the accuracy of the identification of the body said to be Cleo Ipsilanti's and still no one knew the fate of Olympia. So serious was the chaos and apparent bungling surrounding the investigation that the Greek Prime Minister had called for the setting up of an immediate inquiry. On top of all this, there was even a further, as yet unsubstantiated, issue: a rumour that perhaps both Cleo and Olympia Ipsilanti were alive and that the British Secret Service had been party to their illegal abduction from Kardamyli. The Director General had dispatched a Deputy Assistant Director to Athens from RAF Northolt within the last hour.

The Director General heard out Riley and Georgiadis with commendable *sang froid*. He assured them that he 'realized that the situation was extremely grave'. He added that he 'needed more time to familiarize himself with developments as events unfolded'. 'You may be sure,' he emphasized, 'that the senior anti-terrorist officers in the police and their relevant counterparts in MI5 have been alerted. I've spoken to the Prime Minister, who is touch with his Greek counterpart. I've reported to the Foreign Secretary and Home Secretary, who both wish to be kept informed. More than that, there is little I can do at present.'

As the visitors left the Director General's office, his personal assistant was taking a call from Menzies Tunim.

Tunim was asking for an appointment with the Director General alone and in strict confidence. The assistant told him that her chief 'was unavailable'. Tunim was insistent, so she asked him 'to bear with me a moment'. When she came back on the line, she told Tunim that the Director General advised him to speak to Marion Shaw.

59

Menzies Tunim was in a quandary. He told the Director General's assistant that it was in fact Marion Shaw whom he wished to discuss in private with the Director General. With great seriousness, he emphasized the urgency of what it was he had to say. Adding that he would prefer Shaw knew nothing of the appointment, he told the assistant that the essence of the intelligence he claimed to have concerned Greece and Alan Rosslyn.

The assistant asked him once more 'to bear with me a moment'. When she came back on the line, she told him that the Director General would see him. He should bring with him two separate proofs of identity. An entry pass would be waiting for him at the main entrance on Battersea Road.

When Menzies Tunim arrived at Vauxhall Cross, the Director General warned him that he had better not be wasting his time. At his most ingratiating, Tunim offered 'to be of use to the Service', before commencing, 'I take it you know of our involvement with Shaw?'

'Yes,' said the Director General wearily. 'I know.'

'And Rosslyn?'

'I'm familiar with what's happened, yes.'

'And events concerning Cleo Ipsilanti?'

'Yes. Yes. Yes.'

'May I go on?'

The Director General stared at him. 'If you keep it short.'

Menzies Tunim took some time to explain the commission his firm had received from the stockbroker acting on behalf of Air Commodore Knott, the Chairman of Air Technology World Services, in Southampton.

The Director General was making notes in a kind of private shorthand. He wrote with his left hand cupped, like a schoolboy wary of the prying eye of the nearby cheat.

Tunim explained how Knott had been offered shares as the sweetener to ensure his silence. He continued, 'As is standard practice in our business, we followed the money and we arrived at the Thrace Bank in Vaduz, Liechtenstein. One Miltiades Zei, Constantine's partner and a senior employee of the Dragos companies, had recently made numerous arms purchases throughout Europe. Constantine Dragos had approached numerous major companies offering the services of mercenaries in the United States, United Kingdom and elsewhere.'

The circle of what Tunim described as clandestine activity touched many companies and individuals, including Ioannis Ipsilanti.

The Director General was silent, and Tunim waited and carefully watched his listener's perplexed look. The only sound was the low hum of the air-conditioning system. 'Cleo's ex-husband?' said the Director General at last.

'You know him?' Tunim said.

'I'm familiar with him,' said the Director General, without revealing that this was the same Ioannis Ipsilanti who had been shot dead in Piraeus.

'Look,' said Tunim. 'Our world is something like yours, isn't it?'

The Director General gave Tunim a frozen look. 'If you say so.'

'I mean, we all know the main players, don't we? We all, as it were, shelter beneath much the same sort of umbrella.'

'You speak for yourself,' observed the Director General. 'And, thank you, I've heard enough. Don't you think so?'

'What I think is this. I think that you really must hear me out, Director General.'

'Look, even if I wanted to, Tunim, we can't take this much further without talking to Shaw. Now can we?'

'That's the core of what I want to tell you,' said Tunim. 'My view is that you should speak to anyone who has had dealings with Ioannis Ipsilanti. Your officer in Athens, for example.'

'And if we do,' said the Director General slowly, with the look the man who hates being given advice, 'what d'you suppose it is we'll learn, if anything?'

'That Marion Shaw,' said Tunim very slowly, 'has been very far from frank with you.'

'Oh, Tunim, I doubt that very much. I really do. I have to tell you that I happen to know Marion rather better than you do.'

'With respect, Director General, I've known her rather longer than you have.'

'Professionally?' said the Director General, shaking his head.

'Professionally and personally.'

'I think not.'

'I mean very personally,' said Tunim. He broke off, making a circular gesture with his hand, suggesting perhaps that he was cranking up some story in his memory. 'We go back a long way together, and what I am telling you is this. That Shaw is following a personal agenda. She's fighting some secret war to do with her own personal traumas.'

The Director General gave Tunim a slow smile. 'It hardly behoves you, Tunim, to walk in here and play amateur psychiatrist, diagnosing some streak of instability in one of my most senior officers. Now, really, does it?'

Tunim shrugged. 'Take it or leave it'

'I'm asking you to leave it, Tunim. Leave it. . . .'

'Sorry?'

'To leave it *out*,' said the Director General.

'And she's using SIS as the shield –'

The Director General interrupted. 'Look, Tunim, we get about half a dozen complaints of this sort every week from people accusing our officers of improprieties. I have to disabuse you of your suspicion. And these theories of psychoses.'

'Listen, I'm not theorizing. It is not a suspicion. It's an accusation. You must have every biographical detail of Shaw's on file here. You must have made yourself more than a little familiar with senior officers like her.'

The Director General folded his hands on the desk. 'I rather hope, Tunim, you're not suggesting,' he said, 'that I have been remiss.

You'd have to be in possession of some very good evidence to back that up. This is very serious. And I have to tell you that people like you are the last on God's earth who could ever hope to gain access to it.' He stared at Tunim with a look of incredulity. 'Or are you telling me that you have accessed it?'

'Not directly.'

Now the Director General was suddenly in pursuit. 'Well,' he said, 'even if you have indirectly, then you could be in breach of the Official Secrets Act and I am empowered to make sure you don't leave the building until matters are clarified.' He paused. 'Do you follow me?'

'I know what you're saying.'

'Do you?' The Director General gave an empty laugh. 'You realize that I can keep you here indefinitely. You follow me?'

'I follow you entirely. But it isn't your archive that we've penetrated.'

'Is that so? Whose is it then?'

Now it was Tunim who was in pursuit. 'A firm of solicitors in Vienna,' he said. 'In fact, the leading firm of solicitors in Vienna. Look, why don't you boot up your PC there and access Shaw's CV, the Positive Vetting reports, the works, and see if you can find any mention of Naumann Bartenstein.'

The Director General stared hard at Tunim. 'And why are you so keen I do that?'

'Because I want you to be the one to point the finger at Shaw.'

'You won't then?'

'I won't, oh no.'

'Why's that?'

'Because of your unwelcome suggestion that I might be detained in this place indefinitely.'

'I've already told you, Tunim, I hope you aren't wasting my time.'

'I think you'll find that I'm not,' said Tunim. 'By the way, I'd also advise you to have a word as soon as possible with your man in the embassy in Vienna. You can have him check out the credentials of someone called Dr Karl Rudiger Einem. Einem's a senior partner in Naumann Bartenstein and acts on behalf of one of our clients in

Vienna, Austrian Engineering and Construction International. AECI.'

The Director General wrote it down. 'And this Einem, who is he?'

'He asked if we could tell him anything about an employee of his, one Dr Lutz Farenkamp, the AECI man in Zurich.'

'How come?' said the Director General with a note of diffidence.

'Because,' said Tunim sharply, 'he spent two days outside Zurich explaining the workings of Wolff tower cranes to Dragos's man. Miltiades Zei. Nothing wrong in that. Except whatever fees he may have been paid by Zei never showed up in the AECI books.'

'Really?' said the Director General, as if his mind were far away. 'Perhaps he didn't take any?'

'We looked into that for Einem,' said Tunim.

'And then?'

Tunim explained, 'Farenkamp's bank account in Zurich shows that he paid in the sum of 100,000 dollars on the day Zei left Zurich for the UK. The day after that, Zei showed up in Air Commodore Knott's office. So from where else would Farenkamp have got the money?'

'Well,' observed the Director General, 'perhaps there's a perfectly reasonable explanation.'

'Or perhaps there isn't. And when I asked Einem if the name of Marion Shaw meant anything to him, he said it didn't. I put it to him that it was a matter of some importance to me.'

'Why?' said the Director General, his eyes widening with interest. 'Because Marion Shaw gave me the name.'

The Director General looked dumbfounded. 'Marion Shaw did?'

'That's what I said,' said Tunim at his most self-satisfied.

'And tell me,' said the Director General, leaning forwards across his desk, 'in what context did she give you the name?'

Tunim smiled. 'I don't suppose she realized the importance of what she was saying. I'd say she's in one whole lot of trouble.'

'Tunim,' the Director General said in exasperation, 'are you going to tell me about it?'

Tunim summarized his exchange with Shaw outside the London Clinic. He concluded by saying that, in view of Shaw's 'manner and extreme reaction', he believed he had 'scored a bull's-eye'. 'None the less,' he added, 'Einem offered, more as a favour than anything else, in strict confidence to check his firm's archives for me.' He reached inside his jacket pocket and handed the Director General the copy of the fax from Vienna.

The Director General read:

Personal and Confidential
To: *Menzies Tunim, London*
From: *Dr Karl Rudiger Einem*

Menzies,
The enclosed may go some way toward answering your inquiry.
Please don't hesitate to let me know if we can be of any further use.
With best wishes,
Karl

Then the letter from Susan Shaw to her daughter, Marion.

'Who else knows about this?'

'No one,' said Tunim.

'No one at your office? Not even your brother?'

'No.'

'Very well,' said the Director General.

He activated the intercom on his desk and spoke to his personal assistant. 'Would you be so kind as to get Mr Tunim a drink of some sort. And perhaps you'd have someone make him comfortable in Room Two?'

With a look of extreme gratitude, he turned to Tunim. 'I'd much appreciate it if you'd stay on a while. I'd like one of my colleagues to take a short statement from you. Is this all right with you?'

'Absolutely.'

'Good. It shouldn't take too long.'

'I'd be more than happy.'

'Very well, Tunim.'

'Don't mention it.'

'We'll meet again a little later on.'

The personal assistant was standing in the doorway with an obliging smile. Directly the door had closed, the Director General called for coffee and then lifted the telephone to the Commissioner's Office at New Scotland Yard.

'We need an immediate arrest warrant for a man called Campbell Tunim. My people will give you the necessary addresses and those of all employees of the firm of Tunim Security. All of them must be arrested and held until further notice. I believe the offices are in Fitzroy Square. The offices should be put under armed guard with immediate effect and all papers, electronic technology, computers and so forth impounded. Perhaps you or one of your people could report back to me once you've completed matters.'

Then he called his SIS officer at home in Vienna. He was out, but his wife thought he had probably returned to the embassy after a meeting at the offices of the British Council on Schenkenstrasse.

The Director General dialled the embassy's main switchboard and asked for the officer to be paged. Within two minutes he was on the line. The Director General asked him to pay a friendly visit to a Dr Karl Rudiger Einem. Senior partner in Naumann Bartenstein. 'Take him to his firm's offices as soon as possible. And have him open up three personal files. On Marion Shaw. Susan Shaw, who was Marion Shaw's mother. Then, more importantly, establish anything you can on one Alexios Dragos and whatever dealings a Greek by the name of Miltiades Zei may have had with a man called Dr Lutz Farenkamp, the AECI man in Zurich. Offer Dr Einem a fee in Austrian Schillings.'

'How much, sir?'

'Whatever it takes, within reason.'

'And if he's reluctant to cooperate?'

'Call me at once. I'll speak to the chief of the local service in person.'

'I take it you'd like me to report back to you personally?'

'Yes. From your office.'

He sat staring at the framed photograph of his wife and three children, seated in the garden of their house in Wimbledon. They were presently trekking in the Himalayas and he envied them their adventure. His mind turned to Cleo Ipsilanti and he wished he could have talked to her.

Finally, he dialled again and asked to be put through to the governor of HM Prison Whitemoor.

60

The prison where Rosslyn had been taken was set in ninety acres of a former railway marshalling yard in Cambridgeshire. Surrounded by open fenland in grim isolation, some three kilometres north of the town of March, off the Wisbech road, in the light of the full moon it looked bleak and drained of colour.

A high mesh fence surrounded the low buildings and beyond the fence there was a concrete wall. Both were intended to deter escapees. So too were the dog patrols beyond the perimeter of the outer walls. The fences and walls were all over five metres high. Inside yet another concrete security wall, there was the prison within the prison, the Special Security Unit, which at the time housed some dozen exceptional risk or Category A prisoners, those who may be said to 'pose a danger to the public, the police or the security of the state'. The CCTV cameras around the SSU's exterior were monitored from the SSU control room. Since the notorious Whitemoor escape in 1994, security had been further increased. There were still more cameras inside the exercise yard, central association area, corridors, showers, cells and staff and visits area. There were no blind spots.

Isolated from the other inmates, Rosslyn was allocated one of the fourteen single cells. Measuring some two by four metres, the cell contained a bed, a washbasin and a WC.

On her arrival that night at Whitemoor, prison officers subjected Marion Shaw to search by X-ray and metal detectors. CCTV cameras monitored the search.

'You've seen your doctor recently?' the prison officer said.

'Why do you ask?' said Shaw.

'That Elastoplast on your left forearm?'

'Oh, yes. My six-monthly medical,' Shaw lied.

'Blood test?'

'Yes,' Shaw said airily. 'We all have them. The usual.'

She was asked politely to leave her shoulder bag in a secure container. A small paper bag of boiled sweets was temporarily confiscated. The one item she was permitted to keep with her was a small cassette player.

When she entered the SSU, she was subjected to a second search with X-ray equipment and was told there would be a final search when she left. Indeed, she was subjected to all the controls and restrictions that apply to visitors to SSU inmates, and it was explained to her that the visiting area itself would be searched both before and after she left it. No other visitor would be allowed access to the area where she would undertake her interrogation of the prisoner Rosslyn.

61

They faced each other across the bare wooden table. The table, like the chairs, was fixed to the floor and a thick glass screen separated them. Rosslyn's clothes had been taken from him and he wore prison-issue white paper overalls.

On Shaw's insistence and with the verbal authorization of the Director General, the prison governor had allowed one formal concession. Given the 'operational nature of the information that might be yielded by the prisoner Rosslyn and in so far as it related to national security' no monitoring or recording could be made of the evening's proceedings.

Rosslyn refused to make any statement whatsoever unless he was 'provided with immediate legal representation'. Denied permission to make any outside calls, he protested to Shaw about his arrest and its circumstances with great force.

Shaw homed in on Michael Lo.

'I have no comment,' said Rosslyn.

She told him George Vayakakos was dead.

'No further comment,' Rosslyn said firmly.

At this point she was called away to the governor's office to take an urgent call and Rosslyn was escorted back to his cell.

Ten minutes later he was escorted back into the visits area. Again he was alone with Shaw. When she explained what she had just learned, namely that Christiane Prevezer and Ioannis Ipsilanti had been murdered that very afternoon, he understood the agitation in her eyes.

The Americans, she told him, had issued an announcement to US citizens in the United Kingdom and Greece, warning against terrorist attacks. 'You can thank me for keeping you in safety here,' she said.

'No thanks to you.'

'Outside you'd be as good as dead.'

'I doubt that.'

'I'm telling you, Alan, I've been acting in your interests all along. I've already spoken to Lambrakis, as well as Chang and Avolites in Holloway.'

'They know nothing.'

He was in two minds about what she was telling him. He very much doubted that either Chang or Avolites had told her anything. Lambrakis, of course, he had never met. But, in spite of what had happened to Lo, he was confident that Lambrakis and the two women would keep their mouths shut. A man with Lambrakis's professional background and experience would be playing for time. Waiting to see what charges would be levelled against him. And not once did Shaw mention the priest at St Sophia's, the man to whom Vayakakos had been dictating his final testament. However much he had trusted Vayakakos, Rosslyn began to wonder whether that too might have been a fabrication of some kind.

Finally, Shaw said, 'Is there anything you want to ask me, Alan?'

'Yes, there is.'

'Go ahead.'

'Is Cleo still alive?' he said.

'Sooner or later I thought you'd ask.'

'Well, *is* she,' Rosslyn snapped. 'Have they identified her body?'

'If I tell you, Alan, could you possibly find it within you to cooperate with me? I'm here to discuss operational matters. The prison is not allowed to monitor or record what passes between us in here. The DG has authorized it personally. If it were to be recorded, the staff responsible, including the governor, would face immediate suspension and disciplinary action. That, believe me Alan, is the truth.'

Something in her manner of desperation led him to believe it. 'Very well,' he said. 'Try me. Go ahead. Tell me.'

'Do I have your word you'll cooperate?'

'You can decide that for yourself.'

'Let me tell you that Christiane Prevezer struck a deal with the chief of the Athens police to get Cleo out and away from trouble. Cleo put up a fight. There was a violent struggle. The rest you know about. You saw the result. To some extent you bought it. You were supposed to buy it. So was everyone else. Since then, she's been held under the Greek Police Witness Protection Scheme along with Olympia. She's safe. You have my word.'

'Where is she then?'

'That I don't know.'

'*You don't know.* What proof can you give me? Couldn't you arrange a telephone call or something?'

'I tend to doubt that'll be possible,' said Shaw. 'The fact is that Cleo's alive and safe. More than that I can't tell you now. She matters to the Service. Why do you suppose you were sent to Greece in the first place?'

'I have wondered. Oh yes, I've wondered.'

'All I can tell you,' she said, her voice at its lowest, 'is that she's alive and well.'

'You had better be right,' said Rosslyn with harsh impatience. 'When they let me out of here, let me tell you, if you've been bullshitting you'll have all hell to pay.'

'I think that goes for all of us, Alan, don't you?'

He believed that a crack, a very small crack, was showing in her defences.

'I have to admit to at least one failure,' she said. 'I have failed to get anywhere with P17N. So have our friends Riley and Georgiadis.'

'I couldn't give a monkey's shit for them. The hell knows what game you've been playing with your friends. And the Tunims too.' He sighed deeply. 'You know what I believe about you?'

She tried to smile. 'What do you believe?'

'I think you've been barking up the wrong tree.'

She was looking at him with puzzled earnestness. 'You do?'

'That you're using me,' he continued, 'and God knows who else, as the scapegoats. That you're engaged in some personal war of your own devising.'

She grimaced. 'What makes you think that?'

'Let me ask you something.'

'Go ahead.'

'Do you know that there was a second person involved in that climb-in at the British Museum. And I'm pretty bloody sure I know who it was.'

'You know?' she said.

He nodded.

'Share?' she asked nervously, her eyes wide.

'You share with me,' he told her, his face almost touching the sheet of protective glass between them.

'Does the name Demetra mean anything to you?' she said by way of reply.

'Yes, of course,' he said. 'What was she doing in the museum on the Sunday morning. Have you looked at the evidence?'

'Yes. I have.'

'And you people were too bloody dumb to see that there was a second person there. That Nezeritis did fall. That he was alive and Demetra put a gun to his head and blew his brains out. Why? So he wouldn't talk.'

'Why do you suppose she was there?' She asked the question as if she already knew the answer.

'Maybe a recce?'

'Maybe so,' she said mildly.

Here they were interrupted a second time. Once again, Shaw was called away to the governor's office to take the call.

'I'll be back,' she said, with an air of coolness that suggested she had regained something of her confidence.

Once more Rosslyn was led back to his cell under escort. He knew that Shaw was trying to win him over.

62

They were back in the visits area and Shaw was ashen. Her lips were dry and her hands trembling slightly.

'I can't help you any more,' Rosslyn said, 'unless you get me out of here now.' He could not immediately fathom out why, but it struck him that now her head, like his, was on the block.

'My active role in this,' she continued, 'is drawing to an end. Rules have been broken. Broken to such an extent that damage has been done that we can't repair. At least, damage that I can't repair.'

He was unsure what she meant. She was talking in abstractions. He was in two minds about rehearsing what he had seen in the British Museum for her benefit. Maybe Shaw herself had been duped about the interview not being taped. Or should he give her his conclusions? Let it be on the record for all to hear?

'You have to believe me,' she continued. 'I haven't lied to you about Cleo.'

'I need to be assured,' he demanded.

'I am assuring you, Alan. Believe me. I can read her moves now.'

'What do you mean, "read her moves"?'

'She'd do what I would in the circumstances. What you would do.'

'Such as?'

'Get herself out of Greece,' said Shaw, 'if she hasn't already.'

'What makes you so sure?'

'Because no one will stop her,' said Shaw. 'She'll make her way to where she's safe. To London. Why? Because that's what she's been trained to do. She's in no position in Greece to ensure the safety of Demetra.' She was searching his eyes for some reaction.

'Why should I believe you?'

'Why shouldn't you?'

'Because you've lied and lied again. You've been lying through your teeth all along. The P17N cover. You know it simply disguises something else. You've deceived me and God knows who else along the way. That's your job. You're very good at it. But maybe this time you've overreached yourself. Overstepped the mark. That's my guess. And, maybe, you've even deceived yourself.'

'Maybe, as far as you're concerned, I've missed a few things out. But I certainly haven't lied about her being alive, Alan. No. Let's rather say I may have been a little less than generous in giving you the truth of things.'

'So what's it to be, Marion? Do I or do I not get out of here?'

'I'm afraid that's, shall we say, out of my hands.'

'Why should I believe you then? C'mon, Marion, make me believe you. Open up. Tell me. What are you hiding?'

'Listen to me,' she said with a look of defeat. 'Someone, somewhere has been digging up my past. *My* neck is on the block.'

'Tough' said Rosslyn. 'What about *my* past?'

'I'd rather talk to you about our future,' she said, her voice faltering. 'I'd prefer to talk about our *immediate* future.'

'So would I,' he said abruptly. 'And the present too.'

'Listen,' she said, studying her wristwatch. 'I've questioned Lambrakis on exactly the same terms that I've been questioning you. After this I'm seeing him again. And after that I leave for London.'

'And then?'

'I'll be forced to tell the truth, that, as I expected, you've told me nothing. Lambrakis is a different matter, however.'

'Has he told you something?'

'Yes, he has.'

'Like what?'

'The name of the priest at St Sophia's.'

'C'mon. What's he told you *in so many words*? Is it to do with Vayakakos?'

She glanced behind her with the gesture of someone worried that others might be listening. She offered no answer to his question. 'I've drawn up a contingency plan,' she said. 'I don't guarantee, unless you keep your head, that it will work. It may, it may not. It's a question of getting you out of here as soon as possible.'

'That's good. Is this legitimate?'

She looked at him in silence.

He shook his head. 'So I'll be on the run again and you people can fix up some little accident that sees me out of the way. Marion, you misjudge me, you really do. I've been in this game for too long to walk into that one.'

'I appreciate that,' she conceded. 'It's up to you though.'

'And after that?'

'After that, as far as you're concerned, it's oceans wide for both of us. Otherwise, this conversation's never taken place. You'll face charges of assault, conspiracy to pervert the course of justice and whatever else the Service can pin on you. Who will you call in your defence? Lo is dead. Prevezer, what little help she might have been to you, she's dead too. You can't expect assistance from the Tunims or me. Even Cleo. Have no illusions. She'll protect herself. The Service will protect itself.'

'You're wrong about Cleo,' he snapped. 'The rest I can handle. Haven't you caused enough damage?'

'Others can be the judge of that.'

'All right. So what's it to be, Marion? Let's hear it. Why have you changed your spots? What's really persuaded you to turn up this contingency plan of yours at the last minute?'

'What I've just been told by the DG. Namely that according to the embassy in Athens, Cleo and Olympia Ipsilanti have absconded from a secure house.'

He looked at her with astonishment and undisguised mistrust. 'Where are they?'

'No one knows.'

'You must know.'

Rosslyn stared at her intently.

'Why were they let go?' he asked.

'Most probably because the Athens police chief realizes that one or other Dragos is responsible for the murder of Ioannis Ipsilanti and

Christiane. A squalid local murder, the killing of Ipsilanti, is one thing. Killing an accredited British diplomat is quite another. The police chief will in all probability seek to sever all connections with Dragos. Wouldn't you?' She looked at her wristwatch once more. 'The other scenario might put Cleo in greater danger. If Dragos has them, then Dragos has the bargaining tool. Cleo and Olympia as pawns in any counter-attack he may launch when his people reach the British Museum. If things go awry.'

'You believe that?'

'Yes, I'm inclined to.'

'Why?'

'Because I personally spoke to Prevezer and Ioannis on the phone, shortly before they died. Ioannis Ipsilanti told me, with absolute certainty, that the operation to remove the Elgin Marbles from the British Museum will be undertaken this Sunday at between three and four a.m. UK time. He also told me that Cleo and Olympia would, as he put it, be used.'

'*Used?*'

'That was the word. I also spoke to Christiane and I am certain the mission has been aborted.'

Listening to a guard dog barking in the distance, Rosslyn looked at her without expression. Now he began to see the whole macabre plot unfolding before his eyes. Shaw and her cronies were conniving at the theft of the Marbles so her people could catch the criminals in the act and throw the book at the Greeks for major conspiracy to thieve. They *wanted* the robbery to take place so that they could eliminate the Greeks responsible; so that the government could announce that the Greeks were no more than thieves whose actions demonstrated to the world that they had no moral or legal right to the Marbles. But they had, of course, to ensure the silence of those who might show up the mendacity of the Security Services and government. If their strategy and tactics became common knowledge, then they would be the ones exposed for what they really were.

'I need absolute proof,' he told her, 'that what you've said is true. If you have it, I'll listen to you some more. If not, then you'd better get yourself out of this hellhole and back to London. Can you give me hard proof?'

She produced the small cassette player and handed him the earphone extension. 'Listen to this,' she said. 'And note that this phrase is repeated three times: "I believe that to be the case." The signal to me that she was making the call against her wishes. That the exact opposite of what she says is true.'

Rosslyn listened to the tape. To the recorded conversation between Prevezer and Marion Shaw. And the phrase repeated three times by Christiane Prevezer: 'I believe that to be the case.'

'What do you need of me then?' he asked.

Shaw spoke slowly and quietly, as if even her utterances posed a threat to her plan. 'Tomorrow night at dinner, you will be allowed to meet with Lambrakis. He'll very suddenly act violently towards you. Believe me, it'll be temporary. But it'll be enough, if you carry things through, to have you driven under guard by a prison officer to hospital in Peterborough for treatment in Casualty.' She leaned forward across the bare surface of the table with an almost animal quickness. 'One of our people will be waiting in Casualty. He'll be carrying a walking stick.'

'Who is he?'

'A friend.'

'And the prison escort?'

'Leave the rest to our friend.'

Rosslyn remained silent. His unblinking eyes searched Shaw's.

'You can be sure of him,' she said.

'What makes you think so?' he demanded.

'Because like you and me and Cleo, he trusted George Vayakakos.'

'Did he?' said Rosslyn. He looked at her with an awful fascination. 'Vayakakos told me to be very wary of you. I think he was right, don't you?'

She shrugged. 'You'll be driven to London by our friend.'

'And then?'

'After that it will be a matter for the police to deal with whatever happens at the British Museum.'

'And what's your role to be?'

'I will brief you when we meet.' She looked beyond him towards the steel door. 'I have to go now. I have to face my maker, the Master of the Cross of Vauxhall.'

'That's your problem.'

'Perhaps. You won't be seeing me in here again, Alan.'

'I hope you're right,' he said sceptically.

'Believe me,' she said, 'I am *very* right.'

'If things go wrong?' he asked.

'They won't,' she said. 'Unless, of course, something untoward happens.'

'Such as your being taken off the case,' he said. 'Or fired.'

'There's no evidence to suggest I might be.'

'I wouldn't be too sure of anything,' said Rosslyn. He could tell she hardly needed telling.

'If there's an emergency,' she said, 'this is where you can find me . . . Don't telephone though. Come straight to this address. Memorize it.'

The address she gave him was her own. The flat in Frognal.

The prison officer escorted him from the visits area.

Marion Shaw, also under escort, was walking a little way ahead of him along the corridor. When the corridor divided, she quickened her step and turned. 'Remember, Alan. We're on the same side.' She hesitated and then, forcing a smile, she added, 'Good luck.'

63

Shaw's talk with Lambrakis was short and to the point. At first, understandably wary of her, Lambrakis obstinately refused to agree to her request and treated her offer of release with derision. How would he temporarily disable Rosslyn? By what means?

It was only when she removed the Elastoplast from her left forearm and handed it to him that he realized she had thought it out.

'Stick this on your inner arm,' she told him. 'Make sure the substance finds its way into his eyes.'

Before she left Whitemoor Prison, Shaw called the governor from the main-gate telephone. She thanked him for the excellent cooperation of his staff. She said her interviews with the prisoners Rosslyn and Lambrakis had been only moderately successful. She would return again, she said, and, if the governor gave permission, she would like the two men to be given their own clothes to wear and to be permitted a degree of association with other prisoners. At first the governor was reluctant to meet her request.

'I'd like to them to feel,' Shaw said, 'that they are being granted minor privileges. At least, say, at meal times.'

The governor said that was in order. Arrangements would be made accordingly next day. Shaw told him she was grateful and, with that, left for London.

64

The dogs and handlers were patrolling the outside perimeter of the prison. Rosslyn lay on his bed beneath a single blanket and listened to muffled voices in the corridor outside his cell and to the patrol dogs barking at the moon.

He was thinking about Shaw. *If you're right, I'm going to need much more than luck to get out of here alive. Lambrakis will, very suddenly, attack me, but the damage will be temporary. But enough to have me driven to hospital in Peterborough . . . Suppose it's permanent? What deal have you done, black eyes, with Lambrakis? His freedom for my life, my silence? Will he be the one to kill me? Victim of a prison brawl?* He closed his ears against the laughter of the guards outside his cell.

Lying on the bed unable to sleep, he tried to fight the sense of fear, hopelessness and defeat. And began to think his way into Shaw's plot. But his mind offered no explanation of it and his thoughts returned to Cleo, to Dragos and the Greeks. *The Greeks. How can they successfully steal back the Elgin Marbles?*

65

While Rosslyn lay on his cell bed in the early hours in Whitemoor, Constantine Dragos, in Athens, reminded himself of three crucial maxims. Surprise is of the essence. Maintain the fluidity of the timings. Check and check again.

He had combined all three and therefore taken the decision, late though it was, to bring the mission forward to the early hours of Saturday instead of Sunday. For this reason he had already dispatched Miltiades Zei to Altenhall in advance with orders to check the Boeing, Chinook, ordnance and arms.

Similarly, he considered the international press and media interest in Prevezer's death. The American government's warning of renewed terrorist activity in Athens. The increased security measures being taken by the Greek police and Intelligence Service. The combination of all these new developments persuaded him that the assault group must now be assembled at the derelict airfield in the plains of Sparta, the final departure point for London. The way ahead was clear. Nothing now could prevent complete success.

Part Three

To rip the Elgin Marbles from the walls of the British Museum
is a much greater disaster than the threat of blowing up the
Parthenon. I think this is cultural fascism. It's nationalism and
it's cultural danger, enormous cultural danger. If you start to
destroy great intellectual institutions, you are culturally
fascist.

DIRECTOR OF THE BRITISH MUSEUM

Those who support the status quo at the British Museum, and
the retention in London of a great single work of classical
Greek sculpture, have the great advantage of inertia on their
side. Their arguments need not be good; indeed they need
deploy no actual arguments at all. Thus, one may patiently
point out that the sculpture is mutilated by its enforced
separation, that this is a highly unusual not to say unique
situation, and that there exists no court or body that can
enforce any 'precedent' in any case, and *still* be met by the
jeering retort that return of the Parthenon Marbles will empty
not just the British Museum but all British museums.

Still, all efforts to shift the apparently immovable (in this
case, the certainty of its own rectitude on the part of a section
of the British establishment) have had their moments of
discouragement.

CHRISTOPHER HITCHENS

The request for the restitution of the Parthenon Marbles is not
made by the Greek government in the name of the Greek
nation or of Greek history. It is made in the name of the

cultural heritage of the world and with the voice of the mutilated monument itself, that cries out for its Marbles to be returned.

EVANGELOS VENIZELOS,
GREEK MINISTER OF CULTURE

66

The hot breeze carried the scent of oregano across the plains of Sparta to the airfield hidden at the end of tracks between laurels and tufts of pine.

Constantine Dragos and the assault team had assembled, having successfully avoided the roadblocks manned by police and military units watching for suspect vehicles driven by P17N terrorists. They were in the briefing area, an isolated and derelict former Greek Air Force administration block. Stratis and Tselios from Chios: muscular, broad-shouldered and dark. The diminutive and dour Cretan, Abatzi, wearing dark glasses, was fiddling with his worry beads. Kalaris from Hydra, his fair hair cut short, had the squashed profile of the pugilist, his head set bull-like on the physique of the body-builder. Demetra Ipsilanti, in a sleeveless white sweatshirt and jeans, slim and dark like her mother, was the silent one. Only Zei was absent, already in the United Kingdom.

Dragos perched on the edge of a crate. He explained there was no hurry. No rush. He was very cool. There was no sense of either fear or danger about him and his fellow Greeks seemed impressed. He asked them to alter their watches to British time. 'We're looking at complete success,' he said, 'to confuse the likely opposition. The idea's been planted in the minds of the British Security Services that the mission is aborted. As an additional fail-safe it is now rescheduled to Saturday at three a.m. British time. We'll be remaining here until departure. The inward route remains the same. First, from here to Altenhall. Then the rapid transfer to the Chinook. The flight to Colchester. The transfer to the container wagon. Then to London and the British Museum, arriving at precisely 0.300 hours. Shortly, I'll take you through the procedures of entry. The tasks in the museum itself. The exit procedures. And finally the return route. We'll also rehearse emergency combat procedures, in the event of being confronted by British police and Security Service personnel. Demetra here knows the layout of the museum better than anyone does and she will take you through it stage by stage. Questions?'

'Do you have a weather update?' asked Abatzi.

'The latest reports suggest it will be ideal,' said Dragos. 'If there should be any change I will, of course, let you know.'

The mood of the group, in spite of the altered and now confirmed schedule, was surprisingly relaxed.

Stratis, who knew little of London, asked about Bloomsbury. He wanted to know how populated the area was and whether 'local residents, even in the early hours of morning, might alert the police to what they might perceive as something untoward going on'.

Pointing with his metal claw to large-scale maps, Dragos assured him, 'At that time of night, the immediate area surrounding the museum is relatively quiet.'

Yannis Tselios asked much the same kind of question about the landing field near Colchester. Once more, Constantine Dragos offered reassurance. The Chinook's flight path had been designed in such a way as to attract the minimum of attention. 'The local police will not be on alert.'

'Suppose a night patrol approaches us?' asked Kalaris. 'The Chinook is incredibly noisy.'

'I know,' said Dragos. 'But it gives us the speed we need. We have made exact distance and timing evaluations. Precise calculations as to fuel loads. We will be taking the same routes in and out. We will rely on speed and operational manoeuvrability to outpace any potential opposition.'

'And the contours of the terrain?' asked Stratis.

'Trust the pilot,' said Dragos.

'But you haven't answered my question about the approach of some police patrol,' Kalaris said. 'What do we say if they approach?'

'We explain that we have a minor technical problem and have called for help.'

'Who explains?' Kalaris persisted.

'I do,' said Dragos.

'Suppose they check it out?' Kalaris asked.

'Then we alert the container wagon via SW radio and it will proceed to Altenhall direct. And we extend the Boeing's departure time.'

'And if the police cause any other problems?' asked Tselios.

'It depends how serious they are,' said Dragos with a tone of detachment.

'If they pose a real threat?' Tselios said.

'We have weapons,' said Dragos. 'We use them. But that's only an extreme eventuality. We are not expecting to walk into some pre-planned ambush, and the local population is rural and scattered.'

Then Dragos explained in detail where each of them would be positioned on the outward and return journeys. In the Chinook. The Boeing. And in the container wagon. He went on to discuss the exact details of the loading and the securing of the Marbles in the container wagon and aircraft. Abatzi asked whether Dragos could afford to abandon what was his responsibility, the Hanakawa mobile combined forklift and transportation unit.

'We'll have no further use for it,' said Dragos. 'The British are welcome to keep it. And when they impound the Chinook the same applies. Any other questions?' There was none. 'I suggest we have a break for some lunch. Afterwards we'll once more consider the entry to the museum, its interior and our exit route. And then the procedures for the return of the Marbles.'

They left the room talking about the mission. No one mentioned the extent of the risk they were being so well paid to take.

Constantine Dragos's mood of certainty, the absolute conviction he showed in himself and in the ability of the group to succeed, was pervasive. Morale was high.

67

The morning sun sparkled on the Thames at high tide. But in the Director General's office at Vauxhall Cross the air-conditioning produced an artificial chill. He leaned forward across his desk to face Shaw.

'What, in this instance,' he began, 'is the government policy we are prosecuting? I'll tell you. The policy, as far as the Elgin Marbles are concerned, is that they remain in this country. I'm not interested in the arguments against the policy. No. The present position is, very simply, that in order to ensure that they remain here you have pursued certain actions. Knowing that an attempt would be made to remove them by Greeks to Greece, you took the course of allowing the plan to go ahead so that, with prior ground intelligence from Prevezer, the attempt would be halted and the Greeks responsible detained, and then the international community would see that Greece was acting in an indefensible way. Thus the growing tide of opinion would turn in favour of the UK. The success would be very sweet. That, in essence, is what you set out to achieve, is it not? Am I correct?'

'Yes. By and large that is correct.'

'But matters have taken a very dangerous turn.'

'We have lost Christiane, yes.'

'In addition, we have lost Cleo Ipsilanti along with one of her daughters.'

'Yes, we have.'

'And we don't know where the other one is.'

'No, we don't.'

'And finally we have no clue whatsoever as to what the disposition of the Greek syndicate may be.'

'No, we haven't.'

'We cannot even be sure whether they have aborted their operation, can we?'

'No, we can't.'

'And the cover arranged for the dead man Nezeritis as some terrorist isn't really holding firm, is it?'

'Perhaps, if I may say so, that's a matter for the CIA and the Greeks.'

'I know it is. And it happens to be their view. As a matter of fact, mine too.' He began to sweep imaginary specks of dust from the surface of his desk. 'Tell me, Marion, if you were in my shoes, what would you do now?'

'We have nothing to lose,' she said, with conviction. 'No one has acted in bad faith.'

'That's not what I asked you. I asked you what you would do if you were in my shoes.'

'Stick to basic principles. Simple. Don't waiver.'

'Which might be, to use your word, simple,' said the Director General, 'if circumstances were not so very different. I admire your determination. Everyone does. But, Marion, it's not enough, is it?'

'I can only advise you to think yourself into the Greeks' minds. Nothing will have altered the determination of the Athens syndicate to succeed.'

'I'm in no position to imagine what the Greeks think. Is that what Rosslyn told you to do? To think yourself into their minds?'

'He told me nothing.'

'Really. Nothing?' he inquired. 'Nothing. I'd say nothing is about the length and breadth of it, wouldn't you, Marion?' This bordered on sarcasm.

'That's the truth,' said Shaw.

'I don't actually know what the truth is, Marion. Let me rehearse things again. Yours has been a high-wire act. Very risky. But the wire has snapped. With Prevezer gone, we have no more covert access to the Greeks. The Athens police chief is a law unto himself. We have no access to Cleo Ipsilanti and we don't know where she is. Languishing in a police cell? Or altogether somewhere else in Europe? God alone knows. I don't. You don't. Does Dragos?'

'I have no idea. How could I have?'

'Then there you are, Marion. And we must always bear in mind that you were the one who suggested we see to her protection. You signed on the Tunims and gave approval that the man Rosslyn be responsible. Too late. Too late.' He had the habit of repeating himself when he was trying to control his anger. 'Too late. The Greeks are loose cannons, aren't they? They can do quite extraordinary damage, can't they?' He slowly withdrew the copy of the letter from Naumann Bartenstein from beneath the papers on his desk and folded his hands on top of it. 'We can't ignore the inevitability of the questions that will be asked. Unpleasant questions. We can always try to keep the lid on. Unfortunately, the lid is off now. Too many outsiders already know the score.'

'Which outsiders? What people?'

'What people? Oh, I'll tell you very shortly. I mean, the Service will be made to look incompetent, unreliable and irresponsible to an unimaginable degree. We have the Foreign Secretary growing itchy. The Americans are suspicious. Our Greek colleagues likewise. Then we'll have some footling parliamentary committee asking questions. Scapegoats will be found. Heads, or shall we say the head, will be on the block.' He looked at her intently and left her in no doubt that hers was the head he was referring to. 'Haven't you felt, Marion, just once, that you've failed to ensure the proper degree of security to achieve success?'

'Sorry? I don't understand.'

'Then, if I can, I will explain in words of one syllable.' He raised his arms and folded his hands behind his neck. 'Our friend succeeded in gaining the cooperation of one Dr Einem. Is the name familiar to you?'

'No.'

'Einem is an Austrian lawyer,' he said. 'You're quite sure you don't know of him?'

'No, I don't.'

'So be it. Let's turn now to Zurich. The morning news from Zurich is as good or, depending on one's point of view, as bad as could be expected. A Dr Farenkamp has given our man a full and frank account of his dealings with one Miltiades Zei, one of Dragos's senior people. You know of Zei? Have you had any dealings with him?

'No, I haven't.'

'Then let's turn to one Air Commodore Knott, who was paid a visit unannounced at his home outside Southampton. You know of him?'

'No.'

'Pity. The Air Commodore had no alternative but to give a bald account of his dealings with Zei. Money, a great deal of money, passed one way or another from Zei to Knott. Mark you, it isn't the passage of the payments that at once concerns me. No. Rather, it's the nature, let's say, of Zei's purpose. First, from Farenkamp he received instruction in the handling of two Wolff cranes. Second, in Southampton he purchased a Chinook. What do you surmise from this?'

'What I've already told you. It confirms the Athens syndicate will launch the operation.'

'And it also confirms that too many, far too many outsiders have their fingers in the pie. Rosslyn we know about. Then there's Menzies Tunim, who is right now here in the building.'

She looked at him with astonished silence.

'Yes, Menzies Tunim. Right here now. And I have asked that his brother be arrested and held *incommunicado pro tem*. Until we can make very sure those shits keep their mouths shut. God knows what rumours they may have spread already.'

'I doubt they have.'

'Perhaps you do doubt. So do I. It's too late for doubt, Marion. Things have run dangerously out of control, haven't they? What began, I have to say, in your mind as a deception seems to have affected you.'

'I don't follow.'

'Think.'

'Sorry?'

'Oh, for God's sake, don't keep up this charade. You've deceived yourself.'

'I most certainly have not.'

'You have. And you've deceived me.'

257

Shaw was about to comment when the Director General's personal assistant came in. 'Vienna asks me to show you this,' she said.

The Director General thanked her. As she retreated from the office, he glanced at the single sheet of paper. Shaw watched him in silence as he read the contents and confirmation of the Dragos family's purpose:

Codicil to the Last Will and Testament of
Stelio Constantine Alexios Dragos

I, the undersigned, Stelio Constantine Alexios Dragos, wishing to settle my estate after my death, and being of sound mind, am proceeding with the present handwritten Codicil to my Will containing my Last Wishes, and order as follows:

Should my death occur before the restitution of the Parthenon Marbles to the Acropolis, my Estate will provide, inter alia, *finance nationally and internationally to the Secret Organization or Institution or Body with monies in excess of the Nobel Foundation in Sweden for restitution of the Elgin Marbles presently housed in the British Museum, London, being the so-called property of the United Kingdom.*

I hereby direct and order the Executors of my Will, my son Alexios Constantine Stelio Dragos, Eleftheria Jocasta Lazopoulos (my Secretary), Alexander Elias Vayakakos, Stamatis Kostas Ioannis Ipsilanti and Ioannis Ipsilanti (my Lawyers) to establish by whatever means the Organization in Athens or Vaduz, Liechtenstein, with the above-mentioned purposes, as well as similar and other such purposes at their absolute discretion, determined by a majority among them, and also to draw upon the articles and by-laws of the said Foundation, in accordance with the Law for the operation of the same.

Variously witnessed at the Office of Stamatis Kostas Ipsilanti and Ioannis Ipsilanti by the above-mentioned Executors.

Athens, Greece

It confirmed what he already knew. The Dragos family would stop at nothing. But how far had they now got with their planning and preparations?

Shaw was saying, 'Listen to me '

'No, Marion, you listen, you listen to me. There's the murder of Dragos's lawyer, erstwhile husband of Cleo Ipsilanti, the father of her daughters and Prevezer's friend. Don't you see the dilemma of the Athens police chief? Oh yes, he might assist Dragos up to the point of conspiring, if you will, to undertake the crime in the name of patriotism. But murder, if we are to imagine, as I do, that Dragos has been responsible for the deaths of Ioannis Ipsilanti and Christiane, then that's one step too far, isn't it? So what does he do? He starts to clean out the stables. He sets Cleo and her daughter free. If release from the Witness Protection Scheme can be said to constitute a sort of freedom. Think yourself into the police officer's shoes. That's what I'd do if I were him, wouldn't you?'

'I can't tell.'

'But what I can tell you is this. It would not be too late, in normal circumstances, to put the lid on matters. To achieve a degree of the necessary damage limitation. We have Rosslyn off the scene. He remains a signatory to the Act. If, say, he were to talk to the press, if he were to announce that you had conspired to allow the robbery to take place, then we'd press immediate charges and utterly discredit him. I have little doubt, possibly for other reasons, that Cleo Ipsilanti will remain silent. The Tunims we know about. So too the man Knott. But there are others who may not stay silent. Others outside the reach of British jurisdiction. The Austrian Farenkamp for one, and doubtless other beneficiaries of the Dragos largesse. God knows how many they add up to. And there is our American friend, Riley, and the Greek, Georgiadis. Too much, far too much, is creeping out into the light of day, Marion.'

Shaw looked at the floor and shook her head.

'I have no great illusions,' said the Director General, 'about my ability to stem the flow. Or your ability. Or, for that matter, anyone else's. Do you suggest I telephone sympathetic editors of the quality press?'

'No crime has been committed.'

'Quite so. None on British soil. Anyhow, not yet.'

He took a sip from the glass of mineral water on his desk.

'Or,' he said, wiping his lips, 'one could have a word with our friends at Thames House or Scotland Yard, and tell them we believe there'll be an attempt, a violent and armed attempt by Greeks, to enter the British Museum and remove the Marbles. We could advise, say, that some form of indefinite armed protection be put in place. Then, suppose it never happens, and we are asked to foot the bill? We would have to explain away our sources. Rather, I would. I would have to face the charge that I knowingly approved an operation that failed and led to the death of one of my officers. You see, there'll be an inquiry into Christiane's death. And so the unholy mess spreads. Swilling at my feet. That's the essence of it, isn't it, Marion?'

'I really don't see it like that.'

'Oh, I know you don't,' he said shortly. 'Particularly because you have, with great care and deliberation, withheld personal matters from me and pursued the whole thing with an obsession that at first I found admirable in its way, and now find profoundly worrying.'

'How come?'

He sensed the defensiveness in her attitude and the evasion in her mind. She had always been something of the fanatic. The solitary and dedicated hard-working officer. He was not alone in having considered Shaw a brilliant choice for handling Greece. The coldness and ruthless objectivity about Shaw had brought her considerable success. He knew of her ability to exploit other people's weaknesses, and suddenly found himself wondering for a moment whether she reckoned she had him in her sights. Except that he held all the aces.

'Are you prepared to tell me the truth?'

'About what?'

The Director General hesitated, allowing her perhaps to believe he genuinely did not know the answer to the question he was about to put. The answer contained in the supplementary facsimile that his man in Vienna had sent in strict confidence. Confirming what the payment of £10,000 in Austrian Schillings had bought from the legal archive of Naumann Bartenstein.

'To put it bluntly,' he announced, 'the operation is headed towards the precipice.'

Shaw looked enraged. 'You authorized it. What more can I usefully add?'

'I'll tell you what more you can add,' he said. 'You can do me the courtesy of explaining why you have allowed personal issues to get in the way. Personal and private issues which you would've been very much wiser not to have disguised or buried when you first joined the Service. Oh yes, you'll tell me that others should have discovered such matters. But we can't turn back the clock. Meanwhile, others have sat were you are sitting now and they have explained something of your past. I would've preferred, Marion, that it had been you.'

'I'm sorry?'

'Oh, I know the old maxim, once the liar always the liar. You and I are paid to lie. We're trusted, are we not, though, to be the judges of what constitutes the lie? We can dissemble. We can even confess errors of duty to our friends and peers. And when we leave the Service some of us can fictionalize fantasies of persecution and paranoia. But we don't believe in fairy stories, do we, you and I, Marion? But it is the moment of recruitment that is so seductive, isn't it? The moment of knowing that you are truly wanted, that you have talents and abilities that qualify you to lead the secret life. For us, the joining of the happy band of liars is life's turning point. In other words, once the liar, always the liar. The art or science, what you will, is to prevent the lies destroying one's own life.' He paused and smiled. 'You must have heard this before at some time or other. And there are those lies of omission, aren't there, Marion?'

'I have omitted nothing,' she said.

'Would I be right,' he said, 'in thinking that you have some Greek blood in your veins?'

She laughed. 'For heaven's sake.'

'I just want to be sure.'

'You're joking. Check my curriculum vitae.'

'Oh, I have. I have. And it's only a small question I need the answer to. Perhaps, finally, it's of no consequence.'

'You have my answer. No.'

'If it's true, then we have no problem and together we can begin the business of discrediting anyone who may level accusations against us. Accusations that the operation may conceivably be, as it were, driven by some personal agenda.'

She looked at him in bewilderment. 'It is not.'

'Are you quite sure, Marion?' He had closed his eyes. 'Quite sure?'

'Quite sure.'

As though relieved, the Director General relaxed and breathed slowly. 'That's good. Good, Marion. Good. Before we decide upon the next and urgent moves, I'd just like to bring you up to date with something. Here.'

He handed her the facsimile of her mother's letter on the Naumann Bartenstein writing paper. Then he sat back in his chair, held his breath and watched her reactions.

For some time Marion Shaw sat quite still in silence.

'Isn't it true,' the Director General said, 'that Alexios Dragos is your father?'

Her face twitched.

'Think about what I've asked carefully,' the Director General continued. 'Is Dragos your father?' He was silent for a moment. Then he very sharply changed his tone. Now he was prosecuting counsel. 'You have lied and lied again. You have used the vast resources of the Service to bludgeon your way towards settling some sort of vendetta. To take revenge. To use the cover of the Service for your own personal and selfish ends. In the old days, I might now be looking at a species of traitor driven by rabid left-wing fanaticism. But that's not you. Your perverse fanaticism is personal. The feverish plots of a deeply traumatized mind. You are responsible for Prevezer's death and, believe me, I did have some dirt on her that you probably had no idea was in my possession. And I gave you the benefit of the doubt. That benefit has gone. You enjoy no benefit. You have abused my trust and time and again remorselessly betrayed the confidence your colleagues had in you.'

Shaw's fists were clenched. 'I take the gravest exception to what you're saying.'

'But everything I have said is based upon the truth, in so far as you understand the truth.'

'There's not a word of truth in it,' she said. 'In fact, I find what you've said deeply offensive. I can only imagine that someone, for some extraordinary reason, has fabricated the basis of what amounts to serious charges.'

'Very serious charges, Marion. And I'm well aware they will need pursuing at some length. All of which will take time. Time that isn't on our side. Because, you see, I want you to have Rosslyn released. On your word. I want you to see to it personally. After that, well, shall we say that fate is perhaps favouring the Greeks. I suggest you contact the prison and then take yourself home. Wait there, Marion, until you receive formal written notification.'

'Notification,' she asked, 'of what?'

'Dismissal.'

She stared at him unblinking.

'You understand the seriousness of your position,' he said. 'You've failed the Service. Failed me. Failed yourself.'

'May I –'

'May you what?' he interrupted.

'Consult a lawyer?'

'In due course,' he said bluntly. 'Otherwise, is there anything more you want to say to me?'

'What you've said is outrageous.'

'Perhaps. The question is, is it true?'

She was staring at him in anger. No, she was not going to make that call to Whitemoor and secure Rosslyn's release. Why should she?

'Is there anything more you want to say?' he repeated.

'Only perhaps –' Her voice trailed off.

'Perhaps what?'

'Perhaps you'll regret this.'

'I don't think so, Marion. Regret is the refuge of the guilty. It is not a word I very much like.'

But Shaw had already decided to end matters in her own way. To take matters into her hands with dreadful finality.

'You'll see,' she said. Then, standing by the door as she was leaving, she added, 'I wonder. Does Rosslyn know of your relationship with Cleo Ipsilanti . . . and your wife, does your wife know of your infidelity?'

It was her parting shot.

The Director General smiled at her. 'Cleo Ipsilanti is a friend of the family, Marion. A friend of the family.'

68

The attitude of the prison officers towards Rosslyn was neither friendly nor particularly hostile. Since the release of the most dangerous IRA terrorists, Whitemoor had once more assumed its treadmill-like routine. Like museum warders inured to the beauty of the objects they protect, so the prison officers outwardly seemed little interested in the threat their charges might pose.

Rosslyn's cell was clean and free of the usual pervasive prison odours. By night, the silence was oppressive. By day, the rattling of keys and the matey conversation of the officers punctuated the silence. The dehumanizing place reminded him of some hospital for the criminally insane.

He mostly thought of Shaw's so-called contingency plan. If it was carried out, well and good; if not, there was nothing he could do but wait, and face whatever charges the police or MI6 decided to level against him.

The morning after his interview with Shaw, Rosslyn's clothes were returned to him, and although he was denied the opportunity to exercise, to make a telephone call or watch TV in the recreation area, he was at least permitted to eat with his fellow inmates, among them Lambrakis.

Both at breakfast and again at lunch, to his relief, the other prisoners studiously ignored him, just as they ignored Lambrakis. Perhaps they had been told to keep their distance from the two new arrivals. No one offered him any explanation for this and he had little interest in being given one.

The two men asked after each other's well-being. Suspicious of the guards standing within earshot, they otherwise stayed silent.

Then came the evening meal of thinly buttered pre-sliced bread, stewed tea and what passed for a warm chicken salad. Rosslyn and Lambrakis were seated at opposite corners of their table, within easy reach of other. Rosslyn noticed that Lambrakis had his eyes on the movements of the prison officers supervising the meal. The prison officers seemed bored and liverish. Judging from the more comprehensible snippets of conversation, they were anxious to get off duty.

There was no warning whatsoever of what Lambrakis did as the meal ended. He had been solicitous towards Rosslyn, even friendly. Indeed, his movements were so subtle that later no one could be quite sure what happened next. One witness, an Iranian with little spoken English, said that Rosslyn did the violence to himself. Another maintained that a prison officer was responsible. No one saw Lambrakis remove the Elastoplast from his inner arm, squeeze the capsule and rub his thumb and forefinger with the brownish powerful chilli powder in the palm of his left hand. He leaned close to Rosslyn and whispered urgently, 'Let me see. Don't touch. Close your eyes.' As Rosslyn did so, Lambrakis streaked the brownish powder with a single wipe across Rosslyn's closed eyelids.

For a few seconds Rosslyn blinked. The powder worked its way into his eyes. Then he could no longer open his eyes and the agony was excruciating.

'Get water,' yelled Lambrakis. 'There's something in this shit food.' He was on his feet.

So was Rosslyn, moaning, feeling his way like a sightless man.

'Help him,' Lambrakis screamed.

Faced with the seriousness of Rosslyn's condition, which treatment had failed to alleviate, the duty medical orderly called an ambulance. In the company of a woman prison officer, Rosslyn was driven at high speed out of Whitemoor in the direction of Peterborough and the district hospital.

Forty minutes later, the ambulance arrived at the Peterborough hospital entrance in Alderman's Drive.

Handcuffed and complaining that he had been deprived of his sight, Rosslyn was led into Casualty and kept waiting, along with several other new admissions. He could just make out a youth who had apparently severed a finger, a drunk with a bloodied face, a barefoot teenage junkie, two pregnant Asian women and, between the junkie and the drunk, the figure of a man leaning on a heavy walking stick, his face hidden behind a newspaper. He remembered what Shaw had said: 'One of our people will be waiting in Casualty. He'll be carrying a walking stick. A friend. Leave the rest to our friend.'

Eventually, in the presence of the woman prison officer, a young duty doctor gently examined his badly swollen eyes. Rosslyn's vigorous protestations that he could see nothing finally persuaded the doctor that the patient needed to be kept in the hospital overnight.

'We'd prefer he was at Whitemoor,' said the woman prison officer.

'I can't advise that,' said the doctor, bathing Rosslyn's eyes.

'C'mon. C'mon. It can't be that serious,' said the prison officer.

'I'll be the judge of that,' the doctor said. 'So will the eye specialist, which is even more important.'

'When is he arriving then?'

'Some time tomorrow morning,' said the doctor.

'I want the specialist here tonight,' said the prison officer.

'Then you, my friend, had better be the one to tell him.'

'I'm telling you. The prisoner has to be returned to Whitemoor tonight. I have my orders.'

'So do I actually,' the doctor said. 'There's the serious risk of infection. I don't know what this substance is in the patient's eyes. Not until we've had it examined.'

'How long will that take, for God's sake?'

'It has nothing to do with God,' said the doctor. 'It'll be done first thing in the morning.'

'Can we have a talk outside a moment?' asked the prison officer. She sucked her teeth. 'Do you mind?'

'Not at all. But I've nothing else to add,' said the doctor. 'You've seen the people waiting out there. I have to see to them. Like you, I have my job to do.'

From the corner of his eye, through the glass panel in the door,

Rosslyn saw the blurred silhouette of the figure standing outside.

'They can wait,' the prison officer told the doctor. 'You and I need to have a talk. In private.'

'Very well,' said the doctor, unlocking the door to the adjacent examination room.

The doctor left the key in the lock. The door closed and Rosslyn was left alone. He blinked. Though his eyes were watery and swollen, his vision was good enough to see the door handle turn, then the door open, then the heavy walking stick. He recognized the figure he had seen behind the newspaper in an instant. The caretaker from St Sophia's in Moscow Road. The caretaker raised his hand in caution. Rosslyn watched him open the door to the adjacent room.

'There's a major emergency,' Rosslyn heard him tell the doctor. 'Please. You're needed.'

The doctor told the prison officer he'd be back shortly and hurried out to the reception area.

The walking stick twisted through the air, jabbing into the prison officer's open mouth. Rosslyn saw the fingers raised in protection too late to prevent the blow that struck her jaw. She sagged, her bulk overturning a portable waste-disposal unit, the blood from her mouth spreading across the white tiled floor.

The caretaker found the key to the handcuffs restraining Rosslyn's hands and unlocked them. 'Walk slowly,' he told Rosslyn.

In the reception area, people paid them no attention and there was no sign of the doctor. They walked towards the automatic doors, which slid open, then shut. Outside, they walked fast towards the car park. The caretaker dodged between the cars and Rosslyn followed him to a small black transit van.

'Get in the back,' the caretaker said. 'Stay beneath the blankets.'

Rosslyn climbed in, pulled the blankets over his head and felt the van move off.

69

With the setting of the sun across the plains of Sparta came some relief from the heat that had held the derelict airfield in its grip throughout the day. The quiet of the barren landscape gave no hint of the turmoil and confusion in the minds of those in London who might, even at this late hour, have set in motion the measures to entrap and foil the Dragos group.

Zei had returned to Sparta and, along with the rest of the group, he and Constantine Dragos made final preparations. Dragos showed the group over the Boeing now in readiness on the cleared runway. He impressed his subordinates as the hands-on flier.

They returned to the old administration block, where they made the final kit checks. The Kotte belts contained ammunition, survival kit and basic first-aid items. Each member of the group was provided with three syrettes of morphine fixed to a light neckband.

'Remember,' said Dragos, 'if you need to administer morphine to a casualty you use the casualty's syrette and not your own. You may need yours.'

Each was given the necessary climbing gear. The weight of equipment was kept to the bare minimum.

'Finally,' said Dragos, 'the no-smoking rule is to be followed. There will be no issue of rations on the outward flight other than mineral water. A packed meal will be handed out on the return flight.'

Then they returned to the administration block for the final rehearsals. By now they were completely familiar with the layout of the area surrounding the museum, the perimeter walls and the interior of the Duveen Gallery, and the disposition and weight of the Marbles themselves. They repeated the details of each move in, each move out. And the what-ifs . . . What if the police are alerted? What if the light restricts vision? What if the emergency procedures are called for? What if we have to regroup? Once more they double-checked the timings. Their exact positions at any given moment in the zone.

Practices complete, they were certain about how and where each detailed phase would take place. Watches were synchronized. Each watch had two faces. One was showing British, the other Greek time.

Fuelling and pre-flight checks completed, Constantine Dragos and Miltiades Zei took their seats in the pilots' cabin and donned their headsets. The rest of the group crossed the tarmac. There was no rush. They climbed aboard slowly and took their seats.

Dragos spoke over the intercom: 'Prepare for take-off.'

He fired the jets.

Gathering momentum, the Boeing roared down the runway in the barren landscape. Red and green lights blinking, it lifted, leaving a cloud of russet dust in its wake, and was airborne.

Ahead lay the route across Europe to the United Kingdom and Altenhall in Norfolk. The Chinook was waiting there for the flight to the landing strip outside Colchester and there, on stand-by, the container wagon stood in readiness to ferry them to Montague Place in London.

70

In London, Rosslyn and the caretaker were in the transit van, some five minutes away from St Sophia's in Moscow Road.

They had driven fast from Peterborough to London. Rosslyn calculated that the police would already be on the alert and the likelihood was that someone would have given them a description of the van and its two occupants. His eyes pained him but his vision was intact. Neither he nor the caretaker had any idea that the schedule for the robbery had been brought forward to between three and four a.m. the next day.

'Stop here,' said Rosslyn. 'Take a careful look in Moscow Road. They'll already be looking for the van. I'll wait for you across the road.' He indicated the doorway to a bed and breakfast house.

'You know where to contact Shaw?' said the caretaker.

'Yes.'

The caretaker handed Rosslyn the keys to the van. 'If I'm not back here in fifteen minutes you'd better leave.'

'I'll wait,' said Rosslyn. He caught sight of a pair of police officers down the street. 'If anything goes wrong, if the police stop you, put them on to Shaw.'

'Don't worry,' said the caretaker. 'And I'll handle the police if they've shown up. They know me. You can be sure it'll be OK.'

'We can't be sure of anything,' said Rosslyn.

'Maybe, maybe not.'

'And thanks for everything you've done.'

'My pleasure,' said the caretaker, reaching over to the floor in front of the passenger seat. 'Shaw told me to give you this.' He lifted the backpack and Rosslyn took it.

Rosslyn watched him walk down the street and cross it diagonally to avoid the police officers. They were questioning two youths and paid the caretaker no attention. It seemed to be a good omen.

Taking the backpack with him, he left the transit van and made for the doorway to the bed and breakfast house. He unzipped the backpack. Inside it he found a Wildrock climbing harness, gloves, a length of nylon climbing rope, karabiners, pitons and a lightweight hammer. A plastic bag contained a pair of high-friction butyl rubber-soled rock boots, size 11. He had to admire Shaw. She had even got his shoe size right.

The caretaker walked slowly into Moscow Road, his eyes alert. The Byzantium had closed for the night and a few dim lights flickered behind the windows of St Sophia. He looked back occasionally, but the pavements were deserted and he saw no one waiting in any of the parked cars.

He was almost at the entrance to the cathedral courtyard when the lights went on. Dazzled, the caretaker raised his forearm to shield his eyes.

'Police,' said the disembodied voice. 'Don't move.'

Two figures emerged from behind the lights. The first was the woman police officer whom Shaw had charged with responsibility for Rosslyn's 'protection'. Behind her, near the parked Audi, was the SO10 Chief Superintendent. And to his left, in the shadows, stood the Director General of MI6.

The fifteen minutes passed. Rosslyn waited two more and then, uneasy, he crossed the road to the transit van. He was tempted to take a look at Moscow Road, but at once thought better of it. He was tempted too to call Shaw from the nearest telephone kiosk, but she had cautioned him against telephoning her.

The warning voice in his head told him not to use the transit van, but he had no cash on him. The choice was to walk or use the van to get to Shaw's place in Frognal. He decided to risk the latter course. He took the backpack with him.

71

The night traffic was light and twenty minutes later he reached Shaw's flat in the Old Mansion. He drove on past the house and parked the transit van in a side road beneath trees and away from the streetlight. Then he walked downhill the rest of the short way to the darkened house and across the courtyard, his shoes crunching the gravel. There were no cars parked there and the house had a shuttered, deserted look.

He found the bell marked simply 'Top Floor Flat'. But he did not ring it immediately. Instead he moved around the house slowly in the dark, pausing every few steps to listen for untoward noises of anyone else out there on a stakeout, or noises from inside the house; searching for the face at the window or the curtain's movement. At the back of the house, he found a second entrance door. He tried the handle and was worried to find it unlocked. Moving it ajar, he peered inside and saw what seemed to be a narrow and steep staircase. He considered stepping inside, closing the door behind him and turning on the lights, but changed his mind.

Instead, he retraced his steps to the entrance to the annexe, sounded the bell to the top floor flat and then waited, watching the empty courtyard and the trees swaying slightly in the night breeze. There was no reply. *Maybe you are waiting in Moscow Road and this whole thing's the final trap? Or are you up there waiting for me with a little group of your nasty friends from Special Branch?*

He rang the bell a second time, for a little longer than before. And still there was no answer and no lights went on in any of the windows. *If you're out, Shaw, do I wait here for you to return?* But there was the night to face on the London streets without protection as quarry. He had no bolthole. No cash. No weapon. He needed to see Shaw and now.

Keeping close to the side of the house in darkness, he returned once more to the other entrance door and pushed it open. It was on the latch and he decided, in case of unwanted later visitors, to lock himself in. He dropped the latch and slowly climbed the stairs in darkness.

Like the main part of the house, the annexe was of two storeys. What seemed to be the entrance door to the top flat was a hefty door with three Banham security locks. Like the door downstairs, they too were unlocked. It was very quiet and the faint squeal of the door that broke the silence made him start. His mouth dried and he felt the fear rising in his chest.

In normal circumstances he would by now have called out and turned on the lights, but he was safer in the dark. His pulse was beating in his neck and he was afraid. *There's no one here.* The passage led into a kitchen and dining room all in one. There was a smoked-glass-fronted refrigerator with a light on inside. A pilot gaslight glowed on top of the stove. He sensed a staleness about the place. It was as if it had been abandoned in a hurry.

Crossing the kitchen to the high windows, he closed the wooden shutters. Then he opened the door to the refrigerator so that the light partially illuminated this end of the kitchen. There were cooking utensils and some dishes in the drying rack by the sink. And to one side of the sink he saw a telephone answering machine. The red light was blinking and the small window glowing green above the buttons showed that Shaw had received several messages. Perhaps he would listen to them later.

His eyes were now accustomed to the near-darkness. He could see into the room across the kitchen and he made his way towards it. This was her bedroom. It smelled musty and almost familiar. That's it. The recognizable odour. For a brief moment he thought he smelled Cleo's scent. The low bed was unmade. A pillow lay on the floor by the bedside table. He lifted the telephone by the reading lamp. It was still connected.

To the right was the bathroom. He slowly opened the door and felt the familiar wave of coldness numb his spine. His throat and lips were parched. There was the heavy scent of body lotion and, when he peered at the bath, he saw that it was full of soapy water. He dipped a finger in. It was quite cold. From the corner of his eye, he saw his shadowy reflection in the mirror above the washbasin. *Let in the air.*

From somewhere else, further inside the flat, came the sound of an eerie rattling. *Shutters perhaps.* Then he distinctly heard a floorboard creak. *There's someone here.* Again there was the eerie creak; the dull sound of footsteps moving slowly, carefully placed. He could almost feel the slight vibration of the movement. *There's someone here.*

He returned to the passage, where he saw unopened mail on a narrow wall-ledge. There was an open bag of boiled sweets next to the unopened copy of *The Economist*. He ate one of the sweets. The hard sugar coating crackled and the juice of the dissolving sweet tasted bitter on his tongue, like lime or lemon. He scrunched up the paper wrapper and put it in his pocket.

Now he stood in the doorway of the room at the end of the passage. He could make out the closed shutters but little else except a digital clock on the mantelpiece. Closing the door behind him, he stood still and listened. There was silence. But he was sure he could feel the floorboards moving. Very slightly. He turned the door handle and opened the door until it was no more than five centimetres ajar.

Suddenly the silence was broken by the telephone ringing in the kitchen. Once. Twice. Three times. Then the answering machine clicked on. He heard the woman on the telephone clear her throat. Then a pause.

'My friend, if you're there, turn on the lights.' There was a long pause. 'Turn on the lights . . .' The voice was instantly recognizable. It was Cleo's.

The machine clicked off and there was silence again.

This is where you keep your head. Where are you? Outside, with the police, with Shaw, with Special Branch? They must know I'm not armed. They can come here and get me.

He listened. There was no sound. No creak. No tell-tale vibration

275

of the floorboards. No. He wouldn't turn the lights on. Not yet. He wouldn't fall for that one. Rather, take a look-see outside. Cross the room. Open the shutters a fraction. Get a little light in the room. Give things time. Take it slowly. Very slowly.

He moved forward, bumped against a sofa, knocked a table leg with his shin. He reached out for the fastener to the nearest shutter, lifted the metal bar from its slot and then very slowly edged the shutter open. There was more light. But not much. He looked outside.

A car was coming slowly up the hill, its headlights raised. It passed by and then there were several more, and the glare of the passing headlights flashed across the room. His eyes were drawn to the desk at the other side. To the dead computer screen. And the sudden passing light from the car headlights showed the shape in the chair. He froze. Then the room was returned to darkness and at the same moment the phone rang once more.

The answering machine clicked on and again he heard Cleo saying, 'My friend, turn on the lights . . .'

Not until I've seen what that shape is, as if I need to know. I already do. It's a woman's body.

He edged towards the desk and the shape, hoping that his eyes had deceived him. But he had been right first time. The body lay slightly sideways across the desk. He hesitated before touching it. He wanted to look. To be certain. He reached closer and touched the back of the desk chair. It was sticky to the touch, and now the touch and the smell told him that this was cold blood. His foot touched something on the floor. He leaned down in a crouch and felt cold metal. It was a handgun.

He carefully detached the magazine and, fingering it carefully, found it was loaded. Holding it in his right hand, he reached forward with his other hand and touched the hair matted with blood and flesh. A splinter of bone pricked his forefinger. Holding his breath, he winced, involuntarily whispering, 'Holy shit.'

Behind him the door opened. He could just make out the figure in the doorway and some sixth sense told him whoever was there was carrying a gun.

He twisted round, both feet apart, releasing the safety catch, the gun raised. 'Don't move!' he yelled.

The lights went on in a sudden blaze. Blinded, he blinked. When his eyes could focus properly he saw, gun raised, Cleo.

72

Ten minutes later in Norfolk, the Boeing landed at Altenhall. Under cover of darkness, the group of seven transferred unobserved to the waiting Chinook.

With two sets of rotor blades and weighing some twenty-three tonnes, some eighteen metres wide and six metres high, the helicopter was an imposing aircraft powered by two Lycoming turbojet engines. Zei had commissioned a crew from Messinian Air to fly it.

The pilots checked the controls. In turn, outside on the tarmac, a crewman checked the responsiveness of the rotor blades. The first engine on the port side started, spewing acrid fumes, and then the starboard engine. The ground crew retreated. A crewman lifted the chocks into the helicopter and it taxied on its six wheels along the ground, ensuring that the sky above was clear for lift-off.

First the nose lifted off the ground, then the wheels at the rear were raised, and the helicopter hovered some five metres up, above a cloud of dust. It lifted gradually, the airframe juddering, and the speed reached thirty-eight knots. Then it climbed, increasing speed swiftly, up to the cruising speed of 150 knots. The dust settled on the tarmac below.

Coated with plastic and soundproofing material, the interior was sparse and smelled strongly of nauseating aviation fuel. The seven sat on the non-slip black strips on the alloy floor next to their equipment, strapped in place for safety. Dragos, wearing headsets, talked to the pilot. Then he communicated with the others on the intercom and rehearsed the emergency procedures in the unlikely event that the police might be showing interest in the airfield outside Colchester. 'One, we will stay aboard. Two, if we're disembarking, we'll get back in and leave our equipment on the ground.'

73

The kitchen wall-clock in Shaw's flat said it was past one in the morning. In the darkness, stunned by the horror of what she had found, Cleo had been unsure whether it had been Rosslyn there or someone else. From the passage just outside the door, she had used her mobile telephone to call Shaw's answering machine.

Her face was drawn and seemed paler than Rosslyn remembered. They embraced in silence.

'Your eyes?' she whispered. 'What happened?'

He briefly explained about Lambrakis's assault in Whitemoor.

'The damage isn't permanent,' he said quietly. 'How long have you been here?'

'Not long. I couldn't fathom out why Shaw wasn't here. And then I found her. Then I played the messages on the answering machine here. They're from Olympia. For Shaw. You have to hear what she says. Listen.'

MESSAGE ONE: Seven of them left Sparta after nightfall tonight for the UK. The plan is being carried out tomorrow, *Saturday, not Sunday*, between three and four a.m. London time. All the transport they need is waiting in the UK. They are heavily armed.

MESSAGE TWO: Demetra is with Constantine and Zei, along with four other men whose identities I don't know.

MESSAGE THREE: Alexios Dragos has left Athens. No one knows where he is. The police and military are on full terrorist alert.

MESSAGE FOUR: I need to know my mother's safe with you. It is too dangerous for me here. I'm leaving Greece for Paris. I won't call again until I've spoken to my mother.

'What did she mean by writing "pluck it out"?' Cleo asked. She was reading the note that had been next to Shaw's body.

'"If thine eye offend thee, pluck it out,"' said Rosslyn.

The loaded Sig Sauer P226 lay on the kitchen table. 'You don't think there's any chance it could've been someone else?' Cleo said.

'No,' said Rosslyn. He erased Olympia's messages. 'The signs are that she definitely did it herself. The gun was lying on the floor. If someone else had done it they'd have taken it away with them.' He tucked the handgun in his belt. 'We can't stay here. Let's talk outside.'

He turned off the lights and they left the house in silence. He wanted to get clean away with Cleo. To find somewhere to wait it out with her. But where?

He imagined what it would be like at Vauxhall Cross once the news was known. The Director General cursing the outcome of Shaw's obsession, considering every available ploy to limit damage, trying to prevent the measures he would be forced to take from looking ill-considered, the desperate concealment of evidence.

Cleo's hire car was parked a short way from the transit van.

'Do you know what she had in common with me?' Cleo asked him.

'Same firm, same balls-up?'

'More than that.' Cleo unlocked the car. 'Do you know who her father was?'

'Yes, I do.'

'Alexios won't give up, Alan. He never will. Constantine will be here in the UK by now. Demetra's with them and I'm going to get her out of this unholy mess.'

Rosslyn stared at the tree near the streetlight across the road. The leaves seemed to be shuddering in the night breeze.

'You know I want Demetra back safe,' Cleo said. 'Aren't you going to call the police or Shaw's people?'

'It's no use. Dragos's team will be fully armed. If the police are called in, they'll be armed and won't take prisoners.' His face was blank. 'If we go there too, say, if we try and talk her out of it, the same applies. No prisoners. There'll be the God's own shooting match.'

'I'm going there, Alan. I want to be there. I have to be there with her. Don't you understand?'

'What I understand is that if they're planning on completing the robbery in the early hours, then there's nothing we can do to stop it. It's too late, Cleo. You should get out of London and away from trouble.'

For a second Rosslyn remembered the moment he thought he'd found her body in the well. Now, in the warmth of the car, even next to Cleo, he felt cold, almost feverish, and he remembered the awful sensation of the grief rising in his chest in spasms.

'I put up a fight last time,' she was saying. 'Now we have to save Demetra from herself.'

74

The pilot gave the three-minute warning and a crew member began to unfasten the straps securing the equipment. First, the climbing gear. Then the arms and ammunition: the 203s and American MI6 Armalite rifles; the 5.56 light-support machine guns, Minimis, with 500 rounds each; the cylindrical white phosphorous grenades for smoke-screen purposes.

The Chinook was now some five metres above the ground. Its speed zero.

Another crew member in a restraining harness leaned from the starboard exit and checked the ground for unexpected obstacles. He continued confirming the position to the pilot, who had no sight of the ground:

'Forward ten units. Three. Steady.'

The tailgate lowered. Now the pilot manoeuvred the helicopter just above the ground. Its engines roared. The rotor blades thundered. There was the same pervasive smell of aviation fuel. The rear wheels touched the tarmac first, then the aircraft's front wheels. It taxied some way along the ground and came to a stop.

The seven Greeks jumped down to the tarmac. Carrying their equipment, they walked quickly away from the Chinook, across the grass to the open barrier.

The Mercedes Actros was parked under the tarpaulin among a heap of scrap cars. Miltiades Zei climbed into the cabin and took the wheel. Moments later, the wagon pulled out on to the road for London.

75

As the Director General gave no clue as to his identity, the caretaker assumed that this man questioning him was a plain-clothes police officer who knew that Rosslyn had been sprung from the hospital in Peterborough. But, sitting next to him in the back of an unmarked police car, the man never once suggested that the caretaker had a central role in Rosslyn's escape.

'You've come across Mr Rosslyn perhaps?' the Director General said. 'You know him?'

'I've never heard of anyone of that name.'

'He's a highly dangerous man.'

'I wouldn't know.'

'And what about George Vayakakos, did you perhaps know him?'

'He was a regular visitor here to St Sophia's. A member of the congregation.'

'The priest has been most helpful,' the Director General said vaguely, as if he expected the caretaker to follow the priest's example.

The caretaker knew the priest well enough to know he would always be helpful. But he doubted that the priest had said anything private or personal about Vayakakos. He gave the Director General a convincing look of bafflement and made no comment.

'You have been seen by a Ms Shaw, haven't you?' asked the Director General.

'I don't know anyone by that name.'

'She's from the Foreign Office.'

'I wouldn't know.'

'She tells me she has seen you.'

'She must be confusing me with someone else.'

The Director General was getting nowhere. 'Very well,' he said. 'If you wouldn't might waiting here a bit longer.'

'I do mind.'

'For a little bit longer,' said the Director General sharply.

He left the caretaker sitting in the car and went to speak to the Chief Superintendent. 'Either,' he said, 'he's a very good liar or we've got the wrong man.'

'He matches the description the prison officer gave us.'

'Then get her down here to identify him.'

'I'm afraid, sir, she's being kept in hospital overnight. She's in no state to travel.'

The Director General returned to his Rover, parked down the street. He silently cursed the police. It wasn't ponderous detective work that was needed now but action. He felt certain that Shaw held the key to the Greeks' intentions. How far had they got? He had to admit he had no idea. But Shaw? Surely, she must know the full picture. His hands seemed firmly tied. He was in no position to inform the Commissioner that he suspected there was going to be a major incident at the British Museum. Sooner or later, his sources would inevitably be revealed. Then all the dirty washing would have to come out.

It was a fantastic bind. If only he had never authorized Shaw to run matters in the first place. His authorization was a matter of record. If he was exposed, and there seemed every likelihood that he would be, then his world would fall apart. Suppose the Greeks achieved their aim and succeeded in taking the Elgin Marbles. *You knew about it, didn't you?* He imagined the Foreign Secretary's snappy rhetoric. *'And what did you do? You summarily sacked the one woman who could have prevented this government, this nation, being held up to the ridicule of the world. And you did so at the one moment when this could have been prevented. Why, oh why, in the name of God, didn't you make a clean breast of it?*

Then, plain for all to see, there was that Will. The Greek billionaire had been planning this whole thing for what – months, years? And all the while we were employing his fanatic of a daughter, who was out of her tiny mind.

Cracked mind or not, something allowed him still to admire Shaw. There had been plenty of bad apples in the Service, the drunks, the psychotics and the traitors. But never before in its history had anyone used the machinery of the secret world to settle some personal score. Actually, if you thought about it, the wonder was that no one had ever done so before.

And there was Cleo. Would she, he wondered, make her way back to Shaw's place? In one way, he hoped she would do just that. He knew very well that Cleo would cooperate and give him the covert intelligence on the Greeks that he desperately needed. He had to talk to Shaw.

There was still no answer from the telephone in Frognal. All he got was Shaw's voice: 'There is no one here to take your call at present. If you would be kind enough to leave your name and number I'll get back to you. Speak after the beep.'

He killed the call and cursed. Then he dialled his personal assistant's mobile phone. She wasn't answering either.

Perhaps he'd been wrong about Shaw. Should he have tried to win her round to find out everything she knew? Perhaps his action had been precipitous. What was it she had said? 'You'll regret this'? Some sixth sense now told him that she might well have been right.

76

To give her credit, the Director General's personal assistant had decided to use her initiative. Her chief had told her to raise Shaw 'no matter what'. She was privy to what had happened in Peterborough. That someone had sprung Rosslyn even before the Director General's order that the prisoner be released had been passed on. Secretly in awe of her chief, she admired his cunning. They would put a tail on the man Rosslyn and see where it led. Sooner or later he would make a false move. Unfortunately, the escape had now taken place and the legmen had been denied their quarry. She had read the description of the man Rosslyn, the details of the black transit van and the police statement that, though highly dangerous, they believed he was unarmed. She repeatedly telephoned Shaw and still she got no answer.

She rather liked Shaw. Had she come from the same background, who knows, she might even now be more than just the elevated dogsbody. She was aware that the meeting between Shaw and her chief had been a bitter one. Shaw had left the Director General's office in tears and the personal assistant had run after her to make sure she was all right. Shaw, alas, had got to the lift first, and the last the personal assistant had seen of her was just as the doors were closing. Shaw, her back to the doors, had been rummaging in her shoulder bag, presumably for a tissue. The chief could be a bully. And to say that the Service treated women badly was an understatement.

Common sense and the residue of her sympathy for Shaw's predicament told her to collect a car from the car pool and drive across the river to Frognal. Twenty minutes later she parked the Ford Mondeo in Frognal Gardens and made her way on foot to Shaw's address.

77

Rosslyn and Cleo were in the hire car within sight of the black railings next to 1 Montague Place. Rosslyn had only two choices. Either to go in now and discover that the Greeks had called the whole thing off, or to take them by surprise and get Demetra away to safety. He wondered whether Cleo had the strength to go through with it.

'Just follow my moves,' he told her. 'Secure your handgun in your belt. I know the route Nicos and Demetra used. Take it slowly. Once we're on the roofs, we take a different route to the security control unit. If we find the alarm circuits have been deactivated, then we know the robbery will take place very shortly.'

'After that?'

'It's them or us.'

The railings next to 1 Montague Place presented them with no great challenge. Neither did the next wall. Cleo was strong and fit and followed his moves with care up to the first roof. Then they abseiled the ten metres to the ground inside the museum's service area. Landing between a pile of tarpaulins and tall steel garbage drums, Rosslyn unfastened the ropes and took them with him.

They crossed the service area and, at the western side of the museum complex, found the exterior wall of the Duveen Gallery, out of vision of the security cameras fixed to the wall above them. Next to the electricity conduit, just as Nezeritis had done, Rosslyn fastened the rope to the fine black cord hidden behind a downpipe. At the roof's edge, eighteen metres above them, the string was attached to the single small piton driven hard into a crack in the Portland stone.

Rosslyn hauled the rope upwards so that it passed over the piton and he kept on hauling until he retrieved the other end of what was now a loop. He tied the end of the rope to a lightweight karabiner. Leaning backwards, with his feet against the stone wall, he allowed the rope to take his weight. Then he began the ascent of the sheer wall up to the edge of the roof above him. Here he secured his footing, paused a moment, then lowered the rope to Cleo for her to make the ascent.

Moments later they were standing on the northern edge of the glass roof of the Duveen Gallery. They left the rope in place and began to crawl along the surface of the parapet, leaving the roof to the gallery behind them. At the far end they found the maintenance walkways, which led them along two sides of a square until they reached the roof of the building that housed the main security control room, three floors below.

Rosslyn inserted the lightweight hammer in the wooden door jamb, braced himself and pressed hard, working the hammer back and forth until the wood splintered and came away, allowing him just enough room to reach inside and release the chain.

He turned to look quickly back across the vast expanse of roofs. The deserted buildings suddenly looked extraordinarily vulnerable to assault and robbery. And looming over the massive complex stood the two gigantic cranes.

He gestured Cleo to have her handgun at the ready and follow him to the narrow stone stairs that led downwards in darkness to the silence of the lower floors.

78

The Director General's personal assistant hurried across the courtyard and found the bell marked 'Top Floor Flat'. She rang it and
waited, but there was no reply. She stepped backwards and looked
up at the house for a sign that Shaw was in. The windows were
dark. She rang again. And again there was no reply. Then she tried
the door and found it unlocked. Surely people who lived in mansion
blocks like this one locked the doors when they went out? There
didn't even seem to be an alarm. There was no one here. She began
to feel frightened.

She turned the lights on in the main entrance hall and at once saw
the small sign with an arrow pointing right.

'Hello?' she called. 'Is anyone at home?'

She felt guilty, like a thief. Still, if anyone surprised her, she had
her ID card on her. She could explain away her presence.

Beyond the sign to Shaw's flat, the stone corridor passage led past
coat racks and beyond them was a narrow flight of stairs. She
climbed them slowly, pausing once or twice to listen.

In front of her was the door to the flat. She knocked on it and,
getting no reply, tried the handle. It opened easily. Here too she
faced darkness. She reached up and down the wall and found the
light switches. She flicked them on. Then blinked. Here was the
kitchen and dining room all in one. The smoked-glass-fronted
refrigerator. To one side of the sink she saw the telephone answering
machine. She passed the open door to Shaw's bedroom, taking in the
low, unmade bed and the pillow lying on the floor by the bedside
table. Then she headed for the room at the end of the passage and
turned on the lights.

She had never seen a dead body before. Staring at it appalled, she whispered, 'Marion?'

The sight of Shaw lying slightly sideways across the desk was more than she could bear. She was so very still. The upper body and hair were matted with dark blood and what seemed like bits of flesh.

Her heart pounded and she felt faint. She wanted to go, to run away. Unsteady on her feet, her breathing now a series of small gasps, she went back to the kitchen and lifted the telephone. She told the duty operator at Vauxhall Cross to transfer the call to the Director General. 'It's urgent,' she said, shaking. 'Hurry.'

Moments later, the familiar voice said, 'Yes?'

'Marion Shaw is dead,' she blurted out. 'It's terrible. She's in here. At her desk. She's dead. Dead.'

'Where are you?'

'At her flat in Frognal, sir.'

'At *Marion's* flat?'

'Yes. I thought . . .' She could hardly get the words out.

'Easy, easy. Take it slowly. You're quite sure?'

'Quite sure,' she whimpered. 'She's been murdered.'

'Stay there,' he said. 'Keep the doors locked till we get there. Don't touch a thing. You hear me?'

'Yes, sir.'

'Don't let anyone into the flat.'

She felt the need to breathe fresh air. 'Can I wait outside, please?'

'No. Stay where you are. I'll be with you shortly.'

The Director General asked the Chief Superintendent for an urgent word. This was the first time that a senior MI6 officer had been murdered on her own doorstep. The Director General knew he would now have to face the most difficult questions of his life.

Two minutes later, sirens wailing, lights flashing, the first of the fast-response police vehicles was speeding to the address in Frognal. Scene of crime officers were alerted. The Director General had followed the Chief Superintendent to Frognal.

By the time the Director General reached the scene, the police and emergency service presence outside the house was massive. 'Have the whole area cordoned off,' he told the Chief Superintendent.

He hurried into the house without acknowledging the police officers in the hallway or those in Shaw's flat. His first sight of the scene upstairs persuaded him that an intruder had definitely shot Shaw. He looked around the room, then at the body and the blood. He asked one of the officers to give him a pair of transparent gloves. Then he examined the waste bin.

'Very well,' he said. 'I want to talk to my assistant.'

He found her seated at the kitchen table, shocked, and he offered her brief words of comfort. 'I want you to spend a few moments with me, alone,' he told her. 'Come with me a moment.' He turned to the Chief Superintendent, who had followed him. 'If you wouldn't mind, ask your people to leave the room.'

'You won't of course disturb anything, will you, sir?' said the Chief Superintendent uneasily.

The Director General shook his head with an expression on his face that suggested, in the circumstances, he had no need whatsoever of such advice. 'If you would give us ten minutes alone. You'll appreciate that what I have to ask my friend here in confidence is, to say the least, sensitive. Sensitive.'

'I understand,' said the Chief Superintendent.

Once he was alone in Shaw's room with his personal assistant and the door was closed, the Director General asked her to tell him exactly what had happened. 'Your every move. Take your time.' He leaned close to her. 'Stand by the door. I don't want you to be interrupted.' He gave her a smile of encouragement. 'Just keep talking. What happened and when and what you thought of Shaw.'

Hesitantly she told him, and while she spoke in her soft voice, he began to search the room. He moved with great agility, like a tracker, searching for 'signs', the tell-tale marks the violent intruder always leaves. Torn fabric. New scratches on a table. Marks of recent disturbance. Fresh dirt from outside. Mud not yet dry. The trace of urine, even faeces, the mark on the carpet. Simultaneously, his gloved hands searched the drawers of the desk. Shaw's bills. Her stationery. With time against him, he was circling the walls of the room. Tracing the carpet edges. Dropping to his knees to peer beneath sofas. Digging with his fingers in the gaps of the upholstery.

'I can't say I really warmed to her,' his assistant was saying. 'Not that I didn't like her. I did. I admired her. And she could be nice. Yes, she could be very nice when she chose to be.'

The Director General was on his knees where the worn grey carpet had recently been disturbed. He peeled the carpet back and saw the loose floorboard. It lifted easily and he reached among the electric cables in the dust until his hand gripped the felt. Dry cardboard boxes, Lilley and Skinner old shoeboxes wrapped in green felt. Whoever had put them there didn't want anyone else to find them.

He removed the contents of the boxes. The photographs of the woman with the uncanny resemblance to Shaw. The naked woman swimming. A bracelet from Cartier fashioned in heavy gold like one part of a handcuff. The silver napkin ring with a date and the name of St Edmund's Church, Southwold. The name: Susan Mona Maureen Shaw. Shaw's birth certificate and the letter of final proof in the writing paper headed Naumann Bartenstein. He slipped the letter and jewellery in his jacket pocket and the photos inside his shirt.

Back at her desk, he unlocked the slim top drawer and drew out the empty box. Empty except for three rounds for a Sig Sauer P226 handgun and a chamois-leather cloth. These too he pocketed. At all costs, Shaw's past must be buried well out of sight of the police forensic specialists, who would now comb the place as the centre of attention shifted here and nowhere near Bloomsbury and the British Museum.

'We can rejoin the others now,' he whispered to his assistant. 'Whatever we have discussed here and anything you may have noticed you mention to no one. To no one at the office. Not even to the police. When they question you it will only be in my presence. Do you understand?'

She nodded. 'Thank you, sir.'

'Not at all. Thank you. I'll arrange a car to take you home.'

79

To Rosslyn too, the problems that lay ahead seemed overwhelming. If the Greeks struck, they would surely do so soon. If their entrance triggered the alarms, then it would be only a matter of minutes before the police arrived from all directions. It would take too long for him and Cleo to retrace their route along the network of inner passages, while remaining out of sight.

Meanwhile, the noise of their footsteps on the circuitous route they were taking, to the southern area of the otherwise silent complex, was proving well nigh impossible to deaden. At least there were no surveillance cameras in these basement passages that led to the museum's central security control unit.

He remembered the tour he had made of the area nearest the Duveen Gallery with the museum guard. Time spent in reconnaissance is seldom wasted and he clearly recollected the distinctive blue uniforms the guards wore. Now, for his own purposes, he hoped those guards on duty would be wearing theirs. Or, if not, that some uniforms were hanging there in the room that accommodated the security personnel. If units of armed police descended on the museum, he and Cleo needed to be wearing the uniforms to distinguish them from the armed intruders.

He discounted the idea that the guards themselves might be armed. But they would certainly have easy access to panic buttons. Buttons that could all too quickly be hit to alert the local police in Holborn. Even beyond. If the museum was reckoned the world's great treasure house, the alarm system would no doubt be linked directly to New Scotland Yard. *The alarms are the problem.* In this respect, however, he had underestimated the scrupulous planning and preparations already made by Constantine Dragos and

Miltiades Zei, and as yet he knew nothing of their earlier success in disabling the alarms for the sixty-minute zone necessary to achieve their ends. The extent of what the Greeks had already so brilliantly done dawned on him only once he had turned left into the final and brightly lit low corridor. It would work in his favour.

At the end of the corridor, he faced the closed door marked 'Security Control'. He and Cleo were standing eyeball to eyeball with the CCTV camera above the door.

His eyes were fixed on the lens. With his loaded handgun beneath his jacket and at the ready, he stood motionless, with Cleo close behind him. Moving closer to the camera, he saw that the small red bulb to the left of the camera was dead. The camera covering the entrance to the security control room was inactive. It was dead.

With Cleo still behind him, he moved towards the door. He paused and listened. Coming from inside the room, he heard the sound of Sky TV news. Breathing slowly, he touched Cleo on the shoulder and pointed to her handgun. Then he gestured to her to take up position to one side of the door. She stood there, ready to fire.

Slowly, Rosslyn turned the door handle. Then, with great force, he threw it open. 'Police,' he yelled. 'Don't move!'

80

Miltiades Zei brought the Mercedes Actros to a stop outside the British Museum. Apart from Constantine Dragos, all members of the assault team now wore dark lightweight overalls and nylon slit masks. They had their climbing gear in place. Dragos and Miltiades Zei now changed places, Constantine remaining at the wheel of the truck.

Taking their loaded weapons, phosphorous grenades and additional ammunition with them, they left in silence and headed for the railings at 1 Montague Place. Simultaneously, Dragos turned the vehicle around and steered it into position within one of the tower crane's reach. There, within ten minutes, the crane manned by Zei would raise the mobile transportation unit vehicle, swing round and lower the vehicle inside through the gap in the Duveen Gallery roof made ready by the assault group.

By the time Dragos had positioned the Actros and turned off its engine, the remainder of the team, with Demetra as lead climber, had successfully abseiled the ten metres to the ground inside the museum's service area. There was the light westerly wind. Some dust in the air. The meteorologists had it right. The pre-dawn weather was ideal.

Zei eyed the security cameras fixed to the wall above them. He saw the red light was off. It was time to establish radio communication with Dragos.

'Come in, Alpha. Over.'

'Receiving you, Beta.'

The others, still with Demetra in the lead, were making the longest climb, up the eighteen metres of wall to the roof of the Duveen Gallery.

Zei headed to the forecourt of the museum. With the museum director's darkened offices behind him, he cut across the forecourt to the high wooden hoardings at the perimeter of the construction site. He reached the small white-painted entrance door to his left. Using lightweight wire cutters, he cut through the padlocked chain. Then, closing the door behind him, he entered the construction site itself. Ahead of him towered the highest of the immense Wolff cranes.

Skirting piles of metal rods and stacks of bricks, he reached the crane's base. He paused there a moment to check his watch. The assault team, albeit some five minutes behind schedule, would now be inside the Duveen Gallery and the business of loosening the last of the Marbles still fixed to the wall would have begun. Zei braced himself, then levered himself up to the lowest of the tower's platforms and, rung by rung, he began to climb the thirty metres up to the crane's control cabin.

81

Of the terrified guards on duty who up till now had been watching the news, two were men, the third a woman. In the face of Rosslyn's gun, they offered no resistance. Rosslyn and Cleo ordered them to remove their drab blue uniforms and strip to their underwear.

With Cleo covering the guards, as well as the door to the room, Rosslyn used the nylon climbing rope to tie the three guards to the table legs. He blindfolded them effectively with the roll of wide industrial adhesive tape he took from the ledge behind the TV. He would use it to gag them shortly.

He was now holding the telephone receiver in his left hand and indicating the alarm and CCTV control panels with his right.

'You're not police,' the youngest of the two male guards said.

'You think not?' said Rosslyn.

'What are you going to do?' the man pleaded.

Rosslyn pointed at the Sig Sauer on the table.

'What am I going to do? I'll tell you what *you're* going to do. You're going to tell me why the alarms are off. The phones dead. And the CCTV system down.'

There was no response. Rosslyn set the telephone down and picked up his gun, pressing the snout into the panic-stricken guard. 'This is a gun, right? And you tell me now. Why are the alarms off?'

'There's a technical fault.'

'C'mon, who turned them off?'

'They're on automatic,' the woman said. 'They're coming on again at four a.m.'

'They are?'

'It's happened before,' the woman said. 'The time switches. There's a recurrent fault.'

'And I'm saying you turned them off.'

'We did not,' the woman sobbed. 'Please.'

'Then if you knew there was a fault, what the hell are you three sitting in here gawking at TV for?'

'Because it's safe,' the woman said.

'Safe? Listen, I walked in here. And you sit there saying you're safe. You are not safe.'

'What's your game then?' the woman blurted out. 'You're sick.'

Like her male companions, she really had no idea the technical fault had been deliberately engineered by an unseen hand.

The TV newsman was blathering on: 'The headlines this morning. Tributes have been paid to the icon of British pop, who died in . . .'

Rosslyn was staring hard at the control panels. 'How come only areas one to fifteen are inactive?'

'The whole system's down tonight,' the woman said. 'All of it.'

'All of it?'

'It happened before,' the woman said.

'When?'

'When that man died in the Duveen Gallery. It was the same then. That's why no one saw the accident. The alarms hadn't gone off.'

'You mean they were turned off?'

'Please,' she moaned.

Then, beside the main panel, Rosslyn saw the panels showing the circuits of the fire alarms. All of them were active. Forget the links to the police. The fire alarms offered him the means and opportunity. It would be the fire alarms he would use to raise the alert when the time came.

He gagged the three guards with the tape and tightened the rope around their wrists, ankles and their necks. 'Breathe through your noses. If you move the knots'll tighten and you'll strangle yourselves. If I were you, I wouldn't move at all, right? Unless you want to die.'

He handed the woman's uniform to Cleo. 'Put this on. A bit small. You'll have to make do. Fast. Get it on.'

He likewise donned one of the uniforms, before picking up a roll of kitchen paper by the sink. The small can of lighter fuel and cigarette lighter he found in one of the men's briefcases. The short and blunt steel hammer from an open toolbox. Finally, he handed Cleo the crowd-control bullhorn, an emergency flashlight and the third set of uniform clothing.

Had the CCTV cameras been covering the whole site of the museum, its web of galleries containing some 80,000 exhibits, the screens in the security control room would have shown the work in the Duveen Gallery. It was now well in progress.

The last of the main frieze panels had been freed from the walls. The adhesive strips had been removed from around the freestanding sculptures from the east pediment. The next stage was the raising by the crane of the mobile transportation unit out of the Mercedes Actros, then through the vehicle's open roof, upwards and across to the gap now being made ready in the roof of the Duveen Gallery. It would then be lowered in and the loading would begin.

Panning across the gallery itself, the cameras would have revealed Demetra standing and looking up at the four Greeks in black slit masks and overalls now at work on the roof: breaking away the glass panes and slowly, with heavy leverage tools; prising open the network of metal struts that had held the centre section of the glass panes in place. A large square sheet of thick, soundproof fabric had been spread across the floor to dull the sound of the falling glass.

From the control capsule at the side of the Wolff crane's tower, Zei kept up constant and rapid radio communication with Dragos in the Mercedes Actros and with Abatzi, who was up on the roof of the Duveen Gallery.

There were some sharp exchanges about the need for greater speed. According to Dragos, they had once more fallen behind schedule. This time by six minutes. He was chanting, 'Keep moving. Keep moving . . .'

Zei now brought the crane into action. Working the joystick, he manoeuvred the great red arm round towards the north, until the hawsers dangled some twelve metres above the gap in the roof of the Mercedes Actros. There, for the time being, it stayed: motionless.

Dragos had already freed the restraining chocks and clips that had held the mobile transportation unit in place during the journey from the airfield beyond Colchester, and now he fastened the lifting attachments. The next task was to raise the transportation unit. Position it over the gap being made ready in the roof of the Duveen Gallery and lower it to the marble floor, where Demetra would free the hawsers and the loading of the Marbles could begin. The four remaining Greeks would then abseil, and Abatzi would start the Hanakawa. Section by section, the sculptures would be placed on the platform Dragos had attached to the hawsers and Zei had lifted into the gallery.

Depending on the size and weight of each load, there would then follow the final lifting of the Marbles. Out through the gap in the roof. Then down to the open roof of the Mercedes. According to Dragos's calculations, this would take between twenty-five and thirty-five minutes to complete. The assault team would then leave the gallery by the route they had used to enter and return to Montague Place for departure from Bloomsbury to the airfield, the Chinook to Altenhall and the Boeing: ready for take-off and the flight home to Greece.

The distorted voices of Dragos, Zei and Abatzi seemed to be repeating a mantra over the three-way radio link:
'Green . . .'
'Green . . .'
'Green. All is go.'
Otherwise, the Duveen Gallery was relatively silent. Demetra was waiting in the centre of the room. Her loaded Armalite rifle stood propped against the northern wall, just out of reach. The many months of planning were paying off.
Strange Police was Green.

84

Rosslyn and Cleo approached the high, locked plate-glass entrance doors to the Duveen Gallery. They lowered themselves to their hands and knees and crawled forward to peer in.

'They're here. They've started . . .'

In the shadowy interior Rosslyn could see, in dark overalls, staring up at the glass roof, where there was now a gap open to the sky, a masked figure with a climbing rope slung over one shoulder. Beyond the figure in overalls, he saw the shape or profile of what was clearly a high-powered rifle propped against the gallery's north wall.

Cleo touched his arm and leaned close to his ear: 'Demetra –'

Rosslyn was not so sure. The figure was certainly a woman, but Demetra?

'Her climbing boots,' said Cleo, her voice shaking. 'It's her. She's alone . . . Move in.'

Rosslyn shook his head. He raised his hand in warning. *Wait.*

Above, he could see four figures beside the broken roof panel and he pointed to them for Cleo's benefit. They seemed to be having problems with a strut that was resisting their leverage. As far as he could see, none of them was carrying a weapon at the ready. Perhaps they had them near by.

Then he saw the shape of the Hanakawa. The mobile transportation unit appeared to be some five metres above the gap in the roof. The four figures were reaching up to steady it with outstretched arms. It lowered and then, only for a moment, blocked out the sky.

His mouth felt dry. *Time to move.* He nodded to Cleo. She lifted the third uniform in a bundle and held it out in front of her for Rosslyn to drench it with the lighter fuel. He squirted the stuff out in a

303

continuous stream of vapour until the can was empty. Then he violently shook the can, as if to say, 'Done. There, now go.'

Getting to his feet, Rosslyn took two steps back, steadied himself, then raised the heavy steel hammer in his right hand and slammed it against the glass. It cracked like a vast sheet of ice and then, as if it had turned into a wall of water, the whole thing collapsed with great suddenness. Rosslyn stepped back and, with his right hand, lit the bundle of clothes as Cleo tossed it into the centre of the gallery. It immediately burst into a ball of livid fire.

Inside the gallery the woman was running as near as she could to the burning mass, but the flames and fumes forced her back in panic. Rosslyn shone the emergency flashlight beam at her and left it to Cleo to speak into the bullhorn.

'Demetra. Here. Run. For God's sake, *run!*'

Demetra was transfixed, blinded by the powerful beam of light. Then Cleo shone it into her face and began to walk into the gallery, through the billowing gaseous smoke and towards her daughter.

Rosslyn saw Demetra spin round. She was making a grab for the Armalite. She had barely touched it when the fire alarms went off. First they produced a whine. Then they screamed out at full pitch.

He took one deep breath and sprinted straight into the smoke, his feet scrunching the carpet of broken glass beneath his feet.

85

'Hold it there.' Abatzi was speaking on the radio link to both Zei in the crane and Dragos in the Mercedes Actros.

'What's happening?' Dragos asked.

They were now talking over each other. No more Alpha/Beta. Calls signs had been abandoned.

'The fire alarms,' Abatzi was panting.

Dragos swore viciously. 'What fire?'

'The interior doors have been broken.'

'Which doors?' Zei wanted to know.

Dragos began to shout, 'Keep moving in. Keep moving in.'

'Where's the fire?'

'Raise the load . . . The smoke. We can't see. Raise the load. Raise it. We have to get down in there.'

'Turn off the alarms!'

Abatzi yelled down, 'Demetra!'

She made no reply. The other three men on the roof lifted their guns. But they were of little use. The gallery was filled with acrid smoke.

'Raise the load!'

'We can't see. Get out of here. It's on fire. The alarms.'

'We have to *go*,' Zei was saying. 'Constantine, it's Red. Red. Red. We have to go.'

86

Though Rosslyn had no wish to hurt her, there was no alternative. Certainly, Cleo had no time to protest against the violence done to her daughter. Choking in the smoke, Demetra was raising the Armalite when he struck her hard in the stomach. It was a bar-room swing of a blow. From right to left the clenched fist drove the wind from her lungs and she staggered and half-collapsed. The gun fell away to the marble floor. Coughing and choking, he barked at Cleo to hand him her handgun. Together they half-dragged Demetra across the carpet of glass splinters, over the shards of the smashed plate-glass doors. The noise of the fire alarms was deafening.

Beyond the junction of Rooms 8a and 8b, Demetra broke free from her mother's grasp. 'Go,' she screamed. 'Leave!'

Rosslyn pointed the handgun at her legs. 'You're coming out of here with us now.'

'You'll never make it,' said Demetra. 'They'll kill you.'

'I doubt it,' said Rosslyn. 'You walk in front, Cleo. Then you, Demetra.'

They took the route trodden by a million tourists before them. Theirs was in darkness. With the lessening strength of the smoke fumes in their streaming noses and lungs and the screaming of the fire alarms in their ears. Through the galleries of Greek art of the fifth century BC. Archaic Greece. To prehistoric Greece. Through the bookshop. And out into the high front hall. To the locked exit doors.

'Stand back a little,' Rosslyn said, and summarily fired several rounds into the locking devices. He slammed the hammer against the last section of the locks. Then he heaved the door open and they were outside in the air of early morning beneath the dark portico of monumental Ionic columns.

Chucking aside the hammer and torch, Rosslyn tucked the two handguns inside his uniform coat. 'Listen to me,' he ordered Demetra, 'if the fire service people talk to you, you say nothing. You're a staff casualty. I'm getting you to hospital. I do the talking. You say nothing. I say again, *nothing*. There'll be a police presence here within minutes from now. If you make one false move they'll book you. And if they find the guns on me we're in total shit. See?'

As if to substantiate his point, in the distance, apparently from all directions, came the noise of police car sirens and the fire engine klaxons.

Rosslyn saw an armed figure stepping through the painted white door in the hoardings. The man, masked and carrying a rifle, suddenly froze. He had seen the three of them descending the steps from the portico.

'Who's that?' Rosslyn asked Demetra.

'Miltiades Zei. He's armed.'

'So I see,' said Rosslyn. 'Do everything I say. Stay well behind me. Leave this one to me. Here –' He handed back Cleo's handgun, then checked his own. 'Move over there fast,' he told her. 'Stay in the shadows. You have sixty seconds. Fire at the doorway on the move. You draw his fire. I take him. Go. Now.'

87

Peering through night-vision glasses, Zei was talking on the short-wave radio link to Dragos.

'There are three people out here by the entrance. One is moving away. The other two, they're maybe heading for the gates . . .'

'Who are they?'

'One's definitely Demetra. She's betrayed us. Constantine, she's betrayed us.'

'Kill her.'

'I have to get back to you, Constantine. Constantine? Please.'

'Hurry it up. Can't you hear the sirens? Wait out . . .'

There was a pause. Zei focused the field glasses. Now he recognized Cleo. 'Constantine, do you hear me?'

'The others are aboard. We have to go. Move it. Just get out of there.'

'The second person is Cleo Ipsilanti. The third is Rosslyn.'

'Do it. Kill them!'

88

Flattened against the wooden hoarding of the construction site, Rosslyn slowly eased his way towards the narrow doorway in which he had last seen Zei. *Whose nerve would give first?* The emergency services would be all over the place within minutes.

The sixty seconds were up and Cleo fired.

Zei answered with rapid fire. The rounds ricocheted and whined.

Rosslyn edged still further along the wooden hoarding. *Fire again, Cleo . . .*

She did so five seconds later. The rounds smashed into the wood above Rosslyn's head. He was now less than a metre from the doorway.

Sensing movement, Zei took aim, fired again and missed.

Rosslyn moved closer to his target.

'Zei?'

He saw the Greek swivel round and in that second Rosslyn stepped forward and shot him through the chest. And as the first of the emergency service vehicle's headlights illuminated Great Russell Street, Rosslyn shot Zei in the head to make sure. Kneeling down, he lifted the short-wave radio.

He heard Constantine Dragos saying, 'Miltiades? Where are you? The police. We have to go. Miltiades?'

Rosslyn spoke into the radio: 'Dragos, he's dead. And you're as good as –' Then the link was severed.

He looked across the forecourt and saw Cleo running towards him.

The first of the fire officers heaved the gates open and waved the vehicles through. 'Where's the trouble?' he shouted to Rosslyn.

'In the Duveen Gallery,' Rosslyn called back. 'Over there.'

'Anyone hurt?'

'Only these two. I'm getting them across to University College Hospital.'

'What's the damage?'

'A lot of smoke.'

'You need any assistance?'

'No thanks,' said Rosslyn. 'There'll be other guards waiting for you inside. I'd get some people around to the back at Montague Place.'

90

The arm of the great crane pointed to the west. Dangling from the hawsers above the gap in the roof of the Duveen Gallery was the mobile transportation unit. The fire below had burned itself out, leaving the stench of burned fabric.

There was no sign of the Greeks. Driven by Constantine Dragos in the Mercedes Actros, they were heading fast to the north-east and the landing strip outside Colchester.

Clear of the scene, Rosslyn called Vauxhall Cross. He gave his name and said he wanted to speak personally to the Director General.

'Where are you, Mr Rosslyn?' asked the SIS duty operator.

'Tottenham Court Road,' said Rosslyn.

'We'll call you back, Mr Rosslyn. Give me the number.'

Without identifying himself, the man who almost at once returned the call asked, 'Mr Rosslyn?'

'Speaking.'

Rosslyn quickly handed the mobile to Cleo. She listened to the Director General, who was saying, 'I've been expecting your call. I'm speaking from Vauxhall Cross.' She nodded to Rosslyn. 'It's him.' Then she handed the phone back to Rosslyn.

'I'd welcome a chance to see you in person,' the Director General said. 'I suggest I send a car.'

'Demetra and Cleo Ipsilanti are here with me.'

The voice was neutral: 'Really?' There was a brief pause. 'Good. I need to talk to you about Marion Shaw. I suggest I have the car collect all three of you.'

'It depends who's in it.'

'Of course. If it reassures you, I'll come alone in a black Rover. I suggest you wait in the doorway of Heal's department store. And please make sure the three of you are there. If not, I'm afraid I can't be responsible for what action the police may take against you and Demetra Ipsilanti. I'll draw up in front of the American Church in about twenty minutes' time.'

92

Waiting in the entrance to Heal's in silence, they stared across the street to the plane trees, the church and the Telecom Tower on the dawn skyline. A bus passed. Otherwise, the streets were empty. The only movement was the blue tarpaulin flapping against the scaffolding around the Exotic Video store at the junction of Tottenham Street with Tottenham Court Road. Before long Rosslyn saw that shadowy figures were visible just behind the parapets of 85 to 90 Tottenham Court Road, opposite. In the distance, somewhere to the south, he could hear the droning of a helicopter.

'Do you know about Nicos?' Demetra asked. 'You know how he died?'

'I heard it was an accident,' said Rosslyn curtly.

'Say it wasn't an accident?' Demetra said.

'Let's not say anything now,' said Rosslyn.

The helicopter was drawing nearer and Rosslyn could tell it was on surveillance duty. His eyes scanned the buildings opposite, searching for clearer signs of marksmen.

'I know the truth,' said Demetra.

It was perhaps the sole indication she gave of what she intended to do next.

At four-fifty a.m., they saw the black Rover pull up outside the American Church. Immediately Demetra saw it, she pushed her way past Rosslyn to the street.

'Wait,' he yelled. He felt Cleo tense and knew that she was about to run after Demetra. He grabbed her arm. 'Don't,' he said. 'Look up there.'

The marksmen were now clearly visible on the parapets. A voice, greatly amplified, called out, 'Don't move.'

The Director General was standing across the street, by the open door of his car. 'Please cross the road now with your companion, Mr Rosslyn.'

'Demetra,' Cleo was yelling. 'Come back.'

It was no use. Running for dear life, she suddenly darted into Tottenham Street and was gone.

Rosslyn and Cleo walked to the Director General's car. Without offering a greeting, he said, 'You should've warned her against doing anything so stupid. You realize the police will make an arrest?'

Cleo turned on him. 'I'm going to find her.'

Overhead the surveillance helicopter was lowering like a warning.

'Not if I were you,' said the Director General.

'Then I'll get her,' said Rosslyn.

'No, Mr Rosslyn.'

Rosslyn followed the Director General's gaze to the helicopter hovering above them. Further up the street, an unmarked Range Rover was approaching at speed against the one-way traffic system. It turned sharply into Tottenham Street, in pursuit of Demetra.

'If you'd join me now in my car,' the Director General said. He was looking at his watch. 'We have very little time.'

'I'm going to find Demetra,' Cleo said again.

'No,' said the Director General. 'She'll be in our hands by now. Please get into the car.'

Taking Cleo by the arm, Rosslyn got into the back of the car and she followed him, offering no resistance.

94

The Director General drove off. Beyond Warren Street, he headed west. 'I've had a preliminary briefing,' he said, 'as to what seems to have taken place at the British Museum.'

'You mean what *hasn't* taken place,' said Rosslyn.

'It's of no concern to me,' Cleo interrupted. 'Stop the car.'

The Director General ignored her. 'There are awkward and immediate issues to be faced. To say nothing of the death of Shaw and whatever implications that may have for you two down the line.' He glanced in the rear-view mirror and caught Rosslyn's eye. 'The police haven't found the weapon. You realize they're treating it as murder?'

'I have the weapon with me,' said Rosslyn.

'You were at her flat?'

'We were. Cleo can testify to it. Shaw was already dead by her own hand.'

'Then it's still a matter of keeping the lid on things, isn't it?'

Cleo asked, 'Where are we going?'

'Northolt,' said the Director General. 'I want you out of this.'

'Out?' said Cleo. 'Where to?'

'You have no choice,' the Director General said evasively. 'It's the risk that needs to be taken. In my judgement, it really will be for the best that you're left out of things from now on. Out of the inevitable inquiry. Far better that you aren't implicated. You need to know that I'm the one person who can insist upon that on your behalf. I'm the one who can arrange immunity from prosecution for you. Others, in my view wisely, have already accepted immunity. Campbell and Menzies Tunim, for example.' On the right-hand side they were passing Paddington Green police station. The Director General continued, 'The alternative is indefinite police custody. You're facing charges – how many charges, Mr Rosslyn? One, assault. Two, escape from Whitemoor.'

'That was Shaw's idea.'

'Really? Well, sadly for you she's not in a position to confirm that, is she?'

'Ask the caretaker at the Greek cathedral. You must know of his involvement with Shaw.'

'The caretaker. Oh, yes. He tells me he has no knowledge of her. Mind you, if you were to accept our offer of a way out, then . . . well, the future might look altogether different for you. Much brighter.'

'I think not,' said Cleo.

'You think not, Cleo? You of all people. Pity. I'd hoped that you'd both cooperate.' He smiled thinly. 'There's also the issue of Dragos and his people. The situation at the museum and so forth. Marion's operation.' He paused. 'If I were you, I'd keep Shaw's gun well hidden for the time being. If you want to know why. . . glance behind you.'

Rosslyn looked back through the rear window. Following some 200 metres distant were two unmarked Rovers like the one they were travelling in. Unmistakable surveillance and protection cars. They were keeping their distance steadily.

'And again, look ahead.'

Rosslyn saw the unmarked Range Rover.

'My people,' said the Director General. 'And again, above. Perhaps the helicopter is out of sight. My point is that one false move and we grind to a nasty halt. Your handgun will be found. It's awkward evidence against you. Alternatively, we continue to RAF Northolt.'

'And then?' asked Rosslyn.

'Case dismissed,' said the Director General. 'You will be safe. What's happened will be a matter of regret to some of us. You, Mr Rosslyn, may have lost your living and more besides. We may all disagree.' He was glancing into the rear-view mirror again. 'But let's agree that you two have each other, shall we?'

'Where's Demetra?' insisted Cleo.

'Don't worry about her,' said the Director General. 'Our people wouldn't have left without her. She's in one of the cars behind us. There was always the likelihood that one of you would do something stupid. Try and make a run for it. We have a plane on stand-by at Northolt in readiness for your immediate departure. The three of you'll be given the benefit of protection where you're going.'

'Going *where*?' asked Cleo.

'Greece,' he said. 'However disagreeable that may sound to you at the present time. To Greece. To your estate. Local and national police have been fully briefed. It will be necessary for you and your daughters to stay out there with Mr Rosslyn until further notice. You'll be formally and painlessly debriefed out of harm's way. The neat and not inexpensive deal to secure your safety's been done with a good friend of ours in Athens.'

'Who's that?' asked Cleo.

'Simopoulos. Chief of Athens police. Simopoulos is a loyal and needful friend of ours. He needs our friendship and we need his cooperation. I dare say it's the sort of arrangement that you'll appreciate, Cleo.' The Director General glanced in his rear-view mirror at her. Beneath her furrowed brows, her dark eyes were fixed at the road ahead. 'Tell me, by the way, what you know of what happened in the museum. Demetra was there, I understand.'

'She's not to be involved,' said Cleo.

'We went there to make sure she wouldn't be,' said Rosslyn.

'I suppose,' the Director General said blandly, 'you understand the need for complete discretion. If by any chance you do find yourselves being asked embarrassing questions, be sensible. Avoid them. I wouldn't discuss the issue of the Elgin Marbles. Let's say the controversies remain – how can I best put it? – academic. Ones that we can handle.'

'And Dragos?' said Cleo fiercely. 'Who do you imagine murdered Christiane Prevezer. And Ioannis? They were butchered.'

'You say *imagine*. It isn't actually a matter that requires much imagination. The Greek police know who's responsible. And those responsible know we know.' The observation seemed to cause him mild amusement.

Rosslyn remained silent. *You forced Shaw to the brink and she jumped. You've saved your face. The government's. The Prime Minister's. Foreign Secretary's. Got the CIA off the hook. The Greek Intelligence Service likewise. You have preserved the status quo. Nothing changes. You are so bloody pleased with yourself.* He had no idea the man was such a smug and brilliant bastard.

'I can tell what'll be on your mind,' the Director General was saying. 'You'll be wondering about the fate of the remainder of the team at the museum. I don't suppose you know that one of them was shot dead at point-blank range in the courtyard?' There was a prolonged silence. He drew up at some traffic lights. His long and feminine fingers drummed the rim of the steering wheel with the impatience of an orchestra conductor. 'As to the others,' he continued, 'we've traced them on the roads to East Anglia. We have the Americans to thank for that. The Americans at Mildenhall intercepted their short-wave radio communications and brought GCHQ on line.' From the corner of his eye, he was looking at Cleo, who had curled up in the foetal position. 'They've made the mistake of using a place called Altenhall in Norfolk. Almost on the doorstep of the Americans at Mildenhall. Unwise choice. Very unwise. There's even a Boeing in readiness at Altenhall to fly them out. You have to admire the extravagance. The Dragos family, Constantine and Alexios, well, we would all like them out of the way. But . . .'

Rosslyn interrupted, 'You're letting them off the hook?'

'Me? Oh, we're not doing anything of the sort. No. No. I have no powers to do so. None. You know that, Cleo, don't you? The Americans have moved with the greatest care and deliberation. We can rely upon them to tidy things up.'

'Are you saying,' Rosslyn snapped, 'that you're sending us out to Greece and letting the Greeks go free? You might as well empty the jails of the most-wanted terrorists.'

The Director General sucked his teeth. 'It wouldn't be for the first time, Rosslyn, now would it? But we need have no further fear of Greeks. Either bearing or stealing gifts, if you follow.'

They were approaching RAF Northolt. Cleo was staring anxiously at Rosslyn. The Director General was glancing at them in the rear-view mirror.

'Can you give us a cast-iron guarantee of immunity and protection?' said Rosslyn.

'Cast-iron guarantee, Mr Rosslyn? That's a bit of a cliché from a man with your education and experience. There is no such thing, is there? All I can do is my best, Rosslyn. I can do my professional duty, as I've been doing for the past twenty-five years. I suggest you do the same. Frankly, I don't see that you really have any other alternative, do you? I've told you what's happening. The deal's been done to everyone's satisfaction.'

At the security barrier, the leading Range Rover paused. The driver and passenger showed their ID. They pointed back to the car driven by the Director General and the barrier lifted to allow them entry. The Director General followed the Range Rover to one of the empty parking spaces marked 'Reserved' by the administration building.

'It may interest you to know,' he said, 'that I've personally supervised tonight's manoeuvres down to the last detail. We've even arranged a change of clothing for you.' He checked his watch. 'The RAF plane will depart in thirty minutes.' He parked the car next to the Range Rover. 'I've also arranged to be kept in touch with the pilot of your plane en route to Kalamata. I want you to be the first to know the outcome of the mission we've agreed with our American friends. I feel sure the news will come as a relief to you. Now, if you'd follow me, we'll join Demetra.'

Rosslyn saw Demetra standing beside the Range Rover.

95

Once inside the administration building they changed into their new clothes. The Director General then accompanied them across the tarmac to the RAF plane.

'By the way,' Rosslyn said, 'I left the handguns in your car.'

'I noticed,' said the Director General. 'Thank you.'

'You don't miss a trick,' said Rosslyn.

'I hope not,' said the Director General. He looked at his watch again. 'You should be arriving at Kalamata in time for breakfast. Three friends from the Athens embassy will meet you there. You'll be provided with a car and they'll follow you to Tseria. They'll serve as your protection officers *pro tem*. If there are any problems or inconveniences, you should contact me directly. Any time of day or night. By the way, passports and petty cash allowances have all been taken care of.'

At the base of the ramp, he shook each of them by the hand in turn. Rather too firmly, Rosslyn thought, and he noticed that Demetra now, as before, never once looked the Director General in the eye.

'Have a safe flight,' said the Director General. He smiled at Demetra. 'I have a daughter your age. Tell me, what's the Greek for good luck?'

Demetra curled her tongue around her lips, spat on his shoes, turned her back on him and ran up the steps to the aircraft's open door. Cleo and Rosslyn followed her aboard.

In the doorway Demetra turned, choked on her words and called out, 'Evil bastard!'

Rubbing his hands, the Director General was walking quickly away towards the administration block. All he could have heard was the roaring of the engines.

96

Rosslyn felt the plane lift off from the Northolt runway. It tilted into a long and slow arc towards the London sunrise. He looked out of the window at the morning landscape and wondered when he would see it again. Then the plane straightened out eastwards for France. Italy. Then Greece.

The RAF steward served them breakfast. The food was yellow. Fruit juice. Leathery scrambled eggs. Sweetcorn fritters. Rolls and butter and sickly marmalade. Only the coffee was bearable.

Demetra pulled the RAF lightweight sleeping blanket over her head.

'Do you believe that creep of a Director General?' Cleo asked Rosslyn. 'I mean, what he said about you having lost your living and – what was it? – ". . . more besides. But let's agree that you two have each other, shall we?"'

'I'll buy the last bit,' Rosslyn said.

'Or does he have more in store besides the idea that your professional life's ruined?'

It was a melancholy thought but probably true: the Director General's knowing nod and his discreet thumbs-down would prevent Rosslyn from working for any of the reliable European investigation firms again.

'That's his opinion,' said Rosslyn. 'There's been no reasonable accusation. No substantial proof of wrongdoing.'

'If you did the wrong thing,' said Cleo, 'it was for the right reasons.'

'I wonder about what he has in store,' said Rosslyn, 'and what sort of secret deal's been struck with the Greek police. Something more to ensure my acquiescence. My silence. His secret triumph. The preservation of his reputation, stature, standing and career. The failure of the Greeks to get back the Marbles. Dragos and his people are unfinished business. There are still scores to be settled. On both sides.'

'More coffee at all?' asked the RAF steward.

They declined the offer.

Cleo settled her head on his chest. 'I can't sleep,' she said.

'You will,' he told her. 'Later.'

It was later, when they were in Greek airspace, that the co-pilot came down the aisle. 'You're wanted on the radio, Mr Rosslyn. If you'd come forward to the pilot's cabin.'

Rosslyn listened to the voice over the radio without comment.

'We're still awaiting final confirmation,' the Director General told him. 'The US Air Force people confirm there were no survivors.'

'When did it happen?'

'Some forty-five minutes ago. At the Araxos US Air Force base. Thirty kilometres due west of Patras. The Boeing was being flown too low and dangerously close to the flight path of the USAF A-7 planes. It was quite properly immediately intercepted and the pilot warned.'

'You mean it was forced down?'

'Oh, nothing like that. *Talked down.* Standard emergency procedure. Talked down. I gather the most painstaking of emergency procedures were followed in full. To the letter. But to no avail. The Boeing landed too late. Too fast. Overshot the runway. It seems it ignited almost at once. Poor buggers. They didn't stand a chance.'

'Thank you for telling me.'

'Not at all, Mr Rosslyn. I gave you my promise, didn't I?' There was a moment's interference on the link that sounded like static. 'By the way, our people are already at Kalamata. You will be in safe hands. I've ensured that the protection officers will remain with you until I'm totally satisfied that matters are at an end.'

'When will that be?'

'When I give the green light,' said the Director General. 'I want you to stay in Greece until I give the word. Is the Air Force treating you well enough?'

'They're doing their duty.'

'As are we all,' said the Director General. 'As are we all. I hope you enjoy the rest of your flight, Rosslyn. You can take things easy in Greece for the time being. Meanwhile, good luck to you. Good morning.'

The plane was beginning its descent into the airport at Kalamata. Down to the haze and morning heat.

Strange Police

The pale marble world of rock and gold stubble and thistle and silver-grey olive leaves shudders in the midday glare, and one feels prone to test the rocks (like spitting on a flat-iron) before daring to lay a hand on them or to lie down in an olive's fragmentary disc of shade. The world holds its breath, and the noonday devil is at hand.

PATRICK LEIGH FERMOR

xvi

To continue from the start, from where they had left off in the Peloponnese. That was what they wanted. Perhaps it was inevitable that several weeks passed before the world began to resume some semblance of the happier past.

The rest of June and the first week of July in Tseria and Kardamyli were some of the hottest in living memory. The landscape had turned from dark gold to burnished shades of light brown. The grapes ripened early. According to the priest, the olive growers were unusually optimistic that there would be a heavy crop in autumn. The priest's wife offered Cleo a young puppy dog as the replacement for Bruno. But she declined the gift.

Rosslyn felt the sense of unfinished business acutely and the Director General's telephone calls with Cleo did little to remove the anxiety. When he asked her what the Director General had said, she proved more than usually evasive. What secrets, he wondered, did they share that she was unprepared to talk about to him?

It was true that in returning the body of Nicos Nezeritis to Greece, in the pauper's coffin as a security precaution, the British had achieved a minor act of restitution and compassion. How much easier it was to box up a human corpse and return it to its native land than a few loads of marble carvings.

The Americans, meanwhile, apparently for reasons known only to themselves, were taking a very long time indeed in releasing the identities of the corpses of those who had perished in the inferno at the US base not far from Patras, where the bodies still lay in refrigerators.

'Inquiries,' the Director General told Rosslyn briefly, 'take time. Please make sure that Cleo accepts the very real need for security precautions to be taken. Once my draft report is ready, I'll pay you both a visit. You stay put in safety until I give the word.'

Cleo was adamant that she wanted to return to the routine of her previous existence. She wanted the protection officers to leave. So she said. It seemed, however, that the Director General had issued firm instructions for them to remain. The protection officers proved to be agreeable enough. Two of them were British and both former military personnel. The third was Greek.

Rosslyn and the women went about their daily routines. The continued presence of the protection officers seemed to be the warning of trouble hanging in the mountain air.

xvii

Apart from casual visitors to the estate, the priest and one or two of the neighbours, there were the two legal advisers from Vauxhall Cross who debriefed Cleo, Olympia and Demetra. The legal advisers implied that the matter of the original kidnap threats was history. Likewise, the activities of P17N and the wider conflict in the Balkans were not apparently their immediate concern. Or so they said.

They debriefed Rosslyn and he agreed with them that he had been well aware Cleo was the experienced and distinguished former agent of SIS. Someone who could be relied upon to keep a secret. Like her, he was told he must clearly appreciate the particular importance of confidentiality and the serious consequences of defying the Official Secrets Act. During the history of events that the legal advisers outlined, they made scant reference to the Tunims and none to his love affair with Cleo. Otherwise, they seemed surprisingly well informed about the history of the immediate past. The greater part of it had not been made public and doubtless never would be.

They rehearsed what they called the primary purpose of his original stay in Greece: to advise upon the protection and security of Cleo's estate. He agreed that to all intents and purposes he had completed his professional duty. By and large, it was pedestrian stuff.

'Thank you for your help, Mr Rosslyn,' they said.

With that, helping themselves to more ouzo, they finally switched off the tape recorder.

xviii

The nightmares remained. Nightmares bringing with them the sense that relief was transient and the estate, however beautiful, and Cleo, however loving, represented some sort of insecure open jail in which he felt far less fearful of his fellow inmates than unseen others on the outside of things.

Demetra and Olympia seemed restored and Cleo dismissed the past as what she called 'the forgotten country'.

She was once more the proprietor of her own territory and Rosslyn was seemingly content to stay with her indefinitely, cut off from London and the various investigations being made into the several deaths with which he had been connected. It was a curious fact that neither the police nor the Security Services followed up on the debriefings. It was as if an invisible line had been drawn beneath the narrative.

The worst of the tension of being both the hunted and the hunter subsided. Cleo showed no inclination to discuss the events of the recent past: neither the death of Nicos Nezeritis, nor the murder of her former husband, Ioannis Ipsilanti, by the hand of Constantine Dragos. Rosslyn noticed that she had disposed of the photographs of Nezeritis that had shown him standing on summits in the Himalayas, the Alps and the Andes, and in the Taygetos with Demetra. If Cleo once thought about Alexios Dragos, she never mentioned him.

Neither did she discuss the inevitability of Rosslyn's eventual return to London. She would look at him silently with those dark eyes and give him one of her warm, wide smiles.

What was it, he wondered, that she was hiding?

By night they resumed their lovemaking. Mostly, they did so in silence. There seemed to be some unspoken agreement that the days and weeks were part of some process of quiet resting: rehabilitation in the isolation of the land beneath the mountains.

It was perhaps Cleo's silences that unnerved Rosslyn. There seemed to be no rational explanation for her distance. Concerned and uneasy, he frequently woke during the night to find his pillow drenched with sweat.

He made no mention of his feeling that she had deceived him. The pair of lies she told him concerning Nezeritis and Demetra. She had known they were somewhere in Europe, but she refused to confront the reality that he had turned his attention towards her daughter. And still it seemed to Rosslyn to be a measure of her self-control that she never once gave him a clue to this betrayal. Conspiracy, as he observed correctly, was in her blood, like an antidote to the truth's more awkward revelations.

But it was perhaps to her self-control and her consummate ability to control others, Rosslyn included, that she had owed her survival as an agent. He could only guess at what was in her mind. Perhaps she entertained some sense of satisfaction that the love affair between Nicos and Demetra, the result of the other intrigue in which they were engaged, had ended, albeit in such violent circumstances. But her distance troubled him and when he asked her quite gently about it she would simply shrug and smile.

The outside world intruded gradually. There were the accounts in the Greek press of the death of Constantine Dragos and they were fulsome in their praise of him. 'A pioneer of modern commercial aviation,' was what one Athens journalist called him.

Rosslyn also saw the widely syndicated and blurred paparazzi photograph of Alexios Dragos. It showed him apparently being comforted by his Japanese companion on the deck of the *Hellenic*.

It was in strict secrecy, aboard the *Hellenic*, which was moored in Piraeus at the Zea Marina, that the patient, contrary to the diagnosis of the Dragos family physician, continued rapidly to recover.

It had been agreed that Constantine Dragos be held under police protection and it had been made very clear to both father and son that if any detail of their involvement was leaked, they would both face criminal charges. In exchange for Constantine's eventual freedom, Alexios had unconditionally agreed the terms.

Constantine owed his life to two courageous USAF fire fighters at Araxos. Just after the crash-landing of the Boeing and seconds before it exploded, they had dragged him away from the body of the plane, through the billowing spread of fire fighters' foam. Constantine's ribcage, when he jumped from the emergency exit and struck the runway, sustained the worst of the damage to his body. The bruising to his legs and face had been extensive and severe, and he had sprained the wrist of his one good hand as he tried to minimize the impact of his fall. Straight away, he was moved in an unmarked ambulance to Piraeus and stretchered aboard the *Hellenic*.

Alexios and Mitsuko tended him in luxury. He rejected his father's proposal that they put out to sea for an extended cruise to relieve the boredom. Perhaps they should set sail for Road Harbour in the British Virgin Isles or even Panama? Alexios Dragos insisted that they could dispense with the plain-clothes Athens police officer whose duties were as much those of protection officer as jailer. The Athens police took the contrary view. So Alexios watched his son and heir, who brooded by day below deck and only ventured to the deck under cover of darkness late at night or in the early hours to take the air. Alexios watched him resume his exercise routines and, once the bruising to his arms subsided, Constantine started exercising the biceps of the arm with the metallic claw. What a fine figure of a Dragos he was.

There was little conversation between the two of them. They shared defeat resolutely in bitter silence.

The Elgin Marbles had not become the Dragos Marbles. The hope of the Dragos gift to the new museum of the Acropolis had gone and there would be no immediate retribution for two hundred long years of arrogant British vandalism and philistinism achieved by the success of the robbery: Strange Police. Constantine would never share the triumph with young and beautiful Miltiades Zei, whose death he mourned in silence.

But Constantine Dragos remained his obsessive father's son. The practitioner of martial arts. The man against whom those past charges for triple murder had never been brought. Perhaps the unwritten wisdom that it was best to keep in the good books of the family Dragos and, if possible, keep out of their books altogether still pertained.

Constantine was still the driven man and, though he disguised it, that aura of urgency and pent-up violence about him steadily increased. The passionate dislike of Great Britain and the British was undimmed. Now it was real hatred. It found passionate if secretive expression in his abiding determination, no matter what the risk involved, to seek revenge against the killer of Miltiades Zei. Direct action was needed and he was going to take it.

Alexios had accepted the deal with the British Secret Service that, in exchange for Constantine's immunity from prosecution, nothing would be revealed and that when 'the air had settled' assistance would be given to provide Constantine with a new life.

So be it.

He would be a non-person. Some moribund victim of political fall-out, like a defector of little use, living a lie with an assumed identity in the Greek community of suburban Sydney or Vancouver.

So be it.

Yet whereas Constantine Dragos would live in hiding with Strange Police for months and years, the British killer Rosslyn was already back with Cleo Ipsilanti in the Peloponnese, enjoying the ministrations of his lover and the security of her estate, protected by the British. The Englishman had a future. Constantine did not.

He planned in secret, and one night, over dinner with his father and Mitsuko aboard the *Hellenic*, he announced, 'You're right. We should make the best of things. Take a fishing cruise. In Greek waters. Say south? To the Peloponnese. Spear some fish.'

Alexios was very pleased by the suggestion and he finally gained approval from the Athens police to set sail. The police had two conditions. That they report the position of the *Hellenic* by radio every six hours. And that the protection officer travel with them.

xxi

The out-of-date British newspapers Rosslyn scrutinized recorded that there had been a serious accident on the construction site of the British Museum. The Minister for Culture was quoted as saying that such an 'incident was inevitable during the completion of so glorious a scheme of restoration'. No loss of life was reported. No mention made of any untoward alteration to the display of the Elgin Marbles. Only the roof of the Duveen Gallery had been damaged. Really quite severely. Now that too had been restored. If academics and philhellenes wrote to the press about the Elgin Marbles, not one of their letters was published.

Strangest of all, it seemed to Rosslyn, there was not a single mention in either the Greek or the British press of the plane crash at the Araxos US Air Force base.

Then came the call from the Director General. He said that he wished to see them in person and would be pleased if they'd join him at Lela's Hotel and Taverna in Kardamyli.

They accepted his proposal and Rosslyn decided that he would ask him more about the disaster at Araxos.

xxii

Some weeks after their return to the Peloponnese, on the day of the Director General's arrival, Rosslyn stood at the edge of the Kardamyli jetty with Cleo. He felt the sense of *déjà vu*.

She looked as magnificent and seductive as the seascape.

The short swallow dives they executed were graceful. The splashes sent out ripples edged with white and silver. They swam away from the shore and at first the sea felt warm. Then, because fresh water spouted far below from fissures in the volcanic seabed, it turned freezing cold. A surprising and heady mixture of water temperatures, both comforting and bracing. After a few minutes they trod water. It was time to join their visitor.

xxiii

Beneath the shade of the vines on the veranda of Lela's, they drank coffee with the Director General, who had arrived from Athens earlier in the morning. The light breeze stirred the bougainvillaea and giant geraniums.

He asked them how they were and about the protection officers, and said that he hoped their presence wasn't proving too great an intrusion. Then he asked Rosslyn what he thought the long-term future had in store for him.

Rosslyn was silent.

'Intending to stay here indefinitely?' the Director General asked him.

'That was your idea,' said Rosslyn.

'True. At least until the accounts have been settled in London,' said the Director General. 'And now they pretty well have been.'

'But here?' asked Rosslyn. 'Have they been settled in Greece?'

The Director General gave him a look of incomprehension.

'The crash at Araxos?' said Rosslyn.

'Oh, yes. Given the situation in the Balkan area, it isn't something our American friends are prepared to discuss in public.'

'Are you prepared to discuss it?' asked Rosslyn.

'There's really very little I can add,' the Director General said. 'What do you want to know? It removed the opposition and we can be grateful for an act of God in His mercy.'

'But it wasn't an act of God, was it?' said Rosslyn. 'You didn't want them to stand trial, did you?'

'Perhaps,' said the Director General slowly. 'Perhaps not.' He seemed restrained by doubt. 'Take it or leave it . . . I prefer to do the latter. One has to accept that unfortunate things happen. There are still people like us who have to be prepared not to count the cost of one's adversaries' lives. And, believe me, when it comes to erstwhile friends, people like Shaw and Prevezer, the cost can seem very harsh to those on the outside.' He smiled. 'Tell me, Rosslyn, what do you reckon you're facing as far as your career's concerned?'

'I don't know.'

'Perhaps I can be of help. With my support . . . well, a word in the right ears might not go amiss.'

Rosslyn shook his head. He knew the man was lying.

'Well?' said the Director General.

'I'll work for myself.'

'And why not? Why not? Bear in mind my offer, though. We mustn't lose touch.' Flicking aside an angry wasp, he said, 'All that remains is for the final approval of my report. Happily, as far as we three are concerned, this is where we leave things permanently, as it were.'

'I don't believe in permanence,' said Cleo.

'Really?' said the Director General. The wasp settled beside his coffee cup and saucer. 'Let's not disagree.'

'I don't believe in permanence either,' said Rosslyn. 'Neither do the Greeks. There's unfinished business, isn't there?'

'Normally I'd share the conservatism of your view,' said the Director General. He squashed the wasp beneath the saucer and stood up to go. 'There's really no need for me to share your view.' His eyes sparkled beneath the bushy eyebrows. 'I'll be staying here a few more days. Until word comes through from London about the draft report. As to your shared belief in impermanence, let's say that, in the notion of unfinished business, we can amicably disagree, can't we? But in the perfect world, given your shared belief, I'd say you'd make an ideal pair.'

His voice carried the bogus wisdom of the assistant master he'd been at Eton in a previous incarnation. Always glib, always sneering, always the mimic of the inadequacies of foreign-language speakers, he essayed an attempt at colloquial Greek.

'Who knows where,' he said, 'who knows when, perhaps we'll meet before I return to London some sunny day.' Then he added, 'We have much in common, Alan.'

Rosslyn noticed the Director General smiling at Cleo. The smile seemed to suggest more than mere affection.

xxiv

He found Cleo more irresistible than ever. Next day, they returned to the rocks from where there were those breathtaking views of the coastline ribbon and the shimmering lavender-blue sea. They reached out for the past.

Accompanied by one or other of the protection officers on these excursions, they took packed lunches of tomatoes, bread, cheese and carafes of the local wine. Rosslyn noticed that Cleo no longer kept the loaded double-barrelled shotgun carefully concealed within reach, and they laughed about the way she had kept the gun with her before, and the way Rosslyn had found it slightly erotic. She offered no explanation for the disappearance of the weapon.

They travelled the precipitous roads that looped and spiralled through the mountain wilderness, affording sanctuary and calm. There was the same celebrated clarity of light. The fierce blue sky. The relentless heat of day, followed by the cool nights and the expanse of stars.

They returned again to the ruined villages not far to the south. To the tiny churches and the chill caves at Cape Matapan, the mythical gateway to hell itself. To the small pebble beach beside the deserted cove where they had first made love beneath the windless sky. On the return visit the presence of the protection officer prohibited the replay.

That night, Cleo decided to mark her return with Rosslyn to Tseria with the celebration dinner. She told him it would, as she put it, 'lay the ghosts'.

Constantine Dragos made his move shortly after eight-thirty the same night.

Already illuminated, the *Hellenic* lay at anchor offshore in sight of Kardamyli. Scuba-diving, in the company of the police protection officer and on board the light motorboat just lowered to the ocean, Constantine had given no indication to his father of his real intention. There would, of course, be the planned accident for which no blame would be attached to anyone. His father had no prior knowledge of it. After that, Constantine had allowed himself two hours at the outside to make the journey to Tseria and then return. He had arranged for a hire car to be left for him in the main street of the village.

On deck with a searchlight, his father was seeking out fish to fall victim to his spear gun. Mitsuko stood by his side in silence.

The protection officer was wearing shorts. His handgun holster was strapped across his T-shirt. He had told Constantine, even though he was an experienced swimmer, that duty required him to see to Constantine's safety. Anyway, he knew nothing about scuba-diving. He offered to take charge of the motorboat while Constantine went about his underwater swimming.

There was nothing unusual about Constantine's preparations. He removed his hand-claw and set it carefully inside a small flotation case. This he attached to a cord which he fastened to his belt. Then he drew on rubber fins. In his shorts, without a rubber suit, he would be diving free, so he had no need of oxygen tanks.

What the protection officer never saw were the other contents of the small flotation raft. The second metallic hand-claw. The light black climbing boots. The change of clothing, including a black nylon mask.

The sky was clear. The air slightly sharp. The stars already visible. It was a great night for a swim at sea. Now came the moment to start the outboard motor.

'You know how?' Constantine asked the protection officer.

'I think so.'

'Here,' said Constantine. 'Let me show you. See this?'

The protection officer was looking at the outboard engine when the metallic hand-claw struck the nape of his neck. For a moment he seemed motionless. Then, gulping his own blood, he sank forwards across the stern.

The boat tilted at an awkward angle as the protection officer heaved himself round, his hand reaching inside the holster. Momentarily, the angle of the boat caught Constantine off-balance. Floundering, he grabbed at the edge of the seat, his awkward movement giving the protection officer enough time to withdraw the gun.

The protection officer yelled, 'Don't move.'

The shout alerted Alexios Dragos on deck. With one hand, he swung the searchlight, its beam blinding Constantine, who was facing the protection officer in a crouch. In his other hand, Alexios held the loaded spear gun.

'He's going to shoot me,' Constantine yelled. 'He's out of his mind. He's going to shoot!'

Blood was streaming down the protection officer's T-shirt.

The spear from Alexios's gun whistled in a straight line. It grazed the protection officer's thigh and seemed to spin him around, and as he twisted he fired his gun at an angle at Alexios.

Constantine heard Mitsuko's scream. Then he threw himself at the protection officer, so that his full weight drove the metallic claw into the man's neck and his mouth opened and he began to wheeze, his bloodied arms flaying, his eyes twitching and bulging like a fish on a hook. It took Constantine ten more seconds to club him to death.

He yelled up to Mitsuko, 'Stay where you are until I return.'

'Alexios's dying,' she moaned.

'Do what you can for him. Do what you can.'

He started the motor boat and drove it at full throttle in a straight line for the Kardamyli jetty, leaving a widening white wake, the fine spray foam sparkling in the moonlight.

xxvi

With persuasive charm, Cleo had told the protection officers to take a night off. Demetra and Olympia would show them some entertaining clubs in Stoupa, down the coast.

The woman protection officer was the one who seemed the keenest to take the night off. It was she who persuaded her companions that they needed some fun. She insisted that Rosslyn keep her handgun with him until the morning before leaving with her colleagues for Stoupa's nightlife.

A kilometre or so down the road, raised headlights dazzled them. A car passed them by at speed leaving a cloud of dust in its wake.

xxvii

There was the din of the cicadas and dinner for two on the terrace, with moths dancing around the lights beneath the enormity of the night sky pricked with stars.

Rosslyn and Cleo sat side by side at the table beneath the vines and talked far into the night.

The distant barking of dogs seemed to echo across the empty gorges to the summits of the mountains. Several of them were barking at the man who parked the hire car opposite the Aloni Taverna and headed off unobserved on to the narrow footpath above the village in the darkness.

xxviii

Rosslyn and Cleo fell asleep in each other's arms.

The moon was high. The night silent. The breeze seemed to cool the single white linen sheet that covered their exhausted and naked bodies.

At two in the morning, Rosslyn woke with a start. He was drenched in sweat. He remembered he had left the protection officer's handgun on the table of the veranda. Without disturbing Cleo, he left the bed, slipped on his T-shirt and shoes and headed out down the stone steps to the veranda beneath the vines.

The handgun was where he had left it, between the vase of wild flowers and candleholder. He retrieved it, clicked the safety catch off, then on, and headed back to Cleo 's bedroom.

To have forgotten the handgun, you have to have been relaxed.

The night felt good. The stars looked magnificent. The chill air smelled sweet. The silence was perfect. There was the scurrying of a mouse, or a gecko perhaps, something in the scented bush near the door to Cleo's bedroom.

The bush moved again and he saw the black climbing boots and then stared straight into the eyes in the slits of the black nylon mask.

XXX

Where there should have been a hand there was a metal claw and it was raised. It thudded into Rosslyn's shoulder and the handgun fell from his hands.

Dazed, he fell sideways, and Dragos dropped on him, breathing heavily. Using the immense power of his one good arm, he wrenched Rosslyn's head round as if he were searching the bare flesh of the throat to slit it. The claw's sharpened point punctured Rosslyn's neck.

Blood spurted from the wound. He moaned in agony, bit into his tongue, and choked on blood and spat. Twice, he kicked out furiously. It was of little use. The full weight of Dragos's knee pressed into his back driving the breath from his lungs. The tip of the metal claw whipped against his left cheek, peeling back a curved length of skin.

Biting his tongue, Rosslyn was sure he was drowning in his own blood. Dragos's thumb was pressing hard against his eye. The eye was blazing hot, stinging, and seemed to fill with a gush of salt water. Managing to squirm sideways, he struggled to reach up for the black nylon mask and he succeeded in stretching it sideways, just far enough for the black nylon to cover Dragos's eyes and temporarily blind him.

None the less, Dragos was heaving Rosslyn to his feet, the metallic claw now embedded in the flesh to the right side of Rosslyn's waist. He forced him down the steps. Rosslyn could smell the nervousness of Dragos's stale breath. There was the strange and animal whistling from Dragos's nostrils. The pain of the claw embedded in his flesh was searing.

Reaching the well, Dragos leaned sideways, with Rosslyn hopelessly attached to him by the claw. Kicking aside the wooden cover, he wrenched the claw from Rosslyn's side, ripping flesh, and the full throat of Rosslyn's scream echoed into the mountains. Dragos clamped his hand across Rosslyn's mouth and Rosslyn sank his teeth deep into the palm of the hand.

For a moment Dragos moved backwards and then he screamed out in fury: something in Greek that Rosslyn was unable to understand. He seized Rosslyn and lifted him to the rim of the well. Loose stones fell away and splashed into the water far below.

Once again, Rosslyn grabbed at the nylon mask. The effort almost caused him to lose his balance. If he was going to go down, he'd take Dragos with him. He twisted his head and bit hard into Dragos's face at the corner of the open mouth and then a second time, his teeth severing a part of Dragos's bottom lip.

For a second Dragos was motionless. But though in pain, blinded by the mask stretched across his eyes, he had the initiative and now Rosslyn seemed to have lost the feeling in his legs. He was sinking. His vision blurred, he fought to see and to draw Dragos towards him, to feint, then shove him into the well's mouth.

Suddenly he saw the blur of the naked feet and ankles below the hem of white silk. In the next fraction of a second's silence he heard the click of the safety catch. He saw Dragos's metallic claw coming down towards him like a gigantic skewer.

Rosslyn squirmed sideways and, as he did so, Cleo fired two

rounds into Dragos's chest. Then, stepping very close, as Dragos fell backwards, she finally shot him through the open mouth.

Flesh and blood spurted from the back of his head into Rosslyn's face. The claw flailed at the well's edge and vanished. A second later they heard the crash as Dragos hit the surface of the water far below in darkness.

Rosslyn heaved himself away, trying to rid his eyes of Dragos's blood. He raised himself to his knees, the blood pouring from his face and side. Cleo tried to hold him back.

Choking, he leaned over the edge of the well. All he saw was darkness.

xxxi

At cockcrow, the Director General arrived. He had answered Cleo's urgent summons and, as she had asked, he brought the doctor from Kardamyli with him. The doctor cleaned and stitched Rosslyn's wounds and soon after he had administered painkillers Rosslyn was asleep.

The Director General settled the doctor's fee in cash and slipped him an additional sum, saying that he would 'be grateful if he wouldn't mention the call-out to anyone'. The doctor seemed to get the message.

Once the doctor had left, the Director General told Cleo he wanted to take a look at the corpse of Constantine Dragos.

They shone a flashlight into the well. The beam showed Dragos floating in the water. Cleo gave her version of the assault and of Dragos's death, and the Director General listened to her without comment. Leaning against the open well, he said, 'I don't want the protection officers connected with what's happened. Or your daughters. Or, for that matter, you.' He flicked at the cloud of flies buzzing around the well's mouth. Finally he asked her, 'Did he have any idea that Dragos was alive?'

'He didn't say so to me.'

'I suppose not,' said the Director General. 'I had no alternative but to trade Constantine's freedom for his father's silence. Simopoulos was our man.'

'But Constantine was never going to let things rest,' she said.

'I realized that.'

'You realized he might kill Alan?'

'It was always on the cards.'

'You're telling me that you were prepared to let Alan die?'

'I don't have to tell you that I was prepared for any eventuality,' he said. 'On the other hand, don't forget the protection officers. They're trained to do just that, to protect.'

'Only, when they were needed most, they weren't here, were they?'

'I don't think *you* can blame *me* for that,' he said. 'One has to accept that unfortunate things happen. And you've been wise to remain silent. When in doubt, say nothing. Silence is what one's paid for, isn't it? Paid to preserve the silence.'

She looked at him coldly.

'Take care of Rosslyn,' he said. 'If there are further medical costs, let me know. You'll be reimbursed.'

'And what's Alan to do?'

'Rosslyn? Who knows? Oh, I dare say he's in good hands with you here. There are plenty of men who'd envy his position. Few, maybe, who'd have been prepared to pay the sort of price he's paid. Meanwhile, I'm sure I don't have to remind you, there are some things you can't say. Not even to Rosslyn. If I were you I'd do your level best to help him forget what's happened.'

'I don't think that'll be possible.'

'You'll make sure of it, I'm certain. Now, if you'll excuse me, there are practicalities to be seen to. A call or two to London and Athens. The humane return of Constantine to his father and so forth. And then, if you can run to it, I'd awfully like some decent coffee.'

In the distance dogs were barking. Cleo led him to the kitchen to make coffee.

The Director General made a telephone call. Once he'd finished he joined Cleo on the veranda and announced, 'Simopoulos will see to the collection of the corpse. It'll all be done discreetly. By the way, Athens say there's been an unpleasant incident. The police are exercised by some accident at sea.' He was staring at the spider's web dangling from the vine leaves. 'Aboard some motor yacht. As a matter of fact, not far from Kardamyli.'

'This motor yacht,' asked Cleo, 'what's its name?'

'*Hellenic,*' said the Director General.

Cleo's wide, dark eyes stared at him.

'You look surprised?' said the Director General.

'Nothing surprises me here,' said Cleo. 'There are things in Greece that the British will never understand.'

She was interrupted by the sound of drunken voices. The protection officers were returning with Demetra and Olympia from Stoupa, singing:

> 'The old woman still laments
> Her ancient child-bearing
> As if the world's pain and sorrow
> Could ever end, ever end.'

'I suppose I'd better talk to them,' said the Director General. 'I'll speak to them on my own.'

xxxii

Cleo returned to her bedroom and spent some time gazing at Rosslyn peacefully asleep. She adjusted the pillows beneath his head and kissed him lightly on his moist forehead. He stirred slightly.

'You'll be OK,' she said.

There was the flicker of a smile on his swollen lips. Then a shadow fell across the room. Turning, Cleo was surprised to see the Director General standing in the doorway.

'How is he?' he said.

'Fine.'

'There's something I want to ask you . . .' said the Director General.

Rosslyn opened his eyes. He could see the silhouettes in the doorway. He closed his eyes, lay still and listened to the voices.